PRAISE FOR ANDREW KLAVAN

'Andrew Klavan is doing something rarely done... a unique angle on the private-eye novel'

Michael Connelly

'Hide the welcome mat, pull the blinds and take the phone off the hook, because you'll be dead to the world from the very first page'

New York Daily News

'Klavan knows every twist, turn and pothole in the road to hell. And all the travellers you will meet along the way'

Stephen Coonts

'Klavan does tough-guy heroes and sexual tension better than anyone writing today'

Janet Evanovich

'Make no mistake, moral choice is at the heart of this tale'

Philadelphia Inquirer

ANDREW KLAVAN won Edgar Awards and stormed the bestseller lists with *Don't Say a Word* and *True Crime*, both of which were made into films, the first starring Michael Douglas, the second, Clint Eastwood. He is the author of eight other books and has been nominated for the Edgar Award a total of four times.

He was born in New York City and grew up on Long Island. He went to the University of California at Berkeley where he met his wife, Ellen. They have two children, Faith and Spencer, and live in Santa Barbara, California.

DAMNATION STREET

Also by Andrew Klavan

Dynamite Road
True Crime
Don't Say A Word
Hunting Down Amanda
Shotgun Alley
Man And Wife
The Uncanny
The Animal Hour
Corruption

DAMNATION STREET

Andrew Klavan

AN OTTO PENZLER BOOK

Quercus

First published in Great Britain in 2006 by Quercus
This edition published in 2007 by

Quercus
21 Bloomsbury Square
London
WC1A 2NS

A CIP catalogue reference for this book is available
from the British Library

ISBN 1 84724 058 5
(978 1 84724 058 3)

10 9 8 7 6 5 4 3 2 1

Printed and bound in Great Britain by
Clays Ltd, St Ives plc.

This book is for Ross Klavan and Mary Jones

AUTHOR'S NOTE

This is the story of two lost men, two men I used to know. Scott Weiss was the owner of Weiss Investigations, a private detective agency in San Francisco. Jim Bishop was one of his operatives. Between the time I graduated from university and the time I returned east to begin my career as a writer of crime novels, I worked with them at the agency in a minor capacity. This is a fictionalized memoir of that period, which I hope will enable me to depict Weiss and Bishop more completely, and so more sympathetically, than if I had merely reported their actions and never explored their hearts and minds. I depict them in the third person but allow myself to speculate novelistically on their thoughts and feelings. I use the first person only at those moments when I become an integral part of the narrative.

PART ONE

The Case Of The Distant Daddy's Girl

1

Paradise was a crap town. With the summer tourists gone, the main street was deserted after nightfall. Trash rattled along the gutters, blown by the harbor wind. Darkened storefronts stared into the emptiness beyond the far sidewalk. Somewhere in that emptiness, the ocean waves crashed down and whispered away.

Scott Weiss walked past the shops, heading for his hotel. He was a man in his fifties, a big man with a paunch. He had a sad, ugly face. Deep bags under world-weary eyes. A bulbous nose. Sagging cheeks. Unkempt salt-and-pepper hair. He wore a gray overcoat. He kept his hands in the pockets, his broad shoulders hunched. The shop windows reflected him as he went past them leaning into the wind.

His hotel was the only hotel on the street. It was two stories, clapboard, yellow with white trim. It had white pillars holding up a balcony with a white rail. Weiss moved under the balcony to the front door. The door was glass. His reflection was there too. He looked into his own mournful eyes as he approached it. He pushed inside.

The hotel lobby was paneled in oak, stained a deep brown. There was a fire in the large fireplace. There was a heavy oak reception counter in front of the manager's office. There was no one behind the counter, no one anywhere in the lobby. The door to the office was closed.

Weiss stood at the counter and rapped his knuckles on the wood. He waited. The office door opened and a woman came out. She was about forty, short and chesty, frazzled, blonde. She was wearing yellow slacks and a purple turtleneck, a cheerfully loud combination. She hesitated when she saw Weiss. Something flickered in the look she gave him. Whatever it was, it passed. She came ahead to the counter, stood across from him.

'Chilly out there tonight, isn't it?' she said. Her voice was toneless. She didn't look up at him. 'Two-thirteen,' she said, and turned to the cubby holes on the wall behind her to fetch his key.

Weiss had a knack for reading people. He could tell what they were thinking. He could often guess what they would do. Sometimes the smallest gesture could give him what he needed.

Now, for instance, he could see that the woman behind the counter was scared.

He took the room key from her pale fingers. The woman pressed her lips together. It looked like she wanted to say something, to tell him something, to warn him maybe about what was waiting for him upstairs. But how could she? How could she know who the good guys and bad guys were, what was safe, what wasn't? It was smarter for her to just keep her mouth shut. So that's what she did.

Weiss smiled at her with one corner of his mouth. He wanted her to know it was all right. 'Good night,' he said.

The woman tried to answer but it didn't come off.

Weiss moved away from her. He walked to the wooden stairs. He felt the woman watching him as he went. The hotel windows knocked and rattled in the wind. He climbed heavily up to the second floor.

He trudged along the second floor gallery. He shifted the room key into his left hand. His right hand slipped inside his overcoat, inside his tweed jacket, to his shoul-

4

der holster. He wriggled out his old snub-nosed .38. It wasn't much of a gun, a real antique at this point. A relic from his days on the SFPD, back before they shifted over to the Berettas. Slow and inaccurate, it wouldn't be much use against the man who was after him. The man who was after him was a professional, a genuine whack specialist. If he wanted Weiss dead, he would make Weiss dead, ancient .38 or no. Still, Weiss liked the feel of the gun in his hand. Better than nothing. He kept it pressed against his middle as he went down the gallery.

He reached the room, two-thirteen. He tried the knob, but the door was locked, just the way he'd left it. He unlocked it. He pushed it in.

The room was dark. He stood where he was, on the threshold. He reached in and felt along the wall for the lightswitch. He found it, flicked it up. Nothing. The light did not come on.

Weiss felt his heart beat harder. He cursed silently. Maybe that's all the specialist wanted. Maybe he was watching from somewhere, spying on him, playing with him, cat and mouse. Maybe he just wanted to see Weiss pale and sweating and scared.

Well, congratulations, he thought. *You sick shmuck.*

He stepped into the room. He shut the door behind him. An act of defiance: to hell with the dark. The dark got thicker. The curtains were closed, only a pale beam from a streetlamp fell through the crack between them. Weiss moved in that light from shadow to shadow. He made his way to the bathroom, reached inside. When he flicked the switch, the bulb worked, the light came on in there, glinting off the white tile walls. That lit his way back to the main room, to the desklamp and the bedside lamp. He turned those on as well.

The room was empty. A small wood-paneled room, crowded with a bed and a weathered writing table.

Weiss holstered his gun. He moved to the bed, sat down on the edge of it, letting out a sigh. His heart beat hard for a few more seconds, then it eased. The back of his neck felt damp against his overcoat collar.

Might've been nothing. Nerves. The hotel clerk might really not have been afraid at all. He might've imagined it. The light bulb might have blown out on its own. The killer might never have been in the room at all.

Didn't matter. He was here, sure enough. Somewhere. Somewhere close. Watching him. Listening to him. Dogging every step.

Weiss's bottle of scotch, his Macallan, was on the writing desk, beside the blotter. After a while, he got up, stripped off his overcoat, dumped it on the bed. He fetched a water glass from the bathroom. He sat at the desk and poured himself a measure of whiskey. He lifted the glass to his mouth with his left hand. Held it there and let the scent sting his nostrils. With his right hand, he reached into the pocket of his jacket and drew out his picture of the whore.

He laid the photograph on the desk, on the blotter, framed against the green felt. He sipped his scotch and looked down at her.

She was one goddamned beautiful whore, all right. Julie Wyant, her name was. She had red-gold hair and blue eyes. She had an ivory and rose complexion. She had a dreamy gaze. Weiss liked that about her especially: her dreamy, faraway gaze.

Weiss didn't know much about her, but he knew what there was to know. She had worked out of San Francisco. She was especially popular with middle-aged men. Some guys reach a certain stage of life and they get all syrupy and nostalgic. She appealed to guys like that. She was gentle and a little spacey and she had a face like an angel. Her face seemed to remind these men of girls they used to

6

imagine when they were young, girls they made up before they knew real girls. She reminded Weiss of that kind of girl too.

Anyway, she had caught the attention of a professional killer, a whack specialist the newspapers liked to call the Shadowman. Weiss knew this guy. He'd been after him since his cop days. The specialist spent one night with Julie. He hurt her – a lot – that was love's sweet song to this sick piece of shit. He hurt her, then he told her he wanted to keep her with him forever.

Julie believed him. That's why she vanished.

She had phoned Weiss once, at his apartment in Russian Hill. It was the only time he had ever talked to her. She had phoned him and begged him not to try to find her. She knew about Weiss. She knew he was considered one of the best locate men in the business. He could find people because of that way he had of reading them, of guessing what they would do. And she knew he had been hunting the Shadowman for years. Julie was afraid he would come after her in order to draw the killer out into the open. She was afraid he would find her and then the killer would find her too. So she had phoned Weiss and begged him not to look for her.

Weiss had traced the phone call to a pay booth here in Paradise. That's how he knew where to start looking.

Weiss sipped his scotch. He studied the picture. She was one goddamned beautiful whore. He wondered if maybe that's why he was here. Maybe it wasn't because of the killer but just because she had an angel's face and it reminded him of the girls he'd made up in his mind when he was younger. Or maybe it was the fact that his business – his private detective agency back in San Francisco – was failing and he needed to get away. Whatever the reason, he had left the business behind – he had left everything behind – and come here to find her.

7

And the killer was following him. Watching him. Listening to him. Dogging his every step, just as Julie had said he would. Weiss was pretty sure there were tracking devices in his car, maybe even in his clothes. He didn't bother looking for them. If he took them out, the killer would just put them back again. The killer was following him, that's all there was to it. When Weiss found Julie, the killer would find her too, just as she had said.

And then they would settle it. Weiss and the Shadowman. They would settle it between them.

Weiss sipped his scotch. He studied the picture, looked into those dreamy, faraway eyes. He remembered how she had begged him – begged him in her warm voice to stay away. He had tried to do what she wanted. He really had tried.

But in the end, he couldn't help himself.

2

'Three,' said the Frenchman.

The customer said nothing. He snapped open the clasps on one of the black aluminum briefcases on the desk between them, the first case, the one to his left. He opened the lid and peered inside.

The Frenchman stole a glance at him, at his eyes. Strange eyes. Not cold or cruel or deadly. Just empty. Like a machine's. No, like a mannequin's. The Frenchman felt a chill in his belly.

He went on: 'Very wise, very strategic.' He knew he was babbling, but he couldn't stop. Those eyes. He needed to hear the sound of a human voice, even if it was his own. 'Your ordinary policeman feels a great satisfaction when he finds the first. He thinks himself, oh, very smart. When he finds the second, he is a law enforcement genius. That is the end of it, almost always. No one searches for three.'

The customer said nothing. He lifted the gun from the case. It was a 9mm Sig P210 with a modified mag release, the most accurate 9mm available. The customer turned it over in his hand, letting the daylight play on it.

The light was pouring in through the high windows on the wall behind the Frenchman. It fell in two broad beams on the men and the desk between them. They were in an office on the second story of a red-brick townhouse. It was small, cluttered. The customer was sitting in a tubular steel chair. The Frenchman sat in an old, tattered green swiveler. The desk was big, wooden, marked with cigarette burns and scars. All around them, broken crates, cardboard boxes, catalogues and mail were jumbled and piled up on carpet the color of static. There were no decorations, no pictures. Just the piled up garbage against the white plaster walls.

The Frenchman watched the customer for another short while. The chill in his belly grew chillier by the second. Finally, he'd had enough. He swiveled around, his back to the other man. He looked out the window.

Like a ghost, he thought. Despite the cool of the autumn day, he felt his armpits beginning to run under his pearl-buttoned cowboy shirt. He puffed his cheeks, blew out a breath. *The man has the eyes of a ghost.*

The Frenchman was no work of art himself. He wasn't French either – he was Belgian, but the sort of people he dealt with couldn't handle the distinction. Gnomish, hunched, sallow, he had damp lips and rheumy yellow eyes under a wispy blond combover. He was sixty-seven, but he dressed younger, wore jeans and the white cowboy shirt and a blue bandana tied around his turkey-gullet throat. Sometimes he suspected this sort of outfit made him look ridiculous. Jeans riding just beneath his tits. A cowboy shirt misshapen by his sunken chest and his bulging, flaccid belly. But what could he do? This was San Francisco, a young town. You wanted to do business here, you had to look jaunty. This was as close to jaunty as he could get.

He heard the clasps of the second briefcase snap open behind him. The customer was looking at the .45 now. A 1911 retooled into a compact powerhouse. Shoot a man in the guts with that at close range, and there'd be nothing left in the middle of him. He'd just be a head on top of a pair of feet.

The Frenchman waited, killed another minute looking

out at the bright blue day. Across the street were the pastel townhouses of Haight-Ashbury, a half-block row of them. A young mother pushed a stroller along the sidewalk beneath. The Frenchman savored the shape of her breasts in her orange sweater. As he watched her pass, a chorus of men's shouts rose to him through the floor.

'*Heeyai! Heeyai! Heeyai!*'

A deep sound, a strong sound. He drew it into himself with a breath.

It was coming from the dojo directly beneath him, on street level. It was his dojo. They were his men. They were big, muscular brutes, real bully boys, black belts all of them, not just black but with red stripes and Japanese letters and God knew what else. They were practicing their martial arts, going through their motions and routines, chopping the air with their hands, kicking the air. Shouting like that.

'*Heeyai! Heeyai!*'

They were the Frenchman's security system. Nice and legal, nothing he had to pay off the cops for. And there was no way to get to the stairs except through them. Usually just the sound of their voices, their presence, made the Frenchman feel safe up here.

Not today though. Not with this one.

He heard the third briefcase snap open. He swiveled back around to face the other man.

'Remarkable, isn't it?' he heard himself saying. His accent sounded overdone and oily even to himself. 'The very latest thing.'

Again, the customer answered nothing. He only lifted the Saracen and held it before him in his open hand.

'You see the size? It hardly covers your fingers. And the weight, you feel that?' the Frenchman rattled on. 'One and a half pounds loaded. Delayed blowback. Very low felt recoil. But it can pierce standard body armor at three hundred meters. I've seen it done.'

The customer ignored him. He never took that strange, empty gaze from the weapon. He worked the slide. Jacked the magazine.

'Twenty rounds,' the Frenchman said. 'In a weapon that size. Imagine. Twenty.'

The customer ignored him.

The Frenchman felt the sweat trickling down his sides. What the hell was this guy anyway? Some kind of specialist, obviously. A good one too – you could tell just by the way he handled the weapons. But if he was so good, why did he need so much hardware? And the Saracen – that would stop a tank. What was he going up against, an army? Who was he so afraid of?

Adalian had referred him. That was good. That meant security was guaranteed. Usually it also meant you were dealing with businessmen, men concerned with nothing but profit. That was the way the Frenchman liked it. It was cleaner, safer. But three guns? The Saracen? That smacked of a passion job, possibly even something political. Much messier stuff, much more likely to blow out of control, attract attention. The Frenchman wished he had questioned Adalian more closely at the outset. As it was, all he knew about the customer was his name, the name he went by: John Foy.

The man himself gave nothing away. Except for his eyes, he was average-looking. In fact, his features were so ordinary, the Frenchman thought they would be difficult to describe. He wore colorless slacks and a bland, striped shirt. A khaki windbreaker zipped at the bottom. Everything so plain, so commonplace it was almost a form of camouflage. *Like a ghost*, he thought. *Everything like a ghost. Invisible.*

The customer slowly lay the Saracen back in its case,

back in the space cut for it in the cushioning gray foam. He sat in the straight-backed metal chair with his shoulders slightly hunched, his hands clasped between his thighs. He looked from one open case to another, one weapon to another. He said nothing. He just sat and looked with his mannequin eyes.

The Frenchman waited and sweat. Finally, he couldn't take it. 'Three,' he said again, just to say something.

The customer nodded almost imperceptibly. His voice was toneless.

'Yes,' he said.

3

The blue afternoon had dimmed and it was evening now. Mist was gathering and making halos around the streetlamps. The man who called himself John Foy walked under the haloed lamps. He carried his three guns in a brown paper bag, rolled up so he could grip it in one hand, his right hand, held down by his side.

He walked along Eighth Street and it was as the Frenchman said of him: he was invisible. Even the gutter bums didn't ask him for a handout. Boozing at the curb outside the liquor store, squabbling in a litter of torn tickets near the betting office exit, sleeping in bags and boxes in the doorways between the bail bondsmen and the diner, they didn't even look at him as he went by. No one did. No one ever did.

He walked past unnoticed and then, unnoticed, he was gone. Off the streets, climbing a narrow stair between peeling gray walls. In at a scarred brown door. Entering a room with one curtained window.

He brushed the lightswitch up as he shut the door. There was a single bulb in the ceiling covered by a frosted glass plate. It gave off a sickly yellow glow, making hard shadows of the moths and flies that had been caught in the plate and died there. The glow showed a small room, two wooden chairs with foam cushions, a TV on a scratched wooden bureau, and a sagging single bed pushed against the grimy wall.

Murder had been good to the Shadowman. He'd made

millions at it over the years. But he dwelled in places like this almost always, one place like this after another. Restless, indifferent and anonymous, he came and stayed a while and moved on. He would be gone from this room before morning.

He shuffled slowly to the bed. He was breathing a little harder after his climb up the stairs. There was a sheen of sweat on his nondescript face. He sat down on the edge of the bed wearily. He set the brown paper bag on his knees. He opened it, peered inside it like a schoolboy wondering what his mother had packed for lunch. He drew the guns out one by one. The Sig, then the .45, then the Saracen. He laid them neatly on the bed side by side.

Grunting, he bent over. He reached down under the bed. He drew out a battered brown leather briefcase. He set this by his thigh, on the side of him opposite the guns. He worked the case's snaps. Opened it. There was a laptop inside, the machinery set into the case so that the lid held the monitor and the base the keyboard. He turned the computer on.

While it booted, he stood. He peeled off his windbreaker, draped it over the back of a chair. Stripped off his shirt, draped it over the windbreaker. He went to the closet, opened it. There was a mirror on the inside of the door. The man who called himself John Foy looked soft with his shirt on but, bare-chested, the muscle showed, corded, rippling and powerful.

In the closet, on a shelf chest-high, there was a suitcase. He opened it, took out the silicone vest. It was heavy, fifteen pounds at least. He had had it made by a special effects company in Los Angeles. It was decorated with painted latex and hair – yak hair, they'd told him. Whatever it was, the vest looked and felt exactly like human flesh.

15

He put the vest on, slipping it over his shoulders, fastening it in back. It blended smoothly with his own body, rising as a false paunch below his breasts and curving back down to end at his waist. It had a subtle effect. It added only about ten pounds or so to the look of him.

There was more stuff like this in the suitcase: silicone overlays and prosthetics to make his face and arms look a little fatter too so the whole image would fit together. But he didn't need them now. For now, this was enough. He walked back to the bed, trying to move naturally with the extra weight on him.

He picked up the Saracen from where it lay beside the other two guns. The Frenchman was a babbling idiot but he was right about this weapon. It was incredibly light, incredibly small, especially for a gun so powerful. It slipped easily through the slit in the silicone vest. It nestled snugly in the foam pouch fitted inside.

The man who called himself John Foy put his shirt back on. He tucked it in as he went to stand again before the closet mirror. He nodded once at what he saw there. The vest looked entirely natural. It made him just a little fatter, and it hid the gun completely. Not only that, when he pressed on it, even when he pressed in hard, he felt only what seemed to be human flesh. The foam, and an extra layer of rubber, made it impossible to tell the gun was there.

Your ordinary policeman feels a great satisfaction when he finds the first gun, the Frenchman had said. *He thinks himself, oh, very smart. When he finds the second gun, he is a law enforcement genius. That is the end of it, almost always. No one searches for three.*

A babbling idiot, no doubt about it. Weiss was no ordinary policeman. Weiss knew things. He guessed things. That was the whole point.

The man who called himself John Foy had a gift for

moving through the world unseen. He had worked in cities all over the west, from the coast to the Mississippi, and yet he had left barely a trace of himself anywhere. No one knew his real name. Even the people who hired him didn't know what he looked like. The cops in the cities he'd been in, the state cops, the feds – none of them even knew he existed.

But Weiss knew. Weiss had somehow guessed. The man who called himself John Foy didn't know how he did it, but he did.

He examined himself in the mirror. Turned this way, that. He pressed the silicone vest from every angle, as hard as he could.

He nodded again. He didn't think Weiss would guess about the third gun.

Satisfied, he looked back at the bed, at the computer in the briefcase. It was up and running now. The monitor showed a twice-divided screen, four separate readouts. One would pick up the GPS tracker on Weiss's car when it was in range, another would map the pulses coming from the bird-doggers sewn into his belt, jacket and shoes. The other two were for listening devices: phone taps, cell tracking, the distance mikes that could pick up voices through concrete and the laser that read the vibrations on window glass. All of them checked out, up and running.

He was ready to return to the hunt.

He packed his things up slowly, methodically. The computer under the bed. The vest back in the suitcase. The guns inside their paper bag with two holster straps wrapped around them. The bag he put in the suitcase too. Before he shut the suitcase lid, he looked down at the bag, his expression distant, even a little sad. It had been a mistake to get the guns from the Frenchman, he thought. Three guns from one man. A man like that. It was just the sort of thing he never did. He had always

17

spread his business out. He had always covered his tracks obsessively. Once, he had traveled to four different cities just to get the pieces for a single weapon. He had been that cautious at his best. Always planning, always anonymous, always invisible.

But that was over. Everything was over. Everything except the girl. And Weiss.

He shut the suitcase. He plodded back to the narrow bed. He lay down on it, shirtless. He laid his arm across his forehead and looked up at the chaotic web of cracks in the plaster ceiling. Thinking about the Frenchman, about the guns, about the girl, about Weiss – it had all begun to give him a bad feeling, a red, hot feeling spreading through his center. He was making a lot of mistakes now. He knew that. He was getting careless. Because of her. Because nothing mattered to him anymore except having her again. He couldn't think beyond that. He couldn't make his usual perfect plans.

He lay there with his arm across his forehead. He didn't see the cracks in the ceiling anymore. He saw her face. He saw her in her agony and tears, the way she'd been when he was with her. His cock grew hard, his breath grew short, as he remembered. He should've found her by now. He *would've* found her, if it hadn't been for Weiss. Weiss who somehow guessed his plans, who held him up, who gave her time to get away. Now, she was gone, just gone. He'd looked. She was nowhere. He was a man who knew how to find people too. He had tracked down plenty of running targets in his day. But this was different. She was different. Other targets had connections, people they loved, money they needed, places they had to be. Other targets stopped running after a while, convinced they'd eluded him. Not her. In a way, she was as anonymous as he was. She had no history. She had no family. She made her living off her body so she could go anywhere and travel light. She had made exactly one phone call that he knew of since she had vanished from the city. One phone call from Paradise. There, the trail ended.

For him – the trail ended for him. But not for Weiss. Weiss, in some way and for some reason the man who called himself John Foy didn't understand, had picked up a new trail. He was moving from Paradise now to a town called Hannock to the east. He would be there by morning.

The man who called himself John Foy would be there too. Because Weiss knew things. He guessed things. He found people who couldn't be found. And the girl would not run away from Weiss, the way she ran away from him.

The man groaned very softly, one hand moving to his groin. That feeling – that bad, red, hot feeling – it was getting worse in him, redder, hotter. Because of her. Because he was thinking about how he'd had her, the things he did to her, how he would've had her again, if it wasn't for Weiss...

He closed his eyes. He dug his fingers into his cock, dug them in until it hurt, until his cock grew soft again. Then he lay still, breathing, breathing. He imagined a tower. It was a trick he had taught himself to keep the bad feelings away. When he could think, when he could plan, when he could do his work, it was like a wheel in his mind was turning. It was like the wheel powered a lamp and his mind was bright and clear. But sometimes, like now, his mind stopped, the wheel stopped, and the lamp went out. Then bad feelings and bad thoughts closed on him from the corners like scrabbling rats. Laughing voices, red rage, red blood, a little boy crying – like rats scrabbling out of the corners when the dark came down.

So he would think of a tower, a tall castle tower. He would daydream himself up its winding stair and into its battlement. At the top, he felt aloof and calm and the bad thoughts and feelings washed against the tower base far below, the red rage like a tide, the tears like rain, but far below where they couldn't touch him. After a while, the laughing voices would quiet. The slanting rain of infant tears would cease. The tide of rage would recede and he would be able to think again and make plans again and start the wheel turning.

Hannock, he thought. That was the plan. He would follow Weiss to Hannock. He would follow Weiss and Weiss would follow the girl and he would find her.

In the end, thought the Shadowman, they would all meet face to face.

4

Jim Bishop, meanwhile, was at a bar. He was leaning on the rail, his hand around a mug of beer. Behind the bar, above the mirrored shelves of liquor bottles, there were three TVs set high on the wall. There were baseball games playing on two of the TVs. There was news playing on the other one. On the news, there was a video of a beautiful blonde girl – a teenager – in handcuffs. A deputy was holding her arm at the elbow, lowering her into a squad car outside the Redwood City court-house. The sound on the TV was off but the caption told the story: the girl had been charged with four counts of felony murder. The squad car drove out of sight with the girl and the deputy inside.

Bishop smiled his sardonic smile. He lifted his beer mug, toasted the television news, and drank. He did not love anyone, but he did have sort of a thing for the blonde girl on the news. She had had a way of bringing him to the cold still border of himself whenever he was inside her. He would've done a lot for the chance to get a few more hits at her. He would've stolen money. He would've fucked over Weiss, who was not only his boss but his only friend. Whatever excuse for a code of honor he still had, he would've shredded it on the spot. Hell, he'd been planning to do all those things and more. But before he got through the list, she had set him up to be killed. That pretty much put an end to the affair – that, or maybe just the fact she'd gotten herself arrested.

Bishop set his beer down. Leaned on the rail. Went on smiling his sardonical smile. Grimacing, he worked his right shoulder around a little. It still throbbed from where the girl's psycho lover had stabbed him after she'd set him up. He was supposed to be taking painkillers for it. He was drinking the beer instead.

He'd been drinking beer for several days, in fact. He'd been in a lot of bars during that time, an endless series of bars it seemed. This one was – where? – in the Noe Valley somewhere. It was one of those Irish pubs that had dolled itself up for the young professional class. There were wrought iron chandeliers and butcher block tables all over the place. A lot of Tiffany-style glasswork around the windows. The light was too bright, the wood was too blond. And everyone seemed to be wearing cable sweaters and brand new jeans and drinking large bowl-like glasses of white wine or beers with slices of lime in them.

Slices of lime! Well, if you wanted to go from bar to bar forever, you had to take the good with the bad.

Bishop lifted his mug again. As he did, he noticed that a woman had planted herself on the stool next to him. He glanced at her over the mug's rim while he drank. She was his age, thirty or so. Appealing in a desperately-unmarried-businesswoman sort of way. She had shoulder-length brown hair and large brown eyes. A nice shape in her tight-fitting brand new jeans and her likewise tight-fitting cable sweater.

Bishop decided he would take her somewhere and have her. This was a talent of his: he could pretty much have any woman he wanted. Who knows why? Something about his being a cold-hearted bastard seemed to drive the girls wild with desire.

He wasn't tall but he was well-built, square-shoul-dered, muscular. He had a thin, fine nose and pale, almost colorless, eyes. His lips had that sardonical smile on them more or less all the time. He stood out in this crowd tonight, his jeans faded and no sweater on but a gray t-shirt under his leather motorcycle jacket instead.

'You want a drink?' he asked the woman.

She looked him over. 'Yeah, sure,' she said.

He lifted his chin at the bar-guy, an owlish part-timer in big square glasses.

'I'll have what he's having,' said the woman.

Bishop drained his mug. 'I'll have what I'm having too,' he said.

The bar-guy brought them beers. The woman raised her mug to Bishop. She wanted Bishop to clink mugs with her so he raised his mug and clinked. They both drank.

'So,' he said then, 'what's your story?'

'Well…' She licked the foam from her lips and considered. 'My name is Heather, first of all. I'm a financial consultant at Howard Paycock, which is a firm in town. I've been in the city about a year, and before that I lived in Seattle which is also where I went to school. How about you?'

'Well,' said Bishop, with a thoughtful frown. 'My name is Jim. I'm a private detective with Weiss Investigations – or I was until I screwed over my boss for some stolen cash and a couple of hook-ups with a killer bitch who set me up to be murdered. Before that, I was actually kind of a hero but I lost my faith in things which, if you're a hero, doesn't leave you with a whole lot besides your addiction to violence and the habit of putting yourself in life-threatening situations. So that's pretty much it.' He shrugged. He sipped his beer through the silence that followed.

It was a long silence. Then the girl said, 'Wow. Interesting.'

Thirty-five minutes later, they were in her apartment three stories above Alvarado Street. She was bent naked over some sort of work desk and Bishop, cupping her breasts in his hands, was driving into her from behind. She was digging it in a big way and was actually beginning to wonder if there really might be such a thing as love at first sight. Bishop was beginning to wonder if there might be a cold piece of chicken or some left-over Chinese in her refrigerator because he hadn't eaten anything but pretzels since forever.

She cried out his name. He grunted the name of the girl on the TV news.

That's when the cops came for him.

5

Bishop would've known those pounding footsteps any-where. How the hell had they found him here? He was irritated and thrust into the gasping financial consultant with a muttered curse. He thrust again, stubbornly – again and again – and managed to finish just as the cops started pounding on the apartment door.

'Open up! Police!'

'Oh my God!' said the financial consultant – Bishop couldn't remember her name.

Anyway, he was already rolling out of her. He yanked his jeans off a chair, started stuffing himself back into them. At the same time, Heather – Heather; that was it – she was twisting off the desk, stumbling backward, covering her breasts with one hand and her crotch with the other. She stared at the door, open-mouthed. Then at Bishop. Then at the door.

The police started pounding again.

'Open up! Let's go! This is the police!'

Heather's mouth opened and closed a few times. Then she shouted, 'Just a minute! I'm not dressed!'

The police went right on pounding.

Heather glanced at Bishop. He was hopping around, trying to get his boot on. 'Hurry up!' she whispered at him fiercely. She snatched her jeans up off the floor, shouting at the same time: 'I said just a minute! I'm getting dressed!'

The cops pounded on the door three more times – *boom, boom, boom* – hard. 'We're gonna break this down in a second, lady!'

'You do and I'll sue your fucking balls off!' Heather screamed back.

Bishop laughed. He had his t-shirt on now. He grabbed his jacket.

Heather pulled on her jeans. She shot Bishop another fierce whisper, 'Hurry! You can use the fire escape in back!' Her brown eyes were wide with fear and hilarity. Bishop liked that look. He liked the way she gave it to the cops too. He had one arm in his jacket sleeve and, on impulse, he grabbed her around the waist with it and pulled her to him even as he snaked the other arm into the other sleeve. He kissed her. She was still bare-breasted. He savored the feel of her against his shirt. When he released her, she let out a wild, breathless laugh.

'You really are a bastard!' she said, as if she'd just figured it out.

Bishop laughed too.

'Hurry!' she said. 'Go on!'

He went – out the rear window, down the fire escape, through a little backyard garden misty in the cool darkness. Brushing fronds of some sort out of his face and striped with dew, he made his way to a garbage alley alongside the building. He jogged down the alley to a white picket gate. Pushed the gate open, peeked out at the street.

It was a quiet block of Victorian townhouses, street-lamps like bookends at either corner. Two patrol cars were parked against the curb across from Heather's building. Bishop's Harley was corralled between the front fender of one car and the rear bumper of the other. A pair of patrolmen were leaning on the hood of the lead car, chatting, their arms folded on their chests. As they talked, they kept a weather eye on the third story bay window of Heather's apartment.

Bishop didn't hesitate. He slipped out of the alley. He ambled casually but quickly across the street, went right to his bike. He was so smooth, the cops didn't even notice him until he swung himself into the saddle.

Then one of the cops did a startled double-take. 'Hey,' he said.

Bishop made the Harley roar in answer.

'Hey!' shouted the other cop.

Bishop kicked the bike into gear. It screeched and stuttered out from between the two patrol cars. Then it shot away.

The sudden speed, the thundering noise, the pure insanity of what he was doing set Bishop's inner world a-gleaming. He laughed into the wind. Slewed around a corner. Blasted up a hill.

He crested the top. He held the Harley there as it rumbled. He heard the sirens behind him, wild and high, like baying dogs. Still, he hung there on the height and looked out over the scene with his cold, pale eyes.

The air was silver with lamplight and mist. The street dipped down steeply from his front tire, a line of modest brick and clapboard houses to his right descending beside it. Beyond, in the middle distance, lay a valley of freeways. Beyond that, the San Francisco skyline rose in the gathering autumn haze. The city's quirky jags, its blocks and spires, shone through the haze, a patchwork of lighted windows. Its glow rose up and washed the sky to a blue-gray nothingness.

The sirens grew louder. A damp wind passed over him. He breathed it deeply. It was refreshing. It was good.

Slowly, then faster, then faster, like water running to a cliff and pouring off the edge, he and his machine curled over the crest of the hill and cascaded down.

He picked up speed, more speed. A sharp turn – a hell of a turn – rose toward him, quick as a thought. He gassed the bike to forty, fifty. Neared the bend. The mist went red, went blue, went red again around him: the cops. He had only an instant to glance back. He caught only a glimpse of them. The two patrol cars, one after the other, came sailing over the hilltop behind him, catching air, their light racks flashing, their sirens howling at the sky. Their tires screamed as they smacked down onto the pavement. The cars gripped tar and fired after him.

Bishop faced forward and went into the turn. He hardly slowed, just took it. The bike leaned over, leaned over more. He laughed again through gritted teeth. It was practically supernatural – he was practically lying on his side, practically skimming on top of the air. Every moment, he expected to go rubber up, lay the bike down in flames and sorrow. But no, then he was around the curve, pulling up straight, threading a narrow street lined with parked cars on one side and on the other with October roses.

The cops were close behind him. He heard their sirens, louder. He saw the red and blue rack flashers throw their colors into the night. He looked over his shoulder, caught a blurred image through tearing eyes. The lead squad car was ripping around that wicked bend. Its tires smoked. It skidded out to the right, scraped a parked car and threw up sparks. It yanked itself back toward the planted median, raked a roadside trellis so that flowers flew merrily into the air like it was all some sort of big parade. The blossoms hit the windshield of the second squad car as it came wriggling frantically around the corner. The car's brakes shrieked like a hectoring fishwife.

Bishop's heart raced. His eyes were bright as a madman's. He felt a thing inside him that was cold and glinting like a knife blade turning to catch the moonlight.

Looking ahead, he saw the pavement sailing toward him, felt his bike sailing uncontrollably fast down and down and down the constricted lane. At the bottom, the street horseshoed around the rosy median. He could choose to continue forward and let the cops run him to ground in the flatlands of the Mission, or he could try the tight one-eighty, and lose them here and now, racing away back up the hill.

The road swept left. He hit the brakes. He wrenched the bike around. The Harley's rear wheel skidded out from under him. The whole bike skidded, changing direction like a needle on a meter. For a second, the machine went sideways across the macadam, heading for the parked cars. Then Bishop gave it gas and it was off again, rising back up the hill in the lamplit mist.

The squad cars had no chance to make a turn like that. He heard them brake. He heard the bay of their sirens become a sour whine. He looked behind him as his bike climbed and it was great, just great: they were stranded down there, their flashers revolving uselessly. They could only edge, slow and cautious, around the bend. With any luck, he'd be gone before they were even up to speed.

A thrill went through him. It was a sensation of breaking out of darkness into day. He'd been lost in a fog of trouble these last few weeks and now he burst free of it. It all swept back past him. The girl on the TV and the pain in his shoulder and the beer and the bars and Weiss whom he'd betrayed – it all swept back. The way ahead looked clear and bright.

Then a third squad car screamed into his path and cut him off.

It came out of a side street at the top of the hill. It planted itself across the intersection. It sat there, big and silent against the sky. Its red and blue lights circled with a sort of slow, lazy arrogance, the way a hick sheriff chews his gum.

Bishop gave a snarl of frustration. He cursed. There was no way around the thing and no way through. He squeezed the brakes. He let the bike slide sideways. It stopped. He set a boot down on the pavement.

Below, the other squad cars chugged up the hill to block his retreat.

Bishop smiled his sardonic smile.

The door of the third car, the car across the road in front of him, swung open. A grizzled veteran climbed out with a grunt. He hoisted his heavy utility belt over the bulge of his belly. He strolled down the hill toward Bishop with his thumbs in the belt's sides.

He stopped. He cocked his head. He looked Bishop over. He sighed.

Bishop grinned outright. 'Gee, officer,' he said. 'Was I going too fast?'

The veteran bit his lip to keep from laughing. 'Bishop,' he muttered. 'You are such an asshole.'

6

Two hours later; the Hall of Justice. Homicide, Fourth Floor.

Bishop sat in an interview room about the size of an outhouse. The soundproofing on the walls, once white, had gone a depressing gray. There was a wooden table. Three wooden chairs, one on one side, two on the other. Bishop sat in the one, slouched, rebellious, his arm thrown over the back.

He waited. A long time. It had been an evening full of thrills. He waited in the little room until every thrill had died. The fog of dejection settled over him again.

Then Inspector Ketchum walked in, scowling and furious.

Ketchum was a small, sinewy black man. He was wearing green slacks and a blue shirt, a red tie pulled loose at the collar. His gold inspector's star was on the front of his belt. His .40 caliber Beretta was holstered on his hip. He was carrying a thick black binder. It had some numbers on the side of it and a name. It was the name of the girl on TV, the blonde girl in handcuffs. Bishop's girl.

Bishop gave the inspector a bored look. Ketchum was bristling with anger, but so what? Ketchum was always bristling with anger. The son-of-a-bitch hated everyone, except maybe Weiss. Weiss had been Ketchum's partner in his cop days so maybe Ketchum liked Weiss. But that didn't help Bishop any. The way things were set up, that only made Ketchum hate Bishop all the more.

Ketchum dropped the black binder – *whap!* – on the wooden desk. He propped his foot up on one of the chairs, rested his arm on his raised knee. He gazed down at Bishop balefully, like a vulture waiting for lunch to die.

'I hope you think I'm good-looking, Bishop, cause I'm about to fuck you hard,' he said. He had a low, rasping growl of a voice. His scowl was apparently permanent.

Bishop shifted in his chair. He whiffled. He sneered. Just because his life was swirling down the crapper didn't mean he was going to take shit from this chucklehead. 'Give it a rest, Ketchum,' he said. 'This is San Francisco. You can't even bust people here for breaking the law, what do you think you're gonna do to me?'

Ketchum lay a finger on the black binder, the girl's case book. 'Accessory to murder. Receiving stolen goods.'

'Oh, bullshit.'

'Interfering with the police. Oh, and how about DUI and speeding? How about operating a fucking motorcycle without a fucking helmet.'

Bishop gestured with the hand behind his chair. 'Without a helmet. Jesus. I guess I'm a pretty bad guy, all right.'

'You're not even a bad guy, Bishop. You don't rate high enough to be a bad guy. You're just a waste of space with skin on. Too much dick and not enough brains and no fucking heart at all.'

'Oh, for Christ's sake, Ketchum, what do you want from me?'

'Well, now, I'm glad you asked me that question. I was just getting to that.' The inspector took his foot off the chair. He stood straight, one hand resting on his gun butt. 'I want you out of here.'

'Hey, I'd like to help you, but all those mean men with guns out there won't let me leave.'

'I mean out of my life. Out of Weiss's life. That's what I want. I want you out of Weiss's life.'

Bishop shrugged. 'I'm gone already. I haven't been back to the agency since you hauled the girl in.'

'Oh, but you will be back, Bishop. You'll strut around and drink and raise hell a while, but you'll crawl back there sooner or later. Know why? You got nowhere else to go, that's why. No one else would have you. And Weiss knows that. And he'll take you back. Cause he thinks he can save your soul somehow. Now what's your opinion on that, Bishop? You figure Weiss can save your soul?'

'Let me think,' said Bishop. 'What's the right answer? Oh yeah: blow me.'

Ketchum snorted. 'Doesn't matter. Cause it ain't happening. Cause you're getting out of Weiss's life. And when I say out of Weiss's life, I mean out of San Francisco altogether. And when I say out of San Francisco, what I mean is: Get the fuck out of California and stay out. I want you to live fast and die young in any one or all of the other scenic forty-nine states in this great and good land of ours. And I want you to understand with the full power of your maladjusted mind that if you ever come back here, you are going to find an Inspector-Ketchum-shaped misery at the center of your existence as unchanging as the infinite but in your case misguided love of almighty God.'

'I'm sorry, Ketchum, did I forget to mention you can blow me?'

Ketchum's scowl didn't falter, but an unpleasant light came into his eyes. It occurred to Bishop that this probably was not a very good sign.

'I don't think you've been listening,' the inspector said.

Bishop kept up the hard guy routine, never mind his sinking feeling. 'I'm listening,' he said. 'But you got nothing here. Accessory to murder! Come on, man, you can't hold me on shit like that.'

The light in Ketchum's eyes grew brighter. 'Boy, I can hold you on any damned shit I please. For forty-eight hours. Counting from the start of business tomorrow. Except – oops – tomorrow's Saturday, there is no business. So it's counting from the next day except – oops – that day's Sunday, so now we're counting from the day after that. Which means, let's see, I can throw you in CJ for forty-eight hours counting from the day after the day after tomorrow – assuming your papers don't get lost or you don't get transferred somewhere we can't find you, which might slow things down considerably. And this is just the start of what this city's gonna be like for you from here on in, just the start. Now get the fuck on your feet, you miserable piece of shit.'

7

So now Bishop lay on his bunk in the County Jail, three floors up. His jeans and t-shirt and leather jacket were gone and he was dressed in orange overalls. He lay with his hands behind his head. He gazed up at the mattress above him. The mattress above him sagged under the weight of an enormous shaven-headed muscleman. The muscleman was also dressed in orange overalls. There were eighteen other men in the cell, each on one of the bunks on the eleven other double bunk beds. All of the men were dressed in orange overalls – county orange – just like Bishop.

The cell was dimly lit, shadowy. There was a grated window high on the wall. It showed a rectangle of blue-black sky. There was a steel toilet underneath it and a steel sink. There was a strange, empty smell in the place, tainted now and then with shit and sweat and disinfectant. There was a steady wash of noise: doors and voices, ventilation fans, footsteps on stone. Bishop breathed in the smell and listened to the noise and watched the mattress above him move as the muscleman rolled over.

He tried to think about other things. He thought about his Harley, about being on his Harley. He thought about the cops chasing him and how the wind had felt on him as he careered downhill. That was funny; that was all right. He thought about the girl – the one from the bar – he'd forgotten her name again. But he thought about her ass against his belly and her tits against his palms. He thought about that other girl, the blonde who'd nearly killed him. He thought about the moments when he'd been inside her on that cold, still border of himself…

But finally, it was no good. Here he was in CJ. All those thrills were in the past and he couldn't bring back the feel of any of them. He was sick of his life.

The noise came back to him, the smells, the heavy presence of breathing, grunting, cursing men in orange. He tried to think his thoughts, but they became vague and jumbled. The girl's tits in his hands became the feel of the motorcyle handlebars and then his hands were fists and he was in an old dustup with his drunken father, finished long ago. Then he had a bad taste in his mouth and he knew he'd been asleep and time had passed. He thought it was the dead of night. There was still plenty of noise – fans, voices, doors, footsteps – but there was a stillness underneath the noise somehow that gave him the sense of a late hour. Somewhere in the distance someone was screaming for the deputies, screaming for help. No deputies answered. Eventually, the screaming stopped.

Bishop drew a breath, coming fully awake. He shifted, stretched on his bunk.

Suddenly, a hand grabbed his upper arm. A pair of wild staring eyes appeared right beside him.

'Help me!'

It was a sobbing gasp. Bishop glanced toward it. He saw a willowy white kid, the only other white guy in the cell. His face was pale as paper. His lips were dry as dust. And that stare, that wild stare of his, was full of terror.

'He's gonna kill me! Please!'

Bishop put his hand over the kid's face and shoved him. 'Get the hell away from me,' he said.

The kid fell backwards onto his butt. He scrambled onto his knees, grabbed Bishop's hand. 'Please! I don't want to die! My father will pay you! I swear!'

The kid had a round, soft face, a floppy mop of brown hair. He had full sensuous lips and deep sensitive eyes. His hands were delicate with long fingers. They gripped Bishop's hand hard. His voice cracked.

'I didn't mean anything! Really. I was just scared, that's all. They just scared me! Please! You're a white man. Please!'

Bishop yanked his hand free. 'Get the hell away from me or I'll kick you in the head,' he said.

'But he'll kill me!'

Bishop kicked him in the head – not hard, just a few harrying blows around the temple to drive him away again.

Throwing up his arms for protection, the kid retreated in a crouch. He sank onto the floor, his back against the bunk across the narrow aisle. He buried his pale face in his delicate hands. He sobbed, 'Please. Please.'

The Mexican on the bunk across the aisle was lying on his side, his back to them. He looked over his shoulder. 'Shut up, *maricon*,' he said to the kid.

The kid went on sobbing.

Now, with a sort of dreamy slowness, another man hove around the bunk bed at the end of the row. He came lumbering toward them.

This one was a hulking figure, big-bellied, slump-shouldered, broad. His head was squashed and shapeless. It looked like a giant glob of clay that had been hurled down – *splat!* – on top of his neck. Marble eyes glowered out of the clay as he approached. Bishop glanced down instinctively and saw the clay-headed man was gripping a sharp strip of metal in his doughy right fist.

He thought, well, the kid was telling the truth anyway. This monster was definitely out to kill him, all right.

The Mexican on the bunk across the way shook his head in exasperation. He rolled back onto his side, his back to the action. The enormous muscleman on the bunk over Bishop's let out a deep laugh – *heh, heh, heh*. He was happy to have some entertainment.

Bishop lay as he was, his fingers laced behind his head again. He watched the clay-headed man stalking toward the kid step by slow step. He sighed. What a bunch of fucking lowlifes. It depressed him to be locked up in the same cell with them.

The kid looked up from sobbing. He saw this Clayhead guy coming for him. He shrieked like a girl and flung himself at Bishop again. His voice was a ragged, high-pitched scream:

'Ple-e-e-ease!'

He gripped the edge of Bishop's bunk desperately.

But now Clayhead was on him. He let out an animal growl and grabbed a handful of the kid's floppy mop of hair. He yanked it so the kid's face turned up toward him. The kid gaped up at the squashed features with his mouth in a wide frown like a fish's mouth. Somewhere in that shapeless mass of flesh above him, there was a killer smile and those marble eyes gleaming. The kid stared at those eyes helplessly, waiting to die. Clayhead held the metal blade low and aligned it with the kid's jugular, to make sure he cut just the right place.

'Oh, for Christ's sake,' Bishop muttered.

He reached out irritably and broke the clay-headed man's arm.

He broke it at the wrist, grabbing it in both his hands, twisting it back and around. The snap of the bone was like pistol fire. The metal blade pattered quietly against the cell's concrete floor.

Clayhead screamed. He grabbed his broken wrist and started reeling back up the aisle, banging from bunk to bunk, whooping and roaring. At the end of the aisle, he fell down and writhed.

The kid, released from his grip, fell down too. He curled trembling into a ball on the floor, his orange jumpsuit stained at the crotch and bottom.

There was a loud buzz and the cell door opened and the deputies came rushing in, as serious and self-satisfied as if they'd arrived in the nick of time.

8

I'm not sure – I'm never really sure – whether my own story is worth telling here, whether it's worth interrupting the main action with it. The romantic doings of my admittedly callow existence at that time seem pretty unimportant compared with the working out of Weiss's fate and Bishop's. Still, we all did converge in the end, and while I don't know – even all this long time later – whether I had any effect on what happened to the others, I do know that what happened to them, violent and terrible as it was, changed my life forever. In any case, as I say, we all did converge, so I guess my part in these events has to be told. I promise to get through it as quickly as I can.

To begin with, the main thing you have to know is: I was in love. Her name was Emma McNair. She was a student at UC Berkeley, where her father was an English professor. She had an adorable heart-shaped face and witty green eyes and... Well, I guess it doesn't matter what she had, does it? The point is I met her one night in a pizzeria called Carlos. I fell in love with her on the spot, convinced that she was my second soul, fashioned for me at the creation. Before we parted, she wrote her phone number on a Carlos coaster for me and I promised to call her right away. Only I never did. That very night, I became entangled in an affair with my superior at the agency, Sissy Truitt. Day after day, I didn't call Emma, because night after night, I was with Sissy.

Now at this point – the point where Weiss suddenly left town and Bishop got thrown in jail and all – at this point, I was already tired of Sissy in a thousand ways but in one way I wasn't. She was older than I was by at least ten years and she knew some sexual tricks that would've been illegal if the sort of people who made stuff like that illegal had ever heard of them, which they couldn't have or they wouldn't have been that sort of people. Me at that age: I was basically a penis with an idea for a human being attached. I wanted to leave Sissy and be with Emma but I couldn't because of the things Sissy did with me in bed. I despised myself for this. In fact, I despised myself for my entire approach to Sissy, the way I pledged my loyalty to her at the same time I plotted to escape her as if she were some kind of Communist regime or something. Sissy was not a bad person at all. She was sweet and gentle and motherly, and so hungry to have a man in her life she was even willing to settle for me. I liked her. I really did. I was just tired of her, that's all. I was tired of her and I was in love with Emma, my second soul.

Last night, the night before Bishop went to jail, I managed to get away from her somehow. I told her some lie or other. I haven't the stomach to remember what it was. Anyway, I drove out to Berkeley. I went to Carlos. I figured Emma had come in there once, there was at least some chance she would come in again. Somehow, attempting to bump into her 'accidentally' seemed less dishonest than calling her or going to her house while I was still involved with Sissy.

So there we find me, in Carlos, at a corner table. Drinking a beer. Pretending not to watch the door.

It was Friday night. The place was packed, noisy with talk and laughter. The chairs around the chunky wooden tables were full of kids from the university, kids not much younger than I. My gaze – my melancholy gaze – traveled over them: athletes pointing their chins and fingers at one another, shouting friendly insults back and forth; intellectuals talking vehemently nose to nose, as if they were disagreeing rather than working out the variations of a single ideology; outcasts in baggy clothes with sullen frowns and big ideas; and bright-eyed Businessmen and Women of Tomorrow who smiled across their pizzas as if they would be bright-eyed forever.

I gripped the handle of my beer mug, sipped the surface of my beer. I had been one of these very students not so long ago, one of the intellectual ones. I had been planning to continue on through graduate school, to become a college professor and write bad smart novels that critics praised and no one read, just like Emma's father did. God knows what lonely impulse of delight had led me to take a year off, to take a menial job at Weiss's Agency. But there I found myself, working at a place and with people who seemed to have erupted whole out of the hardboiled detective fiction I had loved since I was a boy. I wasn't one of those hardboiled people. I knew that. But somehow being among them at the Agency had taught me something about myself. I didn't want to be a professor anymore. I didn't want to write bad smart novels. I wanted to live in the real world with real people and write the kind of novels I had always loved.

I told all this to Emma the night we met. She was the only one I had ever told or ever could tell. I told her and then I went back to the city and started up the thing with Sissy.

Now here I was and oh, how melancholy it all seemed to me, how rife with personal symbolism. Which woman would I love? Which choice would I make? Which life would I lead?

Of course, looking back on it now, I see only one salient point about any of it, one fact that stood out above all others: to wit, I was a feckless poltroon – truly feckless; without a single feck. I was a moral coward to my bones. No wonder I despised myself.

I lifted my beer mug. Tilted it up. Drained it. I clapped it down on the table. I stood.

She would not come tonight, my Emma. She would never come again.

I drove back to the city in a state of high romantic sadness. I went home to my apartment. I slept alone.

9

I arrived at work the next morning feeling all the stronger and more righteous. Having resisted Sissy for an evening, I was like the drunk who takes a night off alcohol and thinks he's beaten it.

The Weiss Agency was on the eighth floor of a concrete tower on Market Street. With its red mansard roof up top and the electric streetcars snapping and rattling by its base, the building had a pleasingly timeless aspect. As I pushed through the glass door nestled beside the bank on the ground floor, it was easy for me to pretend I was pushing into that old tough guy Frisco of my imagination.

I rode the elevator up to eight. There were glass doors there and a reception desk behind them and a receptionist, Amy, behind the desk. There were hallways to the left and right of her. I took the one on the left and went about two thirds of the way down to a little alcove. That's where my desk was.

Originally, Weiss had hired me as little more than an office boy. My desk and I shared space with a copier, a fax machine and a postage dispenser and most of my time was still spent typing case notes, filing reports and sealing envelopes. Lately, though, things had been changing for the better. Wonderful to relate, Weiss had taken an inexplicable liking to me. He would wander by the alcove now and then and stop to chat and, sometimes at night, when everyone else was gone, he would even invite me into his office. He would pour a couple of Macallans and we would drink together and talk – or, that is, he would talk, and I would listen. I was never quite sure whether he wanted to make certain I got things right when I eventually wrote about him, or if he just considered me a harmless cipher who would take his secrets with me when I left to begin my real life. But whatever his reasons, he confided in me. And, in due course, he began to trust me with small investigative chores. I lived for these. They made me feel like a real detective, as if I too, like Weiss and Bishop, were one of the fictional heroes of my youth.

I was just settling down at my computer when my inter-office line went off. It was Sissy. She wanted me in her office. It was down the other hall so I had to walk back through the reception area to get there. As I passed Amy again, I saw her hide a smirk in her coffee cup and all my sense of strength and righteousness deserted me. Truly I tell you, it is easier for a wealthy camel to enter Heaven through a needle's eye than it is to keep an office love affair secret.

I found Sissy standing at the far window with her back to me. Traffic noise rose up to us from Market. Sunlight streamed in through the staggered city skyline. I shut the door. Sissy turned to face me across her desk.

She was a woman of delicate beauty, starting to fade. She had pale skin and blue eyes and golden hair. She had a whispery voice that inflamed me. She had a small, slender figure that fit wonderfully into a man's hands. She always dressed like a schoolgirl, in pleated plaid skirts and white blouses and pastel cardigans and so on. She had a sweet, motherly way of tilting her head to one side when she smiled. She smiled now, and whispered, 'Hello there, my little puppy dog. Did you get a good sleep last night all by your lonesome?'

That was another thing: she talked shit like that. All the time. Sweetie-pie, puppy dog, baby boy – that sort of thing. When I first met her, I have to admit, it made me want to make love to her. Now that I had made love to her, it made me want to throttle her and then maybe hack her into little pieces with some sort of kitchen implement.

But all I did was grunt, 'Yeah. Okay, I guess.'

'No kiss?' She made a pouty face. 'You're not going to give your mama a kiss?'

Have I mentioned I was a feckless poltroon? I went around her desk and kissed her on command. And I confess when I was doing it, when I was immersed in her clean, soapy scent, when I felt her tongue in my mouth and her fingers on a spot at the back of my neck I hadn't even known I had – I confess I was hers again for the moment and breathless for our next night together.

After a long time – a long time – I drew back – back from her lips but only far enough so I could look into her milky, maternal gaze. My body was still pressed hard into hers.

'Jesus, Sissy,' I panted.

'Hm? What? Whatsamatter with my baby?'

'Aren't we supposed to be at work or something?'

She touched my cheek and pursed her lips and giggled as if I were the cutest thing imaginable. She was happy – she was so happy to be in love and have a man of her own. 'Well, we are,' she whispered. 'We are at work. In fact, I have a very special job for my sweetie to do. That's why I called you.'

She kissed me again, on the nose, then on the mouth, very gently. I lingered, slavish, at her lips, even more excited than before. This was her other hold over me: assignments. Weiss had let it be known around the Agency that I was available for occasional investigative work. Since most of our work came from the attorneys on the two floors upstairs, and since most of our legal work went through Sissy, she was the one who had the most assignments to give out. I wanted them, those assignments. I wanted them as much as I wanted her, maybe more.

We were still in that kiss – I was still at her lips – when she said, 'Scott's been called out of town.' Her breath flowed warm into my mouth.

I breathed back. 'Weiss? Out of town? Where'd he go?'

'I don't know. It was very sudden. And he has a client coming in this morning.'

I swallowed. I moved so that my lips brushed her cheek. My heart beat hard against her breast. 'You want me to take one of Weiss's clients?' I said. I had never done that before. I had never taken a client at all. I had never even imagined doing it – or, that is, I had imagined it, but I had never imagined it could actually happen.

Sissy made a rough noise in her throat. She tilted her face up to me. Our lips came together and her tongue was in my mouth again. My hands felt the shape of her bottom through the pleated plaid. While I ground myself against her, a thought came to me.

'I don't even have an office,' I gasped as we broke apart.

'What? What?'

'To see the client in. An office. Don't I need an office if I'm going to see a client?'

'You can use Weiss's,' she moaned into the hollow of my throat.

'I can use Weiss's?' I buried my face in her wispy hair. 'I can use Weiss's office?'

'Sure. I told you. He's not here.'

'Weiss's office?' I said again, only it came out something like *Whysososo?* as I was simultaneously overcome by Sissy's cool fingers down the back of my pants and the mental image of myself enthroned in the high-backed swivel chair that was the Agency's heroic seat of power.

Now Sissy, her waist against my waist, tilted her shoulders back. She gazed up at me and her gaze was full of meaning. Her whisper was full of meaning as she whispered my name.

It had come to that moment, you see, that moment when you are supposed to tell a girl you are in love with her. Only I was not in love with her. I was in love with Emma McNair. So I couldn't tell her.

I gazed down at her. I tried to make my gaze full of meaning too. I tried to make my voice full of meaning. I said, 'Who's the client?'

I could see the disappointment flood Sissy's eyes. She continued to look up at me but it was a sad look now, wistful. She pressed her lips together. She brushed the back of her hand regretfully against my cheek. I knew exactly what she was thinking. She was thinking that her baby was not mature enough to make a commitment. She was thinking I was still too much of a boy to realize how in love with her I was. Also, she was thinking she would wait for me to come around, she would wait no matter how long it took.

And yes, yes, all this made me despise myself even more, if that was possible. But at the same time, I really did want to get the lowdown on this new client. My first client.

'I just thought I ought to to be prepared,' I told her.

Sissy took a deep breath. She gave a deep sigh. She tugged herself away from me. I released her. She turned and bent over a folder open on her desk. The sunlight coming in behind her touched on wisps of her golden hair and made them shine.

'He's a professor out at Berkeley,' she said. Her tone was a little more distant suddenly.

I nodded. Professors were becoming something of a specialty with me, probably because of my Agency reputation as an over-educated egghead.

'Oh, and you should like this,' Sissy went on drily. 'He's a novelist too. It says here he won the Pulitzer prize.'

A thought fluttered at the edge of my mind like sparrow wings at the corner of my eye, but it flew off before I could catch it. It's odd about things like this. We modern types, we're so trained in skepticism, so immersed in our faithless climate of opinion, that we sometimes stare right through our own destiny when it's smack in front of us. If this were fiction – I mean, the ordinary sort of fiction made up entirely out of my head – I couldn't even tell you what came next. You'd complain, you'd say: *That's pure coincidence; that would never happen*. But, of course, pure coincidence of the most fateful kind happens all the time, every day. Why should we let our theories about life override our experience of it? Why should I waste time wallowing in reasonable explanations? Why can't I simply tell you: it happened as if it were meant to be.

Sissy said, 'His name is Patrick McNair.'

Even then, there was a moment when I stood by the window as if I hadn't heard her, as if I were still waiting for her to speak. There was a moment more when I understood what she said, but didn't realize, couldn't bring myself to realize, what it meant.

My client – my first client – was Patrick McNair. The English professor. The prize-winning novelist.

Emma's father.

10

It was two hours before McNair arrived. A good thing too; I needed that time to recover my senses. At first, after Sissy spoke his name, I couldn't think at all. My head was filled with a noise like wind rushing through a tunnel. I was stunned by a whirling sense of mystic impossibilites.

Of course, like most amazing coincidences, this one was not as amazing as all that. I had met Emma while working on a case involving a lady professor. The lady professor probably knew McNair and recommended Weiss to him. That's what I told myself in any case. Still, the wind roared in my head.

I left Sissy and made my stumbling way back down the hall, back through the glassed-in reception area, back past the smirking Amy, and down the further hall to my alcove, my desk. I sat there a long time, making copies, typing reports, doing whatever the hell I did, I wasn't sure then and I don't remember now. Mostly, I think I watched the digital clock on my desk. With every minute that ticked away, a sensation grew inside me, a feeling between dread and panic. I could think about nothing but my meeting with Patrick McNair.

Why was he coming? What could he want? Could it have anything to do with me? There were no answers in the manilla case folder Sissy had given me. A name, a brief description, an address. I kept turning back to it, opening it, scanning the two typed pages inside, but there was nothing else.

The time of our appointment approached. I got up from my desk with the folder in my hand. I stepped with the tread of a condemned man down the last stretch of hall to Weiss's office at the end. I opened the door slowly. I stepped gingerly across the threshold.

I shut the door. For a long time, I simply stood there, stood where I was. I looked at the place with what I would have to call reverence. Weiss's office. Somehow, just being there began to calm me down.

Weiss was my hero. Bishop was my hero too in his own inimitable mad dog way. But Weiss... there was something about Weiss that had completely captured my youthful imagination. His solitude, his sorrow, his worldly wisdom, his nearly mythic acceptance of life as it was. Just standing there in that empty office – in his spiritual presence, as it were – the wind-tunnel roar in my head grew fainter, my mind grew quieter, grew still.

I didn't turn the lights on – not yet – but the sun through the wall of large arched windows made the place bright enough to see clearly. It was a large room, as Weiss himself was large, a cavernous space with a vast desk on the far side of it, two huge blocky armchairs for the clients and, of course, the famous swivel chair itself with its high, high back and its thick arms flanking an impossibly spacious seat. The wall to my right was made up almost entirely of those windows, the apex of their arches rising to just beneath the ceiling. They seemed to open the room up into the city and to bring the city right inside the room. They showed a sweeping, vertiginous view of the ornately carved stone buildings across the street, and the jagged, gleaming rise and fall of modern towers beyond.

After a while, when I had settled down, I turned the light on. I moved forward, still holding McNair's folder. I went around the enormous desk to stand beside the great chair. I had to take a deep breath before I could bring myself to sit in it.

Then I sat, sat silently a while, swiveling slightly back and forth. Without thinking, I propped my elbow on the chair arm and rested my cheek against my fist – exactly as I had often seen Weiss do. What would he have made of this? I wondered. My first client, Emma's father. What would a down-to-earth ex-cop like Weiss have made of such a wild improbability?

I considered the question and sat and swiveled and leaned my cheek against my fist. Soon, I found that I was even thinking to myself in Weiss's voice. I was thinking, *Hey, it's a mystery, that's all. We think we know what the world looks like, but that's just our own bullshit we're looking at. Past the bullshit, take my word, it's a fucking mystery.*

Just then, I was startled by the ringing of the inter-office phone. I hesitated, then picked it up: 'Uh... Yeah?'

It was Amy. She was still smirking. I could hear it.

'Patrick McNair,' she said.

He was a small man, solidly built, fat in the belly the way drinkers get fat. In fact, as I stepped up to shake his hand, I caught the scent of whiskey on him, though it wasn't yet noon. He was bald with a flyaway fringe of silver hair. He had a round, pug, pinched Irish face. His cheeks were laced with scowl lines that seemed to have been carved into them with a putty knife. He had squinting eyes sunk deep into the flesh – eyes that looked out at me from a remove, withdrawn but watchful, a drunk's eyes.

As I showed him to one of the client's chairs, I noticed that he was dressed in an expensive and formal suit, black with a bright red paisley waistcoat in the English fashion, a bright blue tie. There was a generous sprinkling of dandruff on his shoulders. He somehow managed to come across as austere and unkempt at the same time.

I expected to have to explain to him why Weiss wasn't there, why such a young man was handling his case. I even had a little speech worked out about how I was supported by the full power and experience of the Agency and so on. But none of that was necessary. McNair began speaking even as he sat, even before I'd made my way back around the desk to the swivel chair.

'I suppose I can assume this is all confidential. There are situations in which one hopes never to find oneself, and sitting in the office of a private investigator certainly fits that description.' He spoke like that, in a stilted, old-fashioned way, as if he were a character in a novel. He had a slow, rolling bass voice that added to the effect.

'Of course,' I said, grateful to sink into the chair again, hoping it would steady me.

'The idea that anyone might know I'd been here, talked to you, especially about private family business...' He made a great show of shuddering. He gave a single, bitter laugh. 'It's bad enough I know it.'

I offered him what I hoped was an encouraging gesture. Then I put my cheek back on my fist – a conscious action this time, trying to conjure Weiss's gravity and wisdom in myself. It didn't work. My heart hammered. My mind raced.

Patrick McNair, meanwhile, seemed to gather himself for a great effort. Then he said, 'I want to talk to you about my daughter.'

It's not easy to fall over when you're already sitting down, but I nearly managed it. My elbow slipped off the chair arm and I – leaning on my fist – nearly went over the side with it. 'Your... your daughter?'

'Her name is Emma.' He sat like a pharaoh in the

blocky chair, his head erect, his back stiff, his arms lying flat on the chair's arms. He seemed very conscious of his dignity; disdainful, lofty, fearful that the grime of our grimy business might somehow rub off on him. The more he talked, and the more personal the talk became, the more he seemed to fear he would be soiled. 'She's my only child.'

At this point, I couldn't respond. I couldn't believe what was happening. It even occurred to me this might be some kind of joke or prank. Maybe Emma was taking vengeance on me for not calling her when I said I would.

I had repositioned myself now to keep from tumbling to the floor. I sat straight, my hands folded in my lap. It was silent in the room an uncomfortably long time before I realized McNair was waiting for me to prod him to go on with his story. I managed to stammer: 'What seems to be the problem with her? With Emma. Miss... Emma. With her.'

'Well – I'm not sure,' McNair said. 'I'm not even sure there is a problem. In fact, that's the problem: I'm not sure. I seem to have found myself in a position where I can either lower myself to snooping on her, following her, listening in on her phone calls and so on, or I can resign myself to ignorance.' Without relaxing his lofty pose, he let out three sudden barks of harsh laughter. 'Fortunately, it occurred to me that snooping and following people wouldn't present the same sort of moral dilemma for you. For you, it would just be business as usual.'

It took me a second to work out the insult but the insult was the least of my concerns. With popping eyes, I blurted, 'You want me to follow Emma?'

'I want...'

'I mean your daughter,' I said. 'You want me to follow, um, your daughter, is that right?'

'I want you to find out what, if anything, is troubling her, and I want you to find out without her knowing you're finding out. I'll leave the methods to what I'm assuming, perhaps foolishly, to be your expertise.'

At the moment, I could understand his having doubts. My mind just then was like a demolition derby, the thoughts like stock cars racing every which way, crashing into each other. No matter how hard I tried to think it through, the full breadth and consequence of the situation was beyond me. He wanted me to follow Emma? Spy on her? When I'd already wronged and insulted her so badly? It was impossible. It was madness. To have the perfect excuse to be near her, and yet not be able to tell her I was there? And I would never be able to tell her! And what about him, her father? If ever I got the chance to be with her, how could I ever let her introduce me to him? What would he say when he realized who I was and how he and I had met?

That wind-tunnel roar was rising in my head again. My heart was racing again. I was perilously close to babbling hysteria.

'Maybe we should start at the beginning,' I said, to buy some time, to calm myself. 'Maybe you could explain what brought you here in the first place, what made you think Em... your daughter... needs to be watched.'

I would've thought this would be the point where a client would say something like, 'I hardly know how to begin,' or at least hem and haw for a moment as he worked to get his story in order. Not McNair. He answered immediately, declaiming in such complete and complex sentences that it seemed as if he had composed the whole thing beforehand and was merely reciting it now.

'My daughter recently turned twenty years old,' he

said in his grand bass voice, shifting in his chair to sit even more pharaonically erect than before. 'For most of her life, she and I have been extremely close. I know normally you'd think a girl would form her primary bond with her mother, and my wife has certainly provided her with – ' he waved a hand dismissively – 'all the attentions, food and so forth children need when they're younger. But my daughter had a very lively, quick intelligence from the start. She has the makings of an intellectual, so it was natural she would turn to me as soon as she developed to the point where she could begin to understand the world.'

He had a way of looking at you as he spoke, a sort of suggestive glance up from under the eyebrows. It communicated the idea that he was saying much more than he actually said, that his narrative line was surrounded with a mist of subtleties. Between my own confusion and this talent he had for unspoken implications, I had a hard time following any of it. But I guess I got the general idea all right: he and Emma were close. I forced myself to focus.

'Given the situation – and the fact that we were father and daughter – and I suppose my own inclinations to some extent – well, for any number of reasons – there was always an educational element to our relationship. We were like teacher and pupil sometimes. And like any good relationship between a teacher and a pupil it became something more like a friendship as the years went by, as the age difference became less pronounced. Seems natural to me,' he added, as if I'd objected it wasn't, instead of just sitting there like an idiot staring at him with eyes glazed and mouth agape. 'Since she and I were so much alike, I thought, if nothing else, I could save her some time by helping her learn not only how to think, but what sort of things she might enjoy thinking about. I wish someone had done it for me! By the time she was sixteen, I'd given her a complete course in western civilization. We read our way together from... from the Bible and Homer to Beckett and deconstruction.' He gave that sharp, hard laugh again. '"The realms of gold."'

'Ah,' I said. 'Byron.'

'Keats!' he snorted with contempt.

'Keats! Keats! I meant Keats!'

With an exasperated roll of his eyes toward Heaven, he went on, 'The point is: she and I began with natural, genetic similarities and this education I'm describing tended to emphasize them. If she'd gravitated more to her mother, or been raised by, I don't know, some shoe salesman in Milwaukee somewhere, it wouldn't have happened that way, but she wasn't and it did. When she graduated high school – just to give you an example – her final project was some term paper or other, I don't know. But she turned in an almost book-length treatise arguing that the maturation of western man could be traced in the life and death of the idea of God. It was brilliant stuff, it really was. It could've been a doctoral thesis. She argued that the projection of human personality onto the gods of Olympus and Sinai created a magical, infantile world reflecting the infancy of civilization and that, despite the ups and downs of history, this idea has steadily matured into an understanding of God as a psychological illusion – and of psychology itself – the self itself – as an illusion created by brain function. I mean, I remember sitting and reading this and thinking, "My God – so to speak – I could've written this myself – so to speak!"'

He laughed again, and eyed me carefully to make sure I had caught the high irony of those 'so to speak's.

I hadn't. I was still too busy gaping at him stupidly.

And I was thinking, *Keats! Why the hell did I say Byron? I knew it was Keats! I meant to say Keats!* My one chance to impress him with my literary knowledge, to show him I was more – oh, so much more – than just some sleazy, stupid private eye like – well, like Weiss or Bishop – and I said Byron! Byron when I knew it was Keats!

It must've been easy for him to tell that I had no idea what the hell we were talking about anymore. His eyes fluttered with frustration. He lifted his hands from the chair arms and moved them as if shaping the words in the air for me so I could read along with him. At the same time, he began speaking more simply, slowly, loudly, enunciating each syllable with painful clarity as if speaking to a foreigner or a child. 'So you can understand – right? – given how close she and I have been – you can understand why I might be troubled by the fact that recently, suddenly, Emma has begun to avoid me. For no apparent reason. We haven't argued. We haven't even disagreed. There's nothing domestic – I haven't left the cap off her toothpaste tube or anything. In fact, as far as I can tell, there's been no hostility between us at all. We used to spend several evenings a week together. We used to go to the movies sometimes; talk about ideas; discuss her schoolwork. Now, she keeps to her room or slips out before I come home at night. She gets up early and leaves before I come down to breakfast in the morning. She's a full grown woman and she's going to have her own interests, her own friends – although God knows what she'd talk to them about – but all right, she is. But she doesn't have to run away from me. I thought she *enjoyed* our talks and so on. She never indicated anything else. It always seemed to me that we were the best of…'

His words trailed off to nothing and he shrugged. He looked at the floor and shook his head. I don't think he had meant to be so direct about it all. I think he'd only wanted to make sure he'd been clear enough to penetrate the iron wall of my stupidity. But in stating the simple facts, he had let his simple emotions show as well. Intellectuals hate that. I know them. They hate to be reminded that they are just like the rest of us in all the basic and most important ways. McNair loved his daughter beyond anything, loved her as any farmer or mechanic or – what was it? – any shoe salesman from Milwaukee might love his. Now she was suddenly, inexplicably estranged from him and he was just as hurt and baffled as the farmer or mechanic or salesman would've been.

Exposed in this, he grew, if possible, even stiffer and more formal than before. He straightened again. He seemed to turn to stone in front of me. The silence went on awkwardly between us, long enough for me to gather my thoughts.

Then I said, 'Have you asked her?'

'What?' he said, startled.

'Why she's changed toward you? What's going on in her life? Have you asked her?'

He snorted. The tone in which he spoke next reminded me of the whiskey I had smelled on his breath. 'What am I supposed to do, crawl up to her room and beg for her companionship? Am I supposed to whine to her like one of her girlfriends? "Why don't you like me anymore?" Her behavior's been perfectly obvious. If she had wanted to explain it to me, she would have.'

'You'd...' *rather hire a private detective to follow your own daughter than simply ask her what's up?* I almost said. But looking at the proud, wounded and probably somewhat drunken intellectual across the desk from me, I already knew his answer: Yes; yes, he would.

I was about to speak again when something – a possible explanation for Emma's behavior – occurred to me and I paused. In an instant, my inner state dropped dizzingly from the heights of dazed confusion into the depths of darkness and depression. Raising one hand to my lips, tugging my lips between thumb and forefinger, I considered this new possibility. With every moment that passed, it seemed more and more plausible, until at last it seemed inescapably true. I began to ache – to ache hard. Emma. It was not just McNair who had lost her. I had lost her too and by my own folly.

'She must be in love.' It came out of me in a tone of quiet wonder, spoken aloud before I'd meant it, before I'd fully thought it through. But now I came to myself. I confronted the man across from me. 'I mean, doesn't that seem like the most likely explanation? A young girl acts mysteriously, slips out at night and early in the morning. She must've fallen in love with someone and for one reason or another she's not ready to tell you about him yet.'

The professor answered with a violent snort. 'Why shouldn't she?' he said – but he looked past me. He avoided my gaze. 'She's had boyfriends before. It's never been like this. We've talked about them – openly. Sometimes we've even laughed about them. She's still always found time for a movie or our conversations and so on.'

The darkness in me grew darker, the sorrow deeper. She could've been mine. She would've been. All I had had to do was call the damn number on the Carlos coaster. She had been made for me. Made for *me*.

I had to force myself to answer him. The words were thick in my throat. 'Maybe she doesn't want to laugh with you about this one,' I said. 'Maybe she wants to take this one seriously.'

McNair blustered, making a vague circular gesture with one hand. Clearly, he didn't like this idea any more than I did. 'Well...' His mouth worked. His eyes darted here and there as if he were searching for an avenue of escape. 'Well... maybe. What can I say, since we don't know? Of course: maybe.'

He scowled at the walls, the floor. He still wouldn't look at me. But I looked at him. I sat there with my hands in my lap again. I looked at him and nodded to myself. This was no more mere coincidence, him coming here. This was a cosmic rebuke. This was all the forces of the universe speaking to me in a single voice, saying, *Shmuck! All you had to do was call the fucking number!*

The pain of it was terrible. I hadn't fully realized until then how much I had hoped Emma and I might love each other.

After another long moment of silence between us, the older man sighed. Sitting there as if enthroned, frowning regally down at the floor. 'Whatever,' he said – it seemed to fall from him with a thud. 'Whatever it is, I want you to find out. Whatever it is. I want to know the truth.'

PART TWO

Bishop's Sword

11

That Sunday morning, suddenly, Bishop was set free. He was surprised. He'd been expecting trouble.

Ever since he'd broken the clay-headed guy's arm, he'd been lying on his cell bunk wondering what kind of hell he'd have to pay for it. He figured Ketchum would dance on the Hall of Justice rooftop when he got the news. Before this, the inspector had been keeping him here on bullshit charges that wouldn't hold up ten minutes in court, but there was all kinds of garbage he could throw at him now. Bishop figured he'd be behind bars for a year before he even got a hearing. It was his own damn fault too. He should've kept out of the whole business. He should've let Clayhead cut the punk's head off. What did he care?

But it was too late to worry about it now. He'd done what he'd done, there was no changing it. So he waited on the cell bunk, expecting trouble. Only trouble never came. Deputies came. They took the screaming Clayhead away. Then, a little while later, they came back and took the screaming punk away, the willowy pale-as-paper punk whom the clay-headed guy had been trying to kill. They took him away in his soiled overalls, and Bishop figured they'd come back for him next. But they didn't. All that night and all the next day and all the next night, they didn't. Deputies went past the cell and new prisoners arrived and old prisoners left, but no one said a word to him. If Ketchum was dancing on the roof, it was a long dance. He was still at it. Nothing happened.

Then, about eight o'clock Sunday morning, a towering deputy with a sorry face opened the cell door. He waggled his thumb over his shoulder. 'Bishop,' he said.

Here it was then. With a grunt, Bishop got off his cot. Rolling his shoulders defiantly, he strode out of the cell into the hall.

But it was strange. The sorry-faced deputy didn't cuff him. He didn't even take him by the arm. He just walked down the hall to the elevator. After a second, Bishop followed him. They rode down silently together one floor. They stepped out into Processing. There was a counter and then the big tiled room where Bishop had been searched when he came in. A short, round deputy shoved a plastic bag across the counter at Bishop: his clothes. Bishop took the bag into the tiled room. He stripped off the county orange and got back into his jeans and his t-shirt. The clothes smelled of beer and there were whiffs of that girl too, that bank teller or whatever the hell she was. He was glad to get them back.

When he was dressed, he came out again. The big, sorry-faced deputy returned to the elevator. Bishop followed him. This time, they rode down to the fourth floor, Homicide.

The sorry-faced deputy led the way through the maze of desks and filing cabinets and inspectors in their shirt-sleeves. He led Bishop back to that cramped, dingy interview room the size of an outhouse, the room where Ketchum had harassed him when he was first arrested. The deputy held the door open and Bishop stepped into the room.

'Wait here,' the deputy said.

It was the same as before. Bishop sat slouched in the chair, staring at the grime-dark soundproofing. Waiting for Ketchum to finish dancing on the roof or whatever the hell he was doing, and come down here and charge him with battery or attempted murder or conspiracy to run a criminal enterprise or something and basically throw him into the hole for the next five years or so. The only thing he didn't understand was why they'd given him back his clothes.

Now here came Ketchum, also the same as before – Ketchum and his Baleful Glare of Wrath, exactly the same. Same as before, the sinewy little black man propped a foot on a chair seat and leaned over Bishop, seething and silent.

Finally, Bishop got sick of it. 'What the hell's going on?'

'If it was up to me, you piece of garbage...' Ketchum growled back at him.

Bishop didn't get it, at first. Then the surprising idea occurred to him. 'What? You mean I can go?'

Ketchum couldn't even bear to say it out loud. He nodded. He took his foot off the chair. He turned away, snarling and despondent.

Bishop blinked, scratched his jaw. It was an unexpected turn of events, all right. What do you know? he thought. He hadn't realized how crappy he'd been feeling till just now when he suddenly felt a lot better. He had no clue what was going on, but he wasn't going to ask questions about it either. He got out of his chair. His sardonic smile found its way back to his face.

Ketchum caught that, caught the smile with a sidelong glance. That was too much. He shook his head in disgust. He muttered curses into the knot of his tie. 'Yeah, you can be real proud. You can put this on your resume. You know why? You know why you're getting out of here?'

Bishop shrugged. 'No. Do I care?'

'If it was up to me, you'd be looking at battery.'

'Yeah, I figured that was coming.'

'But you know that fuck? That fuck whose arm you broke?'

'Yeah?'

'The fuck with the knife?'

'Yeah, the clay-headed fuck with the knife, sure, I know him.'

'Punk he was trying to kill?' said Ketchum.

'Skinny white kid, sure. What about him?'

'Name is David Adalian?'

Bishop's mouth opened. He made a little noise, a sort of laugh. The two men were only a couple of feet apart from each other in that outhouse of a room. For a second, he could only stand there, looking deep into Ketchum's steaming brown eyes.

'Like Joseph Adalian?' Bishop said finally.

Ketchum gave a quick nod, jutting out his chin. 'He's Joseph Adalian's son.'

'Whoa,' said Bishop.

'The punk and the fuck were dealing meth together. Punk's an idiot. Fuck's a fuck. Punk got busted, dealt the fuck, fuck didn't like it, tried to cut the punk.'

'Except I broke his arm,' Bishop murmured.

'Except you broke his arm,' Ketchum growled.

Bishop laughed. 'So now Adalian...'

Even Ketchum chuckled once in a dejected, nauseated sort of way. 'Right. Now Adalian calls some of the lawyers he owns, and the judges he owns, and the faggot mayor and district attorney who if you ask me he also owns...'

'And suddenly I'm free as a...'

'...psycho piece of shit in a city run by circus clowns, you got it.'

'Actually I was gonna say bird. Free as a bird. Or maybe a spring lamb,' said Bishop.

Ketchum made that dejected chuckling sound again. He shoved his hands into the pockets of his slacks. His narrow frame was hunched as if he were carrying an anvil on his shoulders or maybe just the weight of an idiot city. 'Congratulations. You now have a friend in organized crime. Like I said, you can be very proud.'

Bishop snorted. 'Yeah, that is embarrassing.' His leather jacket was hanging on the back of his chair. He worked it off and slung it over his shoulder. 'I sure do hate to leave under those circumstances.'

'Yeah, I'll bet.'

'If it makes you feel any better, I'll go home and dress in orange and sleep in a room full of muscle-bound Mexicans.'

'Don't press your luck, prick. You'll be back.'

'It's always a pain in the ass to see you, Inspector.'

'Likewise.'

It was only a single step to the interrogation room door but Bishop managed to put some swagger in it.

'Hey,' Ketchum said.

Bishop paused, looked at him, his hand on the doorknob.

Ketchum said: 'Adalian's the devil. Take my word. Whatever he offers you, you put your hand on it and you won't need me to run you to ground. You'll die in prison as sure as I'm standing here.'

'Thanks,' said Bishop. 'That's a very helpful tip. You should write a book.' He turned back to the door.

'Hey,' Ketchum said.

Bishop rolled his eyes, looked at him again.

Ketchum said: 'Why'd you do it?'

Bishop shook his head. 'Do what?'

'The fuck. Break his arm. Why'd you do it?'

'Hell, I don't know. He had a shank.'

'Yeah, but he wasn't after you. He was after the punk. You knew I'd come down on you for it. You could've just let him cut away. You don't give a shit. So why'd you do it?'

Bishop thought about it a second. 'Because,' he said. 'Because fuck him.'

He walked out and left Ketchum muttering.

12

It was a fine, clear, cold September day. Bishop tooled his bike slowly across the Bay Bridge. His mouth tasted bad and he stank like garbage but, after two nights in lockup, it was good to be outdoors. The water spread sparkling around him. The cities of the East Bay lay before him in a mist of distance. The red rooftops dotted the green hills. The green hills rose against the blue sky. He felt the bike rolling under him. It was a decent feeling.

It didn't last. By the time the bike poured off the bridge into Berkeley, all the crap in his life had come back to him. Having his girl get arrested and screwing over Weiss, losing his job and even that pain in his shoulder from where the psycho had stabbed him which he'd forgotten about while he'd been in the can.

His bike sputtered up the avenue. The shops and streetlights whipped by on either side. There were the white stone buildings of the university up ahead and the green iron of the university gates. He curled the bike to the right, gunned it past the rising hill of campus grass. By now, all his good feelings about getting sprung were gone and he was pissed off and miserable again same as before he'd been arrested.

The Harley went on, down among the tall, faceless, concrete dormitories on the south side. Splitting the lanes, cutting around the slow traffic of old student cars, Volks after Toyota after dusty Chevrolet. Bishop motored left and made his way to Telegraph.

His building was on the near corner, a dingy brown pile of brick and stone, elegant once, but not for a long time. Past the intersection, on the Avenue itself, a steady flow of students and hangers-on slouched past the rock star posters plastered on the windows of a music store. On a billboard hanging above them there was a picture of a sports car and the words, 'Experience Freedom.'

Bishop pulled his bike to the curb. Shut it down. Swung off.

He stepped through the fine old oak doorway of his building into the vestibule. He paused there to open the creaking brass flap to his mailbox, to yank out some fliers, some bills. He pushed into the foyer. Slid back the cage of the old elevator. He rode upstairs, blinking, tired, irritable. He scratched his stubble with the edge of a piece of mail.

Fucking Ketchum, he was thinking. *Fucking Weiss too. Fuck all of them.*

The elevator stopped with a jolt. He rattled open the cage. As he shuffled down the carpeted hall, he sniffed his armpit, made a face. He smelled like something in a frat house refrigerator. *Fucking CJ. Fucking everything.*

He opened his apartment door, went through. He let out a long, whiffling breath as the door swung shut behind him.

The apartment was big but there wasn't much furniture in it. There wasn't much point buying furniture. He never stayed anywhere long. He threw the mail on a phone table just inside the door. He moved into the center of the living room, facing the tall windows on the far wall. He stood there, tired, looking at the view without really seeing it. The windows showed the flat roofs of the Telegraph shops and the blue sky beyond them and the billboard with the sports car on it. Experience freedom.

Good idea. Only his life was crap. *What now?* he thought. What the hell was he going to do now?

Here was something though: patting his shoulder, he found his Marlboros in the slash pocket of his jacket. The bastard deputies hadn't stolen them. It was his lucky day, after all.

He shot a cigarette between his lips. Torched it with a plastic lighter. He drew smoke and felt the nicotine rush all through him, sweet, like a flower opening. It was the best thing that had happened to him since that piece of ass he had been nailing when the cops came for him, the real estate agent or whatever she was.

He took another hit off the cigarette. He closed his eyes. This was good. Fuck everything. This was really good.

The two gunmen ruined the moment. That was the kind of guys they were. He heard them creeping in on either side of him, one coming out of the bedroom, one from the kitchen. He didn't bother to jump back or put up his dukes or anything. Without looking, he knew they had guns. In fact, for another second or two, he didn't even bother to open his eyes.

Then he did. Sure enough, they had him covered with a couple of very serious-looking Glock 31s. Not just guns. Big guns. Catch a slug from one of those, they have to pick up your body with a vacuum cleaner.

Bishop took another drag on his cigarette. He looked from one gunman to the other. The guy who'd come out of the bedroom – he was the good one, the dangerous one. Young, still twenty-something. Tall and lean. Sleek and muscular most likely under his crisp slacks, his red windbreaker, his white cable sweater. Mixed race, with light brown skin, a long, smooth, handsome face with a thin layer of hair over his jaw and up top. He had calm, cold, smiling eyes – a little like Bishop's eyes, in fact. He kept his stance relaxed, kept an easy grip on his gun, kept his left arm casually slung across his belly, casually steadying his right wrist to keep his aim nice and true.

The other guy – the one who'd come out of the kitchen – a stocky, nervous white guy with thinning red hair – he was amateur night, a back alley arm-breaker. A gym rat, judging by the ripples in the muscle shirt under his brown leather jacket. He had a lot of twitches, quick glances this way and that, as if people had been sneaking up on him his whole life.

'Fuck with us and we'll feed you your knees,' he said tensely.

Bishop snorted. He glanced over at the brown-skinned gunman from the bedroom. 'Feed me my knees?' he said. 'What kind of threat is that? What kind of cheap operation is this anyway?'

The brown-skinned gunman shrugged wearily. 'What can I tell you?' He had a smooth, mellow voice, no accent, just Northern Cal. 'Listen, this isn't really a gun play, Bishop, awright? Our guy just wants you to come with us, no problem. It's not a killing thing. Really.'

'Come on, come on, let's go,' said the arm-breaker. 'You wanna do this on your feet or on your face?'

'Is this guy, like, an intern or something?' Bishop asked the brown-skinned gunman.

The brown-skinned gunman laughed.

That made the arm-breaker angry. Twitching, looking this way and that, he moved in on Bishop. 'Oh yeah. Give me an excuse. Make me happy. Give me a reason to put you down.'

Bishop took his gun away and smacked him in the nose with it.

'Ow!' said the arm-breaker. 'Jesus! Fuck!' He grabbed his face with his hand. Blood flowed out of his nose, ran between his fingers.

The brown-skinned gunman sighed. 'Morris, you are such a fucking knucklehead.'

'Oh. Oh shit,' said Morris, cupping his hands under his nose to catch the blood.

Bishop gave Morris's Glock to the brown-skinned gunman. 'Thanks,' the brown-skinned gunman said. He slipped it into the pocket of his windbreaker, still shaking his head. 'You ready?' he asked Bishop.

'Whatever,' said Bishop. 'If we're going, let's go.'

13

The windows in the limo's back seat were blacked out: the side windows and the rear window, and the glass partition that sealed off the front. They were all blacked out so Bishop couldn't see where they were going. That's why they'd come for him at gunpoint probably. Bishop wouldn't have gotten into a blind spot like that if he hadn't been at the point of a gun.

Morris, the knucklehead, was driving, out of sight. He'd been casting a lot of dark looks at Bishop ever since Bishop had busted his nose so Bishop was glad to be rid of him. The brown-skinned gunman rode in the back. The kid knew what he was doing. He sat against the opposite door, as far from Bishop as possible. He held the gun close to his waist, pointed at Bishop but out of Bishop's reach. Bishop knew if he tried to take it, he'd be blown into the middle of next Thursday.

The brown-skinned gunman didn't say anything. He didn't even seem to be watching Bishop, although Bishop knew he was. After a while, it sort of got to Bishop, sitting back there with no one talking, nothing to look at.

Just to break the silence, he said, 'So is this about Adalian?'

The brown-skinned gunman didn't answer.

But it was. It was about Adalian. About half an hour after they started out, Bishop felt the limo slow, heard the growl of a motor, an electric door being rolled back. The car bumped forward and the door rumbled closed behind it. The car stopped and the brown-skinned gunman said, 'Let's go.'

Bishop stepped out into a windowless warehouse. Shelves stacked with brown boxes lined the wall. There was a man with a clipboard talking to a man sitting on a forklift. Other than that, the place was empty.

Morris got out of the driver's seat. He was still giving Bishop dark looks. His nose was swollen and red. His lips were puffy. The dark looks just made his face ridiculous, like the face of an angry child. He drew his Glock again. The brown-skinned gunman had given it back to him after Bishop took it away.

The three men walked across the concrete floor, their footsteps echoing. Bishop and the brown-skinned gunman walked side by side. Morris walked behind them with both his gun barrel and his dark looks trained on Bishop's spine. They reached a white door. The brown-skinned gunman knocked. Someone inside said, 'Yeah?' The brown-skinned gunman opened the door and stood back to let Bishop enter.

He came into a small office. It was crowded with metal shelves. The shelves were stacked with books and papers. There was only one man in the room and it was Adalian. He was standing behind a scarred wooden desk, holding a piece of paper up in front of his reading glasses. He was a big, heavy-set man who might have been athletic once but had gotten out of shape. He had a large head with black and silver hair. He had a hawklike face that was not quite handsome. His gray eyes had a certain flatness to them, like a one-way mirror on the mirrored side. He was about fifty-five years old.

He was wearing slacks and a white shirt, the sleeves rolled up, a blue tie loosened at the neck. His jacket was draped over the back of a cheap office swivel chair. Ketchum had said he was the devil but he didn't look like the devil to Bishop. He looked like a businessman, any self-made businessman. You could tell just by his expression that he had that self-made businessman attitude, that bristling certainty about himself: *Hey, if I'm not right all the time, how come I've made so much money?* That's the sort of guy he looked like to Bishop, not the devil at all.

Adalian glanced up from the page he was reading. He looked at Bishop over the top of his glasses – and got a load of Morris's throbbing red beezer out of the corner of his eye. 'What the hell happened to you?' he asked the arm-breaker.

Morris could only answer with a lame gesture.

'I broke his nose,' said Bishop helpfully. 'He was getting on my nerves.'

'Oh yeah? What was he, talking tough?'

'Yeah – and badly.'

'I know. He does that.'

'Threatened to feed me my knees.'

'Feed you your knees?' said Adalian. He peered over his glasses at Morris now. 'Does that even mean anything? What does that even mean?'

Morris could only make the same lame gesture.

Adalian sighed. 'I don't know. What can I tell you?' he said to Bishop.

Bishop nodded in sympathy. 'Good thugs are hard to find nowadays.'

'You can say that again.' Bishop didn't, and Adalian held a hand out toward a chair in front of his desk, an old steel-framed chair with torn green cushioning. 'Have a seat,' he said. 'You smell like shit, by the way.'

'Thanks. I've been in lockup for two days. Your boys didn't give me a chance to shower.' Bishop lowered himself into the chair.

Adalian lifted his sharp chin to the gunmen. Bishop

glanced over his shoulder to see them leaving, closing the door. As he did, he caught a whiff of himself. He did smell like shit, it was true.

When he faced front, Adalian was settling his big, out-of-shape body into the swivel chair on the other side of the scarred wooden desk. He peeled his glasses off and tossed them down onto the blotter. 'So,' he said. 'You saved my son's life. That was my son – the whiny little dickhead – you saved his life in county.'

'Right. So I heard.'

'So I owe you.' Adalian gave him a hawklike glance from under one bushy white eyebrow. 'What do you want?'

'That's a pretty big question.'

'Give a big answer then.' He gestured at the shabby little office as if it held a glittering display of worldly pleasures. 'Anything you're likely to think of I can probably supply.'

'Thanks, but I don't really need anything.'

'That's not what I asked you.' Adalian leaned forward, forearms on the edge of the desk, hands together, fingers intertwined: the pose of a captain of industry eye-locking an underling for a heart-to-heart. 'You wanna hear what I know about you? You wanna hear what the word is about you on the street?'

Bishop shrugged.

'You were military,' Adalian said. 'Some kind of big-time black ops killer shit, no one knows what. But you got all the weapons skills and hand-to-hand skills. Plus you can fly pretty much anything. Plus you can drive pretty much anything. All things being equal, you oughta be a valuable player, government, private, whatever you want. The only problem is you're all psycho inside, I guess cause of the war shit and everything. So you got yourself into some small time trouble, broke into a house, kidnapped a family, whatever. And Weiss, back when he was a cop, let you off with a beating, right? Cause you've got all those medals, and everyone knows Weiss is Mr Born-on-the-fourth-of-July and all that shit. So now you're his lapdog, running around helping old ladies across the street or whatever it is you do for him. A private eye. They still call it that? Whatta you, take pictures of jerks fucking other jerks' wives, shit like that?' Adalian parted his hands, an almost priestly gesture. 'Hey. To each his own. Don't get me wrong. And I know Weiss. We all know Weiss. I like him. I admire him. Hell, he put me away for seven months once and it was my own judge on the bench at the time. Guy's incorruptible – plus some good friends of mine make a lot of money off his hooker habit. No, listen, really, if I had another life, I'd wanna come back as a guy like Weiss. I really would.'

Bishop nodded politely, but he didn't believe it for a second. He thought if Adalian had another life he'd want to come back as Adalian only with even more money.

'But let's be realistic here,' Adalian went on. He sat back now in his chair, hooking a thumb in his belt, making little motions in the air with his free hand. 'I'm not that guy. And – and this is the point I'm getting to – neither are you. I mean, come on, what is that? What kind of small ball life is that for a big league player like yourself? Are you starting to see what I'm saying?'

'No,' said Bishop.

'I'm saying you should be working for me.'

Well, this was a day full of surprises. Bishop wasn't expecting that at all. 'Oh,' he said.

'This,' Adalian said with another grand gesture at the crummy little room, 'this is what you might call your natural habitat. Being my guy is the job you were born for. So I'm gonna give it to you. That's how I'm gonna pay you back for rescuing my piss-puddle of a son.'

Bishop sat still, in his usual slouch, with his usual ironic half smile on his face. He gazed at Adalian's hawk-like features through his pale eyes and gave nothing away. But he was interested. He was thinking: *Yeah. Maybe. Why not?* He was out of work. He couldn't survive forever without a paycheck. He couldn't even survive a very small part of forever. And Adalian was probably right. This was probably the sort of thing he was made for in the end. It was like his fate catching up to him or something like that.

'What kind of job are we talking about?' he asked.

Adalian made that little motion – a little circular motion in the air – with his hand. 'What do you mean what kind of job? A job for me. Doing what you do. Being who you are. Expressing your inner Bishop, what-ever. Good money too. Real money. Genuine happy-time cash. Plus whatever else you feel like. Girls? I run girls'll suck your dick so hard your socks'll come through it. You like to travel? I got business in Thailand, Russia, China now, the Middle East. Plus there'll be plenty of the kind of psycho violent stuff you get your rocks off on and you won't have Weiss hanging over you, wagging his finger or whatever. Plus the next time that what's-his-name, the nigger, Ketchum – next time he rousts you, you can beat the living shit out of him on me and he won't be able to do a goddamn thing about it. How's that sound?'

Bishop was still sitting in that way he sat, still smiling that way he smiled. And the truth was, it sounded pretty good. The way he was feeling – fuck Weiss, fuck Ketchum, fuck everything – it sounded like just what the doctor ordered.

'Come on, Bishop,' Adalian said. 'You don't belong with a guy like Weiss. Guys like Weiss, they mess with a man's head. They think they make the rules of the world. I mean, I'm talking philosophically here if you can understand me. A guy like Weiss: you cut a man's heart out for the fucking government, he gets all misty-eyed, calls you a hero. You do it for me, suddenly you're the bad guy.' He gave an elaborate shrug and made a sound with his lips like *pffft*. 'Where the hell is that written? It's just him. It's just the way he looks at it. So you look at it another way, I look at it another way. So what? He got on you about that bitch, I'll bet, didn't he? That bitch in the papers who got charged with murder. I'll bet he got way down on you for that.'

For all his self-control, Bishop couldn't help the answer from showing itself in his eyes. Not that Weiss had said anything to him about the girl, but he didn't have to. Bishop figured he knew where Weiss stood.

Adalian pointed a finger at him and laughed. 'Eh? Eh? What did I tell you? He gets in your head, he fucks with your brain. Weiss, see, he's not open-minded. He needs to be more open-minded. This is San Francisco, right? This is a very open-minded town. That's why I've done so well here.'

Bishop frowned, considering. He had often thought similar sorts of things himself.

Adalian sat back in his chair, folded his hands over his belly as if he'd just finished a satisfying meal. 'So what do you say? Good work. Good money. Goodbye bullshit. What's not to like?'

Bishop wasn't sure why he hesitated. It wasn't anything that Ketchum had said about his dying in prison or anything. He was already pretty well sure he was going to die in prison one way or another. This way might be fun, at least. It sounded like his sort of thing. He took to heart what Adalian said about Weiss and his stifling rules and his disapproving attitude. That had always bothered him. Still, he hesitated. This – this job Adalian was offering him – this was exactly what Weiss had been trying to keep him from. This was exactly where Weiss had seen him going when he'd dragged him out under the Golden Gate Bridge that night and beat him senseless and advised him not to live out his life as a piece of shit. Bishop got pissed off at Weiss sometimes, but Weiss was all right more or less. Somewhere deep down, he sort of hated to disappoint Weiss after Weiss had gone and made a project of him and everything.

So he didn't answer right away. He sat there thinking.

That made Adalian impatient. Adalian was a busy man. He only had so much time for this back-and-forth shit. You were either in or out. He leaned forward on the desk again. He dropped his voice to an intimate just-between-you-and-me tone. 'Hey,' he said. 'Let me be frank with you on another score. Speaking strictly career-wise? Weiss is not exactly a long term proposition anyway.'

Bishop shifted in his chair. He worked the corner of his lip under his teeth. 'What do you mean?'

'I'm just saying. If you're looking to invest in the future, his is limited.'

'What do you mean?' Bishop said again.

'How clear do I have to be?' said Adalian.

'Clear,' said Bishop. 'What do you mean? You mean there's a whack on him or something? There's a contract out on Weiss?'

Adalian only shrugged, as much as to say, *You said it, not me*.

Bishop fell silent again another second or two. This also was news. And it probably had a much different effect on him than Adalian intended. It bothered him. It bothered him more than he wanted to admit or even to feel. An electric sense of urgency fanned out from his belly, up through his chest. He was worried about Weiss, about Weiss getting whacked – just the sort of ordinary human emotion he never expected from himself, that always caught him off guard. Only his natural instinct for cool allowed him to speak in his usual ironic drawl. 'Hell, what's that about? Is this because he put you away? You gonna whack him because of the seven months he put you away for?'

'What?' said Adalian. 'Oh no, hell no. I'm not like that. I'm not a spiteful person. Weiss did his job, that's all. Me, I move on, I look to tomorrow. This isn't about me.'

'So what's it about? What, did you hear this?'

'Sure. A man in my position. You know, I pick things up, I hear things, yeah.'

'So it's a rumor,' said Bishop. He was inclined to disbelieve it. Aside from the hookers, Weiss was clean. You never get hit if you're really clean, or almost never.

Adalian still didn't really understand how this was working on Bishop. He thought if he could prove what he was saying, Bishop would see there was no future with Weiss and take the job with him. 'You know the Frenchman?' he said.

'The Belgian guy, sure.'

'I referred a guy to him.'

'So?'

'A guy I know. A guy who did some work for me.'

'A specialist,' said Bishop. 'A whack guy...'

'He was stocking up for a job.'

'Did he say it was Weiss?'

Adalian slowly shook his head. 'We didn't talk particulars.' He relaxed back into his chair again, a little knowing smile on his lips like a cat sitting by an empty goldfish bowl. He waited for Bishop to figure it out.

And Bishop did figure it out, some of it anyway. He figured out which specialist they were talking about. He knew how much Weiss wanted the guy and he knew how much the specialist wanted Weiss. He knew about the missing whore too, some of it. He knew the whore was between them. He knew, if they were going to come down to it, it was going to be over the whore.

Bishop went on looking ironical, looking cool. But he felt that urgency spreading through him, growing deeper. He felt something else as well. He was irritated. He was pissed off – pissed off at Weiss. If the specialist was gunning for him, then Weiss must've made a move to find the whore. That's what the specialist was waiting for, that's the only thing that would bring him out into the open. What the hell was Weiss thinking? Did he think he could take this mutt down, finish it off between them – and maybe get a couple of flutter-eyed thanks from the whore into the bargain? That would be stupid. Stupid? It would be fucking nuts. Weiss was a street cop, a door-to-door, desk and paper man. Tough and all that, fine up against some liquor store shooter. But not this guy. He was no match for this guy. Man to man against the specialist, he would get himself killed and the whore probably with him.

Adalian was still stuck on the other thing, the thing about the job. 'So what do you think?' he said, breaking into Bishop's thoughts. 'You're my guy now, right? I pay you back for my piss-head kid, you work for me and get the life you were made for. Yes? No? What do you say?'

Bishop stood up. The second he saw it – saw the way Bishop stood – Adalian understood his mistake. He threw his hands up and let them fall until they slapped the chair arms. He made a big show of gaping at Bishop with an open mouth. 'Oh, come on,' he said. 'Don't tell me.'

Bishop made a little gesture of regret, a lifting of the hand, a shrug. He would've liked to take the job. He really would've. 'You can consider us clear for your kid,' he said. 'You paid me back with the tip on Weiss, the stuff about the Frenchman.'

'Aw, come on, Bishop,' Adalian said. 'Whatta you think you're doing? You think you're gonna stop this. You're not gonna stop this. Believe me. I know this guy. This guy did work for me. He'll kill you, Bishop, even you, so help me. What do you think? You think you're gonna, like, redeem yourself? Make good with Weiss over the girl? Save his life, get back in his good graces. Believe me. This guy will plain kill you. You and Weiss both.'

'I'll see you, Adalian,' Bishop said.

'I'll see you. I'll identify your body, how's that? And don't expect any help from me with the Frenchman either. You're on your own there.'

Bishop only lifted his chin by way of farewell. He walked to the door.

'And take that shower,' Adalian said behind him. 'I'm serious. You fucking stink. You dumb fuck.'

Bishop waved without looking back. He stepped out into the main bay of the warehouse. The limo was still there, waiting for him. The brown-skinned gunman was leaning against the hood, smoking a cigarette. The other gunman, the arm-breaker, Morris – he was nowhere to be seen – and then suddenly he was. Suddenly he stepped out of a shadow along the wall at Bishop's shoulder. He was hunched and angry-eyed, his bruised face flushed. He had his Glock drawn. He had it pressed close to his side, the bore leveled at Bishop.

'This isn't over between you and me,' he snarled. 'We'll settle up and it's gonna cost you in blood.'

Bishop took his gun away and smacked him in the nose with it. He left him writhing and screaming on the warehouse floor and walked over to the brown-skinned gunman. He handed the brown-skinned gunman Morris's gun.

'Drive me back to my place,' he said. 'I got stuff to do.'

14

Weiss hit Hannock that same day and started tailing a man named Andy Bremer. He hated following people. It was boring and sleazy. You sat in a car and drank coffee till you needed to piss so badly you thought it would kill you. Then, without fail, just as you decided to go find a bathroom somewhere, your subject started moving and you had to hold it in and go after him. Finally, your bladder on fire, you ended up watching the poor bastard try to steal something he shouldn't steal or buy something he shouldn't buy or fuck someone he shouldn't fuck – in other words, you watched him trying to find some pathetic version of happiness even as you knew all the while that he would never be happy ever again precisely because you were watching him and were going to tell the person who hired you, who was probably the person your subject least wanted told. Fucking was the worst. Standing outside some hotel window, needing to piss, snapping pictures of some guy's hairy ass bouncing up and down between some girl's open knees. Weiss had a romantic streak. He knew full well this moment might seem like hearts and flowers inside the guy's head, inside the girl's head too. But outside the hotel window, it was just a bouncing ass and open knees. Some photographs. A screaming spouse. Alimony. Misery all around.

With Andy Bremer, he wasn't even sure he was trailing the right guy. It was just one of his Weissian hunches that had brought him here. And while his hunches were almost always right, he almost never trusted them. They were too vague, too unscientific. He wished he could write out the facts on a whiteboard or something and look them over and tap the pen against his chin and reach his conclusions through logic and deduction. But he never could. He just knew what he knew, so he never felt certain of it.

In Paradise, for instance, he started with the fact that Julie Wyant had called him from a pay phone. There were other calls made from that pay phone as well, but somehow he just had a a hunch they weren't hers. He figured she wasn't using a cell phone because it would be too easy to locate. He figured she wouldn't use the same pay phone twice for a similar reason – Weiss might trace the call she'd made to him and find out who she'd called next. So using an old contact at the phone company from his police days, he collected some calls from other pay phones in the area, calls that had been made within an hour or so of the call to him. There weren't that many pay phones around anymore, but he still managed to come up with more than thirty calls. The call to Andy Bremer in Hannock caught him somehow. He wasn't sure why. It was made about the right time and Bremer lived in the direction Julie was traveling and – well, it just caught him. It was one of those Weiss-type things.

So he set off for Hannock, to the northeast. It was a little oasis of oaks and evergreens and clapboard ranches on the edge of the desert. It was pleasant and shady but every street seemed to end in dust. The dust ended at the snow-capped Sierra Nevadas rising in the distance against a sky made pale by a scudding mist of clouds. With all that nature and emptiness everywhere, the town felt to Weiss like the frontier outpost it had once been. It was the kind of place that made him itch to be elsewhere. He was a city boy through and through.

He drove his drab Taurus down the deserted morning streets, past open playing fields and a silent, flat-roofed school and into deeper shadows under clustered junipers. At the end of one tree-lined lane, he parked outside Bremer's house. It was a gray two-story with gingerbread trim on a peaked roof, one of the few two-story houses in the neighborhood.

No one was awake yet inside. Weiss drank a styro of coffee he'd picked up at a gas station food mart on the edge of town. He watched the house. He wondered if the specialist was watching him or just tracking him from somewhere nearby. He checked up and down the shadowed street. There were cars parked along the curb. He didn't see any people in them but he knew the killer was out there somewhere. Just a question of where, that's all.

Sipping his coffee, he read the pages he had printed off the internet, off the computers in the hotel in Paradise. There was a biography of Bremer from a United Way site and some pictures from his real estate home page. Every time Weiss read the material, his stomach grew more sour and he became more convinced he was following the wrong guy. Bremer looked squeaky clean. A family man in his mid-sixties. Small, barrel-chested, energetic-looking. A realtor. Married to what looked like his second wife, a slim, pert, attractive lady in her forties. Two kids: a girl maybe six, a boy maybe seven.

Weiss finished the coffee. He hauled a leather case up off the floor. He unzipped it and took out his camera, a Canon Rebel. He screwed on a 300mm zoom. He peered through the lens into Bremer's kitchen window. It was a nice, clear view.

The man himself came into the kitchen around half past seven in the morning. His son and daughter were clamoring at his heels. The kids sat at the kitchen table, the boy playing with a toy car, the girl with a doll. They gabbled at their father while he made a pot of coffee. Then he started to stir up some waffle mix in a metal bowl.

After a while, the wife came in, wearing a bathrobe. She kissed her husband and poured herself a cup of coffee from the pot. She drank the coffee leaning against a counter, watching the kids shovel waffles into their mouths. She laughed as they scraped the last drops of maple syrup off their plates. Bremer washed the dishes, meanwhile, and chatted with the missus over his shoulder.

'Uy,' Weiss groaned to himself. Wrong place. Wrong guy. A bad hunch, a waste of time.

Maybe Bremer wasn't what he seemed, but he sure seemed to be what he seemed. Everyone has secrets and everyone lies. But mostly it's nothing. Mostly they're just hiding things that make them feel small and sad. They have less money than they pretend, less sex. They drink more than they say. They watch more TV. They use drugs and pretend they don't. They look at pornography and pretend they don't. They steal in one way or another. Their kids are going bad. They're ashamed of their dreams.

Weiss was sure Bremer had his secrets too, told his lies just like everyone. But sitting in his Taurus, peering through his camera into the guy's kitchen window, it seemed pretty unlikely that this was a man who got phone calls from hookers on the run from contract killers.

After breakfast, the Bremer family got dressed and went to church. Weiss followed them there. When they were safely inside, he returned to their empty house and went in.

Wary of nosy neighbors, he approached the place carrying a clipboard as if he were going to read a meter or take a survey or something. He had a set of burglar picks in the pocket of his tweed jacket, but it turned out he didn't need them. The door was unlocked. He walked right in.

The massive man had to step gingerly across the living room. The Bremer boy's superheroes and the girl's dolls littered the tan carpeting. Weiss reached the stairs. He went up to the second floor. He went down a hall and found Bremer's study, his computer, his cabinets. He turned the computer on.

The computer had no security system. The passwords were stored right on the machine. Weiss went through Bremer's word processing files and emails. Bremer served on the church vestry and worked on a committee for the local United Way. His son had had a problem with a bully at school. His wife had had a breast cancer scare, but was all right. The real estate business was on the upswing. There were other things, this and that. But nothing about Julie Wyant. Nothing about the Shadowman.

Weiss blew out a long, weary breath. He turned his attention to the desk drawers. He found manilla folders full of credit card statements. He laid them on the desk and paged through them. Here finally, there was one small item that caught his attention: an American Express charge for a night at a Super 8 Motel on the edge of town. The charge had been made one week ago. Checking back, he found another Super 8 charge two months before. When he dug up the records for another two months back, there was the Super 8 again.

There was an oak close by the study window. A gold-finch perched on one of its naked twigs. Weiss glanced up from the pages in his hand when he heard the bird's triple chirp and trill. It was a pretty yellow bird, a cheerful sight. His gaze rested on it absently and then wandered back to the room.

He was sitting in the cheap leatherette swivel chair behind Bremer's desk. The desk was a battered crescent, the walnut veneer chipped away in places to show the plywood underneath. The surface of the desk was crowded with framed snapshots of Mrs Bremer and the two children. Left and right of the desk, there were scribbled crayon drawings thumbtacked to the wall paneling. Weiss's gaze lingered on one of them: four stick figures – Mommy, Daddy, sister, brother – standing under a rainbow hand in hand.

The picture made Weiss feel bad: lonesome and lowdown. The whole place made him feel like that. He had no business being here. The empty house around him felt like a stage in a closed theater when the play's over and the actors and the audience are gone. It was charged with traces of an intimate energy that belonged to the people who had been here and left. It was not meant for him. For him, the place was hollow, echoing, dead. He would've liked a family like Bremer had. He was the family type. He would've liked a wife who leaned against the kitchen counter and drank coffee and chatted, children who gabbled at him. But he was never any good with women. He thought too much of them, in spite of everything he'd seen. He'd even had a wife once – a poisonous snake of a woman – the whole thing had been a disaster – and still he held onto his high romantic notions. Somehow that made the simple things impossible for him. The only women he had these days were whores.

He went on gazing at the crayon drawing without really seeing it. He held the pages of the Amex statements drooping from the fingers of one hand. Why did a man get a room in a Super 8 in his own home town? he wondered distantly. For an affair maybe, but there were plenty of innocent explanations too. It might've been for a visiting friend or relative, or for a night away from the kids with his wife, or for a business associate. Weiss moved his hand up and down as if weighing the pages. It probably had nothing to do with Julie Wyant. But it stuck with him, all the same.

A clock chimed somewhere downstairs, bringing him back to himself. The Bremer family would be home soon. Weiss put the pages back in their folders, filed them away. Switched off the computer. Grunted out of the chair and lumbered out of the study. Trudged downstairs. He stepped out of the house into the cool morning. He left the door unlocked just as he'd found it.

He drove slowly through the neighborhood, past sidewalks overshadowed by oak trees and the occasional yellowing sycamore, past low houses on half-acre lawns. He came to the Bremers' church on the corner of a broad thoroughfare. There was a grassy median in the middle of the road, early traffic whizzing by on either side. He parked outside the church and waited.

The church had a square tower of brown brick with narrow arched windows and battlements on top like a castle. With the car window down, Weiss could hear the people singing hymns inside. Now and then, he checked the rearview mirror, looked right and left out through the windows, checking to see if he could spot the assassin he knew was watching him, trailing him. There was nothing. The whizzing traffic. An old couple, bent-backed, arm in arm, walking away from him on the sidewalk. A woman on the median waiting for a bus.

Weiss turned back to the church. He sighed and waited. He still felt sordid and depressed. He was on the wrong trail. Wrong guy. Wrong place. But he kept thinking about the charges for the Super 8 motel. That held him.

The last hymn ended. The minister came out of the church and stood in the entryway. Then the people came out, shaking his hand as they left. There was Bremer with his wife and children in the exiting crowd. The children wore paper crowns they must've made in Sunday school. Bremer and the minister shook hands and smiled and spoke together a moment. Then Bremer took his wife's hand. The children ran laughing in front of them toward their car, a red Buick SUV. Mrs Bremer belted them inside the car and her husband held the passenger door open for her. Then he went around to the driver's side. He got in and the SUV drove off.

By now, Weiss had to take a piss pretty badly. He hated following people.

He started up the Taurus and went after the Bremers.

15

Bremer dropped his family off at the house. Then he drove on alone to his real estate office, a glass-fronted box between a diner and an ice cream parlor on Main Street. Weiss waited outside in one of the slanted parking spaces out front. He could see Bremer moving around inside through the window. Most of the rest of the shops were closed but people came in and out of the diner as the little town woke up. Craggy-faced men in woolen plaids and middle-aged women with their hair dyed blonde. They all seemed to know each other, greet each other as they passed in the diner doorway. It was not like the city.

Half an hour of that, and Bremer was on the road again with Weiss behind him. They drove to a house on a street called Arcadia. It was a long ranch faced with white shingles. It was out by the edge of town, on the edge of the desert, the last empty home in a new development. Bremer hauled an A-frame sign from his SUV and placed it out front. The A-frame sign said, 'Open House. Andrew Bremer, Hannock Homes.' He went inside.

Weiss had hung back at the corner to keep from being spotted on the empty street. But now he edged the Taurus into position so he could watch the house. He needed to piss like crazy at this point, but there was nowhere to go. He sat tapping the steering wheel, chattering his teeth. To take his mind off his bladder, he ate a sandwich he'd bought off the shelf in the gas station food mart. He couldn't even tell what was in it. It tasted like paste.

After a while, househunters began to show up. Over the course of an hour or so, Weiss counted four young couples, one family with children, and a man alone. From time to time, he watched them through the big lens of his camera. The househunters prowled from room to empty room with their hands behind their backs and their chins jutting forward. They stepped warily, as if they might turn a corner and plummet into a hidden pit.

Weiss thought Bremer looked like a good salesman. He seemed to follow the customers and lead them at the same time. He kept a certain distance from them, but he was always near enough to gesture at the house's selling points or deliver some pitch or other Weiss couldn't hear.

The people came and went, and after a while the house was empty except for Bremer. It was now around three o'clock. The sun was descending toward rising groves of pine trees to the west. In the east, the distant mist of clouds was gone. The blue behind the mountains was growing deeper.

Weiss had to make a decision. A man can't go without pissing forever, that's just the truth. He figured Bremer would probably stay at the house another hour or so. There was time to find a bathroom somewhere and come back.

But Weiss decided to go into the house. He'd convinced himself now that his hunch was all wrong, that the call to Bremer hadn't come from Julie at all. And he figured, if it had, there was no better way to find out than to ask him.

He unfolded himself from behind the wheel and headed up the front path in the chilling afternoon air. Dressed in slacks, a dark blue polo shirt and the tweed jacket, he looked like the cop he'd once been. He pretty much always looked like the cop he'd once been. He secretly prided himself on it. When he bowed beneath the lintel of the open door, he stood within the threshold in a small foyer, his hands in his pants pockets, his shoulders slightly hunched – exactly the way he'd stood waiting for hundreds of interviews during his stretch on the force.

'Hi. Welcome.'

That was Bremer. He came out of the kitchen at Weiss's back. Weiss turned to see the short, stocky man approach with a swinging stride, his broad chest leading the way. Weiss shook his offered hand. Bremer had a powerful handshake. He had a direct gaze through crystal blue eyes and a strong, rugged face under shaggy white hair. Weiss, being the way he was, caught something in his glance, some hesitancy or emotion. He couldn't quite figure it out. Whatever it was, it made him wonder about his hunch all over again. He decided to go slowly, play out the househunting routine until he had a chance to take the measure of the man.

So they moved through the place together. It was newly built, unfurnished. Its walls were lined with broad windows and sliding glass doors. In every room, hardwood floors gleamed under the westering beams that fell through the panes. Bremer talked about the durability of red oak, the insulation of dual-pane windows and other things Weiss hardly listened to. Weiss stepped warily with his hands behind his back and his chin jutting, trying to imitate the other prospective buyers he had watched through the camera.

After a while, he asked to use the bathroom. He pissed with great pleasure and relief, closing his eyes and lifting his face to the ceiling. When he was done, he washed his hands and looked at himself in the mirror. His sadsack mug and his cop costume. What the hell was he doing here? What the hell was he doing?

When he came out, he couldn't find Bremer at first. Then he found him in a broad, bright room in back. He was standing in front of yet another wall of sliding glass doors. He was looking out one of the doors at the swimming pool behind the house and the wide, brown valley that stretched out beyond it. The land was dotted with brown shrubs and dull green cactuses. The sky was still changing color as the day died. It seemed to be growing more solid somehow. The mountains were beginning to seem flat against it as if they were painted on.

'Nice view,' said Weiss, still playing the househunter.

Bremer nodded his head up and down a few times, his lips working. Then he said, 'Listen, Weiss, you keep following me and my family and I'm gonna take a crowbar to that rolling hunk of shit you drive and maybe to you too.'

Weiss found he was only half surprised by this. He had sensed something, after all, from the moment they'd shaken hands. He went on looking out at the desert.

'I guess Julie warned you I might show up when she called from Paradise,' he said.

Bremer gave a rough snort. 'Listen to you. "Julie." You don't even know her real name. That's a whore name. That's all you know.'

'All right,' said Weiss. 'What's her real name then?'

'What difference does it make? That's gone. Everything she ever had is gone. All she's got left is her life and that's just running away all the time and now you're gonna take that too. You bastard. What're you doing here? Don't you understand you're gonna get her killed?' The man had a voice like concrete: level, hard, rough. Weiss felt as if it would scrape his skin. He didn't answer. He had no answer. Bremer snorted again. He sneered out through the glass door. 'What is it? You got some old grudge with this guy that's after her. You're

98

gonna settle your grudge over her dead body? Or is it just her? Yeah, I'll bet that's it, isn't it? Guys your age get stupid for her. It happens all the time.'

Weiss stared out through the glass door too, stared hard at the brown valley and the mountains painted on the sky. His hangdog face stayed hangdog and impassive, the way it always did. But he felt what Bremer was saying. It didn't just scrape his skin either. The words landed in his gut like punches.

'One of us'll find her,' he answered after a minute. 'In the end, it's gonna be one of us. Better me than him.'

'Yeah, but you're the one who can do it and you bring him with you. You know you do.'

'That's the thing. He's on me,' said Weiss. 'He's on me like he's on her. I wake up, he's there, I go to sleep, he's there, and it's the same for her, only she's running from it, like you said. She's gonna have to run forever. I want it over. I figure she must want it over too.'

Bremer glanced at him sideways – undiluted disdain – then looked away. 'Not like this. Not over like this. You know what this guy is, this maniac fuck. You know what this maniac fuck will do to her. Christ, he did it to her once already. If he was just gonna kill her, that'd be one thing, that'd be bad enough. But you know what he is. The maniac fuck. So what're you doing? Why the fuck are you doing this to her?'

Weiss stood shoulder to shoulder with the man. They both stared out through the glass. The desert shadows and the light of the sky shifted again, grew deeper. Bremer's reflection began to appear on the pane, Bremer's and Weiss's both, their images transparent, like ghosts haunting the wilderness beyond. Weiss could see Bremer's lips working, his jaw working in the image on the glass. Weiss could feel his own stomach churning as the things Bremer said punched into him.

Still, he insisted, 'I want it over. She's gotta want it over too.'

'Not like this. You're gonna lead him right to her.'

'It's not gonna be that way.'

'Bullshit. It is.'

'All right, look,' said Weiss. His gut was really roiling. He was finished with this. He'd taken enough. 'Look, it doesn't matter. It doesn't matter what you think or I think. I'm here now and he's on me. Watching. Listening. Right now. And what do you figure he'll do if you don't tell me what you know?'

'Jesus Christ. Jesus Christ,' said Bremer with a hard laugh. 'You're using him on me?'

'I'm just telling you.'

'Jesus.' Weiss saw Bremer's reflection, the twisted expression of disgust. He saw Bremer shake his head. 'You dumb shit,' Bremer said. 'You think he won't do it anyway. You think he won't come after me, my family. Look what you did now. You probably got us all killed already.'

'No. That won't happen,' said Weiss. 'Because then it's over. He knows that. Then I'm done and he's fucked. Like you said, I can do this, he can't. Like the way I found you, came here – that's what I can do. He can't. If he comes after you or your family, it's over and he's fucked. That's what protects you. He needs me.'

'It wouldn't have started at all if you hadn't come.'

'Tough shit,' said Weiss. 'I came. It started. Now it's on.'

'You bastard. You dumb bastard.' Weiss heard the other man swallow hard. That was all. Then the empty house was silent around them. It was silent and new and had a fresh, empty smell of wood and paint, and one day a family would come to live here. It seemed very sad to Weiss somehow. It weighed on him with all the rest. 'It doesn't matter,' Bremer said finally. Weiss saw his shoulders sag in the reflection. 'I don't know anything. I don't know where she is. I don't have any idea.'

'You lie to me and I can't help you,' said Weiss.

'I'm not lying. She called me that one time, that's all. You said she called from Paradise. That's more than I knew. I don't even know the name she goes by.'

'What about the motel?'

'What motel?'

'The room at the Super 8.'

'What…?' Bremer started – but then he must've realized what Weiss had done. 'Jesus Christ,' he said again, disgusted.

'What about it, Bremer? Is that where you meet her? Is that where you two get together when she comes? You must pay a lot for her to make the trip way out here. But then guys our age get stupid for her, isn't that what you said?'

Bremer shook his head. Weiss saw it in the glass doors. 'That's not her. That's not about her. The Super 8. That's something else.'

Weiss knew he was lying. And he could look at his face in the glass and he knew Bremer knew he knew. So all that high moral talk was bullshit in the end. All that squeaky clean living. Making waffles for his kids, going to church. Every two months, his favorite hooker came to town and he had her out at the old Super 8. That was Bremer.

'So – what then?' said Weiss. 'She called you to say goodbye? Is that what you're telling me?'

Bremer only nodded.

'She called you to tell you she couldn't see you any more.'

'That's right. Never again. She said she couldn't see me ever again.'

'And she warned you I might come. I might come or he might. That's why she couldn't tell you anything about where she was going.'

Bremer nodded again, swallowed again. 'That's why she said she could never come back. She didn't tell me anything else, just that, I swear.' Now he turned from the glass. He turned to face the detective. He let Weiss see the sneer straight on, never mind the reflection. 'Look at you. You bastard. Going after her. Bringing him with you. You're twice her age. You don't even know her. You never even been with her. It's all just daydreams. You're gonna make her die for your daydreams.'

Weiss sneered back. 'What makes you any better? You'd do the same. And you're just as old as I am – you're older. What the hell makes your daydreams any better than mine?'

Bremer's hard face seemed to go out of focus. His blue eyes went soft, looked lost. He turned back to the glass door. He looked out at the brown desert running to the blue and white mountains, all of it growing dark as the sun westered down.

'That's not what it's like,' Bremer said softly.

'Yeah, yeah. The hell,' said Weiss.

'That's not what it's like,' said Bremer. 'I don't have any daydreams.'

Weiss was about to speak again but he stopped cold. The truth came to him in that flashing way the truth had. *Son of a bitch*, he thought. *He's not Julie's john. He's not her lover at all.* He never knew how he knew these things but he knew when he knew them and he knew this. *Son of a bitch. He's Julie's father!*

The two men's eyes met on the glass – the reflection, the ghost of their eyes met on the glass with the desert visible behind them. Finally, they understood each other.

'Now get the fuck out of here,' Bremer said.

16

It was dark by the time Weiss reached the Super 8. The motel was the last place in town, the last lighted spot on the four-lane before the pavement vanished into the desert night. Against the darkness out there, the motel sign stood out bright yellow with the neon *Vacancy* sizzling bright orange underneath. From the parking lot where Weiss sat, the sign's light washed out the stars.

The motel was a small, single-story building, white, trim, well-kept. It was shaped like an L. The office and coffee shop made the base of the L, and the rooms extended along the edge of the parking lot in the L's arm. There were only five cars in the lot, six now with Weiss and his Taurus. There were lights on behind the white curtains in only three of the motel's rooms. The coffee shop was closed.

Weiss stood out of his Ford. A cold wind was rising. It blew in out of the darkness. He felt it on his face and he heard the flag on the flagpole behind the motel snapping somewhere above him. A TV was playing in one of the rooms. He could hear that too: danger music, as if someone were watching a cop show or something.

A truck rumbled past on the four-lane. When it was gone, Weiss heard the wind and the snapping flag and the music from the TV and the vast silence of the desert that surrounded them.

He walked toward the office, his hands in his pockets, his big frame hunched and huddled against the cold. He wasn't sure what he expected to find here. Bremer had said the place had nothing to do with Julie but he knew

Bremer was lying so that meant it did. He figured maybe this was where Julie stayed when she came to visit her father. He figured she was his daughter by some first wife and she had to come in secret so she wouldn't be seen by his respectable second wife. Something like that. He had wanted to ask Bremer about it. He had wanted to ask Bremer a lot of things. Julie had called her father to say goodbye because she had to run for her life. She had called to warn him that Weiss might come and the killer might come with him. Had she said anything else? Had she dropped any clue to where she was going? Was there anything in her past that might help Weiss find her? The questions had come into Weiss's mouth as he stood with Bremer in the empty house. They had come into his mouth – and he had swallowed them down.

For some reason – maybe the second wife, maybe something else – Bremer's relationship to Julie was his great secret. That's what Weiss had understood when his eyes met the father's on the glass. It was his great secret, and if Weiss asked about it, he would balk, he would lie and he would go on lying.

And then the Shadowman would come.

It was true what Weiss had said. He had a hold over the killer. He could stop looking for Julie and the killer would be lost. But that would only take him so far. If the specialist was convinced he might find her himself, he would step in. If he guessed Bremer was Julie's father, if he thought Bremer was lying and holding back, he would come not just for him, but for his wife and his son and his little girl – all of them until he had what he wanted. Bremer didn't know where Julie was, but the killer wouldn't know that. He didn't know things the way Weiss did. He would come to all of them until he was sure.

Weiss had brought that with him. Weiss would bring that with him everywhere he went.

So he did not ask his questions. He swallowed them down. He came here.

He pushed through the glass door, into the motel office. An electric bell sounded as he stepped in.

The office was neat and bright and soulless. There was a small sofa with flowers factory-stamped on the upholstery and a small Windsor chair and a wooden rack full of vacation brochures. There was no one behind the desk at first, but Weiss heard the TV playing through an open door back there. He heard ironical cartoon voices speaking.

After a second or two, a kid came out, a boy in his teens or early twenties. He was tall and fit. He was wearing jeans and a button-down striped shirt, untucked. He had a round face, his hair sandy, his skin very pale except where it was splotched with red acne. He had earnest, light brown eyes. They went over Weiss, up and down him. They looked wary, uncertain.

'Can I help you?' he said.

Weiss leaned on the counter. 'I'm a private detective. You know what that is, right? You've seen that in the movies.'

'I never saw it in the movies, but I know what it is,' said the kid earnestly.

'You never saw a private detective in the movies?'

'No,' said the kid, 'but I know what it is.'

'All right,' said Weiss. 'Well, in the movies, there's always a scene where the private detective bribes a hotel clerk to give him some information.'

'Yeah?'

'Yeah. And that's just like this. I'm gonna bribe you and you're gonna give me some information.'

The kid blinked, made a small, helpless gesture. 'I don't... How does that work? What is that?'

Weiss suppressed an irritated sigh. The trouble was no

one made detective movies anymore. Everything was about these space aliens and superheroes. Kids never learned anything about real life.

'What do you mean how does it work?' he said. 'It works like I give you some money and you tell me what I want to know.'

'Is that honest?'

'Of course it's not honest. That's why they call it a bribe.' *Idiot kid*, he thought. 'I'll give you twenty bucks. How's that?'

'Cool,' said the kid. So he wasn't a total idiot anyway.

The kid let Weiss come around the desk and look at his computer. They found the charge to Bremer's credit card and then compared the room number to the registration records. The room Bremer had paid for was registered to a woman named Adrienne Chalk. She had a Nevada driver's license and an address in Reno. Weiss wrote the address down on a motel pad.

'You remember this woman?' Weiss asked the kid.

The kid shrugged. 'I don't know. There's a lot of guests. I mean, it's a motel. Let me think about it.'

The kid thought about it. Weiss, meanwhile, went into his jacket pocket and brought out the photograph he had of Julie Wyant. He showed it to the kid.

The kid looked down at the picture. 'Wow. She's hot.'

'She might've had different hair when you saw her.'

'She would've had to. I would remember that hair.'

'Yeah, you would.'

The kid shook his head. 'I'd remember her anyway though. She's hot. I've never seen her.'

'Okay,' said Weiss. So he was wrong. This wasn't where Julie came to see her father. But it was still about Julie somehow. He felt sure of that. He slipped the picture back into his jacket pocket.

'I think I do remember this other woman though, now

I think about it,' the kid said after a moment. 'The woman who stayed here? This Adrienne Chalk? I think I remember her.'

'You don't have to say that. You get your twenty either way.'

'No, but it comes back to me. She was, like, older.'

'Older than what?'

'Older than me.'

'Everyone's older than you. How old was she?'

'Forty? I don't know. She was one of those women who always think people are looking at her.'

'Yeah? Was she hot too?'

The kid gave a dull laugh. 'She was forty!'

'Right. Stupid question.'

'Anyway, she was kind of... you know: cheap, whatever. All dyed hair and tight dresses. Wiggling around like every guy was gonna just, like, fall down for her, you know. It was kind of pathetic.'

Weiss was about to ask the kid if he thought the Chalk woman was a hooker, but he didn't. He didn't think the kid would know a hooker from the Virgin Mary.

'Okay,' he said, 'thanks. Here's your twenty.'

'Cool,' said the kid. 'What did this woman do anyway, cheat on her husband or something?'

'I thought you said you never saw this stuff in the movies,' said Weiss. He saluted the kid and went to the door.

As he stepped out into the parking lot, a car went past him. It went out the driveway, onto the four-lane, and turned left, back toward town. Weiss didn't get much of a look at the car, just a glimpse in the glow of the street-lamp above the lot. The car was navy blue, an American make, probably a rental.

Weiss slipped his wallet back into his front pants pocket. He walked toward his Taurus. There were four other cars in the lot now, minus the one that just pulled out. There were still only three rooms with lights on behind the windows.

It took another second for the math to kick in. If there were five cars when he arrived, including the kid's, shouldn't there have been lights on in four windows? There hadn't been – he remembered. There were only lights on in three windows and there were still lights in three windows now. If one of the guests had just pulled out in that navy blue car, then one of the lights should've gone off. It hadn't.

Weiss walked faster, pulling his car key out as he went. Maybe it was nothing. Maybe the car that just left had been driven by the coffee shop waitress or a maid or a janitor – except none of them would've been driving a rental. So maybe it was a guest and he just left the light on in his room.

Maybe. Or maybe the specialist had just made a mistake.

Weiss strode the last few steps to his car quickly and slipped in. The Taurus shot back out of the spot with a squeal of rubber.

He had the gas pedal flattened as he hit the street. He took off down the four-lane in overdrive.

17

There it was. A block away, at a corner, at a red light. Bathed in the white glow from the Shell station on one side and the car dealership on the other. Weiss got a quick glimpse of the license plates but couldn't read the number. Then the big car turned right off the four-lane onto a side street.

Weiss never slowed, kept his foot on the pedal. Raced to the corner. Swung around it, the old Ford's tires giving a short, sharp scream.

The navy blue rental was up ahead, cruising past a long, low building. Weiss recognized the place: the elementary school he'd passed coming into town. The rental's red brake lights flashed as it turned again, vanished again around another corner.

Weiss barreled after it, barreled past the school, past a stop sign. He streaked through an intersection, trying to reach the spot where the other car had just disappeared. His heart was going like a cop pounding on a junkie's door. Sweat was breaking out clammy at his temples. This was the guy, the killer. He knew it. He felt it. Only yards away behind the rental's wheel. Invisible all this time, silent as cancer all this time, and now there he was, within striking distance. A mistake. That business with the cars and the lighted windows. The killer had made a mistake after all this time.

It was all Weiss needed. He could get him now. He could end it here.

And then the dark blue rental was gone. That quick.

Weiss sped to a second stop sign, past the school. Braked not to stop, but to take the corner. Took the corner and came around onto a dark street of houses. Houselight after houselight glowed yellow in the shadows.

But the red taillights of the navy blue car were nowhere to be seen.

Weiss kept his foot on the brake, bore down. The Taurus moved slower and slower. It had happened too fast, he told himself. The car had disappeared too fast. It couldn't have reached the far corner before he'd made the turn behind it. Which meant it was still here. Somewhere. Somewhere on this street. That's what he told himself.

The cold sweat trickled down Weiss's temple and fell. His eyes searched the shadowy block, left side, right side. Small houses, small lawns. Cars in garages and in driveways, cars parked nose to tail along the curb. Weiss's eyes went over all of them, one by one, looking for the navy blue rental in the dark.

It was no good. Too hard to see. Weiss finally pulled the Taurus up against the line of parked cars. He opened the glove compartment. His .38 was in there, in its holster. He worked the gun out of the leather, slipped it into his jacket pocket.

He left the engine running, and stepped out into the street. The block was quiet. Above the hoarse whisper of the Ford's motor, he could hear the occasional car, the occasional truck going past on the nearby four-lane. Other than that, there was nothing, silence, not even a cricket in the night.

Then – suddenly: a metallic clang behind him. Weiss caught his breath, spun around. His hand slapped against his gun pocket.

But no, it was just a guy, some guy, a homeowner,

closing the lid of the trashcan at the end of his driveway after tossing the bag in.

'Hey,' Weiss said. He walked toward him.

The homeowner guy hesitated, wary as the big detective approached him in the darkness.

'You see a car just now, a blue car?' Weiss asked him. He got closer to the man, closer until he could make out his face in the dim light from the houses. The killer – his killer – had been in prison only once – in North Wilderness, a super-max, impossible to escape. The killer had escaped but, because he'd been there, there was a mug shot of him. Weiss had seen it. Seen the face. This wasn't that face. This was just a guy. Just a homeowner in a brown suede windbreaker. Medium height, round head, dark hair. Weiss asked him again: 'You see a blue car just now?'

'What, you mean go by?'

'Pull over, park somewhere on the street. A navy blue car, a big one.'

The guy looked up along the street as if he thought he might spot it even now. He slipped his hands into the windbreaker's pockets. He frowned, shook his head. 'I just came out to take out the garbage. I didn't see anything.'

Weiss nodded, but went on standing there, looking the guy over. Just a homeowner in a brown suede windbreaker.

The guy shrugged. 'Sorry.'

Finally, Weiss nodded. 'Thanks.'

'Sorry I couldn't help you.'

The guy turned and walked up the path to his house, his hands in the windbreaker's pockets. Weiss turned away. He looked up the street. He scanned the driveways and the garages and the parked cars. It would be easy to miss the blue car here. Easy for the blue car to hide. Or maybe he'd been wrong, maybe the rental really had had enough time to reach the next corner, to get away. He wasn't sure anymore.

Weiss walked back to the Taurus idling in the street. He climbed back in and popped it into drive. He cruised slowly along the street, reluctant to leave it, still turning his head back and forth, back and forth, scanning every driveway, every parked car, every open garage. It was a working class neighborhood. The cars were family four-doors and pickup trucks and aging sports models. The new American rental would've stood out, he told himself. Or maybe it wouldn't have. In this light, with all these models. He just couldn't be sure.

He cruised to the next corner, stopped at the sign. He considered turning around, going over the block again. But it was no good. The killer was gone. He'd lost him. He eased down the gas and turned right. He headed back toward the four-lane.

Later, about an hour later, with the dark at every window, with the desert all around him in the dark, Weiss started to wonder about the homeowner at the trash can. Does a guy put on a windbreaker just to take the garbage to the end of the driveway? And how come he hadn't heard the door to the house open when the guy came out or close when the guy went back inside? Had the guy gone back inside at all? He hadn't seen it. He didn't know.

He wondered about these things later, when his heart had slowed and his sweat had dried and the dark was at the windows.

But by then, he was long gone from Hannock. He was well on his way to Nevada.

18

In the town, on the dark street of houses, the man who called himself John Foy slipped back behind the wheel of the blue rental car. His brown suede windbreaker was thin and the night was cold, but he was sweating all the same.

He sat a long time, just breathing, just gazing out through the windshield with his strangely flat eyes. He did not see the things he was gazing at. He did not see anything outside himself. He was thinking about his tower. He was up in his tower in the calm and empty sky. The red waves of his rage were crashing, crashing against the base of the tower far below. He sat behind the wheel of the car and breathed.

The man who called himself John Foy liked to think of himself as a cool professional. We all have our self-deceptions, this was his. He liked to think of himself as a dispassionate tradesman who did what he did without emotion, without anger or remorse. The truth was very different. In truth, the killer was all rage. What in someone else might be a self or a soul, in him was rage alone. There was nothing else there. Sometimes he remembered his boyhood, the wounds and blood and the faces laughing, and he thought he felt sorry for the child he'd been. But he didn't, not really. Really, that was just his rage disguising itself in a sentimental form. Other times, he felt a lofty, almost intellectual competence in his work, a sense of himself as a living clockwork of plans and action. But that was also just an illusion – an illusion created by his rage.

When these forms and illusions failed him, when the rage rose red in him as nothing but itself, it was agony. It felt as if he were being burned and strangled at the same time. It felt as if some consuming flame within him and the choking malevolence of the cruel world without had become one thing. It was unbearable. He went away from it, climbed away. Up into his tower to stand there, empty, in the empty sky.

It was several minutes before he could come back to himself. Slowly then, his surroundings took shape through the windshield. He was in a garage, the rented Chrysler 300 squeezed in next to a large motorcycle. It was dark, but he could make out the bike and the silhouettes of shelves on the walls, power tools, paint cans, small glass jars.

He had spotted the garage and turned in, headlights off, only seconds before Weiss came around the corner behind him. He had leapt from the car and hidden there, crouched in the shadows, waiting to see what Weiss would do. When Weiss got out of his car to search the street for him, he had come out into the driveway. He pretended to throw garbage in the can to draw Weiss's eyes away from the garage and the blue Chrysler.

It'd been a risky move. If Weiss had caught on he would've had to kill him. He had had his hand wrapped around the compact .45 in the suede windbreaker's pocket the whole time. He had thought, any moment, he would have to pull the trigger, blow a hole in Weiss's paunch.

That's what enraged him – how close the situation had come to going out of control. If he had killed Weiss, the search would've been over. There would be a time for that, but not yet, not before he found the girl. He needed

Weiss to find her. He needed Weiss for that way he knew things he shouldn't have been able to know. It should never have been that close – standing there face to face with him like that, holding the .45 in his windbreaker pocket – it had been a mistake, that's all. Another careless mistake, like buying the guns from the Frenchman. And what infuriated him more than anything was that he wasn't sure exactly what the mistake had been.

He had been as close as a breath to Weiss over a dozen times and Weiss had never noticed him before. No one ever noticed him. He relied on that. He relied on his talent for invisibility, the way he could be with people unseen and then come upon them suddenly, like death – just like death. So what had gone wrong this time? The car wasn't the problem. The car was good. An obvious rental, a tourist car. It fit perfectly outside a motel. The man who called himself John Foy had sat in the car in the motel parking lot with complete confidence. From there, it had been easy to use his laser mike to read the vibrations on the office glass, to pick up Weiss's conversation with the motel clerk word for word. He was even able to see the two of them, clear and close, using a pair of powerful Epoch binoculars. He could even read Adrienne Chalk's address in Reno when Weiss wrote it down on the motel pad.

Weiss had come out of the office quickly but the man who called himself John Foy was ready for him. He was driving away as Weiss came through the door. He should've been able to leave inconspicuously, without being spotted. He'd planned the whole thing perfectly. He had it all worked out in his mind.

Somehow, though, Weiss did spot him. Infuriating. Because Foy didn't know how he did it. Maybe his invisibility was slipping. Maybe Weiss's eyes were somehow adjusting to him, the way eyes adjust to the dark. Maybe

Weiss would soon be able to see him anywhere, pick him out of a crowd...

No, that was crazy, paranoid thinking. That's what Weiss did to him. Weiss got inside his head, made him doubt himself. Weiss made him feel that, with all his plans and experience, he was still always a step behind. He had felt that way even before this, outside the empty house, when he was listening to Weiss talk to Andy Bremer. He had heard that conversation word for word too, watched it too, the same as the one at the motel. He hadn't missed anything – but he felt somehow he had. He felt as if something had passed between the two men without their even speaking and he had missed it. That was the sort of thing Weiss made him worry about. Infuriating.

Before the naked rage could build in him again, he grabbed the car's ignition key, grabbed it and twisted it hard to start the Chrysler's engine. He backed out of the garage. He had to plan his next move. That would calm him. He had to think, he had to be cool, dispassionate, a living clockwork.

He thought. He thought: Maybe he should go back to Andy Bremer's house. He would break in and tie the family up. He would go to work on one of them, one of the children – the girl probably. He would work on her slowly while the others watched and listened to her screaming through her gag. He wouldn't ask them anything. He would just work on the girl while they watched and listened until the girl was dead. Then he would start on the boy. And then – then he would ask them. While he was working on the boy, he would ask them what they knew about Julie. Whatever unspoken business had passed between Bremer and Weiss, he would find out soon enough what it was.

He pointed the car down the street and cruised slowly

past the houses to the stop sign at the corner. There was no hurry. He knew where Weiss was going. There was plenty of time to make a stop at Bremer's. Maybe he would even find out enough to go after Julie himself.

But maybe not. Maybe not – and, as Weiss had told Bremer in the house, if the man called John Foy killed the Bremers, Weiss would call off the search. That was the unspoken deal between them, the silent agreement between Weiss and the man who called himself John Foy. Foy would stay in the background. He wouldn't cause trouble or harm the people Weiss spoke to. As long as there was no trouble, Weiss would go on and find Julie and so Foy would find Julie too. Weiss knew it was going to happen like that, knew they would find her together, but as long as there was no trouble until then, he could tell himself that it would turn out all right. As long as there was no trouble, he would go on, he would find her, even if he had to lie to himself about how it would end. He would go on and he would find her because he had to, because he couldn't stop himself. Just like Foy. It was the same for both of them.

The man who called himself John Foy brought the Chrysler around the corner, and headed back for the four-lane. Reluctantly, he gave up the idea of going to Bremer's house. He would've liked to. He would've liked to watch Weiss's face when he learned what happened to them. He would've liked to pay Weiss back for the way he made him feel and for the fact that he needed him to find the girl. But there were other ways to get at Weiss, even now. Weiss wasn't the only one who knew things. The man who called himself John Foy knew something too. He knew a way that he could pay Weiss back.

So it was all right. It was fine. He could start planning again, planning like clockwork. Here was the four-lane, just ahead. He would leave the Bremers alone and go on to Reno with Weiss. He would change cars before he got there. He would change his appearance in the small ways that changed everything: different clothes, different hair, a different way of moving. He would become invisible again. He would be close to Weiss, as close as a breath, and Weiss wouldn't see him. And he would make his plans to pay Weiss back for the way he made him feel and for the fact that he needed him to find the girl.

The Chrysler turned onto the four-lane. The man who called himself John Foy let his foot grow heavier on the gas. The car gathered speed. He was going fifty when he passed the Super 8 motel, the last business on the street. The city lights fell away behind him quickly.

Darkness and the desert closed in around the windows.

19

It was about eleven o'clock the next morning when Bishop pushed into the dojo. The Frenchman's bully boys were there in force. There were seven of these dick-swingers all told, musclemen with tattoos and sneering smiles. Their faces were different colors, white and brown and yellow, but they were all wearing white gis with black belts.

They were going through a *kata* when Bishop entered – a sort of karate dance. They were sliding in unison across the hardwood floor, pivoting as one, kicking the air as one. Two rows of three and one man in front. Seven arms twisting out together in a corkscrew punch. Seven voices shouting – '*Heeyai!*'

Just within the door, there was a carpeted alcove, a small waiting area with chairs and a water cooler. There was a rice paper divider with a wooden frame separating the alcove from the hardwood dojo.

Bishop crossed the alcove and stepped into the divider's doorway. He leaned against the wood frame and watched the *kata*. He was wearing jeans and a t-shirt. He was wearing his ironic smile too. He held his leather jacket slung over his shoulder. He watched as the seven bully boys spun and blocked and shouted. Their eyes were blazing with focus. Their expressions were set and grim.

As the *kata* wore on, Bishop's gaze wandered. First, he looked to the far side of the room. There was a door there, in the right corner. That was the door he wanted.

When he was done considering the door, he looked up casually at the dojo's walls. They were decorated with weapons: samurai swords, a couple of the long staffs called bos, a couple of the long knives called sais. There were some numchuks, some whip chains, some throwing stars. And there was one particularly vicious-looking Chinese broadsword, its keen, flat silver blade curling almost like a scimitar, a black and scarlet cloth hanging from its pommel.

Bishop admired the array. He had fooled around a little with samurai swords in his youth. He tried to remember the Japanese words for the various parts of them and the various classifications. The cutting edge of the blade was called the *ha*, he remembered, and the part that went into the handle was called the *tang*. There were the long ones, *daito*, and the short ones... which was a longer word. Most of the rest of what he'd taught himself escaped him now. Still, he liked the look of them. He'd always thought that Zen Japanese warrior-type shit was cool.

Another loud '*Heeyai!*' brought his attention back to the room. The men were on the *kata*'s final leg, a flurry of sliding steps and blocks and blows that carried the seven black belts as one from the rear wall toward their images in the long mirror that lined the wall in front. As Bishop watched them, his smile grew distant, his eyes grew blurred and dreamy. That cold, steely edge that sometimes gleamed in his core gleamed now.

The *kata* ended. In a single motion, the seven men pulled back from a final punch, drawing their extended legs under them, bringing their hands together. They bowed once in unison. Then they stood erect, two rows of three and the man in front, their elbows raised, their hands together before their faces, the right hand, the male hand, a fist, planted in the left, open, female hand.

After a long moment, the lead man broke the stance and turned to face Bishop.

Bishop looked the man over. He was a big, evil chucklehead. A white guy, approximately the size of Denver. He had short, blond hair and stupid eyes and a vague, pharmaceutical smile. He had a voice so deep it sounded like an earth tremor. His muscles filled his gi like rocks in a canvas sack.

'Help you, brother?' he rumbled.

Bishop went on leaning against the door frame. He nodded slowly. His own smile was friendly and dangerous. 'My name's Jim Bishop,' he said. 'I'm here to see the Frenchman.'

That got an instant reaction, not just from the evil chucklehead but from his six bully boy pals as well. The chucklehead gaped in surprise. Then he guffawed in surprise, his massive shoulders jerking up and down. The six others, though they were standing rigid at attention, started laughing too after a second, their locked hands quivering in front of them.

Bishop stayed as he was, leaning against the door frame. That cold edge gleamed at his core and a sort of bright metallic singing started up all through him, as if that inner edge were a sword blade whistling endlessly through the air. If he had been thinking anything, anything in words, the words would've been *Here we go*. But he was not thinking anything. He was just leaning there, smiling, waiting for it.

The Denver-sized leader of the pack stopped laughing. Slowly, the laughter of the others faded too. The chucklehead glared at Bishop with his stupid eyes. 'What Frenchman?' he said grimly. 'I never heard of him.'

Bishop breathed out sharply once through his nose. 'That's funny. Thanks – a chuckle always brightens up my day. But listen, I'm pressed for time. You're a flunky

– go flunk yourself upstairs and tell that gun-running Belgian prick I'm coming up to see him.'

At this, all signs of laughter – all signs that he had ever laughed at all – vanished from the evil white Denver-sized chucklehead's face. 'What're you, looking for a fight?'

'No, that's close, very good, I am looking for something. But I'm looking for the fucking Frenchman. Now, either you tell him I'm here, or I walk up and surprise him.'

'Or we cram your head up your ass and use you for a hula hoop,' came a soft, snaky voice from the assembled bully boys.

That got another murmur of laughter out of them. Bishop turned his head their way. He could tell right off which one of them was the wise-ass. Big Asian or maybe half-Asian kung-fu type. Burly yellow fucker with a big round face, long, stringy hair and a sort of modified Fu Manchu moustache blossoming out of his stubble. He stood loose at the hips, his bowling ball fist lightly punching into the maw of his open hand. He had his eyes to the side, watching Bishop. He grinned broadly.

'Oops,' he said, 'did I say that out loud?'

Bishop grinned back at him. 'You did, in fact, yeah. And if you speak out of turn again, I'm gonna make you write "I'm sorry" a hundred times on your body cast.'

That doused the murmur of laughter like a bucket of water douses flame. A sort of collective growl rose from the assembled bully boy multitude. Fu Manchu's grin froze on his face.

'Oops,' Bishop added. 'Did I say that out loud?'

Fu Manchu's eyes narrowed. His hands came down slowly to his sides. But it was the evil white Denver-sized chucklehead who moved first. Hooking his thumbs in his black belt, he swaggered over toward Bishop on bowed, muscle-bound legs.

'Uh oh,' one of the bully boys murmured.

Bishop, even with that bright metallic blade whistling through the core of him, thought pretty much the same thing. He straightened off the door frame as the chucklehead came to a stop in front of him. Smiling, the two men stared death at each other.

This staring death business went on for some long silent time. The chucklehead seemed to be waiting for Bishop to try something. But Bishop stood relaxed, his jacket over his shoulder, and made no move.

Finally, the chucklehead snorted. 'Listen, shit-for-brains. You're too skinny to kill for food and too stupid to kill for fun, so why don't you just get the fuck out of here before you start to piss me off. Awright?'

And having offered this helpful hint, he started to turn away, to turn his back on Bishop.

This was an important moment. It was a long way to that door across the room. Bishop knew that if he tried for it, this bunch would swarm him and bring him down. He knew he needed to goad one of them into a man-on-man confrontation if he was going to bluff his way across without getting gang-stomped. In order to do that, he needed to impress them with the fact that he was worthy of such a fight. And this was the moment in which he would or would not.

Because the chucklehead was only pretending to turn away, of course. Another second and he would wheel oh-so-unexpectedly and put a move on Bishop, probably a punch to the face or the solar plexus. If it was a fake punch and Bishop flinched, he would lose the manhood cred he needed to get the confrontation going. If it was a real punch, and he didn't get the hell out of the way – well, the confrontation would be over before it began.

Bishop decided to stand fast and hope the punch was a fake. He didn't have to wait long to find out. The evil chucklehead was now finished pretending to turn around. Oh-so-unexpectedly, he spun back and drove one of those vicious corkscrew karate fists directly at Bishop's mouth.

But Bishop had guessed right. The punch stopped just short – about a quarter inch short – of connecting. Which left the unflinching Bishop standing with his smile intact and his jacket still over his shoulder, looking very steely-eyed and cool indeed.

The bully boys were impressed, all right. Even the chucklehead frowned and nodded with grudging admiration. He opened his fist and slapped Bishop on the cheek – not hard – just a sort of token slap of condescending appreciation.

Bishop smiled deep into the chucklehead's stupid eyes and kicked him hard in the shin.

The chucklehead went down, screaming, rocking on his back and clutching his leg in his two hands. Bishop sneered down at him. He could hear that bright metallic singing inside him like a sword blade whistling through the air.

Or wait a minute – maybe it wasn't inside him. Maybe it was coming from somewhere to his left – along with another noise – a noise that sounded something like *hwa hwoo hwee hwa*.

He looked in that direction and, sure enough, there was the Fu Manchu guy rushing at him, going *hwa hwoo hwee* and so on – and also wielding that goddamned Chinese broadsword Bishop had noticed on the wall.

Well, this was a surprise. Not exactly the kind of confrontation he'd been looking for. In fact, the sight of that sword stunned Bishop so much, it slowed his reaction time. Meanwhile, the Fu Manchu guy came in low and fast. Gripping the broadsword's handle in one hand, he made the wide, curved silver blade spin and twirl through blurring criss-crosses and figure eights. '*Hwa! Hwoo! Hwee!*' he remarked again. And all the while, the black and red scarf flying from the sword's pommel flapped and spiraled, adding to Bishop's distraction.

The approach took barely a second. Then, as Bishop stood more or less stupefied, the Fu Manchu guy brought the big sword around in a vicious arc and hit him with it alongside the head.

He struck with the flat of the blade – this wasn't a killing situation yet. And at the last moment, Bishop did manage to twist his body, head first, to absorb some of the force of the blow. All the same, the thing smacked into him with brain-rattling force. He saw white sparkles and felt himself falling helplessly through the air, his leather jacket flying out of his hand as he went down. The next instant, he hit the hardwood floor with a jolt that made his bones ache. But he took the shock on his shoulder, and kept rolling, kept rolling, and was on his feet again in a defensive stance before he could even think about it.

Now he found himself facing his attacker in a crouch, his arms up in front of him. Which wasn't going to help him much unless he happened to want his arms lopped off and mounted on a plaque. Which he didn't. And the Fu Manchu guy was still coming after him – *Hwa! Hwee! Hwo!* – a steady, unstoppable onslaught with the silver broadsword in his right hand singing through the air in dazzling patterns and the distracting scarf flashing now black now scarlet as it whipped and fluttered unnervingly out of sync with the rhythms of the blade.

Bishop's face was stinging like ants were on it. His left eye was pouring tears and his brain was still slow and numb from the blow of the sword. Around him, the bully boys were clapping and whooping. And where the evil chucklehead had gotten to, he hadn't the foggiest fucking idea.

But there was no time to think about any of that. The swordsman was on him. The blade was arcing up again, preparing for a second attack that could come at him high or low. All Bishop could manage to do was circle away. Keep the distance between them. Keep moving, circling, circling, staving off the moment when the Fu Manchu guy would strike again.

'Hwa! Hwee! Hwoo!' the swordsman shouted, circling opposite Bishop.

The other bully boys gathered around the two of them, shouting encouragement, clapping, moving as they moved. They loved this stuff. As the blade snaked out in a lashing circle under Bishop's nose, Bishop dodged back and felt one of the thugs put hands on him to shove him toward his opponent. The Fu Manchu guy saw this happen and instantly moved in for another strike.

That turned out to be a break for Bishop. He pivoted, grabbed the gi of the thug who'd pushed him, spun him around in front of him. Blocked by his fellow bully boy, the Fu Manchu guy froze, mid-'Hwa!' Bishop shoved the thug – a dimwitted red-head – straight into his attacker. It only slowed him for a second. The Fu Manchu guy caught the dimwit red-head's arm and hurled him aside.

But by then, Bishop had dashed away. The red-head had left a gap in the circle of bully boys. Bishop slipped through it and rushed for the wall. He grabbed the first samurai sword he could get his hands on and yanked it free of its mount. What he planned to do with it he wasn't sure, but it was better than his bare hands, it had to be. He swept it quickly from its sheath and tossed the sheath away. The blade gleamed bright, a short one – katana, that was the word! Well-balanced and with a full tang, set deep and solidly into the handle.

None of which was any comfort. All he could remember from his casual study of samurai swordplay was some Zen bullshit about having No Mind and being One With The Blade. He figured he'd have No Mind in a big hurry if this crazy Asian fucker hit him in the head with his fucking broadsword again. And as for being One With The Blade – that was exactly what he was trying to avoid.

But he seized the handle of the *katana* with both hands as he recalled you were supposed to. He held it up in front of him, pointing the blade at the Asian's eyes just as he would've done in a knife fight – that made it hard for his opponent to judge the distance of the point and also distracted him from the feints and movements of his body.

As Bishop began to circle again, it came back to him what a natural weapon the samurai sword was, a comfortable extension of the hands and arms. A desperate little hope flared in him. The Fu Manchu guy was so busy putting on a show for his pals, so busy *hwa-hwo-hweeing* and swinging the sword in fancy eights and arcs, that if Bishop could stay focused, he might just have a chance to get in on him quick and drop him.

He circled away cautiously, the samurai sword held out before him. The Fu Manchu guy came charging in, the broadsword dancing in the air. The bully boys catcalled. They caught the uncertainty in Bishop's stance and motions. They urged Fu to finish him off.

'Slice him, slice and dice him!'

'Cut him bad, baby!'

'Make meat out of him!'

Bishop forced the grinning, crowing thug faces into the soft blur of his outer attention. He watched the Fu Manchu guy, saw his eyes flare. The broadsword seemed to spiral out of flashing heights and sweep toward his shoulder, edge first. Bishop twisted his wrists, and his *katana* went horizontal. With a metallic shock, the two blades met. Bishop parried the broadsword, turning his body out of its deflected path. In the same movement, he brought the *katana* around and swung it low at Fu Man's kneecap. He hoped to hit just hard enough to slice the tendon. But the strike was met by the sweeping block of the broadsword. Another metallic sting, and Bishop was pushed back. Fu Manchu stepped in with a direct thrust – a genuine thrust that would've opened Bishop's belly. Bishop was startled by its deadliness. The fight had turned serious, and only a hurried, almost panicked recovery – an inversion of the wrists that turned the *katana* nearly straight down – fended off the broadsword's point and gave him the chance to step back and away.

Both men were in their stances again, both were circling. There was a little less *hwa-hwa* crap coming out of Fu Man now. He was breathing hard and the arcs of the broadsword were slower and less ornate. That didn't mean he was easing up though. Bishop could see the anger contorting his mouth. He knew that last reckless thrust had been powered by raw temper. And he knew the next attack would have the same mortal rage behind it, maybe worse. Even the shouts and jokes of the bully boys had dropped a key, had become guttural and murderous.

This had gone too far. Bishop knew he had to end it quick or he'd go home with his head in his hands. The shock of the first onslaught had worn off. That weird, killer cool of his was coming back. Even with his pulse pounding, even with his eyes fastened on the swinging broadsword, a feeling that could only be described as mirth was pumping out of the center of him, coursing through his veins. This was it. This was the finish of it, one way or the other.

The Fu Man was gearing up for another attack.

Looking for a weak spot. Side-stepping, swinging the silver blade, whipping the black and scarlet cloth poetically through the air. Bishop was still on the defensive, circling away, circling away, ready to fend off the strike and answer with a strike of his own. He knew he wasn't good enough with the sword to make an effective assault, but if he could get the Fu to commit himself...

Then... something... the slightest shift of Fu Man's ferocious gaze. A glance over Bishop's shoulder as if someone were coming up behind him. Maybe it was a trick, but maybe...

With a swift pivot of his arm, Bishop brought the *katana* cross-wise at his own eye-level. There – reflected in the gleaming steel – the furious features of the evil white chucklehead were rushing straight at him.

Bishop released the sword handle with his right hand and drove his elbow backwards into the chucklehead's throat. He heard a liquid gurgle; a thud as the Denver-sized enforcer dropped to the hardwood.

At the same moment, Fu Manchu came at him from the front. He feinted low, slipped Bishop's parry. Then he hoisted the broadsword high and brought it crashing down toward Bishop's skull.

With a cry, Bishop spun to the side. He felt the cold wind on his face as the silver blade sliced down past him. He saw the wide front edge of it hit the floor, notching the shiny surface. The momentum of the strike brought the Fu Man forward. On the instant, Bishop stepped on the blade, pinning it to the hardwood. He put his other foot on the blade above the first, scrambling straight up the edge of the sword toward his opponent's head.

Fu Man straightened, trying to pull the broadsword free. The motion exposed the side of his neck.

Bishop had him. With a rush of savage joy, he hammered the pommel of the *katana* into the thug's carotid artery. The Fu Man's eyes flew up and his body dropped down. He crumpled to the dojo floor as if he were made of string.

It was over. Bishop dropped back, crouched low, turned round, pointing the *katana*'s blade at the circle of leering faces all around him, face by ugly, murderous face. A slow, seething growl seemed to come from all the bully boys at once. Bishop answered them with a slow, seething growl of his own.

He backed toward the door, that door he wanted on the far side of the room. From the corner of his eye, he saw his leather jacket on the floor. He swooped down and snapped it up, held it in his left hand, while his right kept the sword pointed at the bully boys.

The bully boys edged toward him, growling. Growling, he backed away until he felt the door at his shoulder.

Then he was through it, gone.

20

The Frenchman looked up from his desk and saw a man with a sword framed in the doorway. At first, he didn't believe what he was seeing. The man was a silhouette with the light of the hall behind him, and the Frenchman thought: No. But then the gunrunner narrowed his eyes, looked more closely. The man was holding a jacket over his shoulder with one hand, and the other hand held – yes, it was a sword, a long sword pointed slantwise at the floor.

Oh, what now? the Frenchman thought.

The man with the sword stepped into the little office and kicked the door shut behind him.

'Call off your thugs,' he said.

'My...?'

'Your black belts, your thugs. They're coming up the stairs behind me. Call them off.'

The Frenchman hesitated. He felt at a disadvantage. When the swordsman had entered, he'd been examining a picture on his computer screen. It was a photograph of a naked woman trussed in a network of complex and imaginative leather restraints while another naked woman sodomized her with an equally imaginative con-traption designed for the purpose. The Frenchman's careful study of this image had left him in a state that would have detracted from the effect had he attempted to rise and greet his guest with any sort of imposing dignity. Also he was dressed in a purple paisley shirt and white jeans which were supposed to make him look youthful but which he knew only made his gnome-like figure pathetic, further impeding any effort he might make to be intimidating.

So he stalled, hoping help would arrive from the dojo below. But the swordsman came straight at him. Stepped to the desk and casually lay the point of his weapon against the Frenchman's sagging gullet. The Frenchman could see the man's face now – bruised and reddened on one side – and he could see his eyes, he could see what sort of man he was. He knew the type well. You didn't try to bluff a man like this. You either killed him or you played along.

'Call them. The fuck off,' the swordsman repeated.

With that, the door flew open again. One of the Frenchman's treasured musclemen – a massive slab of black flesh in a white gi – charged in over the threshold. Behind him, out in the hall, the rest of the karate gang seemed jumbled together, as if they were all trying to crowd in at once.

The Frenchman thought fast, thought of every possible outcome. He felt the uncomfortable chill of the sword point beneath his adam's apple. He lifted a hand, pressed the air down in front of him as if to say, *Ssh ssh ssh*.

'It's all right,' he said aloud. 'Never mind.'

The black slab looked from his boss to the swordsman, from the swordsman back to his boss. The enormous faces behind his shoulders glared wildly with big white eyes.

'Never mind,' the Frenchman repeated. 'Leave us alone now. It will be all right.'

Slowly, unhappily, the black man retreated, joining the general jumble of thugs. The group faded away down the hall as one, the black man pulling the door shut as they left.

The Frenchman looked up at the swordsman with what he hoped was an ingratiating smile on his damp lips. 'So. You see?' he said. 'All is well.'

After a moment, the swordsman nodded. With a sharp movement that made the Frenchman gasp, he snapped the weapon away from the gunrunner's throat. He took a step back and relaxed into the steel tubular chair in front of the desk.

The Frenchman gave a gallic shrug and let his right hand drift down toward the desk drawer in which he kept a Carpati .32, a very accurate little gun.

'All is well,' he said again soothingly.

Bishop tossed his sword to the floor. It fell on the static-colored carpet with a muffled thud. His face hurt and his head hurt and he was out of breath from the fight downstairs, in no mood to fuck around. He glanced around quickly at the cramped, cluttered space, the catalogues and mail and garbage stacked along the walls, the high windows behind the scarred wooden desk, the pastel townhouses of the Haight outside. Then his gaze settled on the Frenchman. What a gargoyle this guy was. And that combover – someone should've broken the good news to him about the buzz cut. On the other hand, judging by his looks, he was a man with no principles but money and fear. Which was exactly what Bishop was hoping for.

So he got his breath steady and he said, 'My name's Bishop. I'm here about a guy. A customer of yours.'

The Frenchman made a light gesture, a flutter of his left hand in the air. At the same time, his right hand casually pulled the desk drawer open, as if he were looking for something – a handkerchief maybe to dry his lips with. 'I have many customers. I couldn't possibly...'

'Are you really gonna pull that thing?' Bishop interrupted in a tone of wonder. He massaged his face, trying to get the ache out of the place where the sword had hit him.

The Frenchman jutted his misshapen face at him as if to say, *Eh?*

'The gun in the drawer. Are you gonna pull it? Because if you are, I'm gonna shove it up your ass and blow your guts out, just so you know.'

The Frenchman's chin went up, went down. He shut the desk drawer. 'In that case, on consideration, perhaps I will not,' he said.

'Good. Jesus. What're you, some kind of idiot?'

'Well, one feels obligated to make the attempt, you know. Foolish, especially in a man my age, but there you are. The demands of custom and dignity are slow to die.'

'Adalian sent this guy,' said Bishop, who couldn't have given less of a shit.

'This...'

'The customer I'm here about. Adalian sent him to you. He's a specialist.'

The gargoyle knew the man at once. Bishop could see it in his eyes. Still, he put on a little show of ignorance. A couple of Frenchy gestures with his claw-like hands as if he were pulling the memory out of the air. Or Belgian gestures, or whatever they were. Then he started a whole point-of-honor routine. Which was a laugh.

'You have to understand, my friend,' he said. 'A business like mine depends very much on discretion. If my customers can't rely on me to keep their various purchases confidential...'

'I understand,' said Bishop. 'Forget it. I apologize for asking.'

'Truthfully?'

'No, I was kidding. If you don't talk to me, I'm gonna put you in the hospital.'

'Ah. Very witty.'

'Thanks. And listen, I don't envy you. It's a clear-cut choice, but it's not an easy one. You talk to me, this specialist guy will kill you for sure, if he finds out and if he lives. But he might not find out. And he might not live. On the other hand, if you don't talk to me, I probably won't kill you. But I will fuck you up in a seriously painful and permanent way. And I'm sitting here right now and there's no chance I'm leaving. So you decide.'

The Frenchman thought about it. He swiveled back and forth slightly in his tattered green chair. He thought about the man whom Adalian had sent, the ghost with the mannequin eyes. He thought about the way the man's features had been impossible to describe even to himself, impossible to retain in his memory. The ghost man could return tomorrow and the Frenchman would not recognize him. He could walk through the door or approach him on the street or deliver a package to his house and he would not know who he was until it was too late. It was not a reassuring thought.

On the other hand, here was this man Bishop sitting here – sitting here, as he himself pointed out, right now. A lifetime of doing business with mercenaries, hitmen, terrorists and lunatics had given the Frenchman certain insights into their various characters. This Bishop, he thought, had a little bit of all of them in him. And when he said he would cause the Frenchman serious suffering, the Frenchman had no doubt he was telling the absolute truth.

In the end, though, one had to take one's chances. That was business. That was life. If Bishop and the ghost came face to face, the Frenchman judged it even odds which one would survive the meeting. That meant he had a fifty percent chance of being killed by the ghost if he spoke, and a hundred percent chance of being hurt badly by Bishop if he kept silent.

'He purchased three guns,' he said.

'Three?' said Bishop, surprised.

'A 9mm Sig P210 with a modified magazine release. A 1911-based compact .45. And the Saracen.'

'The Saracen.' Bishop obviously knew the gun. He was quiet for a second. Then he said, 'That new Belgian thing, the little one?'

The Frenchman nodded with as much gravity as his purple paisley shirt would allow.

'That's a lot of firepower,' said Bishop. 'That's all for one job?'

'Ah,' said the Frenchman, with a wave of his hand. 'He didn't share with me the particulars, you know.'

'Sure. And he didn't say anything that might've given you a clue.'

'My friend, believe me when I tell you, my customers are very close-mouthed when it comes to their enterprises. And this one...'

The Frenchman didn't have to finish. 'Yeah, yeah, yeah,' Bishop said. He nodded. He sat thoughtfully a while, staring at the Frenchman but clearly looking straight through him.

The Frenchman found it disconcerting and unpleasantly suspenseful. He had told Bishop everything he knew. He worried that Bishop would not believe him and would work him over just to make sure.

But after a moment, the intruder nodded again. He stood to go. 'All right,' he said. 'Anything else you can tell me?'

The Frenchman tried not to sigh too loudly, but he was very relieved. He had judged the man aright. There was coldness and cruelty in him, but a certain fairness too. He had his code, such as it was, the way these people did. Mercenaries, hitmen, terrorists, even lunatics – they all had their codes, or at least they liked to think so. The gunrunner felt a warm flood of gratitude and affection toward Bishop. Getting through the day uninjured was no small thing to him, given his advanced age and cowardice.

'Well, I can tell you this,' the Frenchman offered in the flow of his emotion. 'I have had many dealings with people in this business, yes? I have provided materiel to many men who do what this man does. I have seen men of great competence and expertise and he is no doubt one of them, as are you, I can see. But never – never – have I ever witnessed anyone so... what is the word? *Sans charactéristique*. Nondescript, that is it. You might turn your back on him a moment and turn back and be unable to say it was he.'

Bishop looked down at him, bored, indifferent. 'Yeah?' he said after a moment. 'So?'

The Frenchman leaned forward in his chair, leaned past the image of the leather and sodomy girls on his computer. He set his elbows on the burn-scarred desktop, lay his hands together at his chin as if in prayer. 'So when it is on between you,' he said. 'Be aware, yes? The man is like a ghost. He can be right in front of you – right in front of you, and you will never see him coming.'

PART THREE

Cats And Mice

21

I followed Emma.

I woke up that morning in the white tangle of Sissy's fast embrace, in the smell of her, the older woman perfumed smell that I was drunk on, that had me spell-bound. My face was tucked into the hollow of her throat and my dick was hard as rock against her thigh as she lay sleeping. Almost at once, I started thinking about Emma, fantasizing about walking along some street with Emma, holding Emma's hand, standing on Emma's doorstep at the end of a date and kissing her, drawing her into my arms, moving my hand inside her blouse. And so it went, until I wanted Sissy desperately, Sissy because... well, because Sissy was there – right there in the flesh when I was hard and crazy with love for Emma.

She liked it that I woke her up, that I couldn't wait. It made her laugh that I was so aroused, that I was inside her before she was even fully conscious. I looked down at her, trim and pink and white beneath me, her eyes swimming with tears, her lips parted on her small, whispering cries. I looked down at her and thought if I couldn't have Emma I would die.

When I was getting dressed to leave, she called to me, 'Where are you off to so early, sweetie? Aren't you gonna come in to the office with me?'

I was in the bedroom, standing in front of the full-length mirror on the inside of her closet door. She was calling to me from the bathroom, calling over the noise of running water. Out of the corner of my eye, I could see my clothes in her closet, my jeans, my slacks and button-down shirts, hanging among those schoolgirl outfits of hers, the white blouses, the pleated skirts. It was all so comfortable, so domestic, as if our lives were already thoroughly intermingled, as if the deal were already done. I despaired at the sight of it. I would never get free of her, never.

'I gotta go to Berkeley, remember?' I called back to her. 'On the case for that guy, that professor guy, the one who says his daughter is avoiding him. I'm supposed to follow her.'

I heard her shut the water off. 'What?' she called.

'I have to follow the professor's *daughter*.'

For whom my love – I fretted obsessively as I drove over the Bay Bridge half an hour later – for whom my love had become utterly impossible. Never mind Sissy. Never mind that I hadn't the courage or will to leave her. Now there was Emma's peculiar, intellectual, alcoholic not to mention intimidating father to deal with. If she found out he had hired me to follow her, it would all be over. And if she didn't find out, he would find out that I'd followed her for my own purposes and then he'd tell her and it would all be over. And it was all over anyway, because she was probably seeing someone else already, that was probably what I was following her to find out.

I knew I shouldn't have let it come to this. I should've turned the job down at the very beginning. But I couldn't. Because it gave me a reason to see her again. And by the time I reached Berkeley, that's all I was thinking about. I drove up the hill on the north side of campus, past the bookstore and the coffee shops and the sandwich shops, and the students walking down toward the campus under big white clouds and a bright sun. I drove on into the oak and elm tree shadows of the hills, past the oak and elm tree shaded houses. And all I was thinking about was that I was going to see Emma again.

And then I did. I did see her, up in the leafy neighborhood of the foothills. Not half a minute after I pulled my car to the curb a little distance from her parents' house, she stepped out the front door.

It was a moment of truth. After all my fantasies about her, the actual sight of her might have been a disappointment. She might've been less attractive than I remembered, or I might've exaggerated the quiet shock of connection I felt when I was with her. All that sense of destiny, of completion – it might've vanished before the fact of her like smoke in the wind. I might have watched her through my car window, smirking at myself for a romantic imbecile, sagging inside with sadness and disenchantment.

But oh no. It was not like that at all. She stepped out of the modest peak-roofed clapboard, out of the shadow of the porch into the bright autumn day. I took one look at that long, slim figure, the mischievous, valentine-shaped face, the adorable red beret atop the short, shaggy black, black hair. And, brothers and sisters, the angels sang, the birdies went tweet-tweet-tweet, and somewhere in that nexus of heart and testicle that passes for a man's soul, there was a spiritually audible snap as if all the jigsaw pieces of the world had leapt together in an instant.

So that was one second. Then, the next second, I realized Emma was walking straight toward me, that in yet another second, she would see me watching her from behind the wheel. Grasping the situation at a glance, I panicked instantly. I grabbed the ignition key, twisted it. A scree that sounded like the attack cry of a swooping harpy flew up from under the hood – because the engine was already running.

'Shit,' I observed.

I didn't wait to see if the hellacious noise had drawn Emma's attention. I popped the car into gear and hit the gas. The car let out another screech – the tires this time. It tore away from the curb, roaring up the hill. I muttered a prayer of the please-please-please-please-please variety that she hadn't recognized me as I thundered past.

So began the latest and last phase of my career as a private detective.

I went around a curve, out of her sight. I parked the car. Got out. Went after her on foot.

When she came into view again, she was still heading downhill. She was wearing a long, flaring coat and that beret, the same one she'd worn the night I met her. She was carrying books under her arm, striding purposely beside the winding road toward the campus.

I stayed about a block or so behind her. She moved rapidly under the trees, her figure brightening and darkening as she went from sunlight to dappled shadow. We descended together past small lawns and small houses nestled in foliage.

At first, it all went smoothly. We were soon surrounded by other students on their way to school and older locals heading for the shops. It was easy for me to blend in and remain inconspicuous, easy to keep her in my sights. There was only one problem. After the first moment of passion and excitement was over, I began to feel like scum. Following her, spying on her. Taking money from her father to find out what she was doing on the sly. I felt slimier with every step, guiltier with every step until, by the time we came within sight of that final stretch of stores and restaurants leading to the campus, I wanted to be anywhere other than there, anyone other than myself.

We reached the last residential corner above the commercial stretch. Emma stopped at the edge of the side-walk to let a motorcycle pass.

I stopped too, several yards back, standing close to the trunk of a broad oak, hunkered deep in its shadow. I waited there. I watched her. I yearned to step out into the light, to stride up behind her and take her arm. I wanted her to turn and look up at me with those wicked, witty, incredibly sweet green eyes so I could tell her everything, everything.

I just didn't have the courage.

I stood where I was, hiding behind the oak tree. Waiting for her to cross the street and continue on to the campus.

But that was when things got strange.

Emma took a look around her. It was not an ordinary look. It was a slow, deliberate scan of the crossroads. It was as if she were searching for something or someone suspicious, out of place. It was almost as if she suspected she was being followed. She checked the cars going by, the faces of anyone near her. Then she glanced back over her shoulder to check the sidewalk behind.

I was so surprised, I only just had time to pull back, to pull up and stand at attention behind the tree trunk. My heart started beating hard. My breath started coming fast. An endless second passed, and then another.

Finally, I dared to peek out around the tree. Emma was on the move again.

She'd changed direction. She wasn't heading toward the campus anymore. She'd turned left, headed east, up another street of trees and lawns and houses.

Everything suddenly became a lot more difficult. Because Emma was moving with caution now, looking around her with every step, checking to make sure that no one was moving secretly in her wake.

And since, as it happened, I was moving secretly in her

wake, it was no easy thing keeping up with her. I couldn't exactly creep from tree to tree like a cartoon spy. This was Berkeley, a town to the left of reality, and so feminist you could get arrested for your daydreams. The morning crowds were absolutely peppered with joyless, silver-haired spinsters who looked like they did nothing all day but call the police to report men furtively following women. One false step, and I'd end up in the back room of a station house with some six-foot broad hitting me over the head with *Our Bodies, Ourselves*.

I had to think fast. I spotted an apartment house, a brick building across the street. I ducked between two moving cars to get to it. Dashed up the front steps. Stood studying the mailboxes by the door, as if I were searching for a name. At the same time, I stole quick glances up the street. I watched helplessly as Emma moved farther and farther away. She was almost at the next corner now, looking around, looking nervously back over her shoulder.

Then she reached the corner, turned the corner. Hurried out of sight.

'Shit!' I spat between clenched teeth.

I skittered down the steps. I jogged up the hill after her, dodging and weaving through the oncoming crowd. I cursed myself with every yard. Not only was I a piece of slimy scum for following her, I was an incompetent piece of slimy scum, following her badly.

I reached the intersection. I looked up the street. She was gone. No – there she was, just moving out of the piebald pool of sun and shade under an autumn maple tree. I stood where I was, right out in the open like a fool, staring after her. If she had looked back just then she would've seen me. She couldn't have missed me.

Then she did look – but she was one second too late. Realizing how exposed I was, I had just moved forward to hide myself behind the low hedge dividing one lawn from another. It was from there I watched Emma scan her surroundings one last time. She peered down the hill toward me, then up the hill, then to the left and right. Then, pressing her chin to her chest as if to hide her face, she turned down the front path of a husky brown two-story house. In four steps she was at the door. The door came open before she knocked or rang. A man stuck his head out, glancing around. Then he pulled his head back and Emma followed him inside.

I came out of my hiding place and hurried after her.

Half a minute, and I was at the house. Then I spent another half minute hovering like the stalker I was around the eucalyptus tree on the edge of the lawn. From there, I could see through a front hall window. I saw Emma peel off the adorable red beret, peel off her flaring coat. She handed them both to another figure, a man, the man, I assumed, who had met her at the door. I saw the man put his hand on her arm.

My heart plunged. I'd been right. She was meeting a secret lover.

But the next instant, my plunging heart did a roller coaster climb. I saw Emma and her companion walk deeper into the house, toward the light of an inner entranceway. There, just before I lost sight of them, more people came from the room beyond to greet them. It was not a lovers' meeting. It was a gathering of some kind.

Now, strange as it is to relate, I forgot all my caution. A combination of urgent curiosity and desperate longing overtook me. I was so focused on finding out what was going on – so focused on getting closer to Emma, on knowing her secret – that the need for stealth – the stealth on which everything depended – simply slipped my mind.

Boldly, stupidly, I stepped forth. I crossed the lawn, the

shaggy lawn, the grass above my shoes, the last dew of morning clammy on my socks. I went to the house. I placed a hand on the rough surface of one of its wooden shingles. I pressed my face to the window. I peered through.

I could see shadows – two, maybe three people – just within the inner entranceway. The rest of the room beyond the threshold was out of sight. I heard a voice – a man's voice – speak in there, but I couldn't make out what he was saying. What the hell were they doing in there that had to be kept so secret?

I needed a better view, a window at the rear of the house that looked directly into that back room. I didn't hesitate. In fact, I was so wrapped up in what I was doing now, I barely took the trouble to conceal my movements at all. Like an old friend or a meter reader or the guy who mows the lawn, I sallied forth to the gate in the white picket fence beyond the far wall. Without hesitation – without even covering the noise – I opened the gate and walked into the backyard.

It was just a little square of land between this house and the one behind. Brick paths through shrubs, a lemon tree at the center. The windows here were larger, tall and open and clear. I was completely exposed as I approached them. My footsteps whispered loudly through the pachysandra.

I didn't care. I didn't even think about it. I was too curious, too fascinated. What was this? What was going on?

I heard the people in the house start singing. It sounded like a church choir. In fact, it sounded like church music, like a hymn. What the hell?

Just as I came close enough to make out the words, the singing stopped. That voice, that man's voice, rose again. It sounded steady and sure but it was still too damned low to understand. I had to get closer. I stepped right up to the window. I pressed my face against the pane.

I looked in. I saw everything.

There was a large, open room. There were benches, rows of benches, facing the rear wall, eight or ten benches with maybe twenty-five people sitting on them. There was the man, the man whose lone voice I'd heard. He was standing in front of the others. Standing with his arms half-lifted, his hands open at his sides. Behind him, on that rear wall, heavy purple curtains hung. In front of the curtains, held up by ropes or wires, I wasn't sure which, there was a plain, wooden cross about the height of a man.

I watched. The people slid in unison from the benches and went down on their knees. All of them, Emma too, went down on their knees, clasping their hands in front of them. The man before them lifted his eyes to the ceiling. He began to recite the Our Father, the Lord's Prayer. The others joined in.

By this time, my jaw had fallen nearly to my chest. My mouth was wide open.

They were praying. They were Christians. All of them. Emma too. Emma was a Christian.

I could not have been more shocked if I had looked in and seen her fucking a horse.

How on earth? How in hell? What was she thinking? How could she possibly be a Christian? What happened to all that stuff her father told me? Homer to the Deconstructionists? The realms of gold? What happened to her high school paper about God being an illusion of an illusion of our psychology or whatever?

I mean, no wonder she was hiding from the old man. No wonder she was afraid someone would see her coming here, that word of these religious hijinks would get back to Daddy. He was so proud of what he'd taught her: a whole course on western civilization, he'd said. The enlightenment, modernity, the deconstruction of the old beliefs. It was what connected her to him.

And she had abandoned it, all of it, everything she'd learned, to sink back into medieval superstition and hocus-pocus.

Look at her! I thought to myself wildly, staring wildly, gaping wildly. I was appalled. I was a modern man, an intellectual, sophisticated man. I was appalled to see such a smart, witty, knowledgeable girl kneeling there with her hands clasped like a child's, with those wonderful green eyes lifted like a saint's and that valentine face upraised like the face of some pert, mischievous angel who seemed to give off an almost mesmeric radiance so that I couldn't stop staring at her, standing there at the window and staring and staring through the glass and feeling this tide, this wave, this surge of hunger for a life-time at her lips and in her arms rising up through me, washing away every other thought and caution and con-sideration...

So that it was many long moments – I don't know how many, I don't know how long – before I realized I had been discovered.

22

When I die and go to Hell, they will lock me in a screening room and play the movie of that moment for all eternity. They won't need fire. I'll burn from within.

All this time later, I remember every detail. I can see it as clearly as if I were in Hell already. My breath started it. In my curiosity to know what was going on, I had instinctively held my breath. Then, as the full truth hit me, the air poured out of my lungs in a long huff of surprise. It fogged the glass of the window I was peering through – a circle of mist blossomed on the pane. The preacher caught the movement of it in his peripheral vision. Halfway through an 'Amen,' he turned and saw me standing there.

Some part of my brain must have registered this, but it didn't fully get through to me somehow. I was too busy staring at Emma. She and the rest of the congregation were rising from their knees, settling back into their seats. And one by one, noticing that the preacher had turned his head, they were following his gaze.

Still, I didn't completely realize what was happening. I was staring at Emma. I was thinking about Emma.

Then she turned too. Emma turned too.

Our eyes met through the window. I came to myself with a jolt. The shock I felt was answered by the shock on Emma's face.

I remember thinking: *Ah. Well. That's that.*

Emma stood crisply. She gestured to the others to go

on without her. Calm and stately, she walked out of the room.

The congregation was still staring at me, every one of them. I offered them a Cheshire cat grin of infinite apology and withdrew through the whispering pachysandra to stand abashed in the shadow of the lemon tree.

A moment later, they started singing again. *Why shouldn't they sing?* I thought miserably. *They aren't me.* I stood and waited. I heard the front door of the house open and shut. I saw Emma walking slowly to the garden gate.

She opened the gate and came toward me over the brick path at a thoughtful, deliberate pace. She was not wearing the beret but she'd put the long coat back on. It was unbuttoned, open on the white sweater and jeans, the slim, elegant figure underneath.

It was a cool, crisp day. The sun was bright. The shadows of lofty clouds sailed swiftly over the grass. Emma's cheeks were already turning pink with the weather, a sensational contrast with her black hair and her green eyes. Those eyes were glistening with – what? – mainly bewilderment, I think, and maybe pain – yes, pain.

As for me, I was just sorry, so terribly, terribly sorry I had not called the number she had written on the coaster at Carlos.

She came to stand before me. She looked at me a long time, studied my face, as if she might find some clue there to what was going on. Her lips parted, but she seemed unable to find the words to speak.

'Emma…' I said.

'What are you doing here?'

I couldn't answer. Driving over the bridge, fretting over the disastrous possibilities, I had envisioned this scenario a dozen different times. I had prepared a dozen different lies to tell her if she caught me out. But now that it had actually happened, I was struck silent. Even I could see that a lie here would be quicksand. I would never get out of it. The truth though – even if I weren't professionally bound to keep her father's case confidential, I wouldn't have had the courage to tell her the truth.

'Were you following me?' she asked.

I nodded.

'You were spying on me.'

I nodded.

She shook her head, bewildered. Bewildered, she gazed down at the path beneath her shoes with an expression of wonder. She moved around past me to the lemon tree. There was one of those circular wrought iron benches surrounding the trunk. She sank onto it. She considered the bricks another moment. Then she raised her eyes to me and shook her head and gave a single laugh – bewildered, all bewildered.

'What are you doing here, Emma?' I blurted out.

'Well,' she answered quietly. 'I'm not really sure that's the question.'

'No, I know, but I mean: you looked like you were praying?'

'Did I?'

'I mean, you and I, we – talked... About poetry and philosophy and... I mean, is it a play? Are you rehearsing a play or something?'

Another wondering laugh burst out of her. The sun through the lemon tree's branches laid a filigree of shadows over her cheeks. It had the weird effect of making her seem part of the scenery, at one with the surrounding garden.

'You're a Christian,' I said, appalled.

She nodded. 'I am, it's true.'

'But that... you can't... you can't be. You... I mean, your father...'

I stopped myself before I said too much. Or maybe I already had. Emma arched an eyebrow at me. 'What about my father?'

'Well, I mean, he's... I read his book, he's... I mean, he's an intellectual. *You're* an intellectual. We don't believe in God anymore. I mean, sure, if you want to pretend there's some amorphous, mysterious Oriental crap underlying actual real reality, fine, but this – this is organized religion.'

'It is a little organized,' she conceded, 'but I try to inject my own personal chaos into it whenever possible.'

'No, really,' I insisted. 'Christianity, Emma. It's for those guys on TV who go around telling people not to get laid and then get caught handcuffed to a hooker in a Motel Six somewhere.'

'I guess I haven't quite reached that stage of spiritual development.'

'Nobody believes in this stuff anymore, none of the real people.'

She continued to look up at me, wondering, even amazed. 'You mean, real people like my father.'

'Well...'

Emma gave a slow nod. She looked away, off into the distance, where you could see, through the neighboring houses, glimpses of the tree-lined road. The people, the congregation, had stopped singing inside and the low voice of the preacher had taken up again. The whisper of traffic reached us too, and the songs of birds carried on the vital autumn air.

'Well, my father is a very brilliant man, that's for sure,' she said finally. 'And he's always been a man of deep convictions too. When he was younger, he was convinced that Freudian analysis would set us all free. Then, he was convinced that Communism would save the world, then he amended that to Socialism – though I've never completely understood the difference. What else was there? Feminism was very big with him about ten years ago. And he's still into multiculturalism – you know, noble savages and all that. Then there's the post modern stuff, I guess that's the latest – everything's relative, there's no truth, words don't mean anything. And of course atheism – that was always there, that was a given. You couldn't really have the rest of it without that.'

She spoke all this into that distance between the trees. My eyes went over her profile as she did. I was struck again by the *rightness* of her, by my *certainty* that we were meant to be together. I had never known anything as surely as I knew that my best life depended on her. I loved her.

Now she turned to look up at me again, the filigree of shadows shifting on her heart-shaped face, holding her within the texture of the garden. 'One thing I couldn't help noticing after a while though? Brilliant as he was, everything my father believed in turned out to be untrue. I mean, people don't really have Oedipal complexes, not usually anyway, and labor doesn't actually produce capital. Women are born different from men, some cultures are better than others and on and on. And then, on top of being wrong all the time, he's also miserable. Drinks morning to night, hates his marriage, treats my mother like garbage. I sometimes think miserable people shouldn't be allowed to have philosophies at all, you know. I sometimes think they should have to find happiness first, then at least they can tell us what worked for them.' She waved the thought away with her hand. 'Anyway, the point is, after a while, it made me wonder. The fact that all these deep convictions of his turned out to be, you know, just false made me wonder about the other thing, the God thing. Well, it's a long story.'

I drew my hand along the side of my jaw. I had to admit, it didn't seem as silly as it did when she was praying. 'What about this?' I said, gesturing toward the house. 'All this hush-hush stuff. Is this the catacombs or something? You have to come here to do this in secret?'

Emma seemed about to object. I wouldn't have blamed her. It was none of my business, for one thing. Plus we both knew I owed her more answers than she did me. Still, she seemed to want to explain, to get it out of the way, maybe, before we got down to discussing the real topic of the day, which was why the hell a creepy scummy slimebag like me was following her around and spying on her?

Emma looked toward the house, gave a fond half-smile. 'It's not secret. It's just private, that's all. The people who come here are mostly in the same boat as I am. You know, it's a university town. We all have parents or boyfriends or girlfriends or bosses or whatever who are academics or intellectuals or radicals or journalists – you know, people who have very, very strong convictions that just happen to be untrue. And like most people who have convictions like that, they get very angry at anyone who disagrees with them. Some of us are afraid of losing our jobs or our lovers. Some of us don't want to stop getting invited to the hip parties. Some of us – like me – I just don't want to break the heart of someone I love. It's not being secretive exactly. Most of us aren't the sort of people who would fit in at the mainstream churches anyway. So we organized this and it's private and it gets the job done.'

She finished. She went on looking fondly at the house as the preacher's voice drifted to us and the voices of the people answered. I stood over her, expecting her to say more, expecting her to turn to me, ask me straight out: Why hadn't I called her after that first night in Carlos?

Why was I spying on her now? She didn't. She didn't say anything. She just went on looking at the house.

'Well, it all sounds almost reasonable when you explain it like that,' I said.

She gave a laugh, a sad little laugh.

'Ah, Emma.' I plunked down next to her on the wrought iron bench. 'I'm not some kind of creep, I swear it.'

She nodded, still without looking at me. 'I know that. I know what you are. I think I know what you can be anyway.'

'Emma, from the second I saw you...' I stopped. I couldn't. I didn't have the right.

'I know that too,' she said. She did turn now, brought her face half-around, glanced at me sidelong. It was an awfully nice face. Pug nose, arching brows. Thin lips, but soft, very soft-looking. I couldn't believe I had stayed away from her so long just to avoid this moment, just to avoid telling her the truth.

'That night we met at Carlos,' I said. 'I went back to the city after, and stopped to pick something up at the house of a woman I work with.' Emma shut her eyes, waiting for it. 'I was gonna call you the next day, but... we, this woman and I, we... started up together.' Emma's soft-looking lips scrunched into a trembling frown. I sighed. 'I keep thinking I'll get out of it. I want to get out of it. But I haven't been able to and... I didn't want to call you until I had.'

A tear hung crystal on her eyelashes and fell. She opened her eyes. For the first time, there was a flash of anger in them, an angry tension in her voice. 'Then why are you here?' she said. 'Why are you spying on me?'

Painfully, I forced the words out. 'I can't tell you. I'm sorry. I'll find a way to make it right. So help me God, I will. But right now – I just can't tell you.'

Emma opened her mouth. She made a noise. A whispered sob, I guess. Another tear fell from her eyes and then another ran down her cheek. She pressed her lips together. She shook her head. 'That,' she said, 'is not fair.'

'I know, I know.'

'You're taking advantage.'

'I know.'

'You're taking advantage of the fact that we were meant for each other.'

I seized her hand convulsively in both of mine. I brought it up and pressed it against my forehead. 'Emma!'

She gently drew the hand away. As tightly as I held on, I couldn't keep it. She stood up. I couldn't look at her. I bent forward with my elbows on my thighs, my hands still pressed against my brow.

They began singing in the house again. Knuckleheads. What the hell were they constantly singing about?

'I'm not the new kind of girl,' Emma said. The way she said it, the way she had to work to keep her voice steady – well, it would've broken my heart if my heart had not already broken. 'I'm an old-fashioned girl. I want a man I can look up to and admire. Don't come back until you are one.'

The air came out of me as if she'd punched me. I wished she'd only punched me. It was several long moments before I could lift my head.

When I did, she was at the gate again, slipping through the gate, closing the gate behind her. She walked away, up the path, out of sight, back to the house, where they all continued singing.

23

The canyon highway curled through the barren hills, came out again into barren flatland, wilderness to the horizon. Swaths of gray cloud covered the sky, as if it were a ceiling painted slapdash. Daylight broke through in places as the sun began to rise, but the clouds also gathered and the light slowly died behind an iron monotony. The color of the distance died with the light. There was nothing ahead but the brown of dust and tumbleweed, a faint hazy blue of mountains far away.

Weiss drove wearily. He'd slept badly. He'd had bad dreams. All night in the motel, in a box-like room bare yards from the highway. Tangled in sweat-gray sheets, mere inches beneath the surface of sleep. Trucks had thundered past, headlights had flashed over the ceiling – and in his dreams, the dark was split by lightning and there stood the Shadowman. It was the man from Hannock, the man in the suede windbreaker whom Weiss had spoken to at the base of the driveway. But in these dreams, the killer leapt suddenly at him out of the split darkness – and he had no face. That was the worst part of it. That was the thing that haunted Weiss even after he was awake. The killer had no face. Even here, now, no matter how hard he tried, Weiss couldn't remember what the man had looked like. He had slipped away, had slipped even out of his memory.

'Boof,' he said aloud. Just thinking about it gave him indigestion. He rubbed his gut with one hand as he steered toward Reno with the other.

At eight, he saw the city catch the sun. Wind with a hint of rain in it had thinned the clouds by then. The light came down in beams. The oasis of hotel towers and casinos was held in a pink glow, set apart from the backdrop of white-blue mountains. It looked like a fine place from here.

But with every mile Weiss drove, a little of the luster of the city seeped away. Soon, the dreary outskirts surrounded him. A great barrel-chested rainstorm came rolling westward, darkening the sky. The dreariness spread and overtook him and went on before.

By the time he cruised into downtown, the streets seemed duller to him than the wilderness. This was in spite of the lights, in spite of the morning crowds. The Taurus passed beneath the arching sign: 'Reno,' in large red letters, and underneath in yellow: 'The Biggest Little City In The World.' Beyond that, on either side, were the hotels and casinos outlined in neon now. Thick traffic clogged the way ahead, pickups and hulking SUVs shouldering against each other from intersection to intersection. Late gamblers from the night before and early tourists moved in small groups along the sidewalks under the shadows of domed roofs and the lancing angles of high-rise hotels.

Weiss found himself checking faces as he drove. The sinewy cowboy in the truck alongside him. The obese salesman coming out of the casino with a whore. The bored, irritated honeymooner with his unhappy bride in tow. Weiss examined them without thinking, compulsively trying to prove to himself that the nightmares were wrong, that he would, in fact, recognize the killer if he saw him again. But it was no good. He didn't know what to look for. The killer's face was gone.

He drove on to the address the kid at the Super 8 had given him. Adrienne Chalk's address. Another of his

Weiss hunches, another slender thread of a lead. The woman had stayed in the motel room paid for by Andy Bremer and Weiss had a feeling that had something to do with Julie. That's all he had. That Weiss feeling. But he'd been right about Bremer, it turned out. And if Bremer was Julie's father, maybe Chalk was her mother or something. Or maybe not. Maybe it was nothing, a dead end.

He found the place easily enough. It was just a couple of blocks from the center of town. The Taurus turned the corner onto a long broad boulevard that led out to the low suburbs and the mountains. There were strip joints lining one side of the street. Their shabby signs jutted over the sidewalk, nightclub names in blinking neon: *Fantasy*, *Femme Fatale*, *Gangster Pete*'s. Weiss parked the car under twinkling lights that spelled out *The Black Hand*.

On the far side of the boulevard, there were four- and five-story buildings with glass-fronted shops and taverns at the ground level, brown brick apartments up top. Weiss got out of the car, lifting his eyes to some of the windows above a liquor store. A figure pulled away behind curtains on the third story. Weiss figured: so what? But he felt edgy. He sensed something was coming. Maybe it was just the bad dreams.

He crossed the street, dodging a red pickup with country music booming from its radio. When he reached the sidewalk, he moved to the entrance alcove next to the liquor store. There was a bright red door. There was a line of names on a brass panel next to it, a line of buttons next to the names. The Chalk woman's name was there. Weiss pressed the button next to it. Almost immediately, the door buzzed, unlocked. Fast, as if she were expecting him. Weiss pushed in. He didn't feel good about this. He was sorry he'd left his gun in the car.

He couldn't tell if the lobby was rundown or if it'd just

been built to look depressing as hell. Yellow paisley walls. A long mirror with his large, paunchy figure and his sad-assed face staring out of it. A cheap table under the mirror with throwaway real estate papers and papers advertising escorts – whores. No elevator he could see. Threadbare runners on the stairs. Weiss started climbing.

The Chalk woman's door was halfway down the third-floor hall. That was about the right place if she'd been the one at the window. Was she expecting him? Did Bremer call ahead to warn her the way Julie called to warn him? He knocked. No answer. But the door swung in. It was off the latch. As if someone inside were waiting for him to walk in. What the hell?

He walked in. Nudged the door shut behind him.

The place smelled. Cigarettes: new smoke and the old stuff that sinks into the furniture and stinks like vomit. Other than that, the apartment was a dive. Sofas and chairs with corrugated upholstery. Framed magazine pictures on the cracked plaster walls. A kitchen through an archway, a bedroom beyond a door. Windows onto the street, one open. Traffic noise filtering through and a desperate trickle of damp Reno air. As far as Weiss could see, the dump was empty, but it didn't feel empty somehow.

'Hey,' he said. 'Anybody home?'

No one answered. He cursed silently. He moved slowly toward the bedroom door, looking all around him.

'Hey?'

He stepped into the bedroom. Small, tight space. The double bed filled the center of it. There were narrow corridors of wood floor on one side of the bed and at its foot. The blankets and sheets were in a jumble on the mattress. There were newspaper pages in the jumble too. On the bedside table, there was a pile of papers and manilla envelopes. There was a brass ashtray full of butts. And there was a romance novel with a red cover. *A Ring For Cinderella*.

The smell of smoke was stronger in here, not so stale. The smoker was around somewhere or had been recently. Behind that open closet door to the right of him – that was a good place for someone to hide. Then there was a bathroom ahead of him to his left. Someone could be hiding in there too.

He guessed the closet. He went for it fast. He was light on his feet for a big man and he crossed to it in a heart-beat. He flipped the door shut with one hand, the other hand ready to strike.

'You're fucking dead,' came the throaty voice behind him.

Weiss sighed, annoyed with himself. It was the bath-room all along.

He turned and faced her. She had a gun trained on his belly. Not your lightweight lady's toy either, but a Smith & Wesson 500 revolver. The recoil would probably blow her out into the street, but not before she'd put a hole in Weiss the size of a basketball.

'You're so dead it's not even funny,' she said.

The kid at the hotel had been right about Adrienne Chalk. She thought she was something. Weiss could see it in the way she came toward him along the side of the bed, swaying her hips and keeping her chin lifted as if she were moving into the camera for her big close-up. She had dyed-blonde hair and a mean face. Maybe her face had been pretty once in a cheap kind of way, but now it was just cheap and mean. Her lipstick was too red and she wore too much make-up on her cheeks and too much whatever-that-stuff-was-called – mascara – under her eyes. She wore a blue suit, skirt and jacket, that might've been meant to give her some style. It didn't. She had too much ass for it, especially the way she swayed.

She came to the edge of the bed. She gripped the gun tight, kept it trained on Weiss's midsection. Weiss didn't like it. He had a temper. He got angry when people pointed guns at him. Guns, knives. They just pissed him off somehow. Chalk's smirky little smile didn't do much for his mood either.

'Where do you want it, fat man?' said Adrienne Chalk.

'Put that down or I'm gonna slap you,' Weiss told her.

Adrienne laughed. 'Slap me? I'm gonna shoot you, you dumb shit. No court in the world'd convict me.'

Weiss slapped her – a good one with the back of his hand. She fell over onto the bed. He reached down and took the gun away from her.

'You son of a bitch, you hit me!' she gasped.

He slipped the gun into his jacket pocket. He kept his hand on it. 'So what? You been hit before, haven't you? Sure you have. I'll bet you been hit plenty.'

'You bastard,' said Adrienne Chalk. 'How about I start screaming?'

'You start screaming, I'll shoot you,' said Weiss – which he wouldn't have, but how the hell was she supposed to know?

She touched the side of her mouth. Looked at her fingertips. Either her lip was bleeding or her lipstick was smeared, Weiss couldn't tell which. Neither could she, it looked like.

She sat up on the bed slowly. 'Ya fuck,' she muttered.

Weiss shook his head. What a world. People pulling guns on you. Women pulling guns, for Christ's sake. He could never shake the idea that women ought to be better than that somehow.

If anyone could've changed his mind, it would've been this prize piece of work. He stood, looking down at her. He searched her face for any sign that she could be Julie's mother. He didn't find any, but then he didn't want to find any.

'All right,' he said. He leaned back against the wall. He had his hands in his jacket pockets, one hand on the gun. 'What is this?'

'Aaah,' she said, angry. She wiped her sore lip with the meat of her hand.

'I mean it. You pull a gun on me?'

'I should've shot you. I was going to. I just wanted to see you sweat first.'

'What the hell?' said Weiss with a laugh. 'No, I mean it. What the hell? You leave the door open like that so I walk in and then you're gonna shoot me?'

'I saw you coming. I saw you from the window.'

'So what? You don't even know me, you crazy bitch.'

'Aaah,' she said again. 'I know enough. I knew you were coming, didn't I? Someone like you. Some thug he'd send.'

Weiss made a *ch* sound, air between his teeth. 'I'm a thug now? What is this?'

'I know what you are.' Adrienne Chalk looked him over. Meanwhile, she worked her jaw with one hand to make sure it still worked. Weiss was large and powerful and he'd slapped her hard. 'You're some private investigator type. Am I right? Ex-cop, you look like. I know. Nice, respectable people, they slip you an envelope, you make things go away. Anything that doesn't fit the nice, respectable picture – *poof!* – right? – they pay you, it's gone. He'd like that, I bet. Mr Nice-Respectable. With his wife and kids and his house and his church and whatever bullshit. He'd like it if I just went away. Well, you go back and you tell him he can forget it. 'Cause guess what? I'm his memory. I'm all that's left of Suzanne and I'm the price he pays for his nice, respectable life. And if he don't like it, he can go fuck himself and so can you.'

165

Weiss listened, leaning against the wall. He looked at her. Sitting on the bed with her legs curled under her. Snarling at him with the fat lip he'd given her. What a skank she was. Was it possible she was talking about Andy Bremer? She thought Bremer had sent him to make her disappear, was that it?

Weiss asked her. 'You mean Bremer? You think Andy Bremer sent me? The realtor guy from Hannock?'

Chalk sneered and eyed him sideways. For the first time, she seemed unsure of herself. 'What're you talking about? Obviously Bremer. I saw your plates, the California plates. Who else do I know in California?'

Weiss cocked his head. 'You see a lot, I'll give you that.'

'I knew what he'd try. Fuck you. You tell him: "Fuck you," I said. And fuck you too.'

She massaged her jaw with her hand some more. Weiss considered her. His temper had cooled now. He was sorry he'd hit her. But not that sorry. The skank.

'So let me get this,' he said. 'Every two months you show up at the Hannock Super 8 and Bremer pays the tab. Now you figure he sent me to make you go away?'

Chalk kept eyeing him, snarly and uncertain. 'You trying to tell me Bremer didn't send you? How come you know all about him then? Huh? Who are you? If he didn't send you, who did?'

But Weiss was ahead of her. It was coming clear to him now. 'I get it. You're blackmailing him, right? Is that it? All that stuff about you're his memory. You're the price he pays. You got something out of his past and you're blackmailing him with it.'

'Fuck you. Who are you anyway?'

'What is it? What've you got on him?'

'What're you, a cop?' said Adrienne Chalk. 'You're no cop.'

'Who's Suzanne? You said you were all that's left of Suzanne? Who's she?'

Spit fizzled between Chalk's lips as she glared at him.

Weiss made a noise. He pushed off the wall, straightened. He lumbered along the side of the bed, big in the narrow passage. Chalk scrambled away from him to the far side of the mattress.

'You keep away from me!' she said.

Weiss didn't answer. He went to the bedside table. He pushed the romance novel aside. *A Ring For Cinderella, my ass*, he thought. He lifted the first manilla envelope underneath, opened it, looked at the papers in it. Sex stuff, money stuff, stuff from one of the strip clubs across the street. *Femme Fatale* was right.

'You work in this place?' he said over his shoulder.

'Yeah. So what?'

'You blackmail the guys who come in here too.'

'So what?' she said. 'Some of them.'

He picked up the next envelope. It hit the brass ashtray. The ashtray fell to the wooden floor with a clang. It spilled butts and ash over the floorboards. In the envelope, sure enough: photographs. Guys with topless women on their laps. Grainy printouts, from a phone camera probably. Addresses, web pages. All kinds of information on these poor hardons.

'That's my shit,' Adrienne Chalk protested. 'I got copies. I got plenty of copies, believe me.'

'I believe you. Who's Suzanne?'

Weiss went through the loose papers, tossing them aside. They floated down to the floor to lie on top of the envelopes. Finally the table was empty.

He rounded on Chalk. 'Come here,' he said.

'Stay away from me.'

'This is all small time shit. Husbands getting lap dances. This is penny ante shit. No one pays good money

167

for this. If you think Bremer's coming after you, he's paying you good money. What've you got on him? Who's Suzanne?'

'Fuck you. I don't have to tell you nothing.'

But she was scared. Her eyes moved. Weiss saw it. Her eyes moved to the cabinet on the lower half of the table. She was scared and she couldn't help herself. Weiss pulled the cabinet open.

'Hey,' she said. 'Hey. That's my shit. I got copies.'

He found another bunch of manilla envelopes in there. He pulled one out.

'Gimme that,' said Adrienne Chalk.

She made a move to come toward him on the bed. Weiss cocked his hand at his ear as if he'd hit her again. He would have hit her again. He was well past ready. He'd had enough of her. She scrambled back out of his reach.

He opened the envelope. He pinched the sheaf of papers inside, tugged it out. He scanned the paragraphs, lifted the pages, looked at the photos. He went over the whole story, his stomach churning. *Jesus*, he thought. *Jesus.*

'Suzanne Graves,' he said, reading the name off the newspaper printout. 'What was she? Your sister?' He got no answer. He glanced up. 'Listen, I'm sick of you. Don't fuck with me. What was she, your sister?'

'Half,' grunted Adrienne Chalk, sulky. She touched her hair as she said it. She shifted where she was sitting and sort of posed for him, arching her back, showing off her tits, which were all right. She must've sensed Weiss was looking her over, comparing her to the photos of Suzanne Graves. Graves was prettier, a lot prettier. Which gave Weiss another lurching pain in his belly. Suzanne Graves not only looked like Adrienne Chalk with her pinched, mean features, she also had the high cheeks and the fine complexion and the slightly uncanny gaze that made her look like Julie Wyant too. It was easy to see the truth. Adrienne Chalk wasn't Julie's mother. Her half-sister was, Suzanne Graves was.

'That's a crap way to die,' said Weiss, rapping the printout with his knuckle. 'Got her head caved in with a claw hammer, it says. That's a crap way to die.'

'While she was asleep,' Chalk spat angrily. 'He just crept up on her in her bed while she was asleep.'

Weiss read from the printout. '"Police are hunting the dead woman's husband, Charles Graves."'

'Look at the picture,' said Adrienne Chalk.

Weiss had already looked. He saw how it was. The photo, captioned 'Charles Graves, wanted for questioning by the police in the murder of his wife,' showed Andy Bremer as a younger man. So Bremer had been married to Suzanne. They'd had Julie together and another daughter too, according to the paper. Then, when Julie was maybe thirteen or so, Bremer had murdered the girls' mother in her bed. Crept up on her while she was sleeping with a claw hammer in his hand and pounded her skull until her brains burst out onto the pillow. Nice. Weiss thought about Bremer the way he was now. Doing the dishes in the kitchen. Joking around with his wife and children. Singing in church. Nice.

'He killed her, huh,' he said aloud. 'He killed his first wife.'

'My sister. That's right.'

'In Ohio, this was?'

'In Akron, yeah.'

'Seventeen years ago, it says.'

'So what? She's still dead.'

'Right. She's still dead.'

He tossed the envelope onto the bed. Adrienne Chalk seized it, clutched it to her breast protectively. Weiss walked back around the bed to the window. He looked out and down on the street of strip joints, the blinking signs. *Femme Fatale. Gangster Pete's.* What a world. He checked his gray Taurus, sitting at the curb, dull and dependable as an old nag under the blinking sign for *The Black Hand*. He scanned the faces of passersby, looking for that one face he could not remember.

Finally, he turned to Chalk. Propped his butt on the windowsill. Looked her over.

It made her nervous. 'Who are you?' she said. 'Who sent you, if Bremer didn't? What're you gonna do to me?' It was more than nervous. Weiss could see she was really scared now. She didn't know anymore what he was here for. Maybe he wanted to move in on her, shake her down, steal her stuff. Maybe he even wanted to kill her. She didn't know.

Good, Weiss thought. Let her worry. It'd make it easier to get the whole story out of her.

'You're something, all right,' he said. 'You're a real piece of work. I gotta hand it to you. Seventeen years ago, Bremer kills his wife and gets away with it. Runs off, changes his name, gets married again, starts a new life. And all that time, you look for him, you hunt him down. Seventeen years, you wait for the chance to put the squeeze on him.'

'I didn't look for him,' said Adrienne Chalk. She kept her eyes on Weiss all the while, watching him, scared, not knowing what he was here for, what he would do. 'I wouldn't've known where to start. One of those things just happened. You know the way things happen sometimes? A couple of years ago, I saw Charlie's picture in the paper. Some kind of convention, some kind of charity thing. The Children's Charity, that was the name of it. People from all over the country were in Albuquerque for it and there was some guy from Reno there. So they had him, the guy from Reno, they had him in the local paper. And in back of him – in the picture in back of him – there was Charlie, big as life. With one of those name tags, you know. Andy Bremer. So I went on the computer and found him. That was it. It just happened.'

Weiss laughed. 'Beautiful. So the guy's giving to charity, you figure he must have money, right? You go to California, you find him with his new name and the wife and the house and everything. It's a perfect setup. Enough of this penny ante shit, right? Bremer has to pay you real money and keep paying you or else you send him to the Graybar.'

Adrienne Chalk gave a jerky, nervous shrug, always eyeing him. 'Well, why should he just get away with it? Right? All his Mr Nice-Respectable shit. Like you said. He's got the house, the wife, the kids. He's got money enough to give it away to charity. I mean, my sister's fucking dead.'

'Your sister's dead!' Weiss sneered. What a skank. What a piece of work. 'Your sister's dead, you go to the police.'

'What good is that to me? The police. My sister's dead and he gets the good life? What're the police gonna do?'

He shook his head. 'You're something. You really are.'

'Look,' she said. Her tone changed suddenly, went softer. 'Look. Who are you? What do you want? You want money? I mean, we can work something out. I got this, I got a couple other things going. We could even work together on some of this.' She lifted her chin. She posed her tits for him again. 'You might like working with me, you know. There might be benefits...'

'Yeah, yeah, yeah,' said Weiss. 'You'll blow me, you'll cut me in – whatever. Fuck you. Here's what I want. This woman, your sister, Suzanne. She had two kids, right? Two daughters. The newspaper doesn't say their names.'

'The daughters?' Chalk said – there was a hopeful, calculating note in her voice. She hadn't been thinking about the daughters. She didn't care about the daughters. If Weiss was here about them, maybe it would be all right. 'Mary and Olivia – Livy.'

'Mary and Olivia. What happened to them? Where are they?'

Adrienne Chalk hesitated. Weiss could practically hear her thinking. Trying to figure what she could get out of him for this. 'How would I know about that?' she said.

'You know,' said Weiss. 'This didn't just happen. You kept tabs, kept watch. Sat on top of it until it broke right for you. You're the sister. The aunt. Bremer killed his wife and booked it, left the kids behind. It would've been easy for you to find out where they went, keep watch on them, in case maybe he got in touch.'

Chalk seemed about to lie again, but must've given up on it. 'You see a lot yourself, don't you?'

'Where are they?'

'What's in it for me?'

'I go away.'

She snorted.

'All right,' said Weiss. 'I don't go away. I go to the police. Bremer goes down for murder, you go down for blackmail. It's nothing to me.'

That got her. She thought it through. 'How do I know you won't tell the cops anyway.'

'Because why would I? I just want the girls. You and Bremer can torture yourselves to death, for all I care. You deserve each other.'

Adrienne Chalk thought it through some more. 'They took the daughters into homes,' she said then. 'After Suzanne was killed and Charlie booked it, the daughters got taken into foster homes. The older one, Mary, she went bad, ran off. I don't know where she is. I don't, I swear. The younger one, Livy, Olivia, she's in Phoenix. She's a – whattaya call it? – like a counselor, a shrink or something.'

'Olivia Graves – is that still her name?'

'Yeah, that's right. She's not married or nothing. Olivia Graves.'

Weiss pushed up off the windowsill. 'Thanks,' he said. He took Adrienne Chalk's revolver out of his pocket. He tossed it onto the bed. It bounced on the mattress next to her legs.

In a flash, Adrienne Chalk threw the envelope aside and pounced on the gun. She snapped it up with both hands. She pointed it dead at Weiss. 'You never should've slapped me, you son of a bitch,' she said. She pulled the trigger.

Weiss was already walking to the door. He already had his hand in his jacket pocket again. When the hammer of the 500 snapped down, he paused and turned. He shook his head. He brought a fistful of bullets out of his pocket. He flung them in Adrienne Chalk's face. One hit her, the rest flew all over the room, pattering on the wood floor.

'What a skank,' Weiss muttered.

The bullet that hit Adrienne Chalk fell on the mattress and rolled under her knee. She was furiously trying to dig it out, get a hold of it, trying to shove it into one of the cylinder's chambers as Weiss left the apartment and shut the door behind him.

24

Later, it came to him, in the desert, in the dark. He knew what he had to do.

He'd been driving for hours and hours by then. Pushing on, relentless, through relentless emptiness. Rain came before night fell, a slashing downpour. Then night fell under stuttering thunder. Awesome three-fold barbs of lightning jagged from the core of the vast sky to the horizon. The desolate land lit up – endless desolation at every window, in all directions – and then vanished into desolate darkness... the sheeting rain on the windshield... the wipers working back and forth.

Weiss drove on, tired, tired. It was hard going. Hard to see anything, hard to make any time. Hour after hour, slogging through the rain. He gripped the wheel, peered into the night.

He thought about Julie.

The Graves family had been poor. That's what Chalk's old newspaper stories said. The father, mother and two daughters lived in a cramped, dilapidated house on the edge of the east city. The father had worked in a tire warehouse before the company shut down. Afterwards, he mostly did odd jobs, off the books, hauling and lifting for whatever outfit would use him. The mother, Suzanne, was a drunk and a meth addict – a whore too when she needed money for the drugs. Otherwise, she worked in the local Hoffman's Department store from time to time.

The kids, Mary and Olivia, were thirteen and ten.

The neighbors said Mary took care of her little sister. She played mother to her, made sure she ate, made sure she got to school most days. She took Olivia to their room and hid there with her when the parents fought. The parents fought a lot, the neighbors said. Suzanne brought men to the house when her husband was out – long-haired, tattooed toughs in the drug trade. Charles suspected what was going on and that's what started the fighting. The police had been called in once or twice to break it up.

No one was very surprised when Suzanne woke up dead one morning. She was supposed to go to work that day and her girlfriend found her body when she came to pick her up. 'It was like a broken watermelon, her head; stuff all over the pillow,' the girlfriend told the papers. Everyone said it was shocking, but no one was very surprised.

The husband and daughters were thought missing at first. There was some talk about a drug deal gone sour, a kidnapping and so on. But it turned out the girls were standing outside Olivia's elementary school, unharmed, waiting patiently for the doors to open. Their father had dropped them off there just before dawn. Then he'd driven away. The police found his pickup later that evening. He himself was never seen again. The children didn't seem to know what had happened.

Weiss gripped the wheel, peered into the night. The Taurus pushed through the spattering rain. Weiss thought about the Graves family, Charles and Suzanne, Mary and Olivia. After a while, this thing happened to him, this thing that was always happening. He began to live through the story as if he were in someone else's mind. It was strange. It just came over him. It was part of that weird, Weissian knack of his, that knack of knowing who people were, knowing what they would do. He found himself feeling his way through the past as if he had been there, as if he had been Charlie Graves – Charlie Graves who became Andy Bremer – an odd-jobbing lowlife who hammer-killed his junky wife and became a prosperous church-going family man. Weiss could feel how the one kind of man always lived inside the other somehow, the family man lived inside the lowlife all along. Maybe Charlie Graves didn't know it at first. He married Suzanne and, at first, it was all right. But if Suzanne was anything like her half-sister, she was a seething, vicious bitch. Savage to her husband, making fun of him when he was down. Smacking the kids around. Drunk, drugged. Bringing the tattooed drug dealers into her house and trading with them, a ride inside her for some booze, some coke, some meth. Charlie could've lived with it, maybe, Weiss felt. Lived with it or just skipped out and left it behind. But there was this other man inside him, this better man. And this man, this Andy Bremer, looked out through Charlie's eyes and saw his kids, his daughters. He saw the looks on their faces. He saw ashes and powder on the living room rug and half-eaten food on the sofa. He smelled the sex-stench of strangers, his wife's perfume. And those looks – even in his sleep, he saw those looks on the two girls' faces. It wasn't enough just to leave. He had to get free. He had to get them all free and he had no money and no place to go and he couldn't even think with the bitch screaming at him the minute he came through the door…

The rain thundered down on the Taurus and the thunder rolled and the desert lay invisible at every window. Weiss's right hand closed tight on the steering wheel but he felt the wooden handle of the claw hammer in his hand.

Afterwards, when the hammer slipped from his fingers, there would've been nothing left for Charlie

Graves but the shabby reality of the thing: his wife's crushed skull, the brains on the pillow, the splayed female body, which he had known. And the girls, the two little girls, huddled together in one of their beds, clinging to each other against the horrible noises from the next room, wide-eyed when he opened the door and the wedge of light fell on them, on the looks on their faces...

By then, Charlie Graves was gone, was dead, as dead as his wife. He had killed himself killing her. He went through the rest of it like an animated corpse. He hurried his daughters out of the house, drove them to the elementary school in the pre-dawn dark, turning the steering wheel, pressing the pedals mechanically. He left them at the schoolhouse door with a monotone goodbye. And he drove away and kept driving, the life of Charlie Graves falling from him like rotten flesh with every mile, until he reached California and was Andy Bremer at last.

Weiss let him go. He turned in his mind back to the children. The two girls in the school doorway. Fatherless, motherless, alone. Mary took care of Olivia. She always had, that's how she was. Even later, even after she became the whore Julie Wyant, Weiss had heard she was still like that. She had an other-worldly air of tenderness about her – that's what made lonely middle-aged men fall in love with her, that and the other-worldly beauty of her face.

So she took care of Olivia. But then Olivia was taken away. The state, Child Protective Services, foster homes: the two girls were separated. That's why Mary Graves 'went bad, ran off,' as Adrienne Chalk put it. That's why she became the whore Julie Wyant. She needed to make enough money to save her sister from the system, take care of her, put her through school so she could become a counselor or psychologist or whatever she was. Julie would not have left her sister behind. She would've gone on taking care of her as long as she could. Weiss didn't know how he knew this, but he knew it.

And that's why he knew what he had to do.

He was coming to the end of his search. Olivia was out there. In Phoenix, up ahead, where the lightning touched down. It had taken Weiss and his instincts to get this close to her – that's why the killer had hung back till now, stayed out of it, trailed behind him like a cloud of dust. But now that she was found, the rest would be easy. If anyone knew where Julie was, Olivia did, her sister did. There was nothing to keep the specialist from questioning her himself.

Weiss gripped the wheel, peered through the windshield. Pushed the Taurus on through the downpour.

It was time to meet with him, to meet with the killer. There was no other way to protect Olivia. It was time to talk with the specialist face to face. Just as he had in his dreams last night. Just as he had in his nightmares.

He drove on. He crossed through the rain into Arizona. He thought about the Graves family. He thought about his dreams. He knew what he had to do.

He had to meet the Shadowman.

25

In the morning, Sissy stepped out of her building and found Bishop waiting for her. Later, she would tell me what happened between them, and that would become part of the story. But for now, I was standing at the window of her apartment, watching. I saw Bishop there, three stories below. He was sitting astride his motorcycle at the curb, idling in the no parking zone just outside the door. He was wearing his aviator shades and his ironic smile. He had the collar of his leather jacket turned up. His helmet was hanging on the handlebars. His sandy hair moved in the biting wind that funneled up the narrow street behind him.

When I saw him, when I saw Sissy approach him, I felt a stab of what I thought was disapproval. It was easy to disapprove of Bishop after all he'd done. It was easy to tell yourself you were a better man than he was. But in my case, I don't really think it was disapproval at all. I think I was jealous of him. The words Emma had spoken to me hung from my heart like an anchor. *I want a man I can look up to and admire. Don't come back until you are one.* It was the harshest thing anyone had said to me in my young life, harsher still coming from her, whom I loved. I was jealous of Bishop because I couldn't imagine any woman ever saying anything like that to him. He treated women like toys. He treated almost everyone like garbage. He was violent and reckless and he didn't give much of a damn about anything. But I could not imagine a woman saying to him what Emma had said, and whatever he had that made that true, I wanted to have it as well.

I told myself I disapproved of him, but that was a lie. I wanted to be more like him.

Anyway, that was me, upstairs, watching from the window. Down on Jackson Street, Bishop caught Sissy's eye. He lifted his chin to her. He waited while she walked toward him. She was wearing a long blue overcoat, a woolen cap with blue stripes. Like all her outfits, it was schoolgirl stuff. She wore leather gloves and kept her hands clasped in front of her. She got a frown on her lips when she saw Bishop, like a prim eight-year-old girl watching some boys get muddy.

The look of her made Bishop snort. It made something cold and humorous go through the heart of him.

At his shoulder, the morning traffic on the hill rumbled end to end. The noise of the motors was loud. Sissy had to raise her whispery voice to be heard above it.

'Hello, Jim,' she said. It was a cold, cold tone coming from her.

'I need to find Weiss,' he told her.

'He's gone. I don't know where he is. He left me in charge. Can I help you in some way?'

Bishop ignored the cool voice, the scolding eyes. He couldn't have cared less what Sissy thought of him. If he wanted her to make noise, he'd fuck her. 'No,' he said curtly. 'I need Weiss. I can't reach his cell phone. I sent him an email, I left a message on the machine at his apartment, but he hasn't called back.'

'That's right. He's out of touch.'

'That's it? He's just gone? He just left? There's no way to reach him?'

'He must've had some private business.'

Pissed off, Bishop looked away. Private business.

Bullshit. Weiss had gone to find the whore. He didn't want anyone to know where he was because he'd gone to draw the specialist into a showdown and save the whore and prove he was still some kind of hero instead of an over-the-hill Jew ex-cop picking up scraps as a private detective.

'Christ,' Bishop said under his breath, the word lost in the motor noise from the Jackson Street traffic. He should just let the old man go, he thought, let him get himself killed. Fucking Weiss.

'Is there anything else I can do for you?' said Sissy coldly.

Bishop gave her a look. Her whole priggy schoolgirl routine was beginning to give him a pain. 'If he was gonna leave someone a clue where he went, it'd be you, you or Ketchum.'

'It wasn't me,' she said.

Bishop nodded. 'Well, if you think of anything, let me know. And if he gets in touch, tell him to call me.'

'Well, he might not want to talk to you,' Sissy said primly.

Bishop ran his gaze over her, from her wool cap to the gloved hands clasped in front of her, back up to her dis-approving blue eyes. He didn't say anything but he was thinking it. That was enough. The look made her blush.

'I don't give a fuck whether he wants to talk to me or not,' he said. 'Tell him to call me. If he goes after this guy alone, he's gonna get himself killed.'

'What's that supposed to mean?'

'Just tell him, Sissy.'

He made the sputtering Harley roar. He looked up at me. It was too quick. There was no time for me to pull back. He laughed. He gave me an ironical wave. Then he nodded at Sissy, curled the bike away from her into the traffic, and headed off down the hill.

26

Next, he broke into Weiss's apartment. He flipped the lock with a credit card. Stepped inside. Shut the door behind him.

The living room was in shadow. The window shades were half drawn, blocking out the morning light. He could hear the traffic out on Russian Hill, but it was quiet inside. The unstirred dust of days hung in the air. The place felt abandoned.

Bishop stood just within the doorway. He gave the room what pilots call a block scan, moving his eyes over ten degrees of arc at a time. He started with the corner to his left. An open kitchen door. The white tile of the room beyond. The toaster on the counter. His gaze moved on another ten degrees. A desk, a swivel chair, a computer, a phone, the answering machine with its red answer light burning: no messages.

He went around the room like that, shifting his focus from one object to another. He looked at the wing chair in an alcove across from him, facing the bay window. There was a small round table by one arm. There were pale rings in the table's brown surface, stains left by the bottom of a glass. Bishop could picture Weiss sitting in the chair, looking out the bay window, sipping his Macallans.

The corner of his mouth twitched. *Fucking Weiss*, he thought. His gaze moved on.

To his right, he could see the foot of the bed through

the bedroom door. The bed was neatly made, the bed-spread smooth. Moving on, he saw, on the wall directly at his shoulder, a mirror and another chair. That was the end of the scan.

He went to the desk. He sat down in the swivel chair. The first thing he noticed was the cell phone, Weiss's cell phone, lying right there next to the computer keyboard. Bishop turned it over. The battery was gone. Weiss wanted to make himself that much harder to trace.

Bishop turned the computer on. As he waited for the machine to boot, he pulled open the desk drawers one by one. There wasn't much there. In one drawer, he found a box of bullets but no gun. Weiss must've taken his old service revolver with him, that old snub-nosed .38 he had. There was a twinge in Bishop's gut when he thought of Weiss going after the specialist with his old .38. The specialist with his Sig and his 1911 and his armor-piercing Saracen. He made a face. He slid the drawer shut hard.

He diddled with the computer for a while, but he was no hacker. Weiss had a code on his case files and his mail. Everything else was business letters, home accounting, that kind of thing. No clues to where he'd gone. The phone answering machine wasn't any help either. Bishop pressed the replay button, but all the messages had been erased.

He pushed back from the desk. Crossed the thin hemp rug. Went into the bedroom. Not much there either. A stack of magazines on the bedside table. *Baseball Digest, Sports Illustrated, Baseball America, Newsweek, Law And Order*. A book on the bottom of the pile: *Let Freedom Ring*. He picked up the remote, turned on the television at the foot of the bed. The voice of the anchor-woman was startling in the long-standing silence. Fox News. He turned the set off again.

He went out, back across the living room, back across the thin hemp rug, into the kitchen. He took a quick glance around. Banged through the cabinets. Brought down a drinking glass. He held the glass under the faucet and ran a thin layer of water onto the bottom. He carried the glass back into the living room.

He sat in Weiss's wing chair. He put the glass on the little round table by the chair's arm. He brought his cigarette pack and his plastic lighter out of the slash pocket of his leather jacket. He lit a cigarette. Pressed his head against the chair back and smoked, looking out through the bay window – through the bottom panes, the panes that weren't covered by the half-drawn blinds.

Outside, in the bright, cold morning, the wind was moving in the plane trees. There was a steep hill falling away from a grassy square, townhouse by townhouse lining the street, bay window after bay window, descending. On the sidewalk just across from him, a thickset workman pushed a dolly past the hilltop. A young woman in a white sweater strode into the wind with great determination. On the street, a blue station wagon rolled past, then a red coupe, then a green one. There were long moments between the cars when the corner was empty and still.

Bishop raised the Marlboro and pressed it between his lips. Weiss must've sat in this chair in the evenings, he thought. Drinking his scotch, looking out at the hill. Watching the dusk fall over the city. Alone. Watching the dark.

He drew smoke. He let it trail out of his mouth slowly. What did Weiss think about, sitting here? Did he think about the whore? Alone here, night after night, drinking, watching the dark. Or was it the killer he thought about – the killer out there somewhere, watching him, hunting for her?

Bishop tried to think the way Weiss would. If he was going to catch up to the old man, if he was going to stop the specialist, he had to get into their heads – just like Weiss would. He had to get a sense of what they were planning, what they wanted.

He thought about the killer. He thought about him buying three guns from the Frenchman. It was a lot of hardware, powerful stuff. Just to kill off one middle-aged private eye. What was that about?

Bishop lowered the cigarette. He tipped ash into the water glass on the table. The ash hissed softly, spread and sank, lay black and cold at the glass's bottom. He considered it. Something came to him. A scenario. A reason for the three guns.

Weiss and the killer were different kinds of people – not just because Weiss was a good guy and the killer was a psycho piece of shit. The ways they approached things were different. Weiss had that magical trick he did, that thing where he guessed what you'd do before you'd do it. He'd pulled that on Bishop any number of times. It was annoying as hell, but it worked, no question.

The killer – nobody knew much about him, but from what they'd seen in the past, he was more the methodical type. He made plans. He laid out elaborate strategies and followed them precisely, step by step. He waited patiently – he had endless patience. Then, when he set his machinery into motion, he was relentless, unstoppable.

But Weiss had stopped him once. The last time Weiss and the killer tangled with each other, Weiss's instinct had been one step ahead of the killer's plans. So this time, the killer wanted to make sure it was the other way around. This time, the killer was *planning* for Weiss to outguess him.

Bishop smiled around the filter of his Marlboro. That was it. The three guns. The killer was *planning* for the moment when Weiss would get the better of him. He was planning for Weiss to get in on him somehow and take his gun away – take his gun and search him like the ex-cop he was and find the second gun too. The killer must've come up with some way to hide the third gun, so Weiss wouldn't find it. That would be the Saracen – small, accurate, powerful. He was planning for Weiss to outguess him and take two of his guns away. Then he would kill him with the Saracen.

Bishop narrowed his eyes, peering through the drifting smoke. It was good, he thought. It was a good plan. Simple, but very smart. It would probably work too.

So that was the killer. Bishop had gotten into the killer's mind, just like Weiss would. Now he had to do the same to Weiss himself.

How was he going to figure out where Weiss was? How was he going to get to him before the killer did? Weiss knew everything about finding people, it stood to reason he knew how not to be found. He'd left his cell phone behind. He probably loaded up on cash before he left. He probably wasn't using credit cards or ATMs. He was staying off email. Staying off the phone...

Then it came to him. Another breath of smoke rolled out of his mouth, this one in a billowing rush. It joined the cloud hanging heavy in the still, close air before his eyes.

The message machine.

Bishop darted the butt of his cigarette into the glass. It spit and died with a trailing wisp. He pushed out of the wing chair. He went back to Weiss's desk.

There was the message machine, the red light burning. No messages. They'd all been erased. But Bishop had called the apartment himself, just as he'd told Sissy. He'd left Weiss a message yesterday and now it was gone. That meant Weiss must've phoned in from somewhere, must've picked the message up and erased it. It was careless of him. It was not the kind of mistake he usually made. But maybe he hoped the hooker would contact him here, or maybe there was some information he was waiting for. Maybe he just didn't think anyone would break into his apartment like this. Whatever it was, he'd given himself away.

Bishop picked up the desk phone. He called a lady cop he knew. He flirted with her for about forty-five seconds, then asked her to get him the record of incoming calls to Weiss's apartment.

Then he went out, leaving the glass with the cigarette stub on the table by the wing chair, leaving the smoke hanging in the musty room.

Moments later, he was on his Harley. He motored back across the Bay. The wind was on his face. The sun lay broken, dazzling, on the wind-rough water. He could already feel that cool, metallic presence in him – that presence that meant violence was coming.

When he got to Berkeley, he checked his palmtop. There was a message waiting. The lady cop. There had only been a few calls to Weiss's apartment, she said. All of them were local, except for one. That one call came from the Saguaro Hotel in Phoenix, Arizona. Room 414. It had come in only a couple of hours ago.

Bishop smiled to himself again. It was that easy. The Saguaro Hotel in Phoenix.

All he needed now was an airplane and a gun.

27

The gun was a K9. It was compact and built to sit low in the hand, just the slender matte blue barrel peeking out above the fingers. Bishop kept it in a shoebox in his bedroom closet, tucked in there beside a lightweight shoulder holster. It had been a long time since he'd gone armed. But he shrugged the holster on now, anchored it to his belt. Slipped the pistol in. He checked himself in the closet mirror to make sure the leather jacket covered the outfit. Then, by way of insurance, he brought a knife out of the shoebox as well. It was a tactical Strider folding knife with a fat four-inch blade. He had sewn a leather loop in his boot to hold it. He hadn't used the loop in a long time either. He used it now.

He gathered a few other odds and ends: a lockpick, a sap, a change of clothes. He dumped them into a gym bag and was on his way again.

As for the plane, he got hold of a Centurion, a Cessna Turbo 210. One of the FBOs at Oakland Airport had one on hand. They knew Bishop. He called ahead and the plane was gassed up and waiting for him on the tarmac when he arrived half an hour later.

Another fifteen minutes and he was airborne, westbound. As he drew the 210 up off runway 27R, the windshield was filled with the glittering water and the peaks and jagged falls of the city skyline, its buildings golden and rose in the late morning sun. He banked the plane right over the bay, then right and right again until he was slanting southeast along the freeway in a distant parallel to the state border. As he climbed, he caught sight of the Sierras, golden and green. He followed the misty line of them all the way to Bakersfield. There, he landed, refueled, and took off again, heading easterly now, the foothills to his left.

He set his course for Arizona.

The plane was fast for a single engine. He had it cranked up to 235 knots as he skirted the Mojave. He climbed to nine thousand five. Watched as the brown desert before him slowly became a dozen shades of red. Bulges, arches, cylinders of living rock aspired toward him, almost close, then passed beneath his wing. Long plateaus went under leisurely, so level they seemed shorn flat. Sudden mountains stabbed up at him out of the sage. All – every formation and the long empty earth as far as he could see – were crimson, scarlet, cinnabar – a dozen shades – each color growing more and more vivid as the sun westered and the contrasting sky became a richer blue.

He was close now. But above the escarpments of Maricopa, he saw the cumulus clouds building. He glanced at his stormscope. There were red cells swirling to the north. These were the last of the thunderstorms Weiss had driven through the night before.

Soon, ATC came on the radio, warning him southward. He drifted that way, confident he could outrun the front. But the clouds followed him. He eyed them through his window. Great cottony masses, they boiled up out of themselves like white volcanoes in a doper's dream. Their froth spilled higher and higher. More of them appeared and more.

Then suddenly – it was incredibly sudden – the storm stomped down on him. Bishop's stomach lifted, then did a nauseating dive. In less than ten seconds, the Centurion was driven five hundred feet toward the earth. The plane rocked side to side, one wing dipping drastically then swinging up as the other dropped down. The windshield was swallowed in a sickly green-black. The green-black was laced with skeleton fingers of white light. The wind swept up from under him and hurled the machine skyward as many feet as it had fallen. The rain washed over the windshield in a blinding rush. The darkness flickered behind the rain.

Now the air trafficker was screaming vectors, but his voice was reduced to static by thunder like an explosion. Bishop pulled the throttle fast, dropping the speed to VA, hoping to keep his wings on. But even as he did, he heard a crash against the fusillade – he felt it like a blow in his own side – and he knew that he'd been struck by hail.

Bishop laughed wildly, his pale eyes bright. He didn't have much of an imagination, but the way the stick was jumping in his hand made him feel as if he were arm wrestling the storm for his life. And now vertigo got him. The taste of vomit was in his mouth and he couldn't tell if he was rightside up or overturned and plummeting. He swept his gaze across the instrument panel again and again, trying to get a sense of his position. The digital altimeter had gone blank. Altitude, airspeed, vertical speed indicators – they were all windblown, dancing, unreadable.

Again, the green blackness was lanced by lightning. Another blast of thunder engulfed him. More hail hammered at the wings. More rain gushed over the windshield. There was nothing on the headset anymore but a dim, desperate calling, very far away. Bishop gripped the shivering stick. He felt his stomach come into his throat as the plane was driven down and down and down by another crush of air.

The altimeter blinked on. He was at three thousand feet above the earth, then two. The hard ground was coming up fast. The plane would pancake in another minute, a silver stain in the red dust.

He fell ten more seconds – a hundred feet. Ten more – a hundred more. Then, still in the clouds, the plane steadied. The yolk grew sure and solid in his fingers. He glanced at the stormscope. He was through the red cell. It was blowing south and west of him. There was a break before the next yellow mass moved in. He looked up. The mist shredded and fell away from the windshield on either side...

And there, smack in front of him, was the red terrain. He was piloting straight for a hill of rock. A strange, cold thrill went through him. An image came into his mind: he saw the Centurion buried in the mountainside, nothing left but rudder and blood.

He gave the plane gas, drew the nose upward. He laughed again, shaking his head, as the plane flew over the hill, nosing into thin clouds. He banked to the right and broke through into brilliant blue sky.

As suddenly as the storm had hit, the view was clear, so clear he could make out the gleam of Sky Harbor airport twenty miles in the distance.

Still laughing, he prepared for his landing in Phoenix.

28

Bishop drove away from the airport in a rented Sebring, a silver-blue convertible, the top down. It was afternoon now. A typical October day in the desert city: blindingly bright, ninety degrees. It hadn't occurred to him back in chilly San Francisco it would be so hot here. As he drove, the wash of air swept over him, cooling his face. But the leather jacket was suffocating, and he couldn't take it off with the gun strapped on underneath.

All the same, he was jazzed, wired. The thrill of the thunderstorm was still in him. It had him wound up inside, ready for more action. Sure, Weiss would be pissed off when he showed up out of nowhere. He'd probably be pissed off that he'd tracked him down so easily. But that was too damn bad. Weiss was no match for the specialist and Bishop was. He was going to save the sad-faced old bastard's life whether he liked it or not.

He passed through a low area of sprawling malls, an expanse of concrete with a backdrop of red desert hills. He spotted the Saguaro Hotel half a mile away, a rippling wave of mirrored glass eight stories high. It sat across from a shopping mall on an oasis in the stone: planted grass, jets of water in a marble fountain, a line of towering palm trees standing like sentinels on each side of the reception cul-de-sac. Bishop drove up the winding driveway, under the palms.

He tilted his head back to look up at the hotel through his aviators. He was surprised. It was a fancy, high-end venue. Not really Weiss's style. As the Sebring drew to a stop, a valet – a white-faced kid in a black vest – rushed to open the door for him. Bishop stepped out into the shade of the hotel. Even in the shade, the air was hot and still. He brought his gym bag up from the passenger seat.

'You're gonna want to get rid of that jacket,' said the valet brightly.

Bishop smiled a little. He shifted his shoulder as he lifted the bag and he could feel the shape of the K9 beneath his arm.

Two big glass doors slipped open automatically. Bishop stepped into the hotel, thankful for the cool of the air conditioning. He went up a few stairs and came into the lobby. It was a vast open space, an eight-story atrium. There were glass walls with sunlight filtering through vines and bamboo trees. The broad floor area was thick with people – tourists with their fat asses stuffed into shorts, their big bellies ballooning under flowered shirts. They gathered in clusters around the long reception desk and in the seating areas. They filled the four elevators. The elevators were glass too and Bishop could see the fat people in them gaping out, rising past the galleries on each floor toward the skylight far above.

He passed into the crowd. He moved through the clusters, carrying his bag. He was a glaringly dark figure amidst all those flowered shirts.

'A little hot for a leather jacket,' some guy piped up outside the elevator doors. Bishop glanced at him. An egg-shaped man in a gathering of egg-shaped men and women. They all wore shorts and untucked Hawaiian shirts pressed out by their fat bellies. 'I'm burning up and I'm dressed like this!' said the guy. He did look hot, even in the cool atrium. His face – egg-shaped like his body – was pink and damp with sweat, the skin glistening under sparse hair combed across his dome to hide the bald spot. He was practically panting as he spoke.

Bishop – who managed to look cool and untouchable even in his jeans and leather – didn't answer. He shifted his shoulder to get the feel of the gun again.

The elevator came. Bishop stepped into it in the crush of egg-shaped people. The elevator rose. He held the gym bag in front of him, looked out through the glass wall as the people in the lobby grew smaller below. It was a slow trip. The glass box stopped at every floor. The egg-shaped people got out by twos and threes. When the box reached the fourth floor, Bishop got out. The egg-shaped man who had spoken to him and two egg-shaped women stepped out with him onto the gallery.

'Well – have a good one!' said the egg-shaped man as he and the two women waddled off to the right.

Bishop went in the opposite direction, still without a word.

The gallery wound around the atrium, catching the wave-shape of the building. Then it turned the corner and became a straight hallway. Bishop carried the gym bag to the hallway's end. There was the room he wanted, right next to the fire stairs, Weiss's room, 414.

He stood at the door. He rang the bell, waited for an answer. A maid came up the hall toward him, a heavyset Mexican woman pushing a linen cart, leaning into the effort. No one opened the door. Bishop knocked. The maid and her cart passed behind him. He waited. Still, no one came. He turned his head and watched the maid push her cart to the corner. Then she went around the corner and was out of sight.

Bishop set the gym bag on the floor. He knelt and unzipped it, brought the lockpick out from beneath his clothes. It was a special pick he used for hotels. Modern hotels had electro-magnetic locks with card keys. They could be picked with magnets, but this thing was easier. It was a small device like a metal tape measure. It slipped under the door and then bent up to hook the door handle. Because of the laws meant to protect people with disabilities, the door handles in hotel rooms had to be easy to pull down and had to override the latch. Bishop hooked the handle with his device and yanked it down. The door swung open for him.

He put the pick back in the bag. He stepped into the room, shut the door behind him. The room was broad and shadowy. The far wall was one long curving line of windows, but heavy curtains were drawn across them, keeping out the sun. Peering through the gloom, Bishop surveyed the place. The bed was made. No luggage was in sight. No clothes were in sight, no shoes were on the floor. The air conditioner was going but, aside from that, there was no sign that anyone was staying here.

This was the first moment Bishop suspected he'd been set up for the kill. Even now, it was just a glimmering of suspicion, just a hint of it. Before this, it never occurred to him that the killer was drawing him in. He'd been so focused on finding Weiss, on trying to get here. And then that thunderstorm – that had blown everything out of his mind. Also, truth be told, beneath the hard guy stuff, he'd been eager to do this. He'd been eager to make things right with Weiss. He figured if he could help him take out the Shadowman, it might make up for all the other stuff he'd done, the bad stuff. And no matter what he told himself, he wanted to make up for it. Weiss was the only person on earth who'd ever done shit for him. Weiss was the only friend he'd ever had.

So he'd been eager. He'd been in a hurry. He hadn't thought things through. He hadn't stopped to consider how easy this had been, how Weiss didn't make mistakes like the one with the answering machine, how he wouldn't stay in a fancy place like this. He noticed those things but he hadn't stopped to consider them. And he still wasn't thinking about that stuff, not really. There was just that hint, that glimmering. A tendril of anger and dread drifting through him. An instinct that something was wrong.

He told himself it was nothing. He told himself that Weiss had called the answering machine from the room that morning and then checked out, moved on. But even as he told himself that, Bishop tossed his gym bag onto the bed to free his hands. He pulled the zipper of his jacket down. He slipped his right hand into the gap. He touched the grip of his K9 as he walked slowly across the room to the curtained windows, looking to his left and right.

He parted the curtains with his left hand. The windows faced west. The rays of the sinking sun shot straight through them. Even behind his shades, Bishop squinted at the brightness of the light.

He squinted through the glare and saw a large swimming pool just below him. The sun was reflected on it. It was blinding, a layer of sparkling white atop a depth of blue. Colored bathing suits and pale flesh drifted peacefully in and out of the dazzle, in and out of sight, on the water. Other bodies lay stretched, luxurious, on white lounge chairs around the pool's perimeter. Bishop could hear children laughing, even up here, even through the glass.

He caught a movement reflected on the pane and the truth came over him like nausea. He had been too eager. The hotel was too big. The trail was too easy. It was all too fucking easy.

Damn it, he thought.

He knew he was dead.

He did what he could at the end. With a single motion, he drew the K9 and swung around, yanking the curtains open to let in the blinding sun as he dodged to one side.

The egg-shaped man was standing right behind him. The Saracen was already in his hand. Before Bishop could pull the K9's trigger, the Saracen spit fire.

Bishop felt the bullet rip through him. It was a cold, dull business. The egg-shaped man fired again. Bishop's legs went weak. He stumbled back against the windows. His knees buckled. He tried to get his fingers to tighten on the K9, but they wouldn't. He tried to hold on to the curtains. He couldn't. He couldn't even get his mouth to close.

He dropped slowly, sliding down the wall of glass to the floor, leaving a trail of blood on the sun-bright pane.

29

The man who called himself John Foy moved in to finish Bishop off. It gave him a sense of professional satisfaction. It was a job well done.

Bishop had been good. He was good when the shooting started anyway. Before that, he was just a little hot-headed, a little careless, that's all. That's why it had been so easy to draw him in. The man who called himself John Foy had a small network of watchers and informants who fed him information in a number of elaborate ways. A coded message on an internet news website had alerted him Sunday afternoon that one of these people had something for him. He made contact with the informant on a stolen cell phone and learned that Bishop had roughed up one of Adalian's thugs. In revenge, the thug had spread the word that Bishop was coming after the specialist. It was a good break. It gave him a chance to pay Weiss back for chasing him around outside the Super 8.

It also gave him a chance to try out the fat suit. It worked well. He'd augmented it with some foam, covered it with the Hawaiian shirt, made himself look like a real lardass to blend in with the tourists. And the way the Saracen sat invisible in the vest's pouch – that was perfect. No one could have seen it or felt it there.

In fact, the whole thing had given him fresh confidence after a period of self doubt. The mistakes he'd been making recently had made him feel that maybe his luck was deserting him. This, though – this had gone off exactly as planned. He left a trail and Bishop followed it, simple, efficient. True, Bishop was no Weiss. He wasn't smart like Weiss and he didn't have that way Weiss had of guessing what you'd do. But he was a real professional all the same, a specialist, just like Foy. And he never saw it coming. He never suspected a thing.

Still, he was good at the end. When the shooting started, he was very good. He must've seen Foy coming at the very last second. He had no time at all to react, but he made a close duel of it all the same. When he pulled the curtain open like that, the sun had pierced through the window directly into the specialist's eyes. It had blinded him just as Bishop leapt out of the way. The slugs from the Belgian 5.7 ripped Bishop's left side open at the midsection, but the man who called himself John Foy had been aiming for a center shot, his chest, his heart. The detective should've been dead by the time he hit the floor.

Instead, he sat slumped against the wall. His head hung limp on his chest. His eyes were open, staring at the carpet. His left hand lay motionless in his lap. His right hand lay open on the carpet, palm upward. His finger was still tangled in the trigger of his gun – a Kahr 9mm, a K9, the specialist noted. Not a bad little weapon for this sort of thing. He probably had another in his boot – or maybe a knife. But it didn't matter now. He was almost gone.

There was nothing left but to finish it, and he had to do it fast. The blasts from the Saracen had been loud in the small room. Usually people ignored these things but there was always a chance some shit-for-brains Good Samaritan would decide to investigate or call the police.

For safety's sake, he tried to kick the K9 out of Bishop's hand, but it snagged on the detective's trigger finger. He covered Bishop with the Saracen, knelt down, worked the gun free and tossed it behind him onto the bed. Aside from the rapid, shallow falling and rising of his chest, Bishop never moved. He was dying all right, but not fast enough.

So, kneeling there, the man who called himself John Foy placed the barrel of the Saracen in the center of Bishop's forehead. Then he squeezed the trigger.

30

Bishop moved. It took all the strength he had left. From the moment he'd fallen, he'd been marshalling the violence in him. Now he willed it to explode in this single motion.

As the specialist put the gun to his forehead and pulled the trigger, Bishop's left arm – the arm lying slack on his lap – drove up and forward. His forearm hit the killer's gun hand, knocking it aside. The gun went off. The report was deafening. The bullet whistled over Bishop's skull. It cut through the curtain behind him and shattered the window. Bishop's arm, meanwhile, kept driving forward. His hand, the fingers stiffened, jammed into the killer's eye.

It wasn't a good hit. Bishop didn't have a good hit left in him. But it nailed the eyeball straight on. The Shadowman cried out. Instinctively, he grabbed his eye with both hands, dropping the Saracen. The gun fell to the carpet with a dull thud.

But the killer recovered immediately. Holding his eye with his left hand, he groped for the fallen weapon with his right.

Bishop struggled to rise.

There wasn't much time. Another second, the Shadowman would have the gun in his grasp. Bishop managed to get one foot flat on the floor. He managed to get one hand flat on the floor. He clutched at the cloth of the curtain with the other hand. He pushed himself up and pulled himself up. The cold, dull sensation of being shot was morphing quickly now into a pulsing, spreading red zone of pain. He couldn't be sure, but he had the sense that the scream he was hearing was coming from him. He struggled up an inch, another inch.

And the Shadowman grabbed the Saracen. Holding his hurt eye shut with his left hand, he focused the other eye on the gun. He fumbled with it for a moment. Then he had it, gripped it. He swung it toward Bishop.

Bishop screamed again. He propelled himself upward with his legs. He threw his upper body back against the curtains. He felt the curtains catch him and give way. He felt his guts become a single drilled nerve. He saw the killer bring the Saracen around. He saw the endlessly deep black bore of the gun. The curtain behind him gave way, gave way.

Then the Shadowman fired and Bishop fell.

He threw himself out the shattered window. He felt himself tumbling through the open air. He felt pain and heat and swirling confusion.

He caught a glimpse of the swimming pool beneath him. The glare of the sun on the surface flashed up at him. It obliterated everything. Somewhere women were screaming. Inside him, the pain was screaming, one great red scream. But his eyes, his mind, were filled with that dazzling light coming up to meet him.

Then he hit the water and the light went out.

31

Shit, thought the Shadowman.

He leapt to the window. He shoved the curtain aside as it fluttered back toward him. He looked down just in time to see Bishop plunge into the pool.

The solid sheet of light on the pool's surface splashed up in a fountain of beaded sparkles. The brilliant water at the fountain's center swallowed Bishop's dark form. Blood began to spread from the sinking body. It stained the blue pool with coils of black. Screaming swimmers streamed up over the concrete edges like insects streaming from the hole under a lifted rock. The killer saw two women wading with long strides through the shallow end to grab their startled children. He saw a man push past the fleeing swimmers to dive in and swim down after the sinking Bishop. Two other men were standing in front of their lounge chairs on the pool's far side. Their bellies hanging over their bathing suits, their hands held to their brows, they were peering straight up at the fourth floor window, staring straight at him, pointing straight at him.

Shit, the killer thought again.

He drew back into the shadows of the room. A little tremor was in his throat, a threat of panic. He blinked against the images: Staring men. Pointed fingers. Police, police... He winced at the frantic, whining voice in his head: Why did he keep making these goddamned mistakes? Why did they keep happening? It wasn't fair.

He put a hand to his temple, massaged the corner of

his hurt eye. He wanted the images to stop, the voice to stop. He wanted to climb into his tower, into the blue calm at the top of his tower. No time. He had to move. He had to get out of here. Police...

He crossed the room in a few steps. As he went, he slipped the Saracen through the slit in his fat suit, fitted it back into the pocket under the silicone. He was panting now, feeling the fat suit's extra weight.

He pulled the door open. Already, as he stepped out into the hall, he heard the elevator bell ring around the corner. He heard stern voices growing louder. Men. They were coming, fast. They would rush into view any second now.

He seized the knob to the fire stairs door. It was the reason he chose this room, part of the plan. He was in the stairwell in a second. The heavy door swung shut behind him slowly. As he started down the concrete steps, he heard pounding above him. Fists on the hotel room door. A deep voice shouting, 'Hotel security! Open up!'

The voice grew dimmer as he hurried down and down.

He stepped out of the stairwell onto the mezzanine. He was sweating, gasping for breath. The fat suit felt heavier with every step. He walked as casually as he could past empty banquet halls and conference rooms. He came to the escalator. He rode down in plain sight of the crowd gathering below him in the atrium.

He left the lobby by a side door. The smothering heat closed over him. The silicone vest suddenly felt like an anvil tied to him. The silicone overlays he had used to fatten his face seemed to tighten and squeeze the fluid out of him. Working for every wheezing gulp of air, he dragged himself around the front of the hotel. He humped over the lawn, parallel to the palm trees.

Now police car after police car came pulling into the Saguaro cul-de-sac, their sirens howling like cats in heat.

Their light racks threw glancing rays of red and blue into the desert afternoon. One cruiser stopped at the entrance to the driveway to keep anyone from driving out.

But by then, the man who called himself John Foy had already reached the street. He crossed it in a stumbling jog, reached the shopping mall on the other side.

There was a concrete box of a parking structure on the mall's northern border. His car was parked there on the ground floor. It was a new car. A brown one. A Taurus, the same type Weiss had. The man who called himself John Foy slipped in behind the wheel.

He got the car started. A blast of steamy air rushed out of the air conditioning vents, but in a moment it cooled and he leaned over to bathe his cheeks and forehead in it. It was good to feel the sweat drying on his face. His chest and armpits were still pouring. There were dark stains all over his Hawaiian shirt.

After a while, he straightened. He glanced up into the rearview mirror. A stranger looked back at him. He had fattened his cheeks with the overlays and cut his hair to get the balding tourist effect. Simple changes, but they transformed the look of him completely. He hardly recognized himself.

He pulled out of the lot and drove back toward the city as police cars kept streaming past him to the hotel.

32

The specialist had spent a lifetime killing other men. Women sometimes, a bunch of kids once, but mostly men, over a hundred of them. He had come to the job as easily as dozing in a chair. He had been in a Burger King in his home city, a stark grey city surrounded by flatlands. He was sixteen. He was with a guy he knew, a tough guy who had dropped out of school and was making a living jacking stuff off trucks. The tough guy noticed someone across the room. He lifted his chin and said, 'That fuck needs doing.' And right away, he answered him, 'What'll you pay me?'

That was it. He went home and made a garrotte out of a broomstick and a jump rope. He found the target a couple of nights later walking through a stand of trees in a small park. He didn't even look around to see if anyone was watching. He just walked up behind the fuck and strangled him with the homemade garrotte. Left him lying right there in the grass in his own shit. Strolled over to the tough guy's place to pick up his pay.

It was strange to look back on it. It had been as simple as that. No plans, no worries. What did he know? He was a kid. He trusted his luck. He didn't think about the bad things that could happen if he got caught. He didn't think about anything. He just did it.

But then, later on, he did think. After all, he knew what it was like to get caught. He knew better than anyone what it was like to be punished and humiliated and hurt more than you thought you could stand while people looked on and laughed at you. He didn't want that ever to happen again.

So he learned to be more cautious. It was a gradual process. He learned to plan, to keep ahead of events. He learned to make allowances for the unexpected. After a while, the planning was all he thought about. He was planning every moment right up until he did the job. It was almost a kind of ritual for him. It made him feel safe. It made him feel that nothing had been left to chance. He would never allow himself to be caught, punished, hurt, humiliated – never again.

He drove for the heart of the city. As he went, he reached down under the seat and pulled up his surveillance briefcase. He laid it on the seat beside him, worked it open with his free hand. He got the laptop going.

He picked up Weiss at once. The GPS tracker in the detective's car appeared as a green triangle blinking on a map of the city's south side. The killer was still too far away to pick up the birddoggers woven into Weiss's clothing.

The killer headed for the green triangle. He was getting his breath back now. The runnels of sweat were slowing down on his body. The cry of the sirens was fading behind him. The tremor of panic – and the panicky inner voice – they were fading too. Ahead, through the windshield, the sun was arching toward the top of the skyline. Lights were coming on in the buildings. Windows stood out as yellow rectangles in large gray rectangles set against the rich blue sky. He gazed at them as he drove but in his mind he was far away. In his mind, once again, he was in his own high tower. He was calmer there, calmer.

The city closed over him. He prowled down a dark broad avenue between skyscrapers. Only a strip of blue sky appeared at the top of his windshield here. He began to come back to himself. He was fine now. Everything was fine. Bishop had been a hard case. He'd fought a good fight. But he was dead, or he soon would be. And the man who called himself John Foy had gotten away. His luck was not running out. Everything was fine.

He crossed the city into the south, heading toward the low mountains. The skyscrapers fell behind him quickly. He came into an area of shacks and empty lots and churches, one church after another. The church steeples and their crosses stood high and dark against the rich blue horizon. Lean Mexican men and fat Mexican women walked beneath them. The falling sun gleamed on the white shirts of the men.

The killer heard a noise from the seat beside him. He had picked up the birddoggers in Weiss's clothes. He glanced over at the laptop, seeking out the yellow blips.

He saw them – but for a moment, he didn't understand what he was seeing. Then he did understand, and his breath caught. He stared at the laptop so long that when he looked up, the brown Taurus had nearly veered off the road. He had to wrench the wheel to keep it from smashing into the curb.

He eased the car to a stop at a red light. He stared down at the laptop's screen again. That crawly fear was back at once, that crawly, whispering panic. *Why is this happening? It isn't fair. It isn't fair.*

One of the birddoggers had broken away from the GPS tracker. Only one – P143 – the one in Weiss's tweed jacket. At first, the man who called himself John Foy thought Weiss might have left his jacket somewhere. But the birddogger was still moving. And the GPS showed the car was still moving too. Weiss's car was driving away from the south mountains, heading for the interstate, and

Weiss's tweed jacket was somehow traveling slowly over the southeast corner of the city.

The car's air conditioning was going full blast now, but the Shadowman began to sweat again. What the hell was this? Some kind of Weiss bullshit, some kind of trick. The red light turned green, but the killer just sat there looking down at the screen. Which signal should he follow? What the hell was going on?

A horn honked behind him. He glanced into the rearview and saw some straw-hatted Mexican in a Chevy pickup. He briefly considered getting out of his car, walking back to the Chevy and ripping out the wetback's esophagus with his bare hands. But he was a professional, a cool professional. He fought down the impulse. He hit the gas. He drove on.

He went after the birddog in the tweed jacket. The car would get away quickly, but he could trace the car at a distance. The jacket was less than half a mile away. He could get to it, find out what was happening and get back to the car fast. Anyway, if Weiss was in the car, the killer already knew where he was going.

He turned the corner, putting the sun behind him. The shacks and churches sank away. Now there were empty lots by the side of the road, dust and nothing. Brown hills to the right of him. Brown hills up ahead.

The sweat was in full tide under his shirt again. His heart was hammering again. That lost, childish voice was whining at him again. What was Weiss doing? What was going on?

Then the road ended. There was a diamond link fence, an open gate. He drove through onto an unpaved lane, his tires bouncing over the ruts and rocks. Ahead, some kind of a house stood on a little hill. It was a strange house. A covered balcony of red wood, misshapen gray battlements of rock. A single car was parked nearby. An aging Impala, not Weiss's car. But when the killer glanced over at the briefcase again, the yellow birddog signal was still blipping, not fifty yards away.

The man who called himself John Foy was getting angry now. He thought he knew what was happening and the rage was rising into his throat. He shut the car down. Got out. The heat was bad. There was desert all around him. Dirt and stone crunching under his shoes. When he looked off, he saw a rolling plain of dust, the distant sun touching the top of the gray and sparkling city. He was isolated out here. That Weiss, that fucking Weiss...

He reached into the slit of his silicone vest. His fingers closed on the Saracen. He drew it out. His teeth were clamped together. He wanted to see something die.

He walked up a flight of steps. The broken rock battlements loomed over him. He stepped into the shadows of the covered balcony. He reached the front door. He pushed it. It swung in.

There was a strange stone room, lit dimly with standing lamps. There was rough handmade furniture made of logs and rock. Shelves, tables, benches – and all of them crowded – the whole room packed – with junk and knickknacks. A stuffed bird in a bamboo cage. The skull of a longhorn staring from above the fireplace. The skin of a snake lying on a wooden table under an embroidered pillow that said 'Home Sweet Home.'

The killer jumped as he turned and saw a piano with a woman sitting at it. But she was nothing, a weird stuffed figure. And there was an easy chair with a stuffed man sitting in it.

Then the man moved. The killer leveled the gun at him. He nearly shot him. He wanted to.

The man in the chair was an old black man. He was long and bent. He had a long, sad face with a day's growth of grizzled beard. He was wearing jeans and a t-shirt – and Weiss's tweed jacket.

'He said you'd show up,' the old man said.

The killer could hardly breathe. He felt as if a powerful hand were around his throat, squeezing it shut. 'Who are you?'

'I run this place.'

'What place? What is this?'

'It's the castle. For tourists. Robert Lindley built it. For the woman he loved. Only she never came. I run it now. For the people.'

'What people?'

'The people. You know. The tourists. I give them the tours.'

The specialist's quick, wild glance took in the corners, the rafters. A stuffed alligator. A glass dog. A hangman's noose. Dizzy with the heat, he saw them swirling around him.

'Ain't it strange?' the old man said. 'He put everything in it. Hoping she'd come.'

The killer steadied his gaze on the man in the chair. Shoved the gunpoint at him. 'Come on.'

'All right, all right,' said the old man. 'Here. He wanted you to have this.'

The old man reached inside the tweed jacket. The killer's gun hand tightened.

'Uh uh uh,' said the old man, with a soft chuckle. He didn't seem to care very much whether he died or not. Slowly, he drew out a folded piece of paper. He held it out toward the man who called himself John Foy.

Foy snatched the paper away. 'Did he tell you I'd kill you,' he said in a strangled voice.

The black man shook his head slowly. 'He said you wouldn't do a thing. Not a thing. The people'll be here for the last tour soon and they'd find me. He said you'd take the paper and go or the two of you were finished. He said you didn't want that.'

The killer hated Weiss so much just then he almost shot the old man anyway. But in the end, what could he do? He felt the room closing in on him. Strange shapes in glass bottles. A carved menagerie. A crude painting of a staring face.

'This is a crazy fucking place,' he said, sick and dizzy with the heat.

The old man laughed outright. 'Yes, it is. Robert Lindley, the man who built it, he had a crazy idea of things. But that's what a man builds castles for, isn't it? Some say it's for money, some say it's for sex or love. But really, it's just for his own crazy idea of things, that's all. The woman he loved – she never even came.'

The killer retreated, his heart hammering, his face hot. He drew away from the staring longhorn skull and the stuffed woman sitting weirdly at the piano. He went out the door. Down the steps, across the dirt lot, back to the car. He had to sit behind the wheel a long time before he could focus, before there was anything in his mind but heat sickness and rage. He had to stare at the folded paper a long time before he could bring himself to open it.

Then he did. It was a notebook page, wrinkled. Black ink on it. Weiss's scrawl.

Sky Harbor. Gate 8. 6:30.

The Shadowman crushed the paper in his fist, a growl of rage squeezing out of him. He could barely stand the feeling in him. He thought it would claw him apart. Weiss. Weiss. That arrogant fuck. Weiss had summoned him to a meeting. Sky Harbor. The airport. 6:30. Just a couple of hours from now.

The arrogant fuck. The arrogant so-dead fuck. He had known exactly what the specialist would do. Known exactly, every step – and still knew. It made the specialist hate the detective with a flaming hatred. Worse. It made him afraid of him. Because if Weiss could do this to him now, what would happen when it came time for the end?

The fuck. The arrogant fuck. The arrogant so-dead fuck.

He tried to breathe. He tried to breathe deeper. *All right*, he thought, *all right*. They would meet. Six-thirty. They would meet and the killer would tell him about Bishop. He would tell him how Bishop walked right into it, how he never suspected a thing. He would tell him how Bishop took two in the gut, how he sunk down to the floor leaving a trail of blood on the window behind him. How he sunk into the pool leaving a trail of blood in the water.

That's how it would be in the end too. That's how it would be for Weiss.

He started the car with a quick jerk of the key. He put it in gear roughly. He backed out over the dirt lot.

You arrogant so-dead fuck, he thought. *I am coming for you.*

PART FOUR

Sky Harbor

33

Olivia Graves looked up from her desk when Weiss came to the office doorway. The sight of her made Weiss stop short on the threshold. There was a big window on the wall to her left. There was a lot of light – a sheet of warm afternoon light – late, clear desert light – sweeping across her. It smoothed her features nearly to nothing. So for a moment, Weiss thought she looked exactly like Julie.

Then she stood. She stepped around her desk, came toward him. 'Mr Weiss?'

The illusion was gone. She didn't look like her older sister at all. He'd just expected her to. Maybe wanted her to.

In fact, Olivia was short and slender. Her features were small and sharp. Her hair was boy cut, parted on one side, brown, not Julie's flowing, startling red and gold. She wore a long green skirt and a white blouse. Not an unfriendly look, but a little starched, a little unapproachable. It made Weiss feel underdressed, wearing only his slacks and his blue polo shirt. But he'd left his tweed behind out at that weird house on the edge of the desert.

Anyway, he found Olivia attractive in a compact, efficient sort of way. Twenty-seven years old, as he knew from the newspaper stories. Trying to seem older, he thought. Trying to seem as if she weren't afraid of him – which touched him, made him want to take care of her, protect her from the wind and weather – which was pretty much the way he felt about most women most of the time.

They met in the middle of the room. He towered over her. His paunch alone dwarfed her. She offered her small white hand. His huge hand engulfed it. He looked down at her. He thought of the little girl waiting on the school doorstep with her big sister. Huddled there in the morning dark after their father hammered their mother to death. His sad, baggy eyes went soft for her.

But Olivia Graves's manner was clipped and business-like. She gestured brusquely toward a leather sling chair near the wall across from the window. She marched toward another sling chair facing the first, her blocky heels knocking hard against the Yuma rug.

Weiss followed her to the chairs. He hated sling chairs. He always felt as if his big body were going to sink right through them and smack the floor. He waited for her to sit first, then worked himself down across from her, settling back carefully against the thin leather.

He took a quick glance around the room. The office was big. He was surprised. She was only an associate professor of psychology, but the office was downright spacious. Nothing much in it but the Yuma rug from the door to the blocky blondwood desk. An upholstered swivel chair behind the desk, a bookshelf behind the chair. Jumbo-size books with dark bindings; doctor-type books. That huge window on the far wall with a view of the campus, its green paths and gracefully rounded red and white buildings. Then, set apart against the opposite wall, these two chairs they were in, and a glass coffee table beside them with a huge picture book on it about Native American art.

This, he realized, was the corner where Olivia did therapy and counseling. She had guided him to the chair where the students sat when they came to her homesick or lovelorn or pregnant or whatever the hell students were these days.

And Olivia Graves was in her psychologist chair. And she now made a psychologist-type gesture at him, an unreadable unfolding of the hand which might've been an invitation for him to begin or maybe not.

She had a lot of ways to defend her inner territory, this girl. The starched dress, the clipped manner. Now this I'm-the-doctor routine.

'You know why I'm here, Dr Graves,' Weiss said.

'Ms Graves. On the phone, you said it was about my sister.'

'That's right.'

'I'm interested to know. How did you find me?'

'I find people,' said Weiss.

'That's an interesting job.'

'Sometimes.'

'I mean it's an interesting line of work to go into.'

Weiss smiled a little. 'So is yours.'

'And now you're trying to find my sister.'

'That's right.'

'Why? If you don't mind my asking.'

'There's a man looking for her – a bad guy – a contract killer. I want to stop him.'

'So it's really him you're looking for.'

'And her.'

'I'm confused. You're looking for both of them?'

She was sitting with her legs crossed, with her hands clasped on top of her knee. Her body was leaning toward him out of the sling. Her expression was caring, polite, enquiring. It was the whole psychologist package. She thought she could play him like one of her patients, then send him away with nothing. Weiss, in his protective concern for her, tried not to laugh.

'The man – the bad guy – who wants to find her,' he said. 'He's following me. When I find your sister, he'll make a move to get her. Then I'll take care of him.'

'You'll – take care of him?'

'That's right.'

'I see.' Her expression didn't change. She nodded, psychologist-like, considering. 'You want to use my sister as bait to catch this man.'

'If it comes down to that. But he'll find her eventually anyway. He has people all over the country. She'll make a mistake, walk down the wrong street. She'll have to live afraid every day – and eventually he'll find her.'

'So you're going to save her. You're going to rescue her from this bad man.'

'I'm going to take him out of the equation. Then she can live her life any way she wants.'

Olivia straightened her back, drew in a loud breath through her pert nose. 'I see.' More I-am-the-psychologist stuff. 'Just out of curiosity? How do I know you're not the bad guy? Just because you're you?'

'That and my white hat.'

She smiled blandly. 'Yes, but really: how do I know?'

'You know,' said Weiss. He tried to lean forward too but he was sunk too deep in the damned sling chair. 'You know exactly who I am and why I'm here. You know because your father would've called to warn you…'

'My father…?'

'…and because Julie – your sister – Mary – would've found a way to warn you too.'

If that shook Olivia Graves, she didn't show it. In fact, she tilted her head, narrowed one eye and basically looked him over as if he were ranting, out of his mind. It was a hell of a smooth performance, assuming it was a performance at all.

'That's a very interesting fantasy,' she said. 'I take it you know my history then.'

'Your father killed your mother, deserted you and disappeared. Yeah, I know.'

'And you know I was raised in foster homes separate from my sister.'

'Yes.'

'And that my sister ran away shortly after that, almost fifteen years ago.'

'All right.'

'And I haven't seen her since. And I certainly haven't seen my father – no one has.'

'Miss Graves...'

'So I don't really know who you are. And I can't really help you, can I? Even if I wanted to help you lead this "bad guy" of yours right to my sister's door, I couldn't, because I have no idea where she is.'

It was awfully good, awfully cool. And though Weiss knew she was lying, he had no way to prove it. As usual, he had nothing to go on but being Weiss.

'Miss Graves,' he said slowly. 'I know your father would've called to warn you after I found him.'

'You found him,' Olivia Graves said. 'You found my father who's been a fugitive for seventeen years. The police couldn't. The FBI couldn't. But you did. You want me to believe that.'

'You know it's true. Because he called you. And even if he didn't call you, your sister would've let you know.'

Olivia Graves kept the performance going. She shook her head quickly as if she couldn't quite believe what she was hearing from him. She gave a bemused laugh. 'Well, you have it all figured out, don't you?'

'Yes,' he said.

'My father, who's been missing for seventeen years, has called me. My sister, who's been missing for fifteen years, somehow gets in touch. And all because of you. Is there something that makes you believe all this, or does it just come into your head?'

Weiss did laugh now. He couldn't help it. 'It pretty

much just comes into my head,' he admitted.

'I can see that. Sort of like this fantasy you have of rescuing my sister from a killer. That just comes into your head too, doesn't it?'

Weiss didn't answer. There was color in Olivia's cheeks now, a sparking anger in her eyes. He knew if he just let her go on, she would show herself. He just let her go on.

'How well do you know my sister?' she asked.

'I've never met her.'

'Really. You've never met her?'

'I've seen some pictures of her, that's all. A photograph and a ten-second video loop from the internet.'

'I see.' Her hands clasped on her knee, Olivia Graves leaned forward even farther, jutting her chin at him eagerly. Weiss couldn't help but get the idea in his head that she was moving in to finish him off. 'You saw some pictures of her. And she's very beautiful, isn't she, Mr Weiss?'

'Yes, she is.'

'She always was. And men – ' She gestured at him with one hand. 'Men of a certain mindset have always fallen in love with her at first sight, even when she was a girl. To be fair, I think she fostered it to some extent. She had a habit of becoming whoever men wanted her to be. I suppose that makes her the perfect whore, doesn't it? Especially for someone like yourself who seems to expect the world to correlate itself with your fantasy life.' Weiss saw a faint smile play at the corner of Olivia's lips, a faintly triumphant smile as she leaned in for him. 'Let me ask you something, Mr Weiss. Do you often form such intense attachments to prostitutes?'

'Let me ask you something, sweetheart,' he said. 'How do you know she's a prostitute, if you haven't heard from her in fifteen years?'

The question caught her off guard, pulled her up

straight as if he had yanked on a rope attached to the back of her neck. Weiss, being Weiss, had figured it would be like that. Being Weiss, he had figured this girl out pretty well. She was 'the sane one' in the Graves family. She was the lone member of a shattered clan who lived a normal life, walked a straight path. She wouldn't turn her father in. She wouldn't lead him to her sister. But she had no sympathy for either of them, no time for the messes they made, and no patience for whatever unsavory characters they got themselves involved with. They could play games with contract killers and private detectives all they wanted. She wasn't going to have them dragging her into their foolishness. The whole idea of it got her righteous anger working. And the anger was why she had said too much.

She tried to backtrack now. 'I just assumed she hadn't changed,' she said coldly.

'No. You know. Because you and her – you've never lost touch with each other. You wouldn't lose touch.'

Still, she kept the act going. 'I see. More of your fantasy life.'

'C'mon, lady. You were two little girls who went through hell together. Your big sister was beautiful and kind and she took care of you the only way she knew how. You had the brains, and you always knew you were taking care of her too. And you still take care of each other. You wouldn't lose touch.'

Olivia began to speak – then didn't – then began to speak again, then didn't again. Then – bitterly – she said, 'Well... Well, this has been very interesting. You – you have a very interesting personality disorder, Mr. Weiss, are you aware of that?'

He gave another laugh. 'Only one?'

'You think you understand everything, but you don't understand anything.'

'Yeah, it's that, or the other way around, I'm never sure.'

Her eyes were glistening. It hurt Weiss to see it. The tip of her tongue came out to dampen her lips. 'I think you should leave now,' she said softly.

Weiss nodded. 'Sure. I'll leave. But first let me say what I came to say.'

Twenty-seven-year-old Olivia Graves sat very straight in her sling chair trying not to cry. 'All right,' she said. 'Go on.'

'You have a way of getting in touch with your sister. Nothing direct. Neither of you would risk that. But something simple. A middle-man probably who passes messages between you. Whatever the system is, I want you to use it to send a message for me.' He couldn't tolerate this stupid chair any more. It made him feel like a beached whale. With a tremendous groan, he worked his way out of it. He stood hugely above her where she sat straight fighting her tears. 'Tell her it's up to her,' he said. 'She can run or she can stay. I won't do this forever. I'm close now, but if she goes on running, she can keep one step ahead of me. If that's what she decides to do, I'll stop, I'll walk away and then it'll just be him, the bad guy, because he'll never stop and she'll have to go on running and that'll be her life till he finds her or she dies. If she stays put, if she lets me reach her, he'll reach her too, and him and me, we'll decide it between us. Then it'll be over, either way. Tell her. Let her know. It's up to her.'

Olivia Graves was holding onto herself so severely now that her head trembled. She tried to smile her triumphant smile again, but it just came off as spiteful. 'You see? You think you understand everything,' she said again. 'But you don't. You don't understand any of it. Any of it.'

Weiss didn't answer. He shook his head. He sighed heavily. He put his hands in his pants pockets and lumbered to the door.

Olivia's next words broke from her in a ragged voice. 'Why are you doing this? Why are you doing this?'

Weiss opened the door and stepped through. 'You're the psychologist,' he muttered, 'you figure it out.'

34

Now I have to say just a word or two here about what was happening to me – only because it eventually came to play a role in the central story – a minor role, I admit, but a role all the same.

Weiss, at this time, had just exited Olivia Graves's office and was driving out to Sky Harbor Airport where he hoped to meet with the Shadowman. In San Francisco, meanwhile, where it was an hour earlier, Sissy and I had just returned to her apartment. We had left work on the early side. With Weiss gone and the business suffering, there wasn't much to do. The Agency had become a depressing place to hang around.

When we got in, Sissy went to the bathroom to take a shower. I changed into jeans and a t-shirt and plunked down on her four-poster bed to read. And I tried to read. I went through the motions. Stretched out on her fluffy bedspread, my head propped up on her fluffy pillows with a fluffy cat kneading my belly with her claws and another fluffy cat sleeping on my crotch. I held the book in front of me and my eyes went back and forth over the words. But my mind was too full to pay attention to them, and my heart was too heavy. My heart weighed a ton.

I was thinking about Emma, about what she'd said to me. I could hardly think about anything else anymore. I kept asking myself: How was I supposed to become the sort of man she could look up to and admire? It was not a very comfortable question. The thing was, once I began to consider it, I found myself considering all the ways in which I was not very admirable at all. It's funny, you know: I had always been a sort of self-deprecating person, the kind of guy who made a great fuss about my foibles and tried to be honest about my weaknesses and mistakes. But underneath that, in my heart of hearts, I always figured I was a pretty great guy at the very basic level. Now, as I began to really think about it, to think about how I might be more admirable to Emma, it occurred to me to wonder: How great are you really, even at the basic level, if you don't try, at least, to do the right thing?

I knew what right thing I had to do, of course. I knew the first right thing I had to do anyway. I lay there sunk in smothering fluff and I could hear Sissy singing in the shower, some girl song, some happy girl song, because she was so happy to be in love and have the right man in her life finally, and, sure, I knew exactly what I had to do.

Then the shower stopped. Sissy went on singing. Drying herself now, preparing to come out to me. I was filled with dread.

My eyes continued to move back and forth over the lines of type. The book I was reading, the book I was pretending to read, was Patrick McNair's book, Emma's father's prize-winning novel. It was called *The Celestial Fugue of Bugger O'Reilly*. It was about an alcoholic college professor with writer's block. Go figure. I'd tried to read it once before but I never could get to the end of it. I thought I'd try it again because – I don't know – I thought maybe it would help me understand Emma better, why she'd rebelled against the old man and gone Christian and all that. Anyway, the story followed this professor through a series of dissolute picaresque adventures until in the end he finds himself standing knee-deep in a lake grasping wildly at the pages of his unfinished manuscript as they blow away in the wind. Well, all right, as I say, I never actually finished it, but that's how all these novels about blocked college professors end. The fact that manuscripts don't have pages anymore doesn't seem to make any difference.

The novel was written with that languid acerbic eloquence alcoholics seem to be so good at. And then there were all the usual passages where the languid acerbic eloquence suddenly gives way to a more heartfelt but still acceptably ironic eloquence with which the professor affirms the beauty of this meaningless spark of a meaningless flame that was the life of the imagined soul in the accidental universe which was really only the novel he was writing which was this novel which was this universe and so on. My eyes, as I say, went over the words without really taking them in. I was thinking about Emma instead, Emma in that brown shingled house in Berkeley. Kneeling with her hands clasped before her and her green eyes turned up to the ceiling and her face like the face of an angel.

So now I was not only filled with dread, I was also filled – I was overflowing – with confusion over the purely practical difficulties I had gotten myself into. What was I going to do about Emma's father? I couldn't betray her conversion to him and I couldn't betray to her the fact that he'd hired the Agency. And I couldn't very well keep either secret and actually have a relationship with her. It was a genuine mess, and I had no idea how I could get any of it to work out in a way that would make me 'admirable.'

But I couldn't let that distract me. I knew what I had to do first. I had to break up with Sissy.

The bathroom door opened, it seemed to me, with shocking suddenness. Even the cats jumped off me and ran for cover. Out Sissy stepped. She was wearing a short silver nightie, ready for action. Already, on the way home, in that whispery voice of hers, she had gone on at some length about the things she was planning for us to do before dinner. As always, given the limited number of parts and possible combinations involved, her creativity was impressive.

She came toward me very slowly, putting one toned white leg directly in front of the other. Her spun gold hair hung loose at her cheeks. Her gentle, delicate face was all smiles and fire.

It struck me suddenly, as I lay there in my dread and confusion watching her approach, that her bedroom was like a stage in some ways. The four-poster with its white lace canopy. The fluffy bedspread and the fluffy pillows, at least one of them shaped like a heart. The fluffy white shag rug, the white dressers. The posters on the wall – I remember one was a print of people dancing and another was of a tree-canopied dirt road – which somehow managed to seem fluffy too. It was like a setting she'd created in which we were supposed to play out her wished-for moments. All that white, all that fluff, the heartshaped pillow. It was the furniture of a fantasy – this fantasy of something she had missed, the sort of giddy young girl's love for which, in truth, she had grown too old.

Sissy reached the end of the bed. She took hold of the post and leaned against it, letting it press into the silver nightie, bringing out the shape of her breasts.

'Hi there, Sweetiekins,' she said in that singsong maternal whisper. 'Whatcha reading?'

I had the awful sense that it was not just the fluff I was sinking into, that her very dreams were closing in around me. Yet, for all my honorable intentions, I couldn't help noticing: she looked awfully good, standing there. Plus it was flattering, the way she wanted me all the time. Plus, as I say, her creativity was truly impressive.

'This book,' I said. My voice seemed to come from someplace far away. 'By Patrick McNair, that guy McNair.'

'That professor? The one who came in?'

'Who hired me to follow his daughter, yeah.'

'Mm, right, right.' Her chin went up and down, her cheek rubbing slowly against the bedpost. Then she came around the edge of the bed to me, her fingers trailing over the post until they let it go. 'Well, work is over now, puppy dog. It's time for baby to put his book away...'

She sat down beside me on the edge of the mattress. She smelled good. Have I mentioned that? Sissy always smelled exceptionally good. She lifted the book out of my unresisting hands. She placed it gently on the bedside table. She considered my face fondly, sweetly, her blue eyes bright. She stroked the hair up off my forehead. She gave a satisfied sigh and smiled.

'Oh,' she said, 'you make me so happy.'

She leaned down and kissed me very gently on the lips. I don't know how she did these things: it was absolutely electric. Suddenly, I couldn't remember what it was I'd been thinking about a moment before. Emma – admirable – the right thing to do – what was all that about? Why was I always making such a big deal out of these things? All it came down to was a little sex, after all. What was I, some kind of Puritan, some kind of fogey? Life was short, man, you had to *carpe* the old *diem* while you may. Or something.

She kissed me again, gave me a taste of her tongue this time. She pushed her hand up under my t-shirt. Her fingers were cool and dry against my belly.

'Don't you want to take this off, you silly puppy?' she whispered.

How could I crush her fluffy white dreams?

I often think back on that moment. Actually, it's the t-shirt I think about most, an old, ratty black one I've long since thrown away. I think about the fact that if I had taken that t-shirt off that night, my whole life would've been different. To be precise, all the best parts of it never would have happened. The t-shirt, I guess, was sort of like the coaster from Carlos: a little thing on which a lot of big things depended. I had blown the coaster. I don't know why I got a shot at the t-shirt. It was an unlooked-for second chance.

'No, no, no,' I heard myself say hoarsely. I put my hand on her hand as she tried to push the t-shirt up. I drew it out from underneath the cloth and held it. I looked into her sweet blue eyes. 'You're going to have to fire me,' I told her.

She gave a sort of half laugh. She half thought it was a joke, half knew it wasn't.

'You're going to have to kick me out of the Agency.'

'What are you talking about, goofy? What's the matter? You sound so serious all of a sudden.'

'It's the professor,' I said, holding onto her hand, looking into her eyes. I inclined my head toward the novel on the bedside table. 'McNair.'

'What about him? Do we have to talk about this now?'

I brought her hand down and held it against my heart. She must've felt how hard my heart was beating. She looked to where our hands were and I saw fear come into her eyes.

'Yes,' I said. 'We have to.'

Well, she knew right away what was coming. It had happened to her too many times for her not to know. For one more second, I considered letting it go until another day. But really, there was no stopping now.

'I can't do what the professor hired me to do,' I said. 'I took the case under false pretenses. It was the damnedest coincidence, an incredible coincidence, him coming in, him asking me to follow his daughter. I never should've taken the case – because I already knew her.'

'You already...?'

'I was already in love with her.'

Her gaze, which had clung for all these moments to our hands, our hands pressed to my heart, now flickered back to me, my face, my eyes.

'Emma McNair,' I said. 'I love her, Sissy.'

She crumbled. Just like that. It was horrible. I wished she would've handled it any other way. I wished she would've hit me. I wished she would've given me the hell I deserved. But it was like watching one of those buildings you see get demolished with dynamite on the TV news sometimes. She just collapsed inward, just slipped to her knees by the side of the bed, dropped her head into her folded arms and sobbed and sobbed and sobbed. Every now and then, she would look up and plead with me. She would clutch at my arm, beg me to stay with her. Again and again, she asked me what was wrong with her. Why didn't I love her? Why couldn't I just please love her, just please try?

Who knows what mealy-mouthed garbage I answered her with? Mostly, I lay there and watched her, watched the shuddering top of her head, guilt-ridden and appalled. If I could've magically melted through the mattress and reappeared at a nearby saloon with a whiskey in my hand, believe me, I would've. It was unbearable. It went on and and on and on.

After maybe about twenty minutes – twenty minutes that felt like an hour and a half – the phone began to ring. The phone was right near us on the bedside table, right by McNair's book. It was white and, yes, fluffy:

it had this strip of fluffy stuff glued to the top of the handset. Sissy usually turned the ringer off when we made love but she hadn't gotten around to it yet tonight. It rang very loudly. It startled me.

Sissy though – she didn't even seem to hear it. She didn't lift her face from her arms or try to choke back her sobs or anything. She cried and cried, clutching and kneading the soaked bedspread beneath her. The phone kept ringing and ringing.

Finally, I had to grab the damn thing myself.

'Hello?'

I couldn't hear the woman on the other end of the line at first – Sissy was weeping too loudly.

'I'm sorry?' I said.

I stroked Sissy's hair, hoping it would quiet her, but she only seized my hand in both her hands and held it against her wet cheek. I had to pull free so I could press the heel of my palm to my ear, so I could hear.

The woman on the other end of the line spoke for less than a minute. She spoke in a professional tone of regret. When I hung up, my hand was shaking.

I guess my reaction was visible on my face – I guess she could hear it in my voice – because when I spoke Sissy's name, she looked up at once – and as soon as she saw me, her sobs began to slow at last.

Wiping her nose with her knuckle, she managed to force some words out. 'What? What's the matter? What's happened?'

'That was a hospital in Phoenix,' I told her. 'Yours was the only number they had.'

Sissy stared at me, dazed and exhausted.

'It's Bishop,' I said. 'He's been shot.'

'Oh my God!'

'They think he's dying, Sissy.'

35

By this time, Weiss was sitting in the airport. He was eating cashews from a striped paper bag. He had found a secluded place in a corner by a window. He was seated in a molded blue plastic chair, one of a double row of chairs bolted to an iron stand so that the two lines of seats faced in opposite directions. The terminal was quiet at the moment. The rest of the chairs in the double row were empty.

He watched the jets landing and lifting off into the twilight. He watched them deadpan, as if he were in a trance. He munched away at the cashews mechanically. He hardly noticed how his stomach burned and churned. He hardly noticed there was something in the heart of him very much like fear. He watched the jets. He found them a restful sight.

The big terminal pane was thick and the runways were far across the field so that even the hefty seven-sevens seemed to come and go silently. The silence, in turn, made the jets seem graceful, made them seem to float to the tarmac or glide up from the ground into the deepening blue. Weiss watched, lifting cashews to his lips, chewing the nuts like cud, as landing lights like the first stars grew brighter, closer, and the jets that carried them took shape out of the folding dusk. He watched these jets touch down as others taxied into position for takeoff. Then he watched those begin their roll along the centerline toward the sky.

He wished he were going somewhere. Anywhere. Home or far away. It didn't matter. He yearned for his armchair by the bay window and a glass of Macallan, but he also ached to be in a new place, a small town maybe, where the air smelled of woodfire at sunset and people smiled at you as they passed you on the sidewalk of an evening, walking their collies or their Irish setters or whatever the fuck they walked in towns like that. How the hell should he know? He'd lived in cities all his life.

He sighed and dipped his hand into the paper bag again. It was striped red and white like the popcorn bags he sometimes got at ballgames. He liked that. He liked ballgames. He wished he were at a ballgame now.

Outside, a short-hop twin engine wafted smoothly into the air. Heading for Albuquerque maybe, or maybe LA. Weiss's eyes followed it. What the hell was he doing here? he asked himself. He couldn't even remember anymore why he'd started out. Some bullshit about the Agency, the business going sour. Something about Bishop fucking up his livelihood after he had given him so many chances to go straight. Something about being older than he ever meant to be and about that otherworldly look in Julie Wyant's eyes. Mary Graves's eyes.

Why are you doing this?

Olivia Graves had asked him the same question. She came into his mind now. He thought about her. Her professional manner, her standoffish clothes. Her psychologist pose in the sling chair, legs crossed, hands on her raised knee. Ever since he'd left her, something had been nagging at him about their conversation. Not about what she'd said to him, about what he'd said to her, about the way he'd laid out the Graves family story. It hadn't seemed as sound to him somehow when he spoke it out loud in Olivia's office as it had when he was thinking about it to himself in his car.

You think you understand everything but you don't understand anything.

What didn't he understand? The bond between the Graves sisters. The father's bond to them both. If Charles Graves – Andy Bremer – had abandoned the girls after killing their mother, if he had become a fugitive and disappeared, how did Julie know where he was? How had she known where to call him? And if Julie had become a whore to get Olivia out of the foster system, to pay her way through school, why did she go on with it after Olivia was on her own? Why was Olivia so angry with her – and so bound to her? Why were they all so bound up together?

Something about the Graves family didn't make sense to him. Something about the scenario he'd laid out in his mind didn't make sense.

He sat. He thought about it. He ate his cashews. He watched the planes. In some distant part of him, he was dimly aware of his stomach churning, aware of the time passing as he waited for what was on its way, dreading it.

He watched the horizon, where wisps of clouds turned red, turned gray. The sky darkened. He sat and watched it in a kind of trance.

Then, just as night fell, he came to himself as if from a great way off. A sense of sourness had washed over him suddenly. A stale, rotten heat seemed to spread all through him. He had a weird, nauseating, panicky feeling, as if he'd woken up inside his own coffin, underground.

He swallowed a chunk of cashew, swallowed hard. He understood. The time had come. The Shadowman was here.

36

He saw the killer reflected on the darkness of the airport window: a hulking specter of a man, his features half erased by the night outside. Weiss went on eating his cashews. The figure in the window moved to stand directly behind him.

'If you try to turn around, I will kill you, Weiss.'

He sat down slowly in the chair at Weiss's back. Weiss felt the stale, hot presence of him on the nape of his neck. He caught a scent that reminded him of close, dank spaces.

The killer spoke again, his voice low and featureless. No foreign accent, no local dialect. His tone was conversational, almost friendly. Weiss did not remember the voice from when he heard it last in the driveway in Hannock, and he did not think he would remember it the next time he heard it either.

'What'll happen is that they'll find you sitting here after hours like a sleeping bum,' the killer said. 'With your chin on your chest, you know – sitting here. Someone'll call the airport cops and one'll come and shake your shoulder to get you to wake up. But you won't wake up. Finally, they'll push your head back, tilt your head back. There won't be any marks, no cuts, no blood, not even a bruise. But you'll've been dead for hours. Just sitting here, dead, for hours with no one to give a damn.'

Weiss lifted the striped paper bag to his shoulder. 'You

want a cashew?' There was no answer but a low exhalation. Weiss shook the bag, rattling the nuts. 'They're roasted. Salted too. Take some – do me a favor. I can't stop eating the damned things.'

In the silence that followed, Weiss realized he could actually feel the other man's rage. He could actually feel it settle over him like a great dark thunderhead with a world of flash and fire inside.

'Suit yourself,' he said. He lowered the bag. He began picking cashews out of it again. 'They're good though.'

After a long, breathing moment, the killer murmured, 'This was smart, Weiss. The airport. Make me get a ticket, go through the x-ray, security. I like that. It was smart.'

Weiss shrugged, his hand stopping with a nut halfway between the bag and his mouth. 'I know you could get a weapon through, if you wanted.'

'I don't need a weapon.'

'Yeah. I know that too.'

'All the same. It shows you were thinking. Planning things out. I can appreciate that. Like the jacket you gave to that nigger in the crazy house. That was good too. That was the kind of thing I might come up with. I liked it. You're all right, Weiss.'

Weiss had to fight off a shudder. The friendly, conversational voice – the brooding sense of murderous rage: it sent a chill through him. Close up like this, the killer seemed to give off a kind of atmosphere. It was an atmosphere like houses Weiss had been in as a cop. There were certain houses he had moved through, room to room, holding his gun out in front of him. There were moments when he had seen something up ahead through a doorway – blood spatters on the wall in the next room maybe, or a foot sticking out from behind the jamb – moments when he knew what he would find but before he crossed the threshold and found it, when he was surrounded and filled by a pulsing awareness of *Death, Death, Death, Death*. The killer gave off a pulsing atmosphere like that.

Weiss peered into the dark window in front of him. He tried to pick out the killer's features reflected there. It was no good. All he could see were the runway lights and the jet lights – and his own face, strained and mournful and also afraid.

'So go ahead,' the killer said. 'You wanted this. Here I am.'

Weiss was about to answer when a woman approached the rows of chairs. He saw her image in the window, then glimpsed her in the flesh out of the corner of his eye as she came near. She was old and small and elegant. She had silver hair and was wearing a pink jacket and pearls. She was pulling a wheeled suitcase behind her with one hand and holding a hardback novel in the other.

The Shadowman must have turned to face her. Weiss couldn't see it happen, but he saw the woman stop short. She stood where she was, very still, like a mouse catching wind of a python. Then, without a word, she turned and walked away, very quickly, her luggage wobbling behind her on its unsteady wheels.

Somehow this brought Weiss's own feeling into focus: the boiling in his belly, the tightness in his throat. He dropped the cashew he was holding back into the bag. He couldn't eat anymore.

'What do I call you anyway?' he said.

'Foy. John Foy.'

'Well, the thing is, Foy: we're near the end of this.'

'That's right. That is the thing. We are.'

'You heard what I said to the Graves girl, right? You were listening in?'

'I heard it, yeah.'

'So you know I'm close. I'm really close. And every-thing depends on us not doing anything stupid. Either one of us. You see what I'm saying?'

The killer said nothing. Weiss felt the heat and sour-ness of him.

'What I mean is: these things go step by step. Location work like this – it goes step by step. If you move too fast, if you do too much, you blow it. It takes, you know, patience, or else things go haywire on you. That's what I'm saying.'

Foy laughed softly. It was a cold sound, cold and empty.

'You afraid I'll go to see the Graves girl myself?' he said. 'Is that it? Well, maybe I should. Like you said, she has a number she calls, a way to get in touch with our girl, doesn't she? Maybe I should go ask her what it is.'

'Look...'

'She'd tell me, you know. She wouldn't tell you, but she'd tell me. You know why? I'd stick a tampon in her soaked in gasoline. Then I'd light a match...'

Weiss had warned himself about something like this, but it didn't matter. The anger went off in him like a bomb. He started turning in his seat. 'You filthy fuck, I'll...'

The grip on his shoulder sent a lancing pain up the side of his neck. He gasped, gritted his teeth.

'Careful, Weiss,' said the Shadowman softly.

He let Weiss go. Weiss rubbed the spot, wincing. He settled back in his seat. He found he'd balled the bag of cashews up in his fist. Crushed the nuts to powder. He let the crumpled bag roll from his hand onto the seat beside him. He wiped his palms together to get the salt off. He was surprised how wet his palms were.

'You'll blow it for both of us,' he said finally. 'You'll lose her. You will.'

'Maybe.'

'Not maybe. You will. As long as it's just me, there's a chance she'll stay put. A chance she'll trust me and let me reach her. Once you show yourself, it's over. She'll start running again.'

'She knows I'm here. She might run anyway.'

'She might. But she might not. If all she sees is me, she might not.' Weiss rubbed his hands together till they were dry. He worked to steady himself, to steady his voice. 'Look, Foy. I don't have to tell you this. You know it's true. You've hunted people before, just like I have. If they don't see you, they stop running. Even if they know you're there. They can't run forever so they tell themselves you're gone, they convince themselves you're gone and they stop.'

'Well, that is right,' the killer said thoughtfully. 'They do do that, it's true. That's when you get them.'

'That's right. You touch the sister, you touch her contact, her middle-man, that's it: our girl takes off again. And if she takes off again, that's it for me too: I'm through, I'm done with it.'

He could almost hear the killer sneer. 'Don't give me that. You're not gonna stop. You can't.'

'Try me,' said Weiss. He drew the meat of his thumb across his upper lip, wiped the sweat away there too. 'Look, just stay out of it, that's all I'm saying. Stay out of it until I find her. If she doesn't see you, if it's just me, she'll stop running, then...'

He let the words trail away. And for a while, there was no answer from behind him. Weiss stared into the window at the light on the runway, the lights of the jets rising and falling, the vague, faceless figure hunkering there behind him.

'Then what?' said the Shadowman finally.

Weiss waited, breathing slowly.

'What happens then? Huh? You gonna kill me, Weiss?'
Weiss breathed and waited.

'That the way you figure it? You think you're gonna kill me?'

'No,' Weiss said finally. 'I'm not a killing man.'

Foy laughed that icy laugh again. 'You're not a killing man, huh? Well, I am. I'm a killing man, for sure.'

'I know.'

'And I will kill you, Weiss. In fact, I want her there to see it. In case she thinks you're her hero coming to save her or something. I want her to see what I do to you, how you die. You think it'll be clean? It will not be clean, my friend. I want her to see that too – to see what I turn you into before I'm done. Then she'll know: it's all me for her. It's just gonna be me, nothing else in her life from then on, that's it. All me. Everything.'

Weiss opened his mouth but nothing came out. He was too sick to speak at this point. Just being so near this guy made him dog-sick.

'So what?' the killer pressed on. 'Huh, Weiss? I really want to know. What do you think you're gonna do? What do you think's gonna happen?'

Weiss forced the words out. 'We'll decide it. That's all.'

'We'll decide it,' the killer echoed. 'You think you're gonna send me to jail? You think they can keep me in some jail somewhere?'

Weiss didn't answer. The killer laughed again, with disdain this time. Then, all of a sudden, he stood up. Weiss saw it in the window and tensed. He saw the ghost of a figure rising, hulking, the face obscured by the night. He felt the atmosphere change, felt the heat and the sourness – the rage – lifting away, a burden lifting.

'All right,' the killer said. 'All right.'

'You'll keep away,' said Weiss.

'Until you find her. I'll keep away until you find her. Then I'll be there.'

Weiss nodded once. 'Good.'

There was another moment, the killer hovering over him. Weiss felt his eyes on the back of his neck, felt his ill will burning there, burning.

'Another thing,' Weiss said.

Foy snorted. 'Another thing?'

'The number. The number Olivia called, the sister called.'

'What about it?'

'You got it, didn't you?'

There was only a second's pause. 'Sure. I got it. She didn't even wait till you reached the parking lot. She didn't even wait until the door shut. She picked up the phone the second you were gone.'

'Sure. That's how I figured it. I pushed her and she picked up the phone to contact her sister. And you were watching. You got the number, right? You heard the call?'

'Sure.'

'So?'

'So what?'

'So save me some fucking trouble,' said Weiss.

Weiss saw the reflection of the killer, saw him rear a little, then shake his head. 'Oh, that's something, Weiss. You're something. That's good. That's really good. I guess we're a team now, huh? I guess we're partners.'

'Just give me the number.'

The killer recited it. The number and an address and a name too: Kristy.

'Looks like we're heading back to Nevada,' he said.

'Kristy,' said Weiss. 'You got the name too. That's good.'

'Sure. We make a good team, don't we?' said the killer. Then, before Weiss could answer, he said, 'Oh – and by

243

the way. You might want to check out the news if you missed it.'

Weiss didn't like the sound of that. 'The news?'

'The local news. Something about a shooting at the Saguaro Hotel. Yeah, you definitely might want to check it out, Weiss. It'll give you a feeling for how it's gonna be between us.'

Weiss stared at the reflection on the dark window. 'What...?'

'I'll be seeing you,' the killer said.

The reflection sank away to nothing.

When Weiss finally risked a glance over his shoulder, there was nobody there.

37

With a weary sigh, Weiss pushed into a men's room stall and vomited heavily. The cashews came up out of him, spattering the toilet water. A lot of coffee came up too. Two cups at two bucks a piece. Goddamn airport prices.

Weiss bent over the mess, pressing one hand against the tiled wall. When he finished, he waved the other hand down low in front of the sensor to make the toilet flush. He watched what had been the contents of his stomach swirl slowly down the drain.

For another second or so, he stayed as he was, leaning over. He still felt pretty lousy. He wanted to make sure there was no more. There was no more.

He straightened. Turned. Shoved the door open. Stumbled out of the stall. The lights in the white-tiled room seemed overbright. They made him squint. They made his head hurt behind his eyes. They were like a needle on a naked nerve.

He shuffled to one of the sinks in the line of sinks set under mirrors on the far wall. There was a small, tidy-looking black man washing his hands two sinks over. He gave Weiss a sympathetic nod. Weiss nodded back, embarrassed.

'Airplane food,' the tidy-looking man said.

Weiss managed a smile.

He waved his hands beneath the faucet, catching the sensor, making the water run. He cupped his palms and caught the water and splashed it onto his face. The cool, wet shock revived him. He dragged his hands down over his brow and over his cheeks and chin, wiping the water away. When he was done, he found himself looking into the mirror. The sight was sharp and painful like the men's room light.

The big heavy mournful countenance was pale and unhealthy. The sunken eyes with their dark rings looked ghostly, a dead man's eyes. The hound dog cheeks had a greenish tinge. The bulbous nose stood out as if the face around it were wasting away. The shaggy salt-and-pepper hair seemed pasted on, a wig on a skull.

'For fuck's sake,' he muttered.

A corpse is an unhappy sight to see anywhere, but to find one in the mirror is depressing as hell. It struck Weiss as a premonition. Just what he needed. He already felt sick to his stomach. Now he felt sick to his stomach and doomed.

I will kill you, Weiss. I want her there to see it.

He shook his head and turned away.

He came out of the men's room, moving unsteadily. The airport surprised him, as if it hadn't been there when he went in. The long, broad corridor surprised him. So did the people moving purposefully to their gates. A tired mom shepherding two dancing children. A businessman with a laptop slung over his shoulder. A young couple with their arms around each other. He stood and watched them go by.

There was a flight boarding to his right, a slow line moving past the ticket-taker into the jetway. There was a woman's voice summoning the passengers over the loud-speaker. There were televisions mounted on the wall. It all surprised him. It was all so modern and busy, present and alive. He felt as if he had come out of a fever dream, a dream of a darker, older world. It surprised him to find this world – this bright, loud, modern world – still here.

Still here. Weiss trudged down the corridor. He came to a row of shops and restaurants. He came to a bar. There were brightly colored hangings around the entryway: wooden cutouts of mountains and cowboys and chili peppers – a southwestern decor. Inside, the place was dark, somber. Low light. Chairs and tables dark brown. Solitary drinkers alone with their beers. Travellers passing through.

Weiss moved to the bar rail. He hoisted his butt onto one of the stools. A waitress stepped up to him, wiping his little piece of bartop with a cloth. She was forty or so. She had even features and long blonde hair. Her face was lined and tired but still pretty. Her figure was good. Weiss let his eyes go up and down her. She was wearing a tight black top that showed off her breasts and her firm waist.

It was funny, he thought, how, when the subject came up, you realized how much you didn't want to die.

'Gimme a Rock, willya,' he said.

She brought him the beer in a bottle. Poured it into a glass in front of him. He watched her face while she did it. She knew he was doing it. She liked it. She smiled.

'Thanks,' he said.

'Sure. Can I get you anything else?'

He lifted his chin to one of the television sets hanging above the bar mirror. 'Could you see if there's some local news on?'

He watched the back of her short skirt as she turned to pick up the remote. She switched the picture on the TV from a Diamondbacks game to the news. The sound was turned off but there were subtitles. He sipped his beer and watched the pictures, read the words. The beer made his stomach feel better.

The shootout at the Saguaro Hotel was the lead story. They had already covered it at the start of the program, but they returned to it at the end. Weiss was distracted, thinking about the Shadowman, trying to get rid of the images in his mind.

I want her to see what I turn you into. You think it'll be clean. It will not be clean.

The pictures on the TV snapped him out of it. They showed the hotel and the broken window through which Bishop had fallen. The camera panned down from that to the swimming pool, to show how long a fall it was. There were still traces of blood in the water, or what looked like blood. The camera zoomed in on it.

The newsman didn't know the name of the man who had been shot. The police hadn't identified him yet. But Weiss suspected it was Bishop from the first. Then, when the newsman said the victim had been wearing a leather jacket, Weiss knew for sure.

He was not prepared for what he felt, for the weight of it. It was the end of something and he knew it. There would be no more second chances. He set his beer down on the bar, his hand trembling. He set some money down. His vision was blurred.

'Hey,' said the waitress. 'Are you okay?'

Weiss waved her off. He lumbered out of the bar with his head down, his back bent. He looked like a sick old man.

38

He was there, at Bishop's bedside, when Sissy and I walked into the hospital room. We had come through Vegas on the last plane out. It was nearly three AM when we finally arrived.

The hospital room was a double, two beds. The bed nearer the door was empty. Bishop was in the other bed, the one nearer the window. Weiss was sitting in a chair pressed right up against the bed's side. His big form was hunched over Bishop where he lay. For a moment, right after we first walked in, we could hear him murmuring to the fallen man, a steady stream of words, indistinguishable. Then he must've sensed we were there, because he fell silent.

We waited. Without turning around, he said aloud, 'I'm glad you came.'

I hung back by the door. I felt I had no business being there with the three of them. I had only come because Sissy was such a wreck, in no condition to travel alone. Now I let her move to the bed without me.

'The hospital called,' she said softly. 'I was the only number they could reach.'

Weiss nodded. 'I guess I've been out of touch.'

He turned. Glanced at me over his shoulder, then looked steadily up at her. He was an awful sight. Old and exhausted and pale. After a night of crying, Sissy didn't look much better. They gazed at each other a long, long moment, appalled, I think, at the pitiful spectacle they made. They were always very fond of each other, these two.

Sissy said, 'How is he?'

They both turned to look down at the man on the bed.

Bishop lay on his back in an unconsciousness so deep he seemed almost inanimate. The handsome, tough, ironical face was drained of every expression. It was drained of color. It seemed made of stone. A white sheet covered him to his waist. A white patient's gown covered his torso. There was a tube full of something running into one of his arms, another in the other, a counter of some kind clicking off the doses, a monitor running his numbers with an occasional beep. He didn't even look like himself. He didn't even look like a man. He looked like part of the machinery, pulsing but lifeless.

'He's bad,' said Weiss in a voice infinitely weary. 'The doctor said he's lucky to still be alive. But he's very bad.' He rubbed his chin as if he were thinking. His cheeks were dark with stubble. 'The bullets... I've seen this before. Bullets are strange things. They do strange stuff inside you. Like they go into you and they have a mind of their own. It's – crazy. Anyway, they had to...' His shoulders lifted as he took a deep breath through his nose. 'They had to take out his spleen. Then there was some vein – I forgot what she called it. Ill... Illy...'

'Ileac.'

'Yeah, the ileac vein. This big vein. One of the bullets sliced it. He lost a lot of blood. She – the doctor – she said his heart stopped beating three times on the table.'

'Oh, Christ,' said Sissy. 'Oh Christ.'

Weiss laughed miserably. 'Yeah. Yeah.'

She took a breath. 'Well – I mean: is he gonna make it?'

Weiss lifted his hand by way of a shrug. 'His chances

aren't so good, she said, the doctor said. You know, he's fighting. He's a tough guy but... It's not so good.'

Sissy lifted both her hands to massage her eyes. 'Does he have any family? Do we know? Does he have parents or anything?'

'No, I don't know,' said Weiss. 'His father's dead, I think. I don't know.'

They were both silent then, hanging over the injured man. As if they had nothing else to say about him but didn't feel right talking about anything else.

After a while, Sissy seemed to remember I was there. She looked over her shoulder at me and smiled briefly.

'You don't have to stay.'

I was about to protest, but then I realized: she didn't want me there. Neither of them wanted me there. I was just passing through their lives on the way to a life of my own. This was too real to them for me to stand by watching, making a story of it in my head.

'You can go get yourself a hotel room, put it on the Agency,' Sissy said. 'You can fly out in the morning. I'll get home all right.'

I nodded. 'Okay.'

'Thank you – for negotiating the planes and everything, getting us here. I appreciate it.'

I nodded again. I nodded at Bishop. 'Good luck,' I said.

I left.

For another long time after I was gone, Weiss sat stoop-shouldered over Bishop. Sissy stood over him. He lifted his eyes to her.

'You look like crap, Sis,' he said. He moved his head toward the door through which I'd gone. 'What happened? He dump you?'

She gave a sniffling laugh. She rolled her eyes, fighting

tears. 'It has been a really, really, really bad night,' she said. 'It ought to win some sort of bad night award.'

Weiss frowned down at Bishop again, at the empty, marble face. 'Well,' he said. 'He was right. To end it. That's the right thing.'

She barely got the words out. 'Is it?'

'Oh yeah. Sure. Sure it is. It was no good. He's just a kid.'

'I know.' She laughed, starting to cry again. 'It was very nice though.'

'Yeah. Sure. But he's just a kid, Sissy. That's no good.'

A sob broke out of her. She put a hand over her mouth. 'I'm sorry. It's so stupid. With poor Jim...'

'No, no, no.'

'I just feel like everything's falling apart.'

Weiss nodded without a word and Sissy cried.

Weiss went on nodding. 'Well...' he said then. He stood up slowly. He wasn't wearing a jacket, she noticed, just slacks and a polo shirt. He seemed massive dressed like that. He shuffled toward her, his paunch leading the way. He towered above her.

Sissy wrapped her arms around him. She pressed her face against his shirt. He held her. She wanted to ask him what was going to happen, but it seemed like a childish question. How should he know? So she just pressed against him, breathing the smell of him, rank and comforting.

'I just feel like everything's falling apart,' she said again.

He patted her back awkwardly.

She drew away. She looked at Bishop. 'He was coming to help you,' she said.

'Yeah, I figured. In fact, do me a favor, will you. Tell him that when he comes around. Tell him I figured that.'

'He said you'll get killed if you do this alone.'

'It'll be all right.'

She faced him. Showed him her tears, her mottled cheeks. She knew it affected him. He was very soft for her.

'It's not all right, Scott,' she said. 'Look at what happened to Jim.'

He looked. He nodded. 'It'll be all right,' he repeated.

Sissy put her arms around him again, pressed to him again, held him hard. 'He said this man – this man you're after – Jim said he'll kill you.'

'Eh,' said Weiss. 'He's not gonna kill me so fast.'

She laughed, crying against him.

She felt his grip on her loosen. She held on tighter, refusing to let him go. Gently, he pushed her away.

She looked up at his mournful features. 'Will I be able to reach you?'

'No. Not for a while.'

'But what if...?'

'I'll be back soon.'

'Scott...'

'I'll see you, Sissy. Take care of things here, okay?'

'Scott...'

He lifted one of his huge hands and patted her head clumsily. 'All right,' he said. 'That's it. I'll see you.'

He took a last look at Bishop. Then he moved slowly out of the room.

Sissy watched him until he was gone. Then she watched the door. Then she sighed deeply.

Then she walked slowly over to Bishop's bed and sat down beside it in Weiss's chair.

PART FIVE

House Of Dreams

39

For the first time, Weiss sensed a watcher on the road behind him. Sunrise was still a couple of hours away, but the traffic outside Phoenix was already getting thicker. Lines of big, rumbling semis crowded the right lane. Scattered white headlights glared in the rearview mirror. Cars streamed past him on either side. Red taillights receded into the night beyond the windshield.

Weiss drove to the top of a hill and down the far slope into the desert. The sprawling, glittering city disappeared from view behind him. There was nothing now for miles and miles but the other cars and the broken white line slapping up under his front fender. He drove. And after about half an hour, he picked one car out in his sideview: one pair of headlights that had been with him, behind him, too long, at the same distance from him too long.

What the hell? he wondered. Maybe the killer just didn't care anymore. Now that they'd met in the airport, now that they'd spoken together. Maybe it didn't matter to him anymore whether he was invisible or not. Maybe. Weiss doubted it though. Invisible was the way he was. Anonymous was the way he was. This was something else. An open threat? Incompetence? Stupidity? Who the hell knew?

Anyway, he was too tired to work it out. He'd been up all night. His mind was thick with exhaustion. It was full of whispers – the friendly, conversational voice of the Shadowman.

You think it will be clean? It will not be clean.

He was haunted by images of Bishop lying still as stone. He needed to get some sleep.

He drove another hundred miles. That was all he had in him. He pulled off the highway into a rest stop. There was a parking lot lit by sodium streetlamps, picnic tables on a strip of grass, rest rooms and vending machines housed in a concrete bunker with a cheap rock veneer. He parked the Taurus to one side of the bunker. He cracked the window to get some air. The smell of disinfectant wafted to him from the toilets.

He pushed the driver's seat back. He rested there, waiting, watching the sideview. It took about half a minute for the other car to show.

In the pink glow of the sodium lights, he could see it was a little Jap rental, a Hyundai, puke green. He watched it pull into a far corner of the lot, into a slanted space at the end of a long row of parked semis. He closed his eyes. That was it. He had to sleep.

But he couldn't sleep, not at first. Too much crap still going on in his head. The killer's voice, the images of Bishop, Sissy – poor Sissy and her lonely-heart tears. He forced himself to think of something else. The Graves family. The girls Mary and Olivia, their father Charles, their mother Suzanne. What was he getting wrong about them? He went back to work on it, trying to figure it out as if it were a puzzle. He thought it would help him sleep.

He couldn't sleep. He sat back in the reclining seat with his eyes closed. He thought about what Olivia Graves had said about her sister Mary: Julie Wyant.

She had a habit of becoming whoever men wanted her to be. I suppose that makes her the perfect whore, doesn't it?

There was anger in her voice, Weiss thought, but not just anger. There was guilt too. She was angry at her sister because she felt guilty about what her sister had done, what her sister had done for her sake.

The scene floated through Weiss's mind like a daydream. The mother, Suzanne Graves, drugged stupid in her house in Akron. The tough, tattooed men gathering in her living room while her husband was out trying to drum up work. They brought her booze, they brought her crystal. They traded the drugs for her body.

But that wouldn't have been enough. It never was, nothing was. After a while, the men's eyes would've wandered to the daughters too, the little girls.

She was always beautiful, Olivia Graves said. *Men of a certain mindset have always fallen in love with her at first sight, even when she was a girl.*

That was not just anger, not just guilt either, thought Weiss – that was jealousy too. Sibling jealousy, crazy and everlasting. Men of a certain mindset – these dealers, these tattooed thugs – they had supplied Suzanne Graves with drugs in exchange for sex with her, and then for sex with her daughter. But not with both her daughters. Just the older one, the beautiful Mary. Somewhere in Olivia's ten-year-old brain she was jealous about that, jealous that the men wanted her sister more than her.

She had a habit of becoming whoever men wanted her to be.

The perfect whore, thought Weiss. Sure she was. Because thirteen-year-old Mary must have realized that the men wouldn't stop with her. Why should they? Suzanne would give them anything to get her supply. They would go on and rape the little sister too eventually. Mary knew she had to take care of little Olivia. That's what Mary did, that's how she was. So she did what she had to do to keep the men off her, to keep her sister safe. She taught herself how to be whatever each man wanted. She turned herself into the perfect whore. She kept the men busy, kept them away from Olivia. And now Olivia Graves lived with that, with the guilt and the anger and the weird, unfinished jealousy. She lived with what her sister had become – had become for her sake – had become so that she could have the life she had.

Weiss opened his eyes. He stared at the windshield, at the pink glow on the glass from the sodium lights. It all felt like a weight on him just then. A great heavy weight, all of it. Bishop lying in the hospital, and the rage in the Shadowman's friendly voice, and Sissy's lovelorn weeping and thirteen-year-old Mary Graves forced to whore herself for a bunch of thugs to keep her ten-year-old sister safe. Weiss sat and stared at the windshield and he was weighted down by what people were, by the things people did to one another.

You think you understand everything, but you don't understand anything.

He closed his eyes again. What didn't he understand? How Julie knew where her father was when he was supposed to have deserted her to become a fugitive. Why Julie went on whoring now that Olivia was grown up and free. Who that fucking idiot was following him in the puke green Hyundai...

He woke up suddenly. He felt as if no time had passed at all. But there, beyond the rest stop bunker, were brown hills and a vista of slate-gray clouds above them. The dawn of a dismal day.

He dragged a hand over the thick stubble on his jaw. He yawned, looking in the sideview mirror. The green Hyundai was still there, for fuck's sake, nestled small amidst the giant semis like a tortoise sleeping with dinosaurs.

Weiss shook his head. *Who is this fucking idiot?* he wondered.

He pushed out of the car. Went around to the trunk.

Dug his toiletry kit from his traveling bag. Carried it into the bunker men's room. He pissed, shaved, brushed his teeth, washed his face. Then he went outside to take care of this Hyundai clown.

What was so fucking stupid about the guy was where he'd parked. With all those huge trucks around him, Weiss could get to the Hyundai easily without the driver seeing him. He took his time. Went back to his car. Tossed his toiletry kit back into the trunk. He walked over to the rest stop cabin and pretended to read the map hanging on its wall.

From there, it was easy to move behind the trucks. Enormous as he was, Weiss didn't even have to duck or stoop down or anything. He just strolled casually behind truck after truck and in a few seconds, he was right beside the Hyundai, ready to pounce.

Three steps in the open and he was at the car door. The idiot driver never saw him coming. The door wasn't even locked. Weiss yanked it open. He grabbed the driver by the shirt collar and yanked him out. He looked him in the face.

'Oh, for fuck's sake,' he said.

Exasperated, he shoved me against the side of the car.

40

'Oof. Ow,' I said.

Getting slammed into the Hyundai knocked the wind out of me. Also, I banged my elbow. It really hurt. Really. I rubbed it, wincing.

Weiss stared off into the mountains and the distant clouds. A cool wind moved over him, damp with the coming rain. He shook his head.

'Shit,' I said, rubbing my elbow. 'Am I, like, the worst private eye ever or what?'

'What the fuck are you doing? You dumb fuck. You're following me? What the fuck?'

'Bishop told Sissy you'd be killed if you did this alone,' I said.

Weiss gave a short laugh. 'So what? You want to get killed too?'

I looked down at my sneakers. 'I thought – you know, with Bishop out of commission – I thought maybe I could help out.'

All right, it sounded ridiculous even to me. But I couldn't tell him the whole truth. I couldn't tell him about Emma and what she'd said. I couldn't tell him how much I loved her and how she only wanted a man she could admire, and how I had to find some way to become admirable so she could love me back. I'd been thinking and thinking about it, thinking about what makes a man admirable, what makes him worthwhile. I'd been thinking about how you can feel worthwhile but if you really look at yourself maybe you're not. That's why I broke it off with Sissy. So I could be more honest, more worthwhile.

Then the news about Bishop came. Then I saw Bishop for myself, lying there on the bed, his face the color of death. I saw him and I kept thinking about what I had to do.

After that, I left the hospital. I went back to my puke colored Hyundai. I planned to get a hotel room and fly home, just as Sissy had told me to do.

But I didn't. I sat behind the wheel of the car instead. I looked out through the windshield. I watched the hospital for a long time. I saw one ambulance and another and another come screaming out of the desert city in rapid succession. I watched them pull up tight before the big glass emergency room doors. Attendants carried the sick out of the back on stretchers. And there were other attendants pushing sufferers in wheelchairs into the lobby too.

I could see the lobby through the glass. I could see the patients sitting in plastic chairs, waiting for their doctors. Their faces looked haggard. They looked pensive. They looked afraid. These were people, I told myself, who were kind and unkind to others in their lives, who cheated and played fair. They were people who worried about whether they were going to get promoted at their jobs and whether they were going to get home in time to watch their favorite television shows. They were people who argued over who was right and who left out the milk that had gone sour.

I didn't think they were worried about the milk or their promotions or their television shows now.

Which I guess brought my mind back to Bishop. Lying as I'd seen him, with that shocking, colorless face. And

Weiss too, sitting over him with his shoulders slumped and his wise, saggy features emaciated and gray. I thought about both of them and the things that had happened in these dramatic months since I had graduated university and come to work with them at the Agency. They were troubled men. I knew that. Weiss with his whores and his incurable solitude. Bishop with his penchant for violence, his cold heart. They were lost men in many ways. But I admired them. I admired them both.

I sat in my Hyundai and thought some more about what makes a man admirable.

Then, when Weiss came out of the hospital, I followed him.

I couldn't tell him any of that now, here in the rest stop in the Arizona desert. But of course, it was always difficult to figure out how much you had to tell him and how much he already knew.

In any case, he said, 'Get back in the car. Get out of here. This isn't a story. You could get hurt. Go home.'

'I don't want to go home,' I said. 'I know it's not a story. Let me help you.'

'You can't help me.'

'I'm not afraid,' I lied. 'Let me do something. Please.'

I thought that was it, it was over. I thought he was going to jam me back inside the car like he was packing an overstuffed suitcase. I thought he'd grab me by the scruff of the neck, shove me behind the wheel, and kick my ass for good measure before he slammed the door and sent me on my way.

To this day, I don't know what was going through his mind. Maybe he understood what it was I needed from him. Or maybe he simply saw that he could use me for his purposes. I don't know. But to my absolute amazement, he nodded once.

'All right,' he said. 'You wanna follow me? Follow

me. Only stay right behind me this time, so you're not so conspicuous.'

He went stomping angrily back to his car. I jumped – eagerly – into mine.

41

We drove north together out of Arizona. We wound through Nevada, through a glum wilderness, the sky gray the whole time, a long time, and nothing anywhere but dust and scrub and barbed wire. We stopped for gas in places that looked as if they rose out of the barren earth only once every century. We bought sandwiches wrapped in plastic, sandwiches made by people who had long since died. We never said a word to one another. We got out of our cars and gassed up and got back in our cars and drove on and never said a word. I kept the Taurus's rear bumper right in front of me. I hardly looked at anything else. I hardly saw the daylight rise and fall behind the clouds. I felt the night come quickly, but I wasn't sure when.

The hours passed. I had been excited for a while and fearful for a while, but now I was just tired and dazed with driving. I noticed a glow in the distance, a low dome of light below the clouds at the vanishing point. I didn't think much of it at first, but it turned to be a town. Soon the blackness at the car's windows was broken by a billboard, then a gas station, then a sign for a trailer park. Then the town rolled up over the edge of the land. Union City.

It started to rain as we came off the highway. Weiss stopped the Taurus at a red light on the main drag. I pulled up behind him. I turned on the windshield wipers. Peered through the sweep of them at a desolate stretch of road. Mournfully bland restaurants and motels, hole-in-the-wall casinos, car dealerships, mini-marts. Block after block of them, side by desperate side. I stared down the narrowing corridor, wondering what would happen next, waiting for the light to change.

The light changed, turned green. The Taurus edged forward. I followed. Weiss drove slowly. I could make out the shape of him through his rear window. He was scoping the buildings left and right, glancing down the side-streets left and right. It was hard to see anything much in the rain.

Finally, he pulled into a Mobil station. I pulled in behind him, although the Hyundai's tank was more than half full. A leathery local in a straw cowboy hat was pumping gas into his pickup. Weiss buzzed down his window.

'I'm looking for the House of Dreams,' he said.

The local smiled and pulled a toothpick from the side of his mouth. Pointed with it. 'Over on River Lane.' He winked. 'They call it Damnation Street.'

Damnation Street. I've never forgotten it. It was a little lane around the corner from the last motel on the drag, at the edge of town. It was a stretch of broken pavement going nowhere. It was lined with brothels on either side.

The brothels were shabby clapboards, with white walls and bright trim, bright red or bright blue. Most of them were built like houses. They had pitched roofs and covered porches outside the front doors. One was more in the style of a western saloon, brown, long, flat and low. Each had a neon sign of some sort, fizzing under the ridge of the roof or blinking in the window. *Jenny's Place. The Pussycat Lounge. Isabelle de Paris...* I remember I snorted when I saw that one. *Isabelle de Paris.*

It was early yet. A little after seven. But the slanted parking spaces at the curbsides were nearly full. There were all kinds of vehicles slotted in them. A jeep, an SUV, a Corvette, a luxury model Ford, a clutch of Harleys.

There was a separate, fenced-in parking area at the end of the lane set aside for tractor-trailers. That was crowded too.

I was still looking the place over when I was startled by a knock on my window. Weiss. Standing in the rain, wearing his trenchcoat, the water running down the crags in his face. I opened the window.

'I'm going into that one,' he said. He stuck his thumb at one of the white clapboards with red trim. Its name was written in a window in pink neon script: *The House of Dreams and Joy*.

I reached for the door handle.

'No,' he said, 'you stay here. I gotta see a girl and she may not want to see me. These places share muscle. If there's trouble, reinforcements'll come in from one of the others. Stay in the car. I'll take care of things inside. You watch for any tough guys moving in on me.'

I nodded. I knew I was supposed to be grim and determined, but I was secretly thrilled. This was great. This was exactly what I was looking for. The real deal. Adventure. Experience. The sort of thing you could make a story out of at dinner parties.

I said, 'You want me to give you the heads-up when they come?'

'No,' he said. 'I want you to stop them. Keep them out here till I'm finished.'

I meant to reply but somehow I didn't. I think I was going to say *What?* Or *How?* Or maybe just *Huh?* But somehow I didn't say any of those things. I just sat there, looking at him, with my lips parted.

'I'll need about five minutes once the shit starts flying. Keep them out here as long as you can.'

'Uh...' I finally said.

But by that time, Weiss was already moving across the pavement to the whorehouse door.

42

Weiss stepped up onto the porch and pushed into the brothel.

The House of Dreams and Joy was a dark tavern. Cheap paneling on the walls, a string or two of Christmas lights hanging from the ceiling. Horseshoes and metal cowboy cutouts hung here and there. There was a poster of a woman's lips. There was a painting of a naked woman on the bathroom door.

In front of him, two steps down, there was a sort of lounge, sunk deep in shadow. He could make out a tattered green sofa, some stuffed chairs, a pool table in an island of light. There were a couple of bikers playing pool.

There was a bar to his right. A hardcase cowboy was dealing beer from bottle to glass. A TV on the shelf behind him played *Monster Garage*, no sound. The mirror was rimmed with more Christmas lights.

By the jukebox nearby, there were a couple of high round tables. Three asscrack truckers, maybe four hundred pounds apiece, were sitting on stools at one of these tables, surrounding a pitcher of beer, clutching mugs. There was a small dance floor just beyond them, a raised platform with a metal pole for strippers. There was a whore there now, moving sleepily to the country music. She wore jeans cut off just under the crotch and a sparkly halter top. She was blonde and not half bad looking but no one paid any attention to her. She kept her clothes on. She kept her face expressionless.

A woman approached Weiss as he let the screen door slip shut behind him. She was in her fifties, short, with a pinched, gnarled and pleasantly vicious face under a curling red wig. She was wearing a colorless skirt and a dull brown cardigan. She had implants that made her breasts jut out from her like a pair of footballs.

'Wow, you're a big one,' she said. 'All right, let's line up for the gentleman, girls.'

She gestured, and from the shadows in the lounge, the figures of women began to emerge, began to come forward toward the light where Weiss was standing. He caught the glinting of their eyes. He saw the drifting filmy fabric of their robes.

He didn't like the setup.

'If you don't mind, I'll have a drink first,' he said. 'I'll be at the bar.'

'Sure. Suit yourself.' The woman gestured again, and the girls sunk back into the dark corners.

Weiss sat at the bar. The cowboy slapped a Rock in front of him. Almost at once, one of the girls appeared on the next stool over. That was more like it, one on one.

She was a little creature, with mouse brown hair, and the pale, eager face of a vampire. She was wearing a sheer nightgown with a black bra and panties underneath. She was trim but flabby around the middle, he noticed. She'd had a kid at some point, maybe a couple of them.

'Hi,' she said. 'I'm Eden.'

'I bet you are,' Weiss said pleasantly. He raised his glass, smiled down at her, going through the motions.

Eden went through the motions too, leaning forward, moving her hand onto his thigh. But now that she saw him up close, she caught sight of the cop in him. He could tell from her eyes. Their expression changed. They grew watchful.

'I'm looking for Kristy,' he told her. 'I was here a while back and we had a real nice party.'

Eden pretended to believe him. 'Kristy's partying with a guest right now,' she said.

Weiss shrugged. 'No hurry. I can wait.'

She lifted her chin. 'Let me see if I can find out when she'll be ready for you.'

She slipped off the stool. Holding his beer, he looked over his shoulder, watched her black panties move as she receded into the shadows of the lounge. Something was wrong, he could feel it. The girl was too smooth, as if she'd been waiting for him, as if she'd been told what to say.

Weiss sat at the bar, on edge. His eyes moved, taking in the lounge, the dancing girl by the table, the asscrack truckers knocking back their mugs of beer. He didn't know what he was looking out for, but he was looking out for something. Everything seemed okay though.

Slowly, he faced front.

The cowboy barkeep brought a broken pool cue whipping around at his head.

The cowboy was tall and lean. He was wearing jeans and a white shirt with buttons the color of pearl. The sleeves were rolled up high. He had ropy muscles in his forearms. He had meanness carved deep into the lines of his face. He struck with sinuous speed.

But Weiss was keyed up, ready. He saw the blow coming. He moved fast too, dodging back on his stool, his hands flying up at his sides. The pool cue hissed past his nose. It hit the glass in his hand and shattered it, sending a spray of yellow beer into the dim barlight.

On reflex, Weiss slashed with the broken glass in his hand. The shard ripped through the flesh of the cowboy's forearm like a knife ripping canvas. The cowboy snarled and jumped back. He crashed into the shelf behind him.

A red line sprouted between his wrist and his elbow. The pool cue dropped from his shaking fingers.

Weiss lunged over the bar at him. He grabbed a handful of the cowboy's hair with his right hand and yanked him forward. With his left hand gripping the cowboy's neck, he shoved him down with all the strength he had. The cowboy's face smacked into the bartop with a heavy, liquid thud. The impact crushed the cowboy's nose. Blood squirted over the polished wood. The cowboy shuddered. He became a dead weight in Weiss's grip. Weiss released him. The cowboy slid off the bar and dropped to the floor.

Weiss turned quickly. Was there anyone else? It didn't look like it. The truckers were watching him from their table. One of them scratched his chin. Another drank his beer. The girl on the stage behind them had stopped dancing and just stood there, expressionless as before, while the country music played.

In the lounge, at the pool table, in the island of light, one biker leaned on his stick, frowning in Weiss's direction. The other knocked the nine ball into the far corner.

Weiss let his breath out. His hand stung. He glanced at the mess of it. The broken glass had lanced the web between thumb and finger. The blood was rolling out of the cut. It covered his palm. He looked around for a napkin or a bar towel, something to staunch the flow. But now a movement in the shadows caught his eye.

It was the madam, the woman with the red hair and football tits. She was peeking out of an office door near the entryway. She had a phone at her ear.

'Ah, shit,' said Weiss.

He pushed away from the bar, his stool scraping over the floor. He came around the end of the bar until he could look out the window. Sure enough, two more cowboys had just come out of the western saloon-style brothel across the street. They were striding through the rain toward the House of Dreams and Joy, kicking broken pavement and mud with their pointed boots.

Weiss moved fast, heading deeper into the shadows.

43

The minute I saw them, I knew they were the men I was waiting for: these two cowboys charging out of the saloon. Six feet apiece. Both in jeans and plaid shirts. One guy squinty and barrel-chested, the other with a shaved head on broad shoulders. They both had pale eyes, almost white eyes, glinting with a cruel delight in violence. They were moving fast through the rain toward the House of Dreams.

I sat in the puke green Hyundai and watched them through the rain-streaked windshield as they came. I knew I was supposed to get out and challenge them, but it didn't look like a very good idea. Instead, I tried to convince myself that they might not be who they obviously were, might not be the enforcers Weiss had warned me about. Perhaps they were just customers of the local establishments, said I to my inner man. Perhaps they were just two jolly companions out for a harmless spree among the ladies of the evening. How can one tell, I inquired philosophically, who is a mere reveler and who is a murderous thug come to beat the living daylights out of one's friend?

This is how intellectuals stay out of fistfights. They convince themselves the situation is complex. It's much safer than acknowledging the simple right and wrong of the thing, the need for immediate action.

It's safer, but it's not admirable. And as I was there to become admirable, and as there was no room for me to become any less admirable than I already was, I somehow forced myself to push my way out of the car, to step in front of the porch of the House of Dreams and to plant my tremulous body between these two charging gorillas and the front door they were charging at.

I won't discourse at length upon my fear. Suffice it to say there was a lot of it. My muscles felt gelatinous. My aforementioned inner man had suddenly assumed the stature of a crap-assed, squawling three-year-old. Still, I tried to bolster my confidence. I told myself all was not lost. How much of the outcome of such situations depends on a man's approach to them, after all? How much can be accomplished with the right attitude, a powerful façade? If I could put on a good front, if I could act, I mean, a bit like Bishop, cool and deadly like Bishop, or authoritative and just and inexorable like Weiss, surely these men would hesitate before attempting to get past me. If I could dominate them enough with my sheer presence, perhaps I could even keep them harmlessly at bay for the five minutes Weiss needed inside.

So – quivering within though I was – I set my face as if my soul were made of iron. I hooked my thumbs in my belt. I smiled – I actually smiled a slow, easy, dangerous-looking Bishop-style smile – as the two men pulled to a stop in front of me.

'Sorry, gentlemen,' I said quietly. 'I can't let you go in there just yet.'

Now here's an interesting thing some of you may not know about getting punched in the head. It is thoroughly unnerving. It's not just painful – though, take my word, it is extraordinarily painful. It also completely alters your worldview. In a single instant, you are transformed from a person of varied, multi-dimensional interests to a person whose sole interest on earth is not getting punched in the head ever again. A man's principles, a woman's virtue, a lifelong dedication to the good – all of them, I'm convinced, are susceptible to a good punch in the head. In fact, this is why head-punching is generally acknowledged to be impermissible in a free society and why people who do it must, after civil discussion and agreement, be punched in the head back.

Unfortunately, I was no longer in any condition to implement such retaliatory measures. Because one of these monkeys – the one with the shaved head – had just socked me in the side of the face with a fist the size of a very big fist.

I went reeling backward. My ankle hit the edge of the House of Dreams' raised porch. Down I fell, my backside landing hard on the wooden platform. The barrel-chested ape kicked me in the side for good measure. Then both men stepped over me, heading for the door.

It was now no longer my goal to stop these guys or to help Weiss. My only goal was not to get punched in the head anymore. It was a good goal – I think so even today. But was it admirable? No, I couldn't say that it was.

So I scrambled to my feet. I leapt upon the rear man – the barrel-chested man – grabbing him by the belt and collar. The attack took him by surprise – hell, it took me by surprise. Though my head was ringing like a church-tower bell, though my eyes felt as if they were rattling in my skull like dice, I was able to swing the bigger man around, and hurl him off the porch so that he tripped and fell into the mud and concrete.

I stumbled off the porch after him. I regained my balance just in time to see the shaven-headed thug turn away from the door and come for me. He hit me in the stomach first and, when I bent over with my lunch in my throat, he really clobbered me with another one of those head punches.

I have a hard time remembering much about what

happened after that, but I think I know the gist of it. The barrel-chested guy got to his feet and kicked me a couple of times in revenge. Then, muttering with annoyance, both men headed for the door again.

And I got up again and went after them.

A pattern developed. Again and again and, yes, again, I flung myself ineffectually at these two sadistic gorillas. Again and again and, yes, again, they hammered me to the damp earth and kicked me where I lay beneath the pattering rain. Then we repeated the process. I don't know how many times. By the end, I think, these guys were staying around just to watch the show. Standing there with their hands on their hips, shaking their heads in disbelief, laughing in wonder, as I clawed my way up off the pavement one more time in order to stagger towards them and get myself pummeled and battered and kicked back down.

So it was, in that rainy Nevada backwater, that I became admirable, beaten to jelly in the mud outside a whorehouse door, trying to buy Weiss another second, another minute, to do whatever it was he had to do.

44

Weiss went down the brothel stairs, into the lounge, into the shadows. He grabbed the little madam by the arm and dragged her out of her office. The blood from his hand stained the sleeve of her brown cardigan.

'Hey,' she snarled at him.

'Shut up,' said Weiss. 'Where's Kristy?'

Her eyes flitted to the front door. She was waiting for the two enforcers to arrive from across the lane.

Weiss gripped her arm hard, dragged her closer.

'You're hurting me!'

'Come on,' he said. He shook her. Her football tits stood solid, never wobbled, but her wig came askew, curls covering one eye.

'In the back,' she told him.

'What room?'

'I don't know.'

She knew. He glanced out the door. He saw the enforcers charging. He saw me step in front of them. He figured he didn't have much time. He shoved the madam away.

He plunged deeper into the shadowy lounge. From the corner of his eye, he caught the flutter of fabric on every side of him as girls drew back against the walls. In the center of the room, in the island of light, the two bikers stood straight, holding their pool cues – ready, in a casual sort of way, to beat him to death if the need arose. But he went right by them. They let him pass.

He saw the door at the rear. He went for it. He tried the doorknob. It wouldn't turn. He looked over his shoulder. The enforcers were now pounding me into the mud. He didn't think it would take them long to finish up. He faced front, lifted his foot, and planted a kick just beneath the knob.

The door flew in. He was through.

Now he was in a hallway lit by red light. There were doors on either side of him. He grabbed the nearest knob. Threw the door open. Went to the next door. Threw that open too. He marched down the hall to the next door, then the next. He threw the doors open. In each room, he saw what he saw – quick, chaotic. Tumbling glimpses of raw human meat hinged together. A half second of flesh and confusion, the red light bathing everything. There were snarls and cries. A woman on her hands and knees. A man shackled to bedposts. Dark circles of wide open mouths. Damp patches of pubic hair. Straining limbs, straining faces. Scalding nakedness without tenderness or glamor. Nakedness like a blow.

Voices rose around him. Men shouted threats. Women spat rough, ugly curses. The smell of sweat and sex washed over him. The red light washed over him.

He kept going. Any second he expected the enforcers to barge in behind him, to grab him, beat him down, drag him out. But they didn't come so he kept on. Storming down the hall. Throwing open doors. A woman on her knees, her face impaled. A fat man squatting. A trio of sodomists tangled in a mess of flesh.

Then, up ahead of him, near the end of the corridor, one door opened on its own. A whore in spangled red panties stepped out to see what the commotion was. She was young, maybe thirty. A sharp face framed with long hair dyed blonde. A small body, painfully thin but with large round breasts, implants, bare. She saw Weiss.

Startled fear came into her eyes. That's what gave her away.

He pulled up short, his heart pounding, his lungs working hard. He and the whore looked at each other. Shouts and cries and curses filled the air around them.

'You talk to me or you talk to him,' Weiss told her, breathless. 'You know who's following me, right? You talk to me or you talk to him.'

The fear in the whore's eyes turned to terror.

Then the lounge door banged open and the two enforcers rushed in.

The whore glanced around Weiss's shoulder. He turned to follow the glance and saw the enforcers at the end of the hall. They were lined up shoulder to shoulder to block his way. They were pressing their big fists into their big palms. Their pale eyes were gleaming. They were getting ready to come for him.

But they were too late. Weiss had already said what he had to say. He turned back to the whore.

'It's all right,' she told the two thugs. She lifted her chin. 'Forget it. It's all right.'

Weiss took another look at them. The light died in their eyes. He smiled. The enforcers punched their palms, turned around and went back through the door, and were gone.

The other doors began slamming shut all along the corridor. The cursing stopped. A murmuring quiet fell over the hallway. Finally, Weiss was alone in the red light with the bare-breasted whore. Kristy.

'Come on,' she said.

She slipped back into her room. He followed her.

45

There was a little fat man hopping around the middle of the floor. He was pulling his jockey shorts over his legs, then up to cover his bare ass. When Weiss came in, he grabbed the rest of his clothes off a chair and held them against his chest. Weiss stood aside and the man carried his clothes out into the hall without saying a word.

Weiss shut the door on him. He faced the girl in the red spangled panties.

They were in a narrow box of a room. The bed, a queen size, almost filled it. There was a two-drawer bedside table with a lamp and a radio and a vase of flowers on it. There was a window, covered with blinds, and with some kind of lacy stuff draped over the top of it. Betadine, baby wipes, condoms, and a pair of fur-covered handcuffs were piled discreetly in a little wicker basket in a corner on the floor. A cheap blanket – a trick towel – lay over the floral bedspread. It had a gray stain at the center of it.

Weiss went to the basket. Reached in, pulled out a baby wipe. He swabbed the blood off his hand. The cut wasn't deep. The bleeding was almost done.

He lifted his chin at the whore. He was still out of breath. 'Listen...' he said.

Tense, the whore gestured to the bedside table. Weiss looked. He saw the lamp, the radio, the vase. But he knew how these places worked. There was an intercom in one of the drawers. The madam would sit in her office and listen in while her whores negotiated the price of their party. That way, the madam knew the girls weren't holding back her share.

'I guess everyone can listen then,' he said.

'I don't want any trouble,' said the whore.

'Yeah, I got that message.'

'I mean, you know…'

He nodded curtly. He knew. She didn't want the Shadowman coming after her. She'd tell him whatever he wanted to hear as long as he would keep the killer away.

He looked down at her. He felt suddenly weary. He was weary at the sight of her, skinny as some child on a charity poster, but with that fake blonde hair and those fake tits hanging out as if she didn't give a damn. He could see how scared she was. Julie had warned her he was coming and had warned her about the killer trailing in his wake. She was scared as hell, and Weiss was using that to get her to talk. That made him feel weary too.

The killer's right, he thought. *We make a good team.*

'Olivia called you,' he said.

She nodded eagerly, her sharp ferret features going up and down fast. He wished she'd cover herself.

He tossed the bloody wipe back into the basket. 'Just tell me where Julie is and I'll get out of here.'

The hooker's shoulders came up around her ears. 'Christ, I don't know that. She doesn't tell me that. She just calls.'

'You mean she hasn't called since you talked to Olivia?'

'Right. Not since her sister. Right.'

'So that's why you had them set the muscle on me.'

'I didn't know what to do. Olivia told me you were coming and I didn't know what I was supposed to do. I was scared if you came then… you know… he would come too…'

'So you didn't give Julie her sister's message.'

'She hasn't called,' the whore said again. She was almost pleading.

Weiss rubbed his eyes. Weary. 'She's gonna call you though, right?'

The girl looked around as if she'd find the answer in the little room somewhere. 'I guess so. I guess. I don't know. How can I know? She always does.'

Weiss had his breath back finally. His heart was slowing down. 'All right. I get you. It's all right.'

'She just hasn't called. I'd tell you. I would.'

'All right. I get you. It's all right.' His eyes went around the room as he thought it over. 'I saw a motel on the way in,' he said. 'The Frontier.'

'Yeah, sure,' said the whore. 'I know the Frontier.'

'Call me there. When she calls you, you call me there.'

'Okay. Okay, I will, I swear.'

'And tell her what I said, what her sister told you. She can play it either way. She can stay or go.'

'I will. I'll tell her. And look, this guy...'

'He won't touch you. Just do what I tell you, you'll be fine.'

'I will. I'll call you as soon as I hear. I swear.' She was that afraid of the killer. She'd do anything Weiss told her.

'All right,' he said. He looked at her. He couldn't keep his eyes from going down to her naked tits. She responded with a gesture. It was just a small motion of her hand, but he knew she was offering herself to him. That's how scared she was. She'd do anything.

'Just tell her,' said Weiss. 'She can wait for me or not. Stay or go. Either way, this is the end of it.'

46

A few minutes later, I felt his hand on my arm. He hauled me up out of the mud. He set me on my feet. I swayed there, blinking out through swollen eyes.

'Nice going, kid,' Weiss said. 'You held them. Nice going.'

I nodded stupidly. I swiped a handful of blood and snot off my upper lip. Threw it down onto Damnation Street.

Weiss snorted. 'You all right? Can you breathe?'

I tried it. I clutched my ribs. They hurt when I inhaled. 'Yeah,' I gasped.

'You're all right,' said Weiss.

I grunted. I massaged my jaw. It hurt when I tried to talk.

'You gonna be all right to drive?' he asked me.

I nodded again, wincing. I rubbed the back of my head. It hurt when I did nothing.

'All right,' said Weiss. 'Well, listen, drive the hell out of here. Don't stay in town. Head west, for Reno. Keep to the interstate. You gotta puke or pass out or something, pull over. First motel you see, go in and wash yourself up. Sleep it off. Go home.'

I clutched my ribs and then my face and then my ribs again. I began to shuffle slowly toward my car.

Weiss took my arm, held me up, helped me along. 'Don't worry,' he said. 'It'll feel much worse in the morning.'

I laughed – then cried out in pain.

He opened the Hyundai's door. He lowered me into the seat behind the wheel. I sat there, staring. After a while, I turned on the ignition. Then I sat there, staring some more.

Finally, when I could, I turned. I looked up at Weiss. He looked in at me through the window.

'All right?' he said.

'Yeah,' I said.

'Nice going, kid,' he said again. 'Get out of here.'

I put the car in gear and drove away, heading for the interstate.

Weiss went on alone.

PART SIX

The Midnight Nowhere

47

He came to the middle of nowhere at midnight. He'd been driving for hours through the rain.

He'd spent a night and a day at the Frontier, the Union City motel, waiting for the hooker's call. Lying on the bed, staring at the ceiling, staring at the water running down the window panes, staring at the TV news. It was a long night and a long day. He tried not to think about what was coming, but he did think about it. He thought about how it had felt to have the killer close to him in the airport. He thought about how they would be close again, soon.

Then the phone rang and it was the hooker from the House of Dreams, Kristy. It was sunset by then. Weiss sat on the edge of the bed. He held the phone to his ear. He watched the windows as the lifeless daylight went out of them and the streams of rain began to glitter in the beams of headlights passing on the main drag outside. He listened to the whore's instructions. There would be a house at the end of the drive, she said. Julie would come to him there. She wouldn't run away. She would stay, and that's where they would finish it.

Weiss put the phone back in the cradle. He sat and watched the blackness at the window, the glittering lines of water on the glass. Finally, he pushed off his knees and stood. He pulled his shoulder holster off the back of a chair, slipped it on, secured the .38 beneath his arm. He pulled his trenchcoat on over it. He went out to his car.

He drove north as the whore had told him. North and then east. The roads got smaller and smaller, each smaller road coming off the larger one before it as if they were the branches of a tree. The last road was nothing but broken macadam and stretches of dirt. Rain on the pavement, mud in the spaces between. Nothing, just nothing, on either side. Nothing in front of him, nothing behind. Weiss started to wonder if the whore had sent him wrong. If the killer had gotten to her and she'd sent him out of the way.

Then there it was, just as she said it would be: a town – or a cluster of houses anyway, houses and trailers huddled together in the dirt at the base of a hill. There was no road sign to announce its presence. The place didn't even seem to have a name. The first he knew of it were the shadows at his window: an ancient gas station, an autobody shop, a small hotel – all closed up, all dark. Behind them, there was a small grid of paved lanes tapering into dust and dead ends. Weiss couldn't imagine what the place was doing here. But here it was, the middle of nowhere.

He followed the whore's directions. He drove the Taurus down a street, then down another street. He found the house midway between one corner and the next. It was small, a run-down, gray one-story with fake brick siding. There was a patch of lawn, a couple of aspens growing up around it. The aspens grew straight and stood tall above the low roof.

He parked the car in front of the house. Buzzed down the window. He could hear the aspen leaves whispering in the rain.

He sat and watched the place. It was dark. It had a big front window by the door and a smaller window off to one side. Blinds were drawn down over both windows. There was no light behind the blinds.

He sat like that while midnight came and went. His eyes moved over the area. The other houses all around were dark – dark shapes with no lighted windows. There were cars parked along the street, all empty. There was no light anywhere. There were no signs of life at all.

His thoughts went to the killer. There had been no trace of him on the roads coming here. He might've come ahead. He might already be sitting in one of the parked cars along the street. Or he might be inside the house, waiting for Weiss in the darkness.

Weiss made a noise. He was angry at himself for being so afraid. But there it was: he wanted to go on living, like anyone.

Grunting, he pushed the door open. He hoisted his big body out of the car.

The aspens whispered louder as a soft wind blew. He felt the wind on his face. He felt the rain in his hair. He walked heavily up the front path to the gray wooden door. He tried the knob. The door swung open. He stepped into the house.

He stood very still in the deep shadows just within the threshold. He scanned the unlit room, trying to pick out shapes. He saw a sofa maybe, maybe a chair, a lamp. It was very dark. He wasn't sure of anything.

After a while, he realized he'd been holding his breath, waiting for the blow to fall. He let the breath out. He found the lightswitch on the wall beside him. He flipped it up. A dull yellow light went on in the ceiling. He looked around.

He was in a small living room. Scarred paneled walls. A yellow sofa and a brown chair. A phone on a phone table. A television set on a stand. A wooden floor with a braid rug worn raw.

There was a coffee table in front of the sofa. There was a mug on the table, a yellow mug with brown coffee scum at the bottom of it. There was lipstick on the rim of the mug. That got to him – her lipstick.

He checked out the rest of the house, turning lights on as he went. There was a kitchen off to the right. Linoleum counters, and scarred wooden cabinets. A cardtable set up in a corner with a couple of folding chairs. A couple of windows looking out the side of the house and one on the front, that smaller one he'd seen from outside.

There was a door here with another window, this one uncovered. He twisted the knob. This door was unlocked too. He held it open. Outside, there was a small alley of turf separating this house from the next. The alley led one way to a small patch of backyard, the other way to the front of the house. He could hear the rain falling into the alley grass.

He closed the door. He turned out the light and left the kitchen. He walked back across the living room to the bedroom on the other side of the house.

There was a double bed in here with a white crocheted bedspread skewed to one side. There was a closet with a few skirts and blouses hanging in it, two pairs of shoes and a pair of sneakers on the floor. There was a faint scent of a woman coming off the clothing. Her scent. That got to him too.

He went into the bathroom. There was makeup all around the sink. A toothbrush in a dirty glass. A hairbrush. Strands of hair in the bristles. Julie's red-gold hair.

He went back into the bedroom, switched off the lights. Now the light in the living room was the only light still burning. Weiss went to the threshold between the two rooms. He stood there, looking over the living room again.

He could feel her presence in the house – Julie's presence. She'd made sure he would know she'd been here.

The lipstick on the coffee mug, the hair in the brush, the scent: she had not been gone long. Weiss felt almost as if she were standing next to him, speaking to him, trying to tell him something. She had been here and she had gone out, waiting for him to come – waiting to make sure he was the one who came. Then she would return and draw out the killer. That's how he figured it. That's what he figured she was trying to say.

But there was something else too. His eyes kept scanning the lighted room. There was something else she wanted him to know. He could feel it. The lipstick on the coffee mug, the hair in the brush... She'd had time to choose this place, this house. She had chosen it knowing he would come, knowing it was where they would finish it. She had chosen it for a reason. She had left him something, something he could use.

Then he saw the trapdoor. It was cut into the wooden floor. It was hard to make out. It blended with the floorboards and only a small section of it stuck out from under the braid rug. It ended just in front of the coffee table. The mug – the mug with her lipstick on it – marked the spot.

He stepped to it. He stooped down. He found the iron ring embedded in the wood. He lifted the trap. The smell of damp earth came up to him from the square opening.

There was a steep, rickety wooden staircase. He had to back down it, as if it were a ladder. A string brushed his face as he descended. He pulled the string. A naked bulb went on. He looked over his shoulder and saw a dirt cellar. There were some empty boxes down there, an empty suitcase. Nothing else.

He killed the light. He climbed back up. Closed the trapdoor. He left the rug askew so that the trap was easier to find, easier to get to.

He went to the wall and pressed the lightswitch down.

The little house settled back into darkness. There was silence except for the rain pattering softly on the roof.

Weiss felt his way across the room until his fingers lit on the ridged upholstery of the armchair, next to the phone table.

He settled himself into the armchair, facing the front door. He reached into his trenchcoat and drew out his .38.

He waited.

48

The man who called himself John Foy waited. He was in the brown Taurus parked on the street. He had watched Weiss arrive. He had watched him go inside the gray house. Now he was sitting motionless in the dark, watching the house through the rain-streaked windows of his car.

He had his briefcase open on the seat beside him. He had the computer on. He had the monitor light turned low so it would not give him away. He could see Weiss's heat outline on the infrared readout. He could see Weiss sitting in the armchair, see him right through the walls. He could see that Weiss was alone.

He waited for Julie Wyant. He knew she would come soon. Already, he could imagine the touch of her skin and the scent of her. He could almost hear the sound of her sobbing and taste her tears. He was excited. There was a sort of low thrumming through his whole body.

It was a good feeling. He was not afraid at all. He knew he was going to die soon, but somehow it didn't bother him. It wouldn't be tonight anyway. Tonight, he would kill Weiss. He would make Julie watch while he did it. He would make Weiss into something that disgusted her and then he would finish him. Then she would know he was all there was for her. He was everything in her life.

Then he would take her away. He had a place all ready for her. It was a cabin in Colorado, in the mountains, in the woods. He had used it before. No one ever came near. He would keep her there for as long as she lived. Days, weeks. She might last for months even, if he did it right. Then she would die and, when he was done with her, he would die too. It would be good, he thought. They would die there together. He was excited about it. It was the reason he had done everything he had done.

He had never felt the same things other men felt. He knew that. Passing, unseen, invisible, down streets, through parks, through malls, he'd seen how other men were with women. He'd seen men holding women's hands, kissing them, leaning toward their lips across a table. He'd seen men in movies, their faces moving toward a woman's face on screen. He knew there was something they were feeling that he didn't feel, something they were doing that he couldn't do. He tried not to think about it, but he did think about it. Sometimes it felt as if he never thought about anything else.

Then he met Julie. She was like someone he had made up for himself. She was like someone he thought about when he was alone in his room. He could hardly believe how perfect she was, how much she was what he wanted. That time he was with her – that one time – it was exactly like daydreams he'd had. Watching her twist in his hands, hearing her cry out, he had thought: now – now, he was feeling what other men felt. And he knew even at that moment, he would do anything to feel that way again.

He had begged her to come with him. He had told her he loved her. She had laughed. Still sobbing, she had laughed. Then she had run away. And he knew he would do anything to find her.

He watched the house. He watched the computer. Weiss sat still, sat where he was. That was good. The man who called himself John Foy had checked the house out before Weiss arrived. There were only two doors, the front door and the one in the kitchen. He didn't think Weiss would have time to get to the kitchen but if he did, Foy would get him when he tried to come back in the front. Meanwhile, he was glad to have Weiss's company. They were in this together. Waiting for her together.

It didn't take long. A movement caught the corner of his eye. He turned and looked down the street. A car came toward him, headlights off. He couldn't tell what make it was. It parked half a block away against the opposite curb. The door opened. The top light went on. He saw a woman slipping out from behind the wheel.

As she rose from her seat, he could see it was Julie Wyant.

He only glimpsed her for a second. She had a kerchief tied around her head. She had a raincoat with the collar pulled up to her ears. He could see her face. He could see her hair beneath the kerchief. Then she stepped out of the car into the night. She closed the car door and the light went out.

The man who called himself John Foy had to breathe deep to steady himself. The sight of her brought images into his mind in a dizzying rush. It was too much. It made him feel weak and unsteady. He wanted to climb into his tower and breathe the high, blue air until the rush of pictures and emotions went away.

But there wasn't time. She was walking toward the house. He could hear the heels of her shoes on the pavement. She was walking quickly, her body tense, her eyes scanning the night. He smiled. She knew he was here and she was frightened.

The man who called himself John Foy took a last look at the monitor. Weiss was still there, still alone, still sitting where he had been. He knew he had to time this right, just right. He had to give Weiss no chance to move, no chance to try anything.

Julie Wyant reached the house's front walk. She turned onto it. She walked quickly toward the door, glancing left and right and over her shoulder.

The killer watched her. He felt strange, light-headed. He had waited for her so long – and he loved her.

Now she was at the house. At the front door. Reaching for the knob.

The man who called himself John Foy drew the 9mm out from beneath his overcoat. He opened the car door silently.

49

Jim Bishop opened his eyes. He had to get to Weiss. He had to get to the house in the middle of nowhere or Weiss would die.

He didn't know where he was at first. He had come from darkness into darkness. He had come from somewhere black inside himself into a room that was deep gray with shadow. He was aware of vague rhythms. The click and whisper and peep of machines. His own body, heartbeat, pulse and breath. He felt he had been away from all this for a long time.

Now things came clear. The rhythms, the noises, the blurred shapes in the shadows. There was a bed, tubes, chairs. He was in a hospital room. There was a woman in one of the chairs. She had a newspaper on her lap. Her head was down on her chest. She was sleeping. He recognized her. Sissy.

Bishop felt a rush of energy. The sight of Sissy reminded him who he was. He remembered how he had come to Phoenix, how he had been shot in the hotel. He remembered the fall from the hotel window, the certainty that he was dying, dying.

But he had not died. That was the point. He was alive in the shadowy room.

And he had to get to Weiss. He didn't know how he knew this, but he did. He didn't know how he knew about the house in the middle of nowhere, but he knew that too. And he knew it was urgent. Everything depended on him. He had to get to the house or Weiss would die.

He lost consciousness again, faded from the surface of the world. Even then, the sense of urgency stayed with him. He fought his way back. He forced his eyes open. He tried to remember how things were. Some of it tumbled into place and some of it wouldn't. The sickening sense that he had failed – that came back to him, all right. He had been trying to help Weiss but the Shadowman had set a trap for him and he had walked into it like a prize idiot. That much came back to him, but the rest... There was something he had to say, something he had to tell Weiss that would save him. But what was it? And the house. How did he know about the house? How was he supposed to find it? He tried to remember, but there was nothing. All that was gone.

It didn't matter. He had to start moving. Start moving and he would remember. He would find a way.

So he tried to move. What a comedy that turned out to be. He felt as if he were a tiny little stick figure Bishop trapped inside a full-sized Bishop, trying to lift the full-sized man with his tiny little stick figure strength. There was no chance.

But somehow he had to do it. He had to get to the house, to Weiss. He tried again. He focused on his hand. He closed it into a fist. It took a long time, the fingers slowly curling, clenching. Afterward, he fell back inside himself, exhausted. It didn't matter. He had to keep trying. He didn't know what time it was, but he knew there was no time to fuck around.

He went back to work at it. It took... he didn't know how long. He felt the sweat bead on his forehead. He felt the weakness open at his core like a hole. Slowly, slowly, he filled his hollow muscles with his will. He lifted his arm. He reached across himself. He clawed at the tubes that seemed to snake into his flesh from somewhere in the shadows above him. With a hoarse gasp of pain, he dragged the tubes out of himself. He flung them aside. They sprayed drops of clear fluid and drops of red blood over the white sheets.

Then Bishop sat up. He found his clothes. He got dressed. It was a desperately long process, desperately long and slow. Lucky for him he wasn't there for a lot of it. It came to him in strobic flashes of consciousness. Between the flashes, there was only weakness, nausea, black-outs. He didn't feel pain – not pain in one place or another. It was all pain. Pain was the air he breathed.

But now, somehow, it was done. He discovered himself sitting on the edge of the bed. He was panting, sweating, sick – but he had his jeans pulled on and a t-shirt pulled down over his bandages.

He swallowed. He turned his head. Sissy was still there, still sleeping. She hadn't moved.

Bishop began to think about standing. It was not a happy thought. He was bigger inside than he had been, bigger than the little stick figure man he was before. But still. It was an awfully long way to his feet. An even longer way to the door. And a long way to fall if he didn't make it.

Minutes went by. He sat there, sick just thinking about it. He tried to gather his strength for the effort.

Finally, he wrapped his hand around the rail at the foot of the bed. He pushed himself up. All the pain in the world suddenly spun down in a vortex to center in his belly. Bishop grimaced at the agony, his mouth open, his teeth bare. Bent over, he clung to the bedrail with both hands, trying not to tumble to the floor. He breathed hard. He breathed back the pain. Then, with a low growl, he launched himself in the direction of the door.

Now he was traveling down the hospital hallway. It seemed a weird and ghostly place. Nurses and aides floated by him like white phantoms. The walls fogged and melted from the edges of his consciousness. The floor sloped down into misty nothing. He stumbled along it as if drawn by gravity. At one point, he must've passed a mirror. He saw his own face. Horrible, horrible. Corpse-white with faint under-traces of corpse-green. The eyes had sunk down into two dark holes. He was afraid some-one would notice him looking like that, afraid someone would try to stop him and take him back to bed. But no one did. He stumbled on.

The next thing he knew he was somewhere else, some-where in the night, moving through the night. Everything was shaking, rumbling. He became aware of nausea, an awful dryness in his mouth, awful pain. Then there was the noise. A rushing, whispered roar all around him. His eyes came open suddenly. He saw a strip of light pass over the leg of his jeans. He tried to lift his head off his chest. He managed to hoist it up, then it rolled back against some sort of seat.

He was in the cab of a truck. Out through the wind-shield, he saw two-lane blacktop in the headlights. How had he gotten here? He tried to remember. An image came into his mind. He saw himself stumbling along the side of a road. He remembered how grateful he had been for the cool night air on his cheeks because it kept him from fainting. Now he was in a truck. He must have managed to hitch a ride.

He rolled his head to one side so he could see the driver. The lights of an oncoming car passed over the cab. He saw the driver in the light. By an odd coinci-dence, the driver happened to be an alien monster from a comic book he had read as a child. He had yellow eyes and a long red snout with sharp teeth bared in a drooling grin. This worried Bishop in a distant sort of way. Maybe he had died trying to leave the hospital and this demon had been sent to drive him down to Hell.

His head rolled back on the seat. His gorge rose. He thought he would vomit for sure. The light passed and the cab sank back into darkness. Bishop closed his eyes. That couldn't be right about the demon, he thought. That didn't make any sense. He looked again and, in fact, the driver was not a demon after all. He was a fat white guy with a round bald head and a long, wispy red-blond beard. That was better. He lay back again. He closed his eyes again.

Now all he had to do was remember the other thing. What was he supposed to tell Weiss? It started to come back to him. The hotel. The egg-shaped man in the Hawaiian shirt. The specialist had had nowhere to hide a gun, but he had had a gun. The Saracen.

That was it. The Shadowman's plan. He was planning for Weiss to outsmart him. He was planning for Weiss to take his gun away, to take two of his guns. But he had a third gun, the Saracen, that he could hide where no one would find it.

'This the place?'

The driver's rough voice startled him out of sleep. He felt as if he had slept for a long time. He felt better, stronger. He opened his eyes.

The truck had stopped somewhere in the dark. Bishop looked out the window. There was a house out there, a silhouette in the night. How had he gotten here? How had he known to tell the driver where to go?

Confused, he looked at the driver. The driver inclined his bald pate toward the house.

'That the one?'

Bishop wiped his lips with his hand. He looked out the window again. Was that the house? How could he know?

But he must've told the driver how to get here. He must've known the way in his unconscious somehow.

'Thanks,' he croaked.

'You take care of yourself,' the driver told him.

Bishop shoved the door open, shouldered it open with a grunt. It took all his strength. He began the long, difficult climb down from the high cab to the pavement.

He stood in front of the house. He was swaying like a sapling in a swirling breeze. Behind him, the truck drove away into the night. Bishop started up the house's front walk.

He did not feel like a tiny stick figure anymore. He filled his own body. But there was no strength in him. He was weak, so weak. He drove himself forward step by staggering step. He saw the house lurching and swaying in front of him, looming closer. It was a sickening sight. It filled him with fear. Was he too late? Was it over already? Was Weiss already dead?

He kept walking. He reached the door. He pushed inside.

He could see the shapes of things. Furniture in a room. Table, chair, sofa. No one was there. He felt sick, so sick and weak and full of fear. He wanted to lie down on the floor and go to sleep again. Where was everyone?

Then he saw the door. Somehow, he knew that's where he had to go. How did he know? Who had told him? He remembered a voice whispering in his ear. But whose voice? Who was it?

He didn't know. But he knew what he had to do. He staggered to the door. There was a handle on it. He grabbed hold of it. The door was heavy, hard to move. He didn't know where he found the muscle-power to haul it open, but he did, shouting out with the pain and the effort.

He stood, panting, on the threshold. He couldn't tell

what was real anymore and what wasn't. He was so sick, so weak, so miserable. Everything seemed so weird, so far away. Maybe none of it was real. The cellar stairs, for instance: they seemed to wind down and down forever. He didn't think the stairway was real. He didn't see how it could be. But he wasn't sure. He wasn't sure about his tears either. He felt them, hot, streaking his cheeks, but he didn't know if they were really there.

He went spiraling down and down the stairs impossibly. Finally, he stumbled out onto a cellar floor of packed dirt. Dazed and ill, he looked around, trying to get his bearings. A door slammed, startling him. He looked up. The stairs were just wooden stairs now. And the door at the top of the flight was shut. As Bishop stood there looking at it, he smelled gasoline. Gasoline was spilling down through the door, running down the stairs, dripping onto the cellar floor. The specialist had outsmarted him again, had caught him again. Bishop understood what was going to happen next a second before it did.

The gas caught fire. Of course. Flames spread over the cellar ceiling, and down the stairs, blocking the way out.

Bishop stood squinting up at the flames. He knew this was real. He was trapped down here. And Weiss – where the hell was Weiss?

He turned to scan the cellar. There he was. He saw Weiss's body in the hectic light from the flames. Weiss was lying on the dirt cellar floor. He was lying on his side, one hand stretched up over his head, one resting in front of him. Bishop might have thought he was sleeping there, but for the blood that had run out of the center of him. It was pooled in the packed dirt, black in the firelight.

'Weiss.' Bishop tried to shout the word but it was barely a rasp. He staggered across the cellar to him. He caught hold of a support beam, wrapped his arm around it. He slid down the beam to the floor, kneeling by his old boss.

He glanced over his shoulder. The fire was spreading up the walls and down the stairs toward him. He could feel the heat of it now. It dried the tears on his cheeks. The first tendrils of hot, black smoke drifted into his nostrils.

He wanted to die. He had failed at everything, even this. He wanted to kneel here and let the fire come, and die with Weiss and have their bodies burn together. Crying dry, he looked down at the fallen man.

In the dancing flame-glow, he saw Weiss's big body rise and fall with a breath.

'Jesus,' Bishop murmured.

Weiss was still alive.

With a new feeling flooding into him, Bishop grabbed Weiss's heavy shoulder. He shook it, shouting, 'Weiss! Weiss!' Behind him, the wood of the stairs began to crackle as it burned. The sound of the fire was growing louder. It was like a rushing wind. His voice was almost hidden beneath the noise of it. He shouted again. 'Weiss!'

It was no good. Weiss just lay there. Bishop looked down at the sad, hangdog face, all slack and fleshy and flickering with fire. The sight of the old man made his heart ache. He wanted to tell him how sorry he was, sorry for everything. Sorry he had failed even at this.

But there was no point. Weiss couldn't hear him. Somehow Bishop would have to get him out of here and tell him then.

Bishop took a searing breath. He lifted his face. A black haze of smoke was hanging over him. Coughing, he looked down at Weiss. He had to lift him. That was the only way.

He worked as the smoke sank down toward him, as the fire leapt, crackling, around the stairs. He shoved and dragged Weiss's limp body onto its front. Grunting and hacking, he pushed himself off Weiss's back and stood and straddled him. He wrapped his arms around Weiss's enormous chest.

Holding onto Weiss, Bishop began moving backwards. The effort ripped him open inside. He felt his innards tearing like a paper bag. He screamed with the pain. He kept moving backward. Weiss was six foot four at least. Two hundred and fifty pounds at least. It didn't seem possible his body would keep rising, but it did. As Bishop moved backward, he drew Weiss to his knees. He went on screaming. He went on lifting Weiss. It was impossible, but it was real, like the fire and the tears were real.

Screaming again, he hauled Weiss to his feet. Holding him upright, he got around in front of him and raised one of his slack arms. Bishop bent his knees and pulled the arm over his shoulder. He brought the whole, enormous body across his back, holding the arm with one hand and the dangling legs with the other.

Then, screaming wildly, he straightened, holding Weiss across his shoulders. His insides tore again. He felt hot fluid spilling inside him, spreading through him. He faced the fire on the stairs. The top steps were snapping and crumbling. Sparks were flying upward. The bannister had become a line of bubbling flame.

Bishop charged up the stairs, up into the heart of the fire, carrying Weiss on his back. The flames surrounded him. The heat engulfed him. The smoke was everywhere, crawling over his hands, over his face. He lifted one leg and then the other, climbing. His legs grew rubbery, weak. They wouldn't hold him. He fell to his knees. He rose again, screaming, lifting Weiss. The fire felt as if it would strip the flesh from his cheeks. He climbed. His guts bled inside him. He thought he must be dead already. He thought he must be a corpse animated by pure will.

He stepped on the top stair. It cracked. It caved in under his foot. Only the very bottom of the riser held. His foot came down onto it. He felt it bending with his weight. He had only another second before he broke clean through.

He drove himself forward into the door.

The door flew open. Bishop pushed through it, carrying Weiss. He was out – out in the upstairs room again. The room was ablaze. The whole house was burning. The night was blindingly bright with fire.

He turned, this way and that. The smoke was thick as mud. It smothered him like mud. He was lost in it. He couldn't see the door. He couldn't tell one direction from another. Black smoke was folding over him. Black unconsciousness was rising inside him.

It occurred to him that none of this was possible. It couldn't be real. It had to be a dream. But even then, in the impossible moment, with the black coming down over him and rising up inside him, he was struck with wonder by the fantastic appearance of a child.

He caught a glimpse of the child through the flames. He saw him standing in the chaos of smoke and fire, wonderfully calm, wonderfully still. It was a boy with red-gold hair and a beautiful face, all serene. Bishop remembered him from somewhere. He had seen him before as he had seen the demon truckdriver before. It came to him then. The child was a character in a movie, some crap movie or other he had seen on TV. He had stayed up late one night, getting drunk on beer and staring at it. It was full of clichéd images like this one, like this golden boy. He had watched the entire film. It was a complete piece of shit. He wished he had never wasted his time with it. Now he was stuck with this clichéd kid, standing in the midst of the fire.

Well, maybe he wasn't real, Bishop thought, but there he was, all the same. He must've come in through the door. The door must be right behind him: the way out. Bishop went toward him, slogging across the blackness.

The fire clawed at his flesh. The smoke bore down on top of him. He staggered under the weight of the smoke and under the weight of Weiss. He went on, step by step, his knees starting to buckle. He carried Weiss to the child.

The child lifted his hackneyed and beautiful face. He lifted his white, white hand. Bishop held Weiss steady on his back with his right hand and held out his left toward the child. The child took hold of it. He drew Bishop forward, through the black smoke and the blackness inside him, through the flame and the flaming pain. Bishop gazed at the child, amazed and glad that he had come to him out of the crap movie. Then, he looked up over the child's head. He saw the door. The door was a standing rectangle of white light. The child tugged him by the hand and drew him toward it.

The fire fell away behind him. The smoke and noise fell away. The door grew closer. The white light grew brighter, bigger. The white light surrounded him. The white light became everything.

Bishop opened his eyes. He didn't know where he was at first. He had come as if from light into light. He had been surrounded by that fantastic brightness and now he was in the hospital room and the lights were on and Sissy was sitting over him. She smiled at him. She had a sweet smile. Tears were streaming down her cheeks.

Bishop tried to speak to her. It was hard. He hurt. He hurt a lot.

'Ssh, take it easy, Jim,' Sissy whispered. Bishop remembered her voice and how tender it always was.

'You're gonna be okay. You made it. You made it back to us.'

Bishop tried to speak again. His mouth moved but he hadn't the strength to push the words out.

'It was close there, let me tell you,' Sissy went on, her voice breaking. 'We weren't sure you were going to pull through. You're a pretty tough guy.'

Bishop tried to lift his hand to her. He couldn't. He must've moved it, though. Sissy looked down at it and put her own hand into it. Bishop was glad to feel her. The soft woman skin. The cool woman skin.

His eyes traveled from her face, up and around the room. Chairs, the bed rail, a silver tray, tubes, machines. It was the same hospital room as before. He had never left it. The house in the middle of nowhere wasn't real. The demon wasn't real, and the child wasn't and neither was the fire and the whole business about carrying Weiss. Only the darkness had been real. The darkness and the light. And the tears – he could feel the tears rolling down his face onto the pillow. They were real too.

He was alive. That was the point. He was still alive. Maybe he had failed at everything, but whatever needed to be done, there was still time to do it.

He licked his dry lips. He squeezed Sissy's hand. He wanted to tell her how sorry he was, how terribly sorry. He had not gotten to Weiss. He had not told him about the Shadowman's plan.

'It's all right,' she whispered down at him. 'It's all right.'

Bishop closed his eyes, exhausted. He would live. There was time. But it was not all right. It was not all right at all. He had not reached Weiss. He had not told him the plan.

Weiss was still out there – still out there, in the middle of nowhere – alone.

50

For him, in the end, it was a matter of seconds.

Weiss heard Julie's footstep on the path. That was the first he knew she was there. She was almost at the house, almost at the front door.

He sat stock still in the armchair in the darkened room. The .38 was in his hand, his palm sweaty against the grip. He held his breath, straining to hear. The footsteps drew closer. He knew the killer would have to make his move in the next moment.

Weiss sat still, sat still. There was no room for error. If the killer was still watching him, if he saw him leave the chair, it would be over. He had to go at exactly the right moment.

Julie's hard heels sounded on the paved path. Ten yards away. Then five. Then three.

Then a break in the rhythm of her step.

And Weiss thought: *Now.*

51

The killer moved.

The girl was only two strides from the door. She was lifting her hand to the knob. He had waited for this. People who are nervous or afraid of something look over their shoulders as they approach a door, but there is a moment when they have to open it, when they have to focus forward and they can't look around. That's the moment you can take them. He knew this. He had done it half a hundred times.

He was out of the car in a second, the 9mm Sig held lightly in his hand. He went up the walk behind her without making a sound. In his excitement, the silicone body suit seemed to weigh nothing, the fake flesh seemed to have become his own. He moved easily. He glided through the rain.

Now he was right behind her. She was unaware. It was a fine, electric moment. He was alive to everything: the rain on his face, the feel of the gun, the way his movements seemed to flow, inevitable. Then something else: he caught the scent of her. The musky, flowery scent of her on the cool, wet desert air. It was a joy.

She opened the door quickly. With a fearful, jerky motion, she slipped her hand inside and flicked up the lightswitch. She was about to take one last look behind her.

Before she could, the killer grabbed her.

He slipped his left arm around her throat. He yanked

her close against the left side of his chest. That kept his body protected and his gun hand clear.

He was through the door, in the house, in the living room. It was a moment like music. The smell of her hair filled him. His cheek was close to her cheek. Her soft throat was trapped in the crook of his arm. He held her fast and leveled his gun at the armchair, at Weiss.

But Weiss was gone. The chair was empty.

The killer kept moving. He was ready for this. He stepped to the side, carrying Julie with him. He had her almost off the floor. She was choking, clutching at his arm, but too weak to struggle. With a sweep of his gun hand, he covered the kitchen, the bedroom and the front door – the only places Weiss could've gone.

It all happened in a second, one single second with the girl gasping and the rain pattering and the killer sweeping the room with his gun, waiting for Weiss to come at him.

Then, for the first time, as he turned from one side of the house to the other, he saw the braid rug out of place. He saw the trapdoor in the floor.

A bolt of fear went through him. He hadn't known about the trapdoor. He had missed it when he checked the house earlier. The rug out of place. The trap. Weiss could be down there.

Surprised, he swung to face it, lowered the gun at it.

The moment he did that, he knew Weiss was behind him. Weiss had gone out the kitchen door and come around the house, come back in through the front. Of course he had. He had only needed the man who called himself John Foy to see the trap, to face it for that single instant. He was Weiss – and he had known that's what the killer would do.

The thought went through the killer's mind: swing back around, swing Julie around for a shield, shoot Weiss down as he comes through the door.

But he only had time for the thought. Then Weiss stepped up behind him and drove the butt of a .38 into the base of his skull.

The man who called himself John Foy crumpled to the floor, unconscious.

52

The killer let go of Julie Wyant as he fell. She staggered away from him, deeper into the room. Rubbing her throat, she looked up at Weiss where he stood hulking and breathless just within the doorway. The killer lay on the floor between them.

Weiss looked at her. The sight of her made something catch and hesitate inside him. He knew that sweet, rose, white and wistful face – the dreamy eyes – he knew them so well from the pictures he had of her – now here she was before him in the flesh.

She seemed about to speak. He stopped her with a gesture – a movement of his head toward the open door.

Julie Wyant swallowed, rubbing her throat. She looked down at the man on the floor. She nodded. She moved to the door, passing close to Weiss, so close he smelled her and felt the heat of her. Without pausing, she reached for him, gently pressed his arm through his trenchcoat. He ached.

Then she was gone.

With a grunt, Weiss dropped down on one knee beside the fallen gunman. He retrieved the 9mm Sig from where it had dropped from the gunman's hand onto the braid rug. As he slipped the weapon into his raincoat pocket, he heard a metal door shut in the night outside. Julie had gotten back into her car. He heard the engine turn over.

The killer was already stirring. Weiss held the .38 on him and searched him quickly with his left hand. He reached inside his raincoat, feeling his sides, under his arms, the small of his back, the waistband beneath his paunch. He ran his hands down one leg, then the other. He found the compact .45 in an ankle holster on his right leg. He waggled it free.

Weiss stood up. He had his .38 in one hand and the killer's .45 in the other. As he stood, he caught a glimpse of headlights from the corner of his eye. That was Julie Wyant driving away.

He would probably never see her again, he thought.

He moved heavily across the room, back to the armchair. He sank down into it. He lay the .45 on the phone table beside it. He trained the .38 on the man on the floor, the man who called himself John Foy.

It was the first good look he'd had at him. The first good look he'd had, knowing who he was. He couldn't remember how he'd looked the other time he saw him, in the driveway back in Hannock. He had the sense he looked totally different now. Bigger somehow – or fatter maybe. He wasn't sure. He had the sense if he ever saw the guy again, he'd look different then too.

The killer groaned. He shifted on the floor. He moved his hand to his head and rubbed the spot where Weiss had hit him. His eyes fluttered open.

'Oh God,' he said.

As Weiss watched, he slowly pushed himself up into a sitting position. He shook his head as if to clear it. He breathed in deep. He looked around until he saw Weiss sitting over him in the armchair.

Then he smiled.

Weiss held the gun steady on him.

Good, the killer thought.

This was what he had planned for. He'd hoped to get Weiss on the ground fast, but he'd known what Weiss was, he'd known what Weiss could do. So now the detective had the Sig Sauer and the .45. But the Saracen was still nestled in the pocket of the killer's body vest. In a minute or so, the man who called himself John Foy was going to pull it out and blow Weiss away.

Good, he thought.

But the rage – the rage burned in him. He didn't care about the thudding ache in his head. He could ignore that. But not the rage. Sure, he had known Weiss might outguess him, might trick him somehow, but now that it had happened, he didn't like it one bit. And the trapdoor – that was almost as if Julie had been in on it with him, as if they had planned the thing together, laughing at him the whole time. And then – why had Weiss let Julie go? He was aware of it, aware of her driving away, even as he came back to consciousness. That was the one thing he hadn't planned for. He wanted her to be here. He wanted her to see what was going to happen next. He had assumed Weiss would want her to see that too. He thought that was the point of the whole thing, that she was the point. It had never even occurred to him that Weiss might let her run away.

Now she was gone. He would have to find her all over again. It wouldn't be hard this time. There was only one road out of here. He would track her down before she even reached the interstate. He just had to get this over quickly and get on her trail. But he had wanted her to see this, and the rage burned in him.

He rubbed his head. He made a big show of it. He grimaced, as if the pain were killing him. Then he flinched and moved his hand to his belly. He showed Weiss a rueful smile.

'You really clocked me, Weiss,' he said. 'I feel kind of sick.'

'That's tough,' said Weiss.

The killer made a face again. It was all a big show. He

didn't feel sick. His head hurt, but his belly was fine. He just wanted Weiss to get used to him putting his hand on his mid-section like that. Soon he would reach inside his raincoat and rub his fingers back and forth over his shirt and Weiss would get used to that too. Then, he would reach into his shirt, reach through the slit cut in the t-shirt underneath, reach into the pocket of his body vest, and pull out the Saracen. Then Weiss would be dead.

Good, he thought. The rage ate at him, burned him. *Good*.

Weiss shifted the .38 into his left hand, picked up the phone with his right. He pressed the buttons – 9-1-1 – then held the handset to his ear.

A woman's voice, sleepy, drawling: 'Police emergency.'

'Oh, Jesus,' the killer murmured. He grimaced. He bent over as if he were gagging. He clutched at his belly. Slipped his hand inside his shirt, rubbing his stomach.

Weiss's eyes flicked down to follow the hand. He kept the gun on him. But the killer took a deep breath as if the pain had passed. He brought his hand out of the shirt again. It was empty.

The woman's voice again: 'Hello? Police emergency.'

'Get somebody over here,' said Weiss. 'I'm holding an intruder. I took two guns off him.'

'What's your location, sir?'

'Damned if I know. You got my number on your computer, right?'

'Hold on, sir, stay on the line with me…'

'Just track it down,' said Weiss. 'Just get here.'

He hung up the phone. Shifted the gun back to his right hand.

'I think I'm gonna puke,' said the killer. He bent forward. His hand went inside his shirt again.

Weiss watched him, deadpan. He didn't care if he

puked or not. He kept the gun on him, but his mind was distracted. He was thinking about Julie, about her face and the smell of her and the way she pressed his arm as she went by him.

He shook it off. Some things were like that, that's all. You saw them and you thought you would die if you didn't have them, but you could never have them and you didn't die, not from that anyway. Olivia Graves was right: Julie had some kind of knack for being whatever a man wanted her to be. It was a whore's talent, the talent she'd learned while seducing her mother's boyfriends so that they'd leave her little sister alone.

Once again, the man who called himself John Foy took a deep breath as his pain seemed to pass. He straightened, his hand still resting on his middle. He offered Weiss another smile, a weak, bland, anonymous smile.

Weiss could see the rage and hatred in his eyes.

The killer rubbed his belly, pretending he felt sick. This time, he slipped his hand into his shirt a little further. His fingertips touched the razor slit in the cotton of his t-shirt. He knew he could reach into the slit fast, go fast into the pocket of the body suit. He knew he could get the gun fast and come out with it fast.

But not yet. Weiss was still watching too closely, still keeping the gun trained on him.

The killer gave a tight laugh – the sort of laugh you give when you're in pain but you're trying to laugh anyway. 'Bet they're over an hour away,' he said.

Weiss blinked at the sound of his voice. The killer could see his mind had drifted. He'd been thinking of something else. *Good.*

'The cops,' the killer said. 'I bet they won't be here for over an hour.'

Weiss shrugged. 'You got some other appointment?'

The killer flinched and clutched his stomach, made a big show of it. 'No,' he said, almost gasping. 'No.'

'Me either,' said Weiss.

The killer groaned. Yet again, he reached into his shirt. Weiss's eyes followed the movement, but his own hand remained loose on the .38. He was getting used to it now. Good. The killer's rage was so strong he could hardly wait anymore. He wanted to do this. But he brought his hand out empty yet again.

'You let her go,' he said.

'She did her part,' said Weiss.

'Now it's just you and me, right?'

Weiss didn't answer.

The Shadowman grinned, clutching his belly. 'You'll never have her that way.'

Weiss didn't answer.

'I had her,' the Shadowman said.

Weiss snorted.

'I bet you think about that,' said the killer. 'I know you do. That's what this whole deal is. I had her and you didn't. That's what all this is about.'

'I guess you're a big man,' said Weiss.

'I had her.'

'I know what you did to her.'

'She wanted it that way.'

'Yeah, yeah, yeah.'

'Anyway, I had her, that's what I'm saying.'

'So you're a sick fuck, so what?'

'So I had her.'

'Ah, you're a sick fuck.'

'You know what I'm saying,' the killer said. 'You know what I'm talking a...' He grunted, pretended to flinch. He put his hand in his shirt and rubbed his stomach. This time, Weiss didn't even watch his hand.

Good, the killer thought. It was almost time.

Weiss pressed his lips together. He was sorry he'd said anything. He should've known better than to start up with that shit. But he couldn't help it. He had his own anger. It felt like a fist had hold of his gut and was twisting it. When he thought about Julie, when he thought about the killer, when he thought about the look of her just now and the way she touched his arm and the way the killer was... well, he had his own anger.

She had a habit of becoming whoever men wanted her to be.

Yeah, so what? Weiss thought. *That's how she kept the bastards off her little sister.*

But that was what bothered him. Her little sister was in the clear, her little sister was fine – so why did she go on with it? Why did she keep on whoring? Even when she was a kid, the routine wouldn't have worked forever. Eventually, no matter what she did, no matter how good she was, her mother's dealer boyfriends would've wanted more, would've wanted to go after little Olivia too. Julie must've known that.

You think you understand everything, but you don't understand anything.

Then, suddenly Weiss did understand. With his stomach churning, it suddenly came to him – came to him as if it had been hidden in the back of his mind all along: why Julie went on whoring, how she knew where to find her father, why Olivia was angry at her sister even though she'd saved her from the men who would surely have raped her.

He understood all of it.

The killer watched him. He saw Weiss's eyes close and open. He saw the tip of his tongue touch his lips. The detective's mind was wandering. He was thinking about something else. His focus was slipping. The man who called himself John Foy could see it. He could see that his moment was almost here.

He did the whole show one last time. He groaned. He gritted his teeth. He bent forward. He put his hand inside his shirt and pushed it all the way through the slit in his t-shirt. He rubbed his belly and slipped his hand in further, into the pocket of his bodysuit.

He touched the handle of the Saracen.

It was Julie, Weiss thought. His stomach was churning, and he thought: It was Julie – thirteen-year-old Mary Graves. She had learned to play the whore for her mother's men. She had kept them off her little sister by offering them herself. She had learned to be whatever they wanted and at first she thought that would be enough. But finally she must have realized: nothing was enough. There was no holding the men off forever. Eventually, they would go after the younger girl too. That was just how things worked. Bad men did bad things and if you didn't stop them they did more bad things and more.

Thirteen-year-old Mary Graves couldn't stop the bad men, but she could make it so they would go away.

So it was Mary – it was Julie – who picked up the clawhammer, who went on tiptoe into her mother's room, up to the bed where her mother lay sleeping...

Weiss felt he was there. He slipped into her feelings. He felt the weight of the hammer – her father's heavy hammer – as the child lifted it with both hands. He felt the quickening arc as she brought the thing down on her sleeping mother's forehead. And brought it down again. And again. Until the forehead caved in. Until the blood spurted, then burbled out in a steady flow onto the white pillow.

Now there would be no more bad men...
You don't understand anything.

But Weiss understood. He understood Charles Graves
– Andy Bremer. He hadn't run away because he was
guilty. He ran because he wanted to look guilty. If the
police caught him, if they grilled him, if he confessed, he
would make a slip, miss a fact: they would know he was
lying. But if he ran, the cops would just assume he'd done
the murder. He coached the children in what to say. The
cops would believe them because they were just kids. A
little girl doesn't crush her own mother's head with a
clawhammer. It was obviously the missing father who
had done it. The cops would assume he was guilty and
spend their resources hunting for him. He ran to protect
Julie, and he called her, checked on her, to make sure she
was safe. They played out the lie together. She never lost
touch with him.

Weiss gazed down at the man who called himself John
Foy – he gazed down and held the gun on him – but his
mind was far away, on Julie now. He couldn't put it into
words exactly, but he saw what had happened to her, to
her and her whole family. They'd been frozen in time,
stuck in the moment of Suzanne Graves's murder, repeat-
ing the moment of the murder endlessly, endlessly. Andy
Bremer had a different name, a different life, but he was
still Charles Graves taking the blame for his wife's
killing, paying off the blackmailing Adrienne Chalk, not
just to protect Julie, but as penance for the things he had
allowed to happen in his house. Olivia Graves had grown
up, had gone to school, had gotten a profession, but she
was still the little girl full of anger and envy and terror
and guilt at what her sister had done on her behalf.

And Julie. Julie went on living the life she had lived
before the moment she picked up the hammer; she had
gone on whoring, had gone on becoming whoever men

wanted her to be, as if she could somehow convince herself that the moment had never happened, that the hammer had never come into her hands.

Weiss gazed down at the killer. He understood why Julie had waited for him here, why she hadn't run away. Because she had never left that old moment and the old truth had at last come back to find her: bad men do bad things and they'll do more bad things forever unless you stop them.

Once again, she had done what she had to do. She had waited here. She had picked up the hammer. Only this time, the bad man was the man who called himself John Foy. And this time, the hammer was Weiss.

Weiss let out a long sigh. His hand – his gun hand, went slack. The .38 strayed from its target. It pointed down at the floor.

He lifted his body to one side, reached his left hand into his trenchcoat pocket.

'It's gonna be a long wait, Foy,' he said. 'Have a cigarette.'

Good! the killer thought.

It was the perfect moment. The .38 was pointed away from him. Weiss was lifted clumsily in the chair, reaching into his trenchcoat pocket for his cigarettes. The killer's hand was already inside the pocket of the body suit. His fingers wrapped themselves around the butt of the Saracen.

In one clean, lightning-quick instant, he pulled the pistol free.

Weiss, his left hand in the pocket of his trenchcoat, took hold of the 9mm Sig Sauer he had put there: the killer's other gun.

———

The killer brought the Saracen to bear. So quick, Weiss had no time to move. So quick, the killer himself had no time to think.

Then, as the barrel of the gun came around, as the sight centered on Weiss's chest, he did think.

He thought: *Wait a minute! The son-of-a-bitch doesn't smoke!*

Weiss shot him. He shot him with the gun in his trench-coat pocket, the killer's own gun. The blast was loud as hell. The 9mm slug ripped into the Shadowman's chest and blew a hole the size of a man's fist out the back of him. The blood and flesh and shattered bone spattered on the wall behind him.

The Shadowman gaped, a sick, startled look on his face. He dropped backwards onto the floor, hard, like a post falling over. He lay on his back and stared up at the ceiling. His mouth opened and closed.

Weiss watched him, deadpan.

He was dying. The killer could feel it. He was dying fast. His mind was racing crazily, trying to grasp what had happened to him. *Have a cigarette, Foy.* It was a trick... Weiss had known... Somehow Weiss had guessed even about the Saracen. He had tricked him. Tricked him – and shot him – Christ, he'd shot him right to fucking death – and with his own gun and in self-defense... He was fucking dying and Weiss was free, free with nothing to fear from the law, with nothing to fear at all.

The killer's rage and the helplessness of his rage felt like white-hot fire. He couldn't stand it. It was worse than anything.

The tower. He had to climb into the tower in his mind. He had to get to the blue peace up there and breathe. Down here there was nothing but the fire of his rage, waves of fire pounding him, surrounding him, an ocean of fire that went on forever, fire and pain and red lips laughing. He tried to climb, to get away. But he couldn't. He was too weak. The calm, blue, serene spaces were too high, too far away. He was stuck down here in the burning ocean of his rage.

Fading, he was seized with fear...

Weiss stood slowly out of the armchair. He felt sick to his stomach. He hadn't known it would end like this until it did. Or maybe he had. Maybe he had known and he hadn't faced it. Anyway, now that it was done, he wasn't sure why he'd done it. He wasn't sure why he'd done any of it from the start. Was it to get Julie free or to get himself free or just because the killer pissed him off? He didn't know. Or maybe he did. Anyway, he felt sick to his stomach.

He moved past the dying killer. He went to the door. He took hold of the knob.

'You told...' The killer tried to speak. He coughed. He gasped. Weiss glanced back at him. The killer lay staring up at the ceiling. There were bloody bubbles on his lips. 'You told me you weren't a killing man,' he whispered finally.

Weiss watched death pass over the other man's face like a shadow. He pulled the door open.

'I lied,' he said.

He stepped out into the rain.

EPILOGUE

It was one of those nights – the last one of those nights – when Weiss and I sat alone together in his office. He was in the huge leather swivel chair behind the massive desk. I was in one of the two blocky armchairs the clients used. The halls were dark around us and the other offices empty. Weiss's desklamp surrounded us with light, a little island of light in the pool of shadows. At the big arched windows on one wall, the skyline rose and fell, its pale glow seeping into the violet sky. The snap and rattle of the streetcars down on Market drifted up to us. The high winter wind made the panes knock in their frames. I had that sense, that sense I often had on nights like this, that Weiss and I were sitting in the one still corner of the cold and frantic world.

Weiss kept a bottle of Macallan in his desk drawer, just as if he were a detective in one of the old novels. He had poured us each a glass of scotch and now the bottle stood on the desk between us, glowing amber in the lamplight.

I swirled the whiskey in my glass. I drew in the scent of it.

'It's a wonderful thing to imagine,' I said.

Weiss laughed softly.

We were talking about Bishop. He was getting better, stronger, all the time. Two weeks before, he had left the hospital in Phoenix and come back to a rehab center in San Francisco. They held him there for a few days, until the insurance ran out. He was still too weak to take care of himself, so Sissy took him in.

It was, as I said, a wonderful thing to imagine. All the dangers Bishop had faced, all the adventures he'd had, the things he'd done and the things we thought he might have done – none was more amazing to conjure in the brain than the mental image of him sunk in the white, fluffy recesses of Sissy's apartment, lying all but helpless amidst white, fluffy valentine pillows and a white, fluffy comforter while the white, fluffy cats made a bed of him.

I admit I felt a little jealous when I thought of it – a little. Sissy would lavish all her tenderness on him, and I knew well how tender Sissy could be. She would coddle and nurse him, feed him and mop his fevered brow until he had to get well just to keep from killing her.

The outcome seemed to me inevitable. Bishop's wounds would heal. His vigor would seep back into him, then flow back in a strengthening stream. Alone with Sissy and with few distractions, he would become increasingly aware of the sweetness of her smile, the delicacy of her features, the whiteness of her skin – the smell of her; she smelled great, as I think I've already had occasion to mention. She would come and go from the kitchen, from the bathroom, bringing whatever he needed for his comfort, and he would watch her come and go. The girlish whisper and the maternal endearments that annoyed him at first would soon come to reveal what was true gentleness in her. He would think: she was really not so bad, not half bad, after all.

As for Sissy – well, I can't imagine anything so trivial as her experience with me would have lessened one little bit her propensity for the Impossible Man. Bishop's helplessness, his gratitude, his slowly growing realization of her undeniable charms would all work their magic on the pent-up longings of her over-romantic nature. She would begin the familiar process of convincing herself that he was other than he was. She would tell herself that she had overstated his detachment and aggression, unfairly denied his charisma and heroism, and momentarily lost faith in the possibility that a man's personal defects might be reformed by the love of a good woman.

Thus there would come a day – who could help but think there would come a day? – when as she was bustling past his couch to do some errand on his behalf, he would reach for her, his strong fingers closing around her slender wrist. I could see her stopping, looking down – him looking up, his pale, sardonic gaze on her blue eyes.

I could hear her thinking: *Maybe he was right in front of me all this time and I didn't see it.*

And I could hear him: *What the hell? Maybe I'll stick her once before I go.*

And so they would continue, as we all continue more or less, each in his or her own way.

That was my imagination of it anyhow. Weiss, of course, read my mind.

'It'll make her forget you in a big hurry,' he muttered into his scotch glass. He laughed.

I laughed too, although not without a stabbing pain in my ego, I admit.

I'm sure Weiss was aware of that too. 'Well,' he consoled me, coming out of his whiskey with a small gasp. He tilted his glass my way. 'You've done all right yourself.'

I smiled, consoled. I tilted my glass back at him.

I had done all right – much better than just all right, as the years would prove – although it was some while after I got back from Nevada before I could finally deal with Emma and her father. It was a while before I could simply get the various parts of my body to move in some semblance of working order.

When I did, I called Professor McNair. It seemed only fair to go to the old man first. There was no good way to straighten the whole mess out, but that seemed the only fair way to begin. I knew it wasn't going to be easy. I wasn't going to tell him Emma's secret, and I knew he wasn't going to like that. And I was going to have to betray his confidence and let her know he'd hired me to watch her, and I knew he wasn't going to like that either. And if he didn't like that stuff, he sure as hell wasn't going to like it when I explained the reason for it all: that I was in love with his daughter and I suspected she was in love with me.

In the event, it was worse than I could have imagined. I can still remember feeling what seemed like a big iron ball lodged in my throat as I stood on the porch of the small clapboard house in the Berkeley hills, waiting to be admitted. It was Emma's mother who answered the bell. She looked startlingly like her daughter – physically anyway. She had the same long, lean figure, the same heartshaped face. But any spark that had ever been in her eyes, any hilarious wickedness that had ever appeared in her lips had long since been worried out of her. Every feature, every line and angle of her seemed to have been drawn down, down, down by the gravitational pull of a wearying sadness. I couldn't swear to myself that Emma would never come to look like that, but I swore right then and there that she would never come to look like that on my account.

She led me up the stairs and down a hall. I've seen both those stairs and that hall many times since then but they somehow were never again as long or as completely overhung with such a threatening gloom. At the end of the hall was a door and when Emma's mother swung it open, I saw – I thought I saw – a deep and wondrous expanse of a sanctuary with booklined walls running forever toward a towering oak desk in the far distance. In fact, it was quite a small room as I later found out, with books and files and papers stacked in every corner. But at that moment, I felt as if I'd come into the Library of the World and the Great Librarian himself was rising imperiously behind the Great Circulation Desk of Life.

McNair was as I remembered him – including drunk. Those eyes set in their nest of deep-cut wrinkles had a serpentine dullness, a film of whiskey and pure meanness that made the ball in my throat grow larger, heavier. If I had harbored any hopes that good will would somehow transform the discomfort of the situation and put our common errors to some happy use, those hopes sank bubbling to the bottom of my heart as I approached the desk.

Likewise any hopes I had of pity. The bruises I had sustained outside the *House of Dreams* were healing by then, but they looked even worse than they had when they were in their bruise prime. My cheeks were swollen, purple and yellow, the flesh around my eyes was puffed and livid, my lips looked as if they'd been attacked by an insane plastic surgeon with a syringe full of collagen – which was not to mention the fact that I was bent and limping from all the kicks I'd taken to my ribs and legs.

McNair didn't even mention it. He simply stood behind the desk and waited. He didn't even offer my poor broken body a seat.

'Well?' he said.

Well – I won't tell all of it. He was furious. He swore he would have me fired. When I told him I'd already quit, he actually shook his fist at me, too enraged for words. Then he found the words and railed against my dishonesty and stupidity for going on half an hour.

I weathered it. There was nothing else for me to do. Finally he subsided, sinking into his chair, muttering dark imprecations into his sleeve.

'The question is: do you want to tell her or should I?' I said.

'Oh, there's no question at all. You'll tell her. You'll tell her. It's your mess, you imbecilic bastard.'

'All right. Well, sir... I hope this will be the beginning of a beautiful friendship.'

'Get out.'

I did – and with no small feeling of relief, let me tell you. But even better than that, I left in the understanding I had been given a great gift. To wit, I was not the man I was. I was not afraid as I had been. All the time McNair was yelling at me, I stood before his desk – I felt his hot, alcoholic breath washing over me – I felt the flecks of his spit pattering against my face – and I was immovable. What could he do to me, after all? He was not an old man, though he seemed like one to me then. He was in his prime really. I suppose if he had charged at me, I would have had a fight on my hands. But, as I say, I was not afraid. Perhaps I could have handled him in a fight, perhaps not, but that didn't matter.

What did matter – and what has mattered ever since – was that, if the worst came to the worst, I knew I could take a punch.

When I was done there, I phoned Emma. Rather coolly, she agreed to meet me on the university campus. She chose Sproul Plaza just within Sather Gate. That was the arch of bronze framed by concrete pillars through which students passed to enter and leave the university. It was so crowded we were guaranteed not to have a moment alone. Which I guess was the point.

'Oh my God, my God, oh my God!' I believe were her

exact words when I presented myself. She gaped at me with gratifying concern. 'What happened to you?'

'I got beat up outside a whorehouse,' I told her.

'Oh… damn! That's no good. What the hell were you doing in a whorehouse now?'

'I wasn't in a whorehouse, I was outside a whorehouse.'

'Well, what were you doing outside a whorehouse?'

'I was getting beaten up – I told you.'

Then I did tell her, not about the whorehouse, not right away. First I told her that it was over between me and Sissy. I thought I saw her fight down a smile at that.

'Well, that's something I guess,' she said coldly.

Then I told her about her father and the Agency and why I'd followed her to her secret church.

Emma let out a low moan. She leaned against one of the gate's bronze uprights. The students flooded past us, into the campus, onto the street.

'I suppose that's my fault as much as anyone's,' she said. 'I should've had the courage to come out with it.'

'It was just an amazing coincidence. I mean, that he came to the Agency – and that I was the only one there to deal with it.'

She cocked her head. This time, the smile showed. 'Not so amazing.'

I had forgotten she believed in God.

'All right,' she said. 'So what about the whorehouse? That's new.'

So I told her about that, about Weiss and the Shadowman and Bishop and pretty much the whole story. For the sake of brevity, I left out the parts about how I was trying to make myself admirable to her, and it's possible I added a few bits for dramatic intensity, narrative style and to make myself admirable to her.

She covered her mouth with her hand. When she

finished laughing, she said, 'Well, I guess that was actually kind of heroic in a sleazy sort of way.'

I laughed too – which felt as if a Republican had gripped one side of my face with a wrench and a Democrat had gripped the other, and each was attempting to twist it into the shape he deemed correct.

'Stop laughing,' said Emma, 'you'll kill yourself.'

'Listen,' I told her. 'That's it; I'm done. Are you gonna kiss me or not?'

'I might.'

'Come here.'

I grabbed her around the waist and pulled her to me. It was without exception, as I remember to this very day, the single most painful kiss I have ever experienced in my life.

They got better, though, after that.

'So now…' said Weiss. He smiled at me across the island of lamplight. The roar of a bus rose up to us from the loud city streets. The cold wind swept down Market and the arched windows rattled.

I sipped my scotch. I stole a glance at his face. The heavy, baggy cheeks, the deep eyes, that small smile: I thought he looked sad. But he always looked sad.

'Yeah,' I said.

'You're gone.'

'I am.'

'You're history.'

'Now I belong to the ages.'

He turned his sad smile into his glass, waggled the glass a little in his hand. 'It's too bad,' he said. 'I liked having you around, kid.'

'Yeah,' I said. 'It's been great, Weiss. Thanks.'

'You're gonna become a book writer, huh.'

'I'm gonna try. To write novels.'

'Detective stories,' he said.

I shrugged, embarrassed. Laughed.

'Well, let me tell you something,' Weiss said.

Then he did. For the next three hours or so, he told me a lot of things. Other times, we had sat here together and he'd gone over cases or given me some exciting anecdotes from his life as a cop. And there was some of that tonight too. But there was also other stuff. The real stuff.

He sat swiveling slightly back and forth in his chair. He held his whiskey glass on his belly with his two hands. He told me about Bishop and how they'd met. He told me about the nights he had prostitutes come to his place because he had no way with women. He told me about the nights he'd spent alone, sitting here in his office, looking at his photograph of Julie Wyant and watching the ten-second loop of video he had of her. Finally, he told me about the Shadowman and about the last meeting between them in the little house in the middle of nowhere at midnight.

I don't know what moved him to tell me those things. It pleased me, because I knew he wouldn't tell them to just anyone, but I don't know why he told them to me. I wonder about it sometimes, even now. I had no plans to write anything but fiction then. I never imagined I would tell these stories, the true stories about the Agency, *Dynamite Road* and *Shotgun Alley* and now finally this. But I wonder sometimes if Weiss knew, if he knew already. He might have. He knew a hell of a lot, did Weiss, in his Weissian way.

I listened to him as if in a sort of dream. I could see everything, every person, every incident he described as if I were there. Then – all at once it seemed to me – he was done. He drained the last of his scotch and set his glass down with a thunk on the desktop.

'All right?' he said.

I blinked. I came back to myself. 'Yeah,' I said. 'All right. Yeah.'

He folded his hands on his belt buckle. He swiveled back and forth. He smiled with one corner of his mouth.

I sat for another moment with nothing to say. Then I stood. I wanted to get out of there before I got choked up, but I paused a moment to take one last look around the place.

It was all so large, larger than life. The vast office and the wall of soaring windows and the soaring city against the night. The enormous desk with the enormous chairs in front of it and the even more enormous swivel chair behind it and Weiss sitting there, enormous too.

'Well,' I said. I cleared my throat. 'It was fun.'

'Hey,' said Weiss. 'Life's a comedy.'

'Is it?'

'Sure,' he said. He smiled. 'And I'm the King of Romania.'

When I was gone, Weiss poured himself another drink. He brooded over it. He swiveled back and forth in his chair. He listened to the traffic noise and the noise of the wind against the windows. He felt the city out there, beyond the light that fell over him, and beyond the shadows that covered the rest of the room.

After a while, he swung around to his computer. He called up the image of Julie Wyant on the monitor, that little ten-second loop of video he had. It was from an internet advertisement. It showed her leaning forward in a white blouse, crooking her finger at him, beckoning. It played over and over. He watched it for a long time. He didn't know how long.

Then, finally, he sensed something – someone – a presence in the room with him. Startled, he looked up.

There she was. Right there, right in front him. Julie

Wyant. She was standing in the doorway, leaning against the frame. She was watching him. She was smiling. The shadows of the room fell over her, but he could make her out in the glow of the desklamp. She was wearing an overcoat belted at the waist. Her red-gold hair hung down loose. Her eyes were deep and dreamy. She had the face of an angel.

Weiss sat still and gazed at her. For a long moment, he wasn't sure whether he was awake or dreaming...

ACKNOWLEDGEMENTS

I'd like to express my heartfelt thanks to the many people who helped me in the writing of this book. Carolyn Chriss did an excellent job as researcher. Lieutenant John Hennessey and Homicide Inspectors James Spillane and Thomas Cleary of the San Francisco Police Department were extraordinarily generous with their time and expertise. The talented and deadly Sensei Will Silliker of the United Studios of Self Defense in Santa Barbara gave me a wonderful sword fighting lesson; and I thank Chief Instructor Jody Neal for the loan of him. General Surgeon Gary Hoffman was very helpful on the matter of gunshot wounds. Robert Divine of Anatomorphex Special Effects and makeup effects man Barry Koper were instrumental in designing the fat suit. Tom Bartlett, the managing director of XLence Technologies Inc., helped with the listening and tracking devices. Ron Zonen of the Santa Barbara District Attorney's office answered my legal questions. Shandra Campbell of Village Properties answered my questions about the real estate business. Andrea Read of Spitfire Aviation helped me fly Bishop's plane and Larry Mousouris helped me drive his motorcycle. And a couple of informal chats with the ladies at some Winnemucca brothels helped in the creation of the House of Dreams. None of these people is to blame for those sections of the book where I bent facts and geography to the service of my story. I should also mention that, while there is a Paradise, California, it's not the town I describe.

My personal thanks are particularly due to my friend and editor, the unparalleled Otto Penzler. My agent Robert Gottlieb at Trident Media has been great, as has Chris Donnelly and all the agents at Endeavor.

For Ellen, my only ever love, thanks simply aren't enough.